THIS IS THE ONLY KINGDOM

ALSO BY JAQUIRA DÍAZ

Ordinary Girls

THIS IS THE ONLY KINGDOM

A Novel

JAQUIRA DÍAZ

ALGONQUIN BOOKS OF CHAPEL HILL
LITTLE, BROWN AND COMPANY

The characters and events in this book are fictitious. Any similarity to real persons, living or dead, is coincidental and not intended by the author.

Copyright © 2025 Jaquira Díaz

Hachette Book Group supports the right to free expression and the value of copyright. The purpose of copyright is to encourage writers and artists to produce the creative works that enrich our culture.

The scanning, uploading, and distribution of this book without permission is a theft of the author's intellectual property. If you would like permission to use material from the book (other than for review purposes), please contact permissions@hbgusa.com. Thank you for your support of the author's rights.

Algonquin Books of Chapel Hill / Little, Brown and Company
Hachette Book Group
1290 Avenue of the Americas, New York, NY 10104
algonquinbooks.com

First Edition: October 2025

Algonquin Books of Chapel Hill is an imprint of Little, Brown and Company, a division of Hachette Book Group, Inc. The Algonquin Books name and logo are trademarks of Hachette Book Group, Inc.

The publisher is not responsible for websites (or their content) that are not owned by the publisher.

The Hachette Speakers Bureau provides a wide range of authors for speaking events. To find out more, go to hachettespeakersbureau.com or email hachettespeakers@hbgusa.com.

Little, Brown and Company books may be purchased in bulk for business, educational, or promotional use. For information, please contact your local bookseller or the Hachette Book Group Special Markets Department at special.markets@hbgusa.com.

ISBN 9781616209148
LCCN 2025934253

1 2025

MRQ-T

Printed in Canada

Para Rafael Díaz Matos, who passed down all the stories.

Pal pueblo, mi gente del Caserío Padre Rivera.

Para Jeannette Doval Sánchez, who loved me hard. Siempre.

It is the dead,
Not the living, who make the longest demands:
We die forever.

—Sophocles, *Antigone*

Listen to me. I am telling you
a true thing. This is the only kingdom.

—Aracelis Girmay, "Elegy," from
Kingdom Animalia

THIS IS THE ONLY KINGDOM

HOURS BEFORE THEY find him, everything burns.

Smoke rising in black clouds, the golden cañaverales, the dark sky. An explosion of birds and mongooses, lizards, snakes, everything bolting from the fires. Dry leaves crackling, embers, ash. The slow crawl, the body heaving, groping for something steady in the cane. The coquíes fading, quieting, and then silent.

Late morning out in the fields, a cane cutter from La Central pushes aside the burnt stalks with his gloved hand, his protective headgear and thick coveralls weighing him down. After last night's controlled burns, the ground smolders in some places, the heat rising under his heavy boots. It's May 1993, and by noon it already feels like midsummer.

He swings his machete, cuts through a stem, swings it again. He tosses the burnt stalks aside as he takes them down, keeps moving, leaving them to be collected by the other guys. He wades through the charred debris, reaching for the next stalk. He works at a slow, steady pace, striding through the cañaveral. Breathe, swing, strike. He can't move too quickly, because he might faint in this heat. Slow and steady. Swing, strike, toss. Stop. Breathe. Start again.

The other guys call out to one another behind him. This morning's factory crew must be out for lunch.

"Whoa!" someone hollers.

Swing, strike. Breathe.

Suddenly, the voices quiet. Nothing moves. Only the sound of his breathing, the heat all around him, and the smell.

He steps around the edge of a row, cutting stalks as he goes, tossing them, kicking aside the piles of ash and burnt leaves.

"What in the hell is that?" someone else shouts.

Every season after the burning, they find animals in the cane. Snakes, iguanas, bats, all kinds of birds, cane toads. He found a dead dog once, burned to a crisp. Couldn't get the smell out of his head. Everywhere he went, he smelled dead dog. Didn't eat meat again for weeks.

"Is that...?" he starts to ask, then stops. All these years, all the burning seasons, he's never seen something like this. He has an urge to cross himself. *En el nombre del Padre, y del Hijo, y del Espíritu Santo.* He squeezes the grip on his machete.

One of the guys backs away, turns toward La Central. A few others follow.

But he can't move. The sky is hazy, gray with smoke.

"Jesus," he says, turning away from the body. "Jesus." He heads back, following all the other men. Somewhere in the field, he drops his machete. He leaves it behind, walks faster, starts loosening the straps on his headgear, his goggles.

In the sky, above the stacks of La Central, a plague of grackles circles.

PART ONE

"Las Caras Lindas"

1975–1981

"El Cantante"

THE END OF summer in el Caserío Padre Rivera meant the end of freedom. It meant back to Padre Rivera Elementary for the little kids, and the teenagers hoofing it to el pueblo in their scuffed loafers and starch-ironed hand-me-down uniforms. No more sleeping 'til noon for Cano, in his last year at UPR Humacao, and a return to early days at the parish for his older brother, David, a deacon soon to be an ordained priest. It meant long, quiet mornings in the neighborhood again: satos roaming the streets in packs, women sweeping their balconies in silence while the café brewed in la greca, men playing dominoes in la plaza, hustlers throwing dice under the shade of the flamboyán.

Every day after school, sixteen-year-old Maricarmen and her younger sister, Loli, walked past the basketball courts on their way home. Loli was only fourteen, but she was supposed to have dinner ready when their mother came home from work. While Loli finished her homework, a pot of arroz con salchichas simmering on the stove, Maricarmen went off to one of her after-school jobs. Some days, Maricarmen took care of the neighbor's eight-year-old twins. Some days, she cleaned apartments. She'd speed past the basketball courts as she headed to work, the ballers pausing their game just to get a good look, calling out to her, "Mira, nena, where you going in such a hurry?"

One afternoon, Maricarmen was on her way to clean Doña Matos's apartment when she walked past the guys dribbling on the blacktop. She heard one of them wolf-whistle. She was still wearing her high school uniform, maroon skirt and white button-down shirt. She cut her eyes at him, kept walking.

"Leave that girl alone," she heard Cano say. He was Doña Matos's youngest son. He was in college, and barely spoke to Maricarmen when she was over at their house.

"I was just trying to talk to her," the other guy said. "Hey, girl! Come here!"

"She's in high school," Cano said. "What's wrong with you?"

"She's in your house like every day. You mean to tell me you never even *tried*?"

Maricarmen climbed the steps to Doña Matos's apartment, paying them no mind.

"Bye, Mari!" one of the guys called out.

She ignored him. It was always like this with them. A lot of jokes, flirting. She never took them seriously.

Doña Matos had already left for her shift at the hospital when Maricarmen let herself in. David was polishing off a bowl of sancocho at the small kitchen table, dipping bits of pan sobao in the broth and popping them into his mouth.

"Buenas tardes, Padre," Maricarmen said, smiling as she shut the door behind her.

"I'm not ordained *yet*," David said. He pointed at the bread on the table. "Sit. Eat, if you're hungry."

"I'm all right," she said. She opened the storage closet and pulled out the cleaning supplies: a spray bottle, a pair of plastic gloves, and a cleaning towel. Maricarmen came every couple of weeks, two or three days in a row, depending on how long it took to finish the entire three-bedroom apartment. Usually, if she worked quickly, she could finish a room in half an hour, maybe two rooms in forty-five minutes. But when David was around, she took longer, talking as she cleaned, listening to his stories about mission trips to Cuba and Nicaragua, about priests telling jokes over red wine in Portugal.

Maricarmen waited for David to finish his sancocho before clearing the table. "So when's the big day?" she asked. She sprayed and wiped the table.

"A few months." David, who wore thick prescription glasses and a dress shirt, looked up at Maricarmen, nodding thoughtfully. "Just a few months now."

Maricarmen smiled. He was gentle, David the deacon. Soft-spoken, sometimes a little nervous, but laughter always came easy to him. Sometimes, when he wasn't telling her stories that made her throw her head back and roar, he was like this, pensive. What did they do all day, those priests? she wondered. Pray? Think?

"Do you think it's hard?" she asked.

David slid back in his chair. "What do you mean?"

"You know. Like, never getting married. Never having children." She considered how to say the rest, holding the towel and the spray bottle tightly. "Never being with a woman?"

David studied her. "Aren't you a little too young to be worrying about those things?"

She thought about it. By the time her mother was sixteen, she was already married and pregnant with her. "No."

David laughed. "Don't try to grow up too soon, Mari."

Maricarmen felt her face grow hot. David was twenty-five, nine years older than her, but he'd never made her feel like a kid before. She knew he hadn't meant any harm. He was just looking out for her.

"Okay, old man," she said. She smiled once more, sprayed the counter.

They were both unusually quiet after that, Maricarmen cleaning methodically and David retreating to the living room to watch TV.

On her way out, she stashed away the cleaning supplies and avoided saying goodbye to David. He'd fallen asleep on the couch, and she didn't want to wake him.

Outside, instead of rushing past the basketball courts, she stood on the sidewalk, watching. The guys were still playing, but no one noticed her. She looked for Cano on the court, ran her fingers through her hair.

She watched them chase each other from one end of the court to the other, dribbling the basketball, taking shots. She unbuttoned the bottom of her shirt, then tied a knot high up on her waist, showing off her navel. She considered crossing the street to sit at one of the benches, but she didn't think she was brave enough. She ran her fingers through her hair again.

"What the hell do you think you're doing?"

Maricarmen jumped at her mother's voice. She tugged on the knot on her shirt, tried to hide her belly with her hands, but her mother was no fool.

Blanca, red-faced and sweaty, carried her three-inch heels in one hand, her purse strapped across her body. She was barefoot on the sidewalk, breathing hard, her dark bob messy and stringy with sweat.

"What happened to your shoes, Mami?" Maricarmen asked, trying to distract her.

Blanca looked her up and down, ignoring the question. "You done parading yourself in front of the whole block?" She pulled Maricarmen's shirt down, then pointed toward the basketball courts. "You think that these bandoleros are going to respect you?"

"I'm just heading home," Maricarmen said. She turned for their building, but her mother grabbed her by the elbow.

"Don't let me catch you with any of them, you hear me?" Blanca said, squeezing.

Maricarmen pulled away, forcing Blanca to loosen her grip. She was sick of her mother always grabbing her, humiliating her in front of her friends, their neighbors, yelling at her in front of whoever happened to be passing by. And she was sick of her mother always talking bad about "those people" in front of anyone who could hear her. Maricarmen's family was one of the few white families in el Caserío, and Blanca thought that made them better. The truth was, Maricarmen and Loli were ashamed of the way their mother talked down to anyone who was even a shade darker than her. Maricarmen couldn't wait to leave home.

Maricarmen gave her mother a look, one look, and hoped that Blanca understood exactly how she felt. She turned toward their apartment building, leaving her mother on the sidewalk alone.

BY THE TIME Cano met Rey Ojeda, Rey had already been arrested at least three times. He'd spent two years in a work camp for juvenile offenders, out in the country, cleaning chicken coops and pigpens, shoveling shit all day. The same day they released him, Rey turned eighteen.

Cano, Ismael, and some of the neighborhood guys were shooting hoops one afternoon when Rey came walking down the avenue, past the post office and la plaza. His hair was shaved down to the scalp, his gray trousers loose and faded, a matching gray shirt two sizes too big. He was skinny and dark—you could tell he'd spent days working the fields under the hot sun. The guys paused the game when they saw him. He'd been gone so long, it seemed, some of them had forgotten what he even looked like.

"Rey! My brother!" Ismael called out. He walked off the court as the other guys watched, gave Rey a quick hug and pulled back to get a look at him. "What happened in juvie, man?" Ismael asked. "Didn't they feed you?" They were all tall, muscular Black boys, but compared to Ismael and Cano, Rey looked *skinny*.

Cano tucked the ball under his arm and walked over. He didn't know this kid, but he figured any friend of Ismael's, especially in el Caserío, he had to know. Out on these streets, you needed as many friends as you could get.

"When did you get out?" Ismael asked.

"Just got home," Rey said.

"It's good to see you, brother," Ismael said. He turned to Cano. "This is Rey, man. Don Ojeda's nephew, who owns the candy store?"

Cano gave him a quick nod.

Cano knew Don Ojeda—everybody knew Ojeda, who'd been a music teacher but now owned a small colmado just outside the gates to el Caserío, where boleros were always blaring from the speakers of a rusted old radio. Officially, he sold candy, cigarettes, sodas, milk, eggs. But most of the neighborhood guys went to him for Ron Cañita, beer, the occasional bag of weed, and to gamble. All weekend long, Don Ojeda opened up the back of the store and turned it into La Gallera Sin Nombre, where any Fulano could bring his fighting cock, bladed spurs and all, and let it loose in the cockpit. On Friday nights, he also ran a card game—$100 minimum to get a seat at the table.

"So you gonna work for your uncle now?" Ismael asked.

Rey shook his head. "Got something else."

"What, like a music thing?" Ismael turned to Cano again, smiling. "This kid can play, man. Best drummer I ever heard. And he can sing too."

Rey laughed. "Nah. Another thing. But I need a ride. Something cheap, just to get to work every day, you know?"

Ismael smiled, wiped his sweaty forehead with the back of his hand.

"Know anybody selling a cheap ride?" Rey asked.

Ismael shot Cano a glance. Ismael was a mechanic, and procuring cheap old cars was one of the things he did best. He'd been working on cars his whole life, since he was a boy handling oil changes in his father's shop.

"We might have something for you," Ismael said.

Cano scratched the back of his head. "I have an old hooptie. Un Volky. It's in Ismael's shop, been there for months. Doesn't run."

"Needs some work," Ismael said.

"How much we talking?"

"I can get a used transmission in there for about a hundred," Ismael said.

"You can have the car for two hundred dollars if you pay for the transmission," Cano said.

Rey extended his hand to Cano and they shook. When he reached his hand out to Ismael, he pulled him in for a hug. "I'll bring you the money," Rey said, "soon as I get it." He headed back toward the front gate.

Ismael and Cano watched him go.

Cano bounced the basketball, and as all the other guys went back toward the courts, he said to Ismael, "I've known Ojeda since I was a kid. How come I never met his nephew before?"

Rey had already disappeared past the gate.

"That kid," Ismael said, "he's spent his whole life hustling, fighting, in and out of lockup. I tried to keep him clean, off the streets. He's got real musical talent. He can play, and he can sing his ass off! But he can't stay out of trouble."

"Maybe he's back for good," Cano said.

Ismael shook his head. "Some people get caught up in all this."

"Caught up in what?"

Ismael pointed at the buildings, the basketball courts. "All this. El Caserío. But you can't stay here forever. This can't be your whole life."

Cano's mother was a widow who'd raised two boys, and she'd spent the last twenty-five years in el Caserío. He'd spent his whole life here, too, and even though he was trying to finish up his degree at la Upi, he hadn't thought about what he'd do after that. He always assumed he'd get a job teaching, but he never considered leaving. "What do you mean, man?"

"If you can get out," Ismael said, "you do it. Go. And don't ever come back."

"This is the neighborhood," Cano said. "You can't talk that way about your own people."

Ismael touched Cano firmly on the shoulder, looking into his eyes. "What are they teaching you down at la Upi, brother? This? This is not people." He pointed at the buildings again, turned back toward the courts. "This is the project of la colonia. This is how they keep us poor, keep us in line, while they take the oceanfront land to build their hotels and shit. If you can't get out, if you decide to stay here, what will happen to *you*? What will happen to your children?"

"I don't have any children," Cano said, laughing. "I didn't know you wanted to go into politics. I thought you wanted to make music."

"You don't think salsa's political? Haven't you been listening?"

"You talk a lot of shit, brother. Don't act like you know more than me. I listen to the same salsa you listen to!"

The guys went back to their game, Cano dribbling and passing to Ismael, the two of them like blurs zooming up and down the court. It was late afternoon, and the smells of early fall were hanging in the air as the granos vendor pushed his cart back toward the gate: rice and cheese granos fried to a crisp, the overripe passion fruit falling off the hanging vines that ran along the outskirts of the neighborhood, clean laundry drying on the lines, motor oil, dog shit, the sweaty guys running around on the court, red beans on some nearby stove.

They shot hoops until the park benches filled with guys waiting their turn for the next pickup game, all swag and loud mouths and muscles. There were no girls around, not a single woman on the street. This court, these streets, this whole barrio belonged to them.

After, Ismael and Cano sat on the park benches, shirts off, wiping sweat from their faces, when they saw Rey again, strutting across the avenue toward them, a smile on his face.

Cano didn't say a word. Rey just came up, slapped two hundreds into Cano's palm, then handed Ismael a stack of fives and tens.

"Back so soon?" Ismael asked.

"Pick it up in a couple days?" said Rey.

"I'll let you know when it's ready," Ismael said.

They watched Rey leave. On the court, one of the guys shot a layup, jogged back across to the opposite side.

Cano's stomach felt uneasy, empty. "Where did this kid get all this cash?" he asked.

Ismael laughed softly, then exhaled, put the money in his pocket as all the air left his body. "Where do you think?"

OTHER THAN ISMAEL, nobody knew exactly what Rey's job was, except that it was out en el campo. He left el Caserío in the afternoon and came back en la madrugada, after the coquíes had gone quiet.

A few weeks after he bought Cano's Volky, there was a rumor that the cops were looking for Rey. Nobody knew why, only that if they'd seen Rey, they all decided to forget. Nobody in el Caserío talked to los camarones. They just wanted to raise their families in peace. Cano figured that Rey was wild, that he was probably out there robbing liquor stores or something crazy like that. Ismael told him not to worry about it, not to get involved.

Rey was also generous, Cano came to find out. Rey remembered when people had been kind to him, and he always came back with gifts to repay a favor.

Cano's mother told him how a few weeks after the cops came knocking on every door looking for Rey, she'd caught sight of him as she was hanging laundry. There he was, out by the chain-link fence, picking parchas off the vine. He was hungry, she realized. Probably hadn't been home in days. Probably *hadn't eaten* in days. So she went back inside her apartment and came out with a mortadella sandwich on pan sobao, a mug of café con leche. Something she put together quickly.

She called out to him, offered him the food. Rey looked around, then jogged over.

"Gracias, Doña Matos," he said. He ate fast, like he had somewhere to be. But Doña Matos knew he was just a boy living the kind of life not meant for a kid his age. Cano, her youngest, was twenty-two, not much older, and he'd had his own run-ins with los camarones, who showed up every other day—pulled over wherever they saw Cano, parked the car, frisked him. Doña Matos didn't know what they expected to find, but they never found a thing. She was sure they knew they wouldn't find anything on him—they just wanted to intimidate him and the other kids around here. Rey shouldn't have to live like this, running from the cops, going hungry, working whatever odd jobs he could find. His poor mother, Doña Iris, who'd just lost her husband and had a baby at home, was battling cancer. Doña Matos wasn't sure how Doña Iris would survive it if something happened to her Rey.

The next morning, when Doña Matos opened the door to the back balcony, she found a vase of bright yellow girasoles on the little table in the corner, two twenties tucked underneath. Had to be Rey, she thought.

After that, whenever she saw him, she gave him a cup of coffee, leftovers, whatever food she could scramble together quickly, put on a plate. Rey always thanked her, ate fast, handed her back the cup and plate, then went on his way, singing some song under his breath. And in the morning, she'd wake up to find a gift. A box of pastries left on the table, a sack of rice by the door, a pair of budgies in a wrought iron birdcage. Always a couple of bills tucked somewhere for her to find.

Sometimes, when she didn't see him for days, she worried that maybe los camarones had finally caught him, or worse. After a while, she started leaving food on the little table on the back balcony: a sandwich in a paper bag, or bread and butter and a mug of café covered with a small saucer, or a mango, or a bowl of rice and beans, or a piece of pastelón, or some arroz con salchichas. Every morning she left something. Every afternoon, when she went back there, the mug was empty, the plate was clean, the food was gone. She hadn't seen him, but he had eaten, and she was glad. She hoped that if her Cano were ever in trouble, somebody's mother would look out for him too.

MARICARMEN ARRIVED EARLY one afternoon, before Doña Matos left for her shift at the hospital. The front door was cracked, and the balcony door was open all the way.

"Come on in!" Doña Matos called from the kitchen. "And will you leave that door open? I'm trying to air this place out."

Maricarmen pushed open the door. "Smells good!"

Doña Matos was frying chicken, from the smell of it. She rushed into the living room in a housedress, drying her hands on her apron, her afro covered with a pañuelo tied at the nape.

"Mari, I'm so sorry, but will you do me a favor?"

"Of course." Maricarmen nodded, listening closely. Doña Matos never asked for favors. She was always the one people went to when they needed help.

"You don't have to clean today," Doña Matos said. "You do such a good job, the house is clean anyway."

Maricarmen smiled.

Doña Matos put a hand on Maricarmen's shoulder. "But I need you to do me a favor. It's important." She looked into Maricarmen's eyes. "Instead of cleaning around here today, would you look in on Doña Iris? See if she needs help? There's fried chicken and batatas on the stove. Take her some of that. See that she has something to eat. And make sure that baby eats too."

"Don't worry," Maricarmen said. "I will."

"You know where she lives? Second floor?"

Maricarmen nodded. "I cleaned for her once."

"Don't let her tell you that she doesn't need anything. You get in there and tell her not to give you any trouble. Tell her I sent you."

"I will," Maricarmen said.

"There's an extra five in the drawer for you," Doña Matos said, and rushed into the bathroom to get ready for work.

In the kitchen, Maricarmen found a large empty plastic butter tub that Doña Matos used to store leftovers and filled it with pollo and batatas. Then she pulled some dishes from the top cabinets and made two plates, one for David, one for Cano, and covered them with paper towels. She left them on the counter.

At Doña Iris's building, she could hear the baby crying as she climbed the stairs to the second floor. When she knocked, the crying got louder. Doña Iris came to the door right away, pulling it slowly and holding the screaming child in her arms.

Maricarmen tried to smile, but Doña Iris looked like death. She was a brown-skinned woman, but she looked pale, with dark circles under her eyes. Her lips were colorless and chapped. Her brown curls were thinning and stringy. Iris was her mother's age, but she looked much older than Blanca.

"Hola, Doña Iris," she said, holding up the food. "Doña Matos sent me. Says you gotta eat."

Iris moved aside to let her in, and the baby screamed again. She bounced him lightly, leaning on the door as Maricarmen walked past her and into the living room.

"Why don't you let me take him? I can feed him, give you a chance to sit."

Iris handed over the baby, then rushed toward the back of the apartment.

In her arms, the baby felt hot, sweaty. He was heavier than he looked. Solid. She made her way to the kitchen table, put down the food container, and held the baby out in front of her. He was cute. Brown, with soft curls, plump cheeks, and the longest eyelashes she'd ever seen on anybody in her life. He would not stop crying, hiccupping and coughing as Maricarmen wiped the tears off his cheeks.

"You're okay, baby," she said. "Do you eat solid food?" With one hand, she pulled the lid off the butter tub, then reached inside for a drumstick. She touched it but decided it was too hot. Instead, she pulled a small strip of meat off the bone and blew on it. "You like chicken?"

The baby kept crying.

She blew on it some more, then offered it to him.

Somewhere in the apartment, Maricarmen could hear, Doña Iris was throwing up.

"You're okay, baby." She held the piece up to his mouth, and he opened up, ate it quickly. He was hungry, she realized. Jesus Christ. She picked more meat off the bone and blew on it.

"Doña Iris? You okay?"

Iris moaned. "I'll be fine. Couple hours."

"Okay." Maricarmen sat at the table, the baby on her lap, and fed him small bits of chicken, bite-size pieces of fried batata.

She sat with him a long time, talking to him as she fed him, until he didn't want another bite. Once he was done, she covered the food, listening for Doña Iris. She'd stopped vomiting, as far as Maricarmen could tell.

She adjusted the baby on her lap. "You want some juice or something?"

The baby just babbled.

"Okay, then," she said, and picked him up. "Doña Iris? You okay in there?" She went around the kitchen table toward the refrigerator and found four baby bottles already filled. Two with water, two with some red juice. Water it was, she guessed. She picked one up and shut the refrigerator. The baby reached for the bottle immediately, trying to take it from her hand. She let him have it and watched him put it to his mouth.

"Look at you!" she said to him. "You're already grown! How old are you? You got a job yet?" The baby pressed into her, holding the bottle tight. She held on to him and headed toward the back of the apartment.

Iris was already in bed, lying on top of the blanket, resting on several pillows. In the corner of the room, up against the wall, was a wooden crib. Maricarmen sat him down on the mattress and took his bottle, still more than half full.

"God, he's heavy," Maricarmen said, laughing.

"Tito never stops eating," Doña Iris said. "And he's already eighteen months."

"Where's your other son?" Maricarmen asked.

On the bed, Doña Iris opened her eyes. "You don't have to stay. I'll be okay."

"You haven't eaten."

"I will. Just leave the food. I'll eat it later."

"Will you be okay? Really?"

In the crib, the baby was already asleep on his back.

"Don't worry," Doña Iris said. "He sleeps through the night. And Doña Matos drops by when she gets off her shift. She has a key."

Maricarmen looked around the room. "Do you need another blanket or anything?"

"No no no. It's hot as hell in here." Doña Iris laughed, waved her hand, shooing her away.

"Get some sleep, then. I'll come check on you in a couple of hours."

Doña Iris closed her eyes. "Gracias, mamita."

Maricarmen watched her a few seconds before closing the bedroom door behind her. In the living room, as she was heading out, the door swung open.

The eldest, Rey, who she'd only ever seen from across the street while he played basketball, bumped into her, almost knocking her down. She backed against a wall, steadying herself.

"Sorry," he said. "Didn't know you were there."

It took her a moment, but she managed to stand up straight, rubbed her elbow where it'd scraped the wall.

"Your mom's asleep. The baby ate, but she hasn't eaten. Can you—"

"Don't worry, I got it."

He stood there looking down at her, his soft curls haloing his head. The first time she ever saw him, his head was shaved. Now she had to fight the urge to touch his curls. She was glad he'd grown them out.

Later, she would spend hours recalling this moment, going over all the things she should've said, how she should've introduced herself or asked him if he wanted her to stay or asked him *anything*. Why los camarones had been looking for him, and how he'd managed to avoid them, and where he spent his days other than on the basketball courts with the guys, and how come the cops had never picked him up there, or had they? She would remember all those conversations with all those other boys, with men, with David, who she considered a friend, all those times she'd been confident and funny and so damn smart. But she couldn't come up with a single word.

She nodded, slipped out the door.

AFTER A FEW weeks, the cops stopped looking for Rey. They forgot about him or moved on to other guys, other cases. He started coming around again, joining Ismael and Cano on the basketball courts, then they'd walk over to Cano's apartment for drinks, and Doña Matos would pour them tall glasses of Kola Champagne, offer them food. During those afternoons, they'd sit around Doña Matos's kitchen table, shooting the shit, sometimes play cards. Rey had learned to play poker with his uncle Ojeda, but the guys never had more than a couple dollars to gamble. Rey didn't mind, though.

One afternoon, Rey brought out the deck, but Cano wasn't interested. He didn't have the money. He told Rey and Ismael how he was supposed to finish his degree, but things had gotten *hard*. He had his part-time job at the library, but that wasn't enough for tuition, for books. It would take him an extra year to finish. He didn't feel like playing.

"Besides," Cano said, "I don't feel like losing my last two quarters to a kid."

Rey laughed and left the deck on the table, sipping on his Kola Champagne.

"I've been writing songs," Ismael said. He was trying to get his band together. Ismael was always trying to start a band, but nobody ever took him seriously. "There's this guy up in San Lorenzo. They call him the Carpenter. He's a drum maker, works with mahogany for custom-made congas."

Cano smirked. "Custom-made? Who has that kind of money?"

"Not me," Ismael said. "I got a pair of used ones from Don Ojeda for like thirty dollars."

They all laughed.

"So you're really doing it," Cano said, just being nice. He knew that Ismael could play, but the band thing would never happen.

"I'm doing it," Ismael said. "Watch. When I get famous, all you sorry fools will come running."

"I could play with you, you know," Rey said.

Ismael smiled, slapped him on the shoulder. "You can sing too."

Nowadays, Rey wrote these ballads that he sang all over el Caserío, busting out in a falsetto whenever he saw a group of girls walking home from school, serenading the abuelas whenever he worked the register at Don Ojeda's store, making the schoolgirls blush or giggle, the older women saying things like *If only I was thirty years younger.* Everybody called him Rey el Cantante.

"But you gotta stay out of trouble if we're gonna make this happen."

"Listen," Cano said. "I don't know if you two will get famous, but if you get some gigs, I have my van. It's old, has no seats in the back, but it works. I can drive you."

Ismael raised his glass. "It's a deal, then. When we make it big, I'll get some fucking custom congas and I'll buy you whatever you want. Hell, I'll pay your fucking tuition."

Cano raised his glass of Kola Champagne. "To Maelo Conga."

"To Maelo fucking Conga," Ismael said, reaching for his own glass.

"Who the hell is Maelo?" Rey asked.

Cano and Ismael laughed.

"How long you known me, man?" Ismael said.

"All right, then. To custom congas and Cano's tuition." Rey drank, put his glass down hard on the table, then shot up out of his chair. "Wait here. I'll be right back." He took off. Cano watched him fly out the door.

When he came back a few minutes later to Cano and Ismael still sitting at the table, Rey pulled out a stack of bills, started counting, laid the pile on the table in front of Cano.

Cano kept his head down. He hadn't asked for money, especially from a kid. He pushed the money back across the table. "What are you doing, man?"

"It's for your tuition," Rey said. "And for our ride. How we gonna start this band if we have no ride?"

"I'm not taking your money," Cano said.

"You take care of me, I take care of you," Rey said. He wouldn't hear any more. He left the money on the table and walked out.

REY AND ISMAEL practiced for months while they found other musicians for their band. Eventually, they had a guy on trumpet, a trombonist, a bassist, a guy on keyboards, and Ismael's cousin Edgar as the temporary lead singer until they found someone better. Rey and Ismael were always at practice, but some guys came and went with the hurricane season. They couldn't find a good lead singer, and Rey didn't want to sing. He was a drummer, no matter how much Ismael insisted he should sing.

"*You* sing," Rey said every time Ismael brought it up. "This whole thing was *your* idea. It's *your* band."

"But you're a singer," Ismael said.

"I can sing, but I'm not a singer. I freeze up, man."

Ismael had heard this story. Rey was just a kid at church, singing with a choir full of church girls. He was talented—everybody knew he was talented—but he could only perform with a group. Until one day, he was supposed to get up and sing a solo in church. He'd been nervous, he told Ismael later, but he never expected that when the time came, he would just *freeze*. And that's exactly what happened. He froze. But that was a long time ago. "If you can sing all over the streets, you can sing onstage," Ismael said.

They managed to keep Edgar on vocals, Ismael and Rey and the rest of the band practicing like every day, five days a week, for months. But they had nothing to practice for, no gigs. Until Cano's older brother, David the deacon, who'd moved into the Catholic parish in el pueblo as he prepared to be ordained, came home for a visit. Doña Matos was so happy to have him home, so proud that her son would soon be a priest, she cooked all his favorite foods: mofongo con camarones, arroz con gandules, pernil, tembleque. It was just the three of them, but she made enough food for a party. That's how Cano got the idea, then went to find Rey and Ismael at the basketball courts.

"A party for your brother?" Rey asked. "Is it his birthday?"

"Nah. He's getting ordained. He's going to be a priest."

"They have parties for that?"

Ismael clapped his hands. "This is el Caserío, my man. We have parties for everything!"

Rey went to his tío Ojeda's store for the beer, Cano and Ismael went to get the band, and an hour later, news of the party had spread all over el Caserío Padre Rivera. Maricarmen and Loli brought a charcoal grill and a bag of charcoal. Ismael brought meat for pinchos. Evelyn from down the street brought a pastelón, and her son, Maricarmen's friend Carmelo, brought two coolers full of ice. Soon everybody was out in the street with whatever they could afford to bring. A six-pack of Kola Champagne for the kids, some ice, potato salad, a pack of hot dogs, plastic cups, paper plates, hot dog buns, more beer than they could possibly drink in one night. People called their friends down in Patagonia, who arrived ready for a party—everybody knew Doña Matos from the neighborhood or the hospital. And everybody knew her eldest son from church. David the deacon, the good one, called by God, destined to be a priest.

So Rey and Ismael and their band played their first gig, a spontaneous Catholic block party. Rey on timbales, Ismael on congas, Edgar on vocals. Ismael and Rey played like they were stars, all eyes on them. Nobody knew that, to them, this felt exactly like living a dream. People just knew that while David stood outside, smiling and chatting and shaking hands with all the neighbors, a band played salsa. They weren't great, but they weren't embarrassing either. They were boys, nineteen, twenty-two, twenty-three, with a little talent and a lot of guts, who decided they would do something nobody in el Caserío had ever thought they could do. And that night, the neighbors, their friends, *everybody* danced.

Maricarmen danced with Carmelo and Loli, the three of them laughing and singing along and spinning each other late into the night. The neighbors were still dancing in the street, even after Evelyn and most of the women went home, leaving only the girls behind, after David the deacon went to sleep in his childhood bed, long after the band had stopped playing and Ismael had turned into a DJ taking requests, playing Héctor Lavoe, disco hits, and old boleros.

As Loli started dancing with Carmelo, Maricarmen went to get a drink. That was the first time she had a real conversation with Rey, who handed her a Medalla from a cooler and asked her name. He'd been watching her awhile. She'd noticed him while he played, younger than all the other musicians, dark skinned and baby faced, with dark fuzz over his upper lip (that maybe could someday be a mustache), and all those curls.

"How long have you been playing?" she asked him.

He took a moment, then shrugged. "I don't know. Always."

"Always? You mean like your whole life?" Maricarmen asked.

"Something like that."

"Did you take music lessons?"

"Yes and no," he said. "I taught myself. My uncle's a musician too. You know how sometimes there are things you can just *do*, and nobody has to teach you?"

"I guess."

"I had a music teacher, but the lessons didn't teach me anything I didn't already know."

Maricarmen studied his face. She'd taken a few music classes, a handful of voice lessons with Don Ojeda that she paid for with money she made cleaning apartments. She'd dreamed of being a singer once, like Lucecita Benítez, or Blanca Rosa Gil, or like La Lupe on the Myrta Silva show, hips swaying from side to side, singing "La Tirana," beautiful and irreverent and free. But that had been a dream.

He continued. "Music is like that for me. Just comes naturally."

"You mean the timbales, or like any instrument?"

"Timbales, congas, bongos, singing—"

"Singing?"

He nodded.

Maricarmen laughed. "How come you have *that* guy singing, then?" She pointed toward the band's abandoned instruments, where Edgar was smoking a cigarette. "He's not even good."

They both laughed.

"How's Doña Iris doing?" Maricarmen asked, changing the subject.

Rey shrugged. "You know. Not great. Sleeps a lot."

"And your little brother?"

"Tito. Runs around all day. *Sooo* much energy."

She nodded. "Must be hard for your mom."

"I'm around, and so's my uncle, but, yeah. It ain't easy."

They kept talking while all their friends danced in the street. Loli and Carmelo didn't skip a single song, while Cano and Ismael danced with all the neighborhood girls.

Maricarmen occasionally cut in to twirl around with Loli, turning her this way and that way, then handing her off to Carmelo when she went to the cooler for another drink—an excuse to get back to Rey. Over by the cooler, Rey and the rest of the band, all of them drunk, were gathered around the last of the beer.

"Saved you one," Rey said, handing her another Medalla.

"No, thanks," she said, and waved it away. "Got anything else?"

Loli came up and took it for herself. "Thank you!"

"Loli!" Maricarmen snatched the beer out of her little sister's hand.

"What's the matter?" Rey asked Maricarmen. "Your mom doesn't let you drink?" When Maricarmen told him she was still in high school, and that Loli was only fourteen, he threw his head back, laughing.

The guys joined him, laughing their asses off.

Maricarmen took a sip of her beer, her face growing hot.

Loli extended her hand, asking for a sip.

"Just one," Maricarmen said, tipping the can so Loli could get a quick drink.

Carmelo headed their way and everybody turned.

"Who's that? Your bodyguard?" Rey asked. The guys exploded with laughter.

Carmelo didn't say anything, just lit a cigarette. He was younger than the other guys, a quiet skinny boy who had exactly two friends: Maricarmen and Loli.

"That's my pana, Carmelo," Maricarmen said, and quickly changed the subject. "So you guys write your own songs?"

Ismael smiled, put his hand around Rey. "This guy right here. He writes most of them." He smacked his friend's chest lightly. "Rey el Cantante. Isn't that what all the girls call you?"

"Rey? That's you?" Loli asked. "I thought Rey el Cantante was supposed to be *sexy*."

Rey covered his face with one hand but couldn't stop laughing.

"Loli!" Maricarmen said, a little too loudly.

"That's what all the girls around the neighborhood are saying," Loli said.

They talked and talked, late into the night. Ismael told them about Rey coming home after two years in a work camp for juveniles, how he'd had a real hard life but finally got his shit together, and now there he was. There they all were. And one day, they'd be able to leave this place.

"I would toast to that," Ismael said, "but we're out of beer."

Nobody wanted to go home. They had turned the music down, but it was still playing. And when a song they liked came on, they all swayed a little, everybody waiting for something—*anything*—to happen. And then something did.

Cano saw them first, put his empty can of Medalla on the ground. "Hey, man. Here come los camarones," he said to the group, and took a few steps back.

Everybody did the same. Spread out, put down their cans.

Loli immediately started walking home, as if she hadn't seen the cops at all. Her mother would be mad as hell if los camarones brought her home at three in the morning.

"Mari, come on," Loli said, then kept walking.

But Maricarmen stayed behind.

All those years later, they would all remember this moment. How they stood there watching as the two cops strutted toward them, trampling the moriviví that covered their front lawns, one of them holding his club, ready to strike, the other reaching for his sidearm. How nobody moved, all of them frozen where they stood, where they had been their whole lives, where their families had lived since the beginning of the colonial project that bulldozed their ancestral homes and sent them off to live in the caseríos públicos all over Puerto Rico, places built for the poor. Places for people like *them*, and their parents before them, and their children after. Maricarmen and Loli and their mother. Carmelo and his mother, Evelyn. Rey and Tito and their mother, Iris; and his tío Ojeda; and his dead father. Rey's friends, Ismael and Cano. David the deacon asleep in his room, and Doña Matos, his mother, already working her nursing shift at Ryder Memorial. Loli already inside the apartment, watching from the window as her mother slept. Their neighbors, their friends, their families. How they all let themselves believe that their homes, their bodies, were their own. That they had a right to dance and sing in the street, drink a beer.

Once, el Caserío Padre Rivera had been a place of fairy tales, promises of new beginnings and urban renewal. But it wasn't long before they all understood that everybody else didn't live with the American factories dumping waste into their drinking water, with black ash snowing over them a few months a year. They'd come to understand that nothing was random, everything was connected, everything was *deliberate*. That the violence of their neighborhood would always echo the violence los camarones brought with them.

Los camarones, who arrived late into the night, who caught Cano and Rey and Maricarmen and their friends as they laughed together a few steps from their front doors, a few feet from their beds. The cop who lifted his pistol, Officer Altieri, as they stood frozen in front of Cano's building. Altieri, who told them all to put their hands in the air. Who jumped, startled, when Rey laughed nervously. Who brought down his gun on the side of Rey's face, knocking him sideways onto the dirt. And as they all scrambled, reaching for Rey, as Maricarmen screamed, threw herself to the ground where Rey fell, holding him against her, all the other guys between Altieri and Rey, it was Cano who tried to reason with the cops, his hands still raised in the air.

"Hey, you know me, man," Cano said to Altieri. "You know my mother. She's a nurse at Ryder Memorial?" Cano waited for some sign that Altieri had heard him, his hands shaking uncontrollably. "My brother's a deacon. He's going to be a priest. David. This party's for him."

Cano looked to the other cop, who'd stepped beside Altieri. He wasn't sure what else to say.

"He's just a kid, man," Altieri's partner said.

Slowly Altieri's gun came down, turned toward the sidewalk, finger off the trigger.

Cano looked them both in the eyes, his hands held high, his knees locked. But Altieri was looking *through* him, down at the ground, where Maricarmen was pressing her hand to the side of Rey's bleeding face, and Carmelo was pulling off his T-shirt, handing it over to her. Altieri was watching Maricarmen. Cano knew it. He didn't need confirmation. Altieri had his eyes on her, this white girl among a group of Caserío kids—a group of Black boys—and all the man could see was the story he'd told himself about who they were. And Cano didn't need anyone to tell him what that story was.

"El Ratón"

PRESSING CARMELO'S BLOODSTAINED T-shirt against the cut on Rey's eyebrow—Rey fading, eyes closed—Maricarmen summoned all her courage and turned to look at los camarones.

"He needs to go to a hospital," she said, her voice firm.

"We can drive him to el Ryder," Cano said.

Carmelo reached down to lift Rey up, and Ismael helped him. Cano ran across the street to get his van.

The other cop took Altieri by the arm and pulled him toward the police cruiser.

Between Carmelo and Ismael, they carried Rey, hoisted him gently into the back of Cano's van.

Sitting on the floor, Maricarmen felt the rusted-out walls of the van against her back, Rey's head on her lap. She kept the T-shirt pressed against his face. Ismael sat with her while Cano drove. Carmelo, shirtless, rode shotgun.

"Ese cabrón broke his face," Maricarmen said, trying to keep her voice steady.

Ismael nodded. "He could've killed him."

Maricarmen met Ismael's gaze. She hadn't had that much to drink, but los camarones had sobered her up. "Why would they do this? He didn't do anything wrong."

"Look around, Mari," Carmelo said from the front seat. "You're a white girl surrounded by Black boys from el Caserío."

"So what? I'm from el Caserío too," she said.

Ismael met her eyes.

"You know what I'm saying," Carmelo said.

Maricarmen kept her hand on the T-shirt, but it was covered in blood. She wasn't sure if it was helping. "I'm sorry," she said to Rey.

Rey held his hand up slowly but didn't speak.

"This is what they do," Ismael said.

When they pulled up to the emergency room entrance, Ismael jumped out of the van to get a wheelchair. The guys lifted Rey and set him down, wheeled him into hospital reception, where Cano told them he was Nurse Matos's son. A nurse pushed Rey's wheelchair to an examination room while the friends stayed behind, just stood in the waiting room not knowing what to do. Maricarmen covered in blood, her head spinning. Carmelo shirtless and shivering, smaller than the other guys. Ismael and Cano pacing like worried parents.

Maricarmen sat down quietly, looking at her bloody hands. *I'm sorry*, she wanted to say. *I'm sorry* for Carmelo's shirt, for Cano's van, for the blood on her hands. For all the things she'd been so willing to overlook.

Ismael patted her on the back. "Doña Matos will patch him up."

It was then, in that hospital waiting room, that she felt it for the first time. Surrounded by Rey's friends, and Carmelo, who'd always been like her brother. These guys, who cared about Rey, who'd thrown him into the van and rushed him to the hospital. It was just a feeling she didn't have the language for. Not yet. But she was glad they were there.

THEY LET REY out of the hospital two days later. Sent him home with sixteen stitches, a fractured eye socket, and a lacerated eyeball. He was *lucky*, they said. He'd almost lost his left eye.

Maricarmen went to see him every day after school, stopped by his place at the north entrance to el Caserío. The apartment seemed darker than it had when she'd been there before, dusty and messy, like nobody was looking after the family. These days, Doña Iris hardly left her room, Tito crawling all over Rey while he lay in his own bed, his head bandaged, eye covered with gauze and an adhesive eye patch. When Don Ojeda or Doña Matos weren't taking care of Tito, he had to stay with Rey.

Maricarmen came by because she was worried about Rey, but also Tito. She hated to think of him left behind. The poor kid toddling around while his brother was convalescing and his mother was locked away in her bedroom.

That third day, she finally worked up the courage to ask, "How's Doña Iris?"

Tito climbed onto the bed.

"She doesn't sleep anymore," Rey said. "Medication doesn't help."

"Has Doña Matos been by to see her?" she asked, picking up the baby.

"She comes by every day. Gives her an injection. Looks in on me and Tito."

"She's gonna get better, Rey," Maricarmen said. Tito played with her earrings.

"Mari, I want that more than anything. But she's not going to get better."

Somehow, hearing him say those words stung, even though Doña Iris was not her mother but his.

"Don't say that," she said. "You don't know that." Tito pulled on her earring, and she took his fat little hand in hers.

Rey watched her with his one good eye.

She didn't know what Rey was thinking, but after a while, a single tear rolled down his cheek. She wanted to wipe it off. "What about your uncle? Has he been around?"

"He's always around. Looking out for us. Takes care of Tito. Makes breakfast and shit."

"He's a good man," she said.

"He's been like a father. My real father, all he ever did was drink."

She glanced down at her Mary Janes, felt her face flush. She'd heard the story: Rey's father, everybody said, drank himself to death. He'd broken into Ojeda's store and started pulling bottles off the shelf. The next morning, when Don Ojeda opened el colmado, he found his brother passed out behind the register. Ojeda called the ambulance. The brother died that night.

Tito smiled up at her, put his hands in her hair. She took one of his chubby fists, kissed it, and he laughed.

"I can make you guys something to eat," she said. "What do you have?"

Rey shrugged. "There's bread. Eggs, maybe. Some ham."

She made them revoltillo with pan sobao, café con leche for her and Rey. She fed Tito while he sat on her lap and Rey watched.

"You're amazing," Rey said to her that afternoon, and took her hand.

She came back every day after that, even on the weekends, rain or shine.

ONCE THEY FOUND out that Maricarmen was taking care of him, Rey's friends didn't visit him until late afternoon. She usually went over after school, made an early dinner for Rey and Tito, fed Doña Iris. When Maricarmen arrived, Doña Iris always complimented her.

"You're such a good girl," Doña Iris told her every day. "Your mother is so lucky to have you." She would pray for Maricarmen,

Doña Iris said, that God would protect her and her mother and her little sister.

Every day, Maricarmen made sure to get Doña Iris into the shower, scrub her back, dry her, dress her in clean clothes. She changed her bedding and put it in the washer, then hung the laundry out to dry. Rey tried to help. As he got stronger, he did a little more around the house, washing the dishes and bathing Tito.

Every afternoon, as Maricarmen left Rey's building, she'd run into Cano and Ismael walking up the front steps.

"You guys always wait for me to leave before coming up," she said one day.

"Yeah," Ismael said.

Cano bounced the basketball once, looking down at his shoes.

"How come?" She knew the answer but wanted to hear it from them.

"Don't you and Rey need privacy?" Ismael asked.

Cano smacked Ismael's chest lightly with the back of his hand, and Ismael laughed. Cano palmed his basketball.

"Privacy?" Maricarmen crossed her arms.

"Look," Cano said, "Rey asked us not to come up until you left, that first time you went over. After that, we just figured he wanted to be alone with you."

Maricarmen smiled. It was exactly what she expected. "Okay." She turned to leave, and then—

"Also. I don't know if I should say this, but"—Cano searched her face like he was trying to decide if he should say what was on his mind—"your mom."

"My mom?" Maricarmen felt the hair on the back of her neck stand up.

"Don't take this the wrong way," Cano said, "but your mom

doesn't like people. Or, you know." He gestured to himself and then Ismael. "She doesn't like *our* people."

"Your mom's been coming around here," Ismael said, his voice direct, serious.

Maricarmen felt her face burn with heat. "What?"

"She walks by on her way home from el pueblo, every day after work. You get what I'm saying?" Ismael reached for Cano's basketball.

She did get it. Maricarmen had told her mother she was cleaning houses in the afternoon, not that she was taking care of Doña Iris and her family. Blanca had no reason to walk by Rey's building on her way home from work. The road from el pueblo, from her job, was in the opposite direction. Maricarmen's building was on the other side of el Caserío. Blanca, she understood, suspected something was going on with Rey.

Ismael continued. "A couple of times, she stopped at the bottom of the stairs."

"She stopped because we were here, Mari," Cano said. "Standing *right here*."

"But your mom is scary, you get what I'm saying?" Ismael said. "We can't stop her if she wants to go upstairs."

"How you gonna say that, man?" Cano shook his head. "I'm sorry, Mari."

She didn't know what he was apologizing for exactly. She was sure she was the one who needed to apologize for her mother, or would need to, eventually.

MAYBE IF HER mother knew how sick Doña Iris was, Maricarmen thought, Blanca would realize how much the woman needed help.

"I've been cleaning Doña Iris's apartment," she told her mother as they sat down to dinner. "She has cancer."

"I know," her mother said. She didn't look up from her rice and beans.

Loli exhaled. "Can we go one day without some sad shit coming up?"

Loli had just turned fifteen, and could not stop talking about how she would not be having a quinceañera, because they couldn't afford it. Maricarmen had turned seventeen two months before, and she didn't get a party either. Blanca had never thrown her a party. Never. Not a single birthday celebration in seventeen years.

"You know she's going to die," Blanca said.

Maricarmen didn't know what to say to that.

"So make sure you get paid *before* she dies." Blanca cut a large piece of chuleta and stuffed it in her mouth.

"Jesus, Mami," Loli said.

AS THE MONTHS passed and the days got hotter, Maricarmen kept working. She cleaned apartments, took care of Doña Iris and Tito, spent time with Rey. She saved as much money as she could after helping her mother with the bills. Summer in el Caserío meant there would be more kids to take care of, more cleaning for the elderly people, but Maricarmen also looked forward to having her days to herself while her mother was at work at the hair salon. Maybe, Maricarmen thought, she could even get a real summer job. But jobs around el Caserío were almost impossible to find. She didn't have a car, and if she wanted to find something, she'd have to find a way to get down to the beach, where all the tourist spots were.

That summer, Rey and Ismael started playing at fiestas patronales, weddings, and a couple of beachside spots, covering La Sonora Ponceña and El Gran Combo de Puerto Rico. Maricarmen didn't think Rey should go back to playing so soon after his injury, especially with his mom so sick, but he wouldn't listen. Some days, she'd hitch a ride in Cano's van, or take Loli on a carro público to catch their shows. They went almost every day for a week. She'd told Blanca that they were going to the fiestas in Fajardo, but then, Maricarmen had no idea how, Blanca found out that the guys would be playing.

"I won't have you following some cocolos around like you're their fucking cueros!" she said when Maricarmen and Loli came home from one of their shows.

Loli threw herself on the couch. "So, what, you want us to be prisoners in this house?"

"It's just music and dancing!" Maricarmen said.

"Not anymore!"

Maricarmen cried herself to sleep that night, and every night she wasn't allowed to see Rey. For weeks, she imagined the small stages at the carnivals, the outdoor parties, Cano hauling their instruments from one pueblo to another to play las fiestas, Guánica to Loíza to Santa Isabel. Until one afternoon, before their mother was home from work, Loli came in with some news.

"Cano got me a job," Loli said, her face lit up in a bright smile. "The guys are playing at El Paseo, this tourist spot, a beachside restaurant. They need servers."

El Paseo was a big place, with a small stage for live music for tourists and families, some outdoor seating. Maricarmen had only heard of it. Blanca had never taken them.

"So what? You came to rub it in my face?" Maricarmen was sitting on her bed in a long T-shirt she'd been wearing for three days straight. Her hair was a tangled, greasy mess.

"¡No seas pendeja!" Loli said. She sat on the bed. "You know Mami won't let me take the job unless you're there too. And if the two of us are there together, we can look out for each other."

Maricarmen uncrossed her arms, sat up straighter. "Nobody got *me* a job. What do you want me to do?"

Loli pulled back her sister's bedsheets. "Get up, sucia. Wash yourself, get dressed. Cano's gonna drive us to talk to the owner."

Maricarmen didn't move.

"He just needs to take one look at you, see you clear a table, bring over some plates and shit...whatever. Just get dressed!" Loli walked to the mirror over Maricarmen's bureau. "Wear something sexy. Rey will be there."

That made her get up. Maricarmen was dressed—her hair blow-dried, her makeup soft, her neck and wrists perfumed—in under an hour.

On their way out the door, Blanca came in.

"Where do you two think *you're* going?"

Maricarmen was determined. She was going to see Rey. And there was nothing her mother could do to stop her. "Loli and I have job interviews. We have to go."

"A job interview where?" Blanca asked. "Looking like that?"

"It's a chinchorro, Mami," Loli said. "They just need people to work the fryers for the summer."

"Bendición," Maricarmen said. She didn't wait for her mother's response, just pulled the door shut.

Maricarmen and Loli started working every Thursday, Friday, and Saturday afternoon into the night, slinging drinks and serving mofongo con camarones, bacalaítos, alcapurrias, and ensalada de pulpo to gringos from New York and Philadelphia. The food was good, since all the cooks were local, but it was expensive. At El Paseo, Mari and Loli pretended they were women, spraying themselves with too much perfume, hitching up and knotting their shirts to reveal their midriffs, reapplying their red lipstick during every break. Once the sun set and the men crowded around the bar, Mari and Loli smiled at all the half-drunk men, called them all *papi*. They accepted every drink offered to them, letting the men believe that they were in control, but only took sips here and there. When Ismael and Rey played a song everyone loved, they let the men take them out on the dance floor in front of the stage, grab them by the waist, and pull them close.

Mari and Loli kept an eye on each other, Mari making sure Loli didn't drink too much, and Loli making sure the drunks didn't get too close to either of them. Maricarmen was smart, but Loli was bold, brave. All the other waitresses were older, women in their twenties or thirties, mothers with kids in school, and they all called Mari and Loli *mamita* or *mi amor*, never by their names. Maricarmen and Loli had stopped spending Fridays and Saturdays at the beach with friends, hanging out in the neighborhood. They'd traded their bikinis for aprons.

For seventeen-year-old Maricarmen and fifteen-year-old Loli, El Paseo felt a little closer to freedom, making more money in one week than they'd ever held in their hands. In el Caserío, they'd known only poverty. They'd always depended on the money Blanca brought home from her job at the salon, which wasn't much, and the money Maricarmen made from cleaning and babysitting. Outside their neighborhood, in their classes at Ana Roqué, everybody talked about people in el Caserío Padre Rivera like they were lazy, all drug dealers and drug users who were up to no good and didn't work, since they paid only a few dollars in rent a month. But all the people she knew worked *hard*, fixing cars, changing tires, repairing refrigerators, cooking food to sell at kioskos on the weekends. There were also nurses and teachers, bus drivers and factory workers, a lot of cane cutters, and the guy who sold granos at seven o'clock every single morning. But you were lucky to find a job, everyone knew this, and so she and Loli treasured their days and nights at El Paseo.

Maricarmen and Loli worked long shifts, and at the end of each night, after they'd washed all the dishes and wiped all the tables and counters, swept and mopped the whole restaurant and cleaned the bathrooms, they spread out their money on a table and counted their tips along with Ismael and Rey and the rest of the band. They waited for Cano to pull up in his van at the end of the night, some of the other guys in their cars, and then, after El Paseo, they'd all caravan up the coast toward Naguabo and park in el malecón. They became inseparable then. They did everything together, passed a joint around with the radio blasting, rolled down the windows, the wind blowing, the salt in their hair. And it was there, Cano's van parked in el malecón, all of them strolling the path in front of the rocks, watching the moonlight over the ocean, the girls chewing spearmint gum, Loli blowing a bubble wide as her face, the guys passing around the joint, that Rey reached into his backpack, pulled out his kit. Another baggie, needle and syringe, cotton balls, spoon, lighter, tourniquet.

Maricarmen wasn't sure what she was staring at. She looked up at Rey.

"Don't worry," he said. "I can do it for you."

THAT SUMMER, PERICO and H spread around el Caserío like wildfire. Whenever she walked by la plaza or the basketball courts, Maricarmen spotted the tiradores hustling, selling to a neighbor, a family friend, a postal worker she'd seen around the block. Men, young and old, she recognized from the neighborhood as grandfathers, friends' fathers and brothers. Occasionally, she also saw women. Every time she recognized one of the women from her neighborhood, she burned with shame as she remembered that night with Rey, when she tried H. How when she woke up in Cano's van, there was Loli, sitting in the driver's seat, staring at her, eyes narrow, disappointment all over her little sister's face. How that look told Maricarmen all she needed to know about being a good sister, that even though they were their mother's daughters, all they really had was each other, and Maricarmen had let Loli down.

I won't do it again, Mari had said immediately. And Loli had pursed her lips, gotten out of the van, and before slamming the door shut, said, *You better not*. She'd felt awful after that, sick for a whole day. Before, Maricarmen had thought of people who used drugs as lost and faceless addicts, destined for prison or early deaths. But now she saw them differently. It could be anybody. It had almost been *her*. She never wanted to feel that again.

That summer, as the weeks passed, she saw that it was not just perico and H, but other drugs tearing through el Caserío. And los camarones were everywhere, the entire neighborhood under surveillance. Police cruisers rolling up to la plaza in the middle of the afternoon, after los tiradores had a whole day of slinging, their bundles of cash spread on the sidewalk as they were handcuffed and thrown in the back. Ambulances screaming through the front gate, paramedics wheeling out stretcher after stretcher. Later, Maricarmen would read all about the weekend's overdoses on the pages of *El Mundo* or *El Imparcial* and discover that there was a heroin epidemic sweeping *all* of Puerto Rico's caseríos.

MARICARMEN HAD STARTED noticing things. She noticed that until that summer, most of the people she'd seen every day of her life had not changed. They'd always lived in the same place, never traveled outside of Puerto Rico, never got to think about having more. Of course, they wanted money to feed their families, clothe their kids, send them to school. But usually you didn't get to leave. If you were lucky enough to find a job, the pay was shit.

Nearly everyone she knew in el Caserío had been sent there after they lost their land to the government: When she was a kid, her mom had had to move them there after the government said she couldn't prove she owned her land, where Blanca's family had been for generations. Maricarmen remembered the day they were evicted, how the cops arrived with two guys from el pueblo, how they had put the little furniture they owned on the dirt road in front of their house, the uniformed cops threatening to put Blanca in handcuffs when she refused to leave the property. And how their neighbors watched them through their windows, everyone too afraid to come outside, to say anything. Maybe everyone suspected they would be next.

Their old neighborhood, the whole seaside community, was bulldozed to make room for a hotel. Their old house was now part of the hotel's parking lot. Families had lived en el campo or on the beach since before Puerto Rico was a Spanish colony, but the American government didn't recognize handwritten documents in Spanish and didn't recognize verbal agreements. Maricarmen had seen photographs of other zinc-roofed, one-room houses on the coast that were demolished. Shantytowns, the government called them. Their wooden barns and houses on stilts were torn apart. Eminent domain, the government said. But there was no compensation. Instead, they'd all been sent off to live in el Caserío Padre Rivera. Maricarmen's family; Doña Matos and her two sons, Cano and David; Evelyn and Carmelo; Don Ojeda and his brother—all of them had been displaced there. But they had made el Caserío theirs—they had made it *home*. Maricarmen remembered that when she was a kid, it had been safe. She'd had no idea that they were poor, only that they were happy. Nowadays, most people left el Caserío in a police car or a body bag or a celebration, their story all over the local papers.

THAT SUMMER, AS Maricarmen and Loli served food and drinks in El Paseo, they spent more and more time with the guys. Maricarmen got used to seeing Rey during her shift, to feeling his eyes on her as she cleared a table, as she picked up the bills and coins left for her by customers, as she wiped the tables and chairs. One Saturday afternoon, as she placed drinks on a table, Loli caught her eye from the bar. Loli's eyes were wide as she mouthed the words, *Look! Rey!* and pointed toward the band.

Maricarmen held her empty tray with one hand, like she'd forgotten what to do, then caught herself. She took the tray back to the bar, dropped it on the counter for the bartender, and watched the band. El Paseo was full, customers sitting at every table, sipping their drinks, smiling and swaying to the music. They started with keyboards, and she recognized the chords immediately—they were covering Cheo Feliciano's "El Ratón." But what struck her was that it was Rey on the mic, about to sing. She'd *never* heard him sing.

Loli was hopping around on her feet, ready to dance—she couldn't help her excitement, Mari realized. They smiled at each other nervously. Nobody had heard Rey sing with the band before. This was a first for all of them.

As Rey leaned toward the mic, the scar above his left eye visible in the spotlight, Ismael playing the congas, a soft steady beat accompanying the keyboards, the whole restaurant went quiet, only the sounds of the music. Maricarmen's heart hammered in her chest. And then, when Rey sang, *Mi gato se está quejando / que no puede vacilar*, the crowd sprang, clapping and woo-hooing like they were listening to a star. Everybody loved Cheo Feliciano, especially this song, and everybody loved Rey's cover.

She scanned the crowd, all the customers singing along, like they were at a concert. They weren't just at a restaurant by the beach—they had been transported. The horns blaring, the bass's low rhythmic rumbling, the stroke of Ismael's congas. Rey closed his eyes and sang, his body swaying. He was there, but he wasn't, Maricarmen realized. He was somewhere else, somewhere far far away. He was feeling every note, not at a beachside restaurant with guys from the neighborhood. When

Rey sang, his voice was aimed at the sky, at *her*, at every woman sitting there watching. He was lifting them up with his song. They were flying.

And as she listened, Maricarmen grasped something about his body, about the way he moved. How her own body would feel against his, underneath his weight. It was then, for the first time in her life, that she understood something about love—the ache deep in her chest, Rey in front of that mic, everything she wanted, the scar on his face like a reminder of how she had held him. And how come he never wanted to sing when he'd always had that voice inside him? That voice, that song, how it pulled at the seams of her. He seemed so out of reach then. If she tried to touch him, would he disappear?

He wasn't hers—she saw that then. He was everybody's, and he would be a star. He would never be hers. Even though she loved him, she understood that she also hated him. Just a little. Just enough for it to hurt.

LATER THAT NIGHT, after they closed up the restaurant, Maricarmen and Loli swept and mopped the floors, wiped off every table and chair, cleaned the restrooms, washed all the glasses at the bar, and counted their tips.

"Are the guys waiting for us?" Loli asked.

Maricarmen nodded. She picked up her purse from where it usually sat on the bottom shelf behind the bar. She hadn't said a word to Loli most of the night. She'd avoided her, avoided Rey, talking only to customers when it was expected. She couldn't really explain why, but after the band played their set, she'd needed time to think.

"They're out there smoking weed, aren't they?" Loli asked. She stuffed her tips into the front pocket of her shorts.

Maricarmen folded her stack of bills, put it in her purse, then threw the strap over her shoulder. "Remember, when Mami asks, one of the girls from work dropped us off," Maricarmen said. "Don't even think to mention weed, or the guys, and especially not Rey."

"Do you think I'm an idiot?"

Maricarmen patted Loli's back, smiled. "Nah. You're the smart one."

They rode to el Caserío in the back of Cano's van, the guys and Loli laughing their asses off, Maricarmen sitting quietly on the floor, her arms hugging her knees. She felt every bump, her butt bouncing on the hard metal floor, her back against the side of the van. Rey sat next to her, laughing with the rest of the guys. As she watched him, watched all of them, she felt that hollow in the pit of her stomach again. Their time together would end—it was just a matter of when.

In el Caserío, Cano parked his van in front of Rey's building, and everyone got out. Maricarmen went into her purse and pulled out a few dollar bills. "Hang on," she said to Loli.

Loli turned back to her. "What's up?"

She put the small stack in Loli's hand. "Tell Mami I had to stay late and that one of the girls will drop me off later."

"What?!" Loli inspected the money, folded it, and stuffed it in her pocket. "You can't bribe me!"

"Just do it. Tell her they asked me to help clean. Tell her it's for the money!"

Loli shook her head, punched her softly on the shoulder. "You better be home in an hour."

Maricarmen hugged Loli. Rey waited for her by the stairs, the guys already scattered back to their own apartments. Together, Maricarmen and Rey watched Loli cross the street, then turn the corner, disappear around one of the buildings. Rey took Maricarmen's hand, led her up the stairs.

Inside Rey's apartment, she let him pull her past the living room, where his uncle Ojeda was asleep on the couch, and into his bedroom. His mom and Tito must've been asleep, she thought, since she didn't hear any sounds coming from Doña Iris's bedroom. Rey shut the door behind them and sat on the bed. She let him pull her close.

They kissed for a while, Rey pressing against her, his lips soft against hers. She pulled back slightly, then tried to breathe. She was out of breath, she realized. This was all too fast—a couple of hours ago, she'd been watching him onstage, and he'd been a boy with the whole world in the palm of his hand, who could get whatever he wanted, whoever he wanted. And now they were here, on his bed.

"You all right?" he asked.

No, she wanted to say. No, she was *not* all right. He was a shooting star and she was just a girl on his bed. What the hell had she been thinking?

He kissed her again, softly, then smiled. "We don't have to do anything. Just be here with me." He put his arms around her and pulled her in for a hug.

She didn't know how to tell him what she wanted, that she wanted *him*. That she wanted *everything*.

"Hey," Rey said, taking her face in his hands. "It's you and me. And no one else." He caressed the side of her face, put his hands in her hair.

She liked the sound of that. Rey and Mari. "You're mine, then," she said.

"I'm yours." He kissed her again.

She relaxed, finally, and decided she didn't need to say the words—she could just take what she wanted. She looked into his eyes, ignored the way she felt: like she was just some simple girl who cleaned apartments around the neighborhood, who waited tables and put up with drunk men hitting on her all night for the possibility of a two-dollar tip. She wasn't just a girl. She was *his* girl, and he was hers. She pulled her shirt up over her head, tossed it aside. He stripped his own shirt off quickly. She reached down and unbuttoned his jeans. She was a woman, and he was a man, and they were in each other's arms, and they were two kids out in front of her building trying to talk to each other at a party, and he was a boy bleeding in her arms, and she was a girl pressing her hand against his bloody face trying to keep it all inside, and they were inside each other, all sweat and hair and teeth against her neck, and she could see that he *was* hers. She could see everything they were, everything they would be.

WHEN CARMELO STOPPED by a few days later, Maricarmen tried not to let him see it on her face. The way Rey had kissed all down her back as she lay naked on his bed, all the things he'd done to her, the things she'd done to him. How he'd walked her home afterward, waited across the street for her to go inside, her mother be damned. She'd been lucky that Blanca was asleep when she got home.

She let Carmelo in and closed the door behind him. He gave her a quick hug. He smelled clean, like soap and cologne, and he was sporting a fresh haircut. His afro was trimmed, oiled, and neat.

"You look nice," she said. "Where you going?"

"What do you mean?" he said. "I came to see *you*."

"I have to go to work soon," she said.

Carmelo ignored that and headed toward the back balcony. They sat in the ratty old plastic chairs, Carmelo lighting a joint and droning on about some car he wanted to buy, how his father wouldn't buy it for him, because he had a new wife and a baby to take care of, how Evelyn didn't want to hear a word about his father's new family. Maricarmen watched the cañaverales and let her mind wander—all she could think about was Rey.

"I barely see you nowadays," Carmelo said. "You never come by anymore."

"Work," she said. She wiped her sweaty face with her forearm.

"It's Rey, isn't it?"

"It's work," she insisted. She wasn't sure why she felt guilty—Carmelo was her best friend. They'd known each other their whole lives, since they were kids in elementary school. But he wasn't her boyfriend.

"You're over his house like every day." He held out the joint for her like he always did, but she shook her head.

"I have to go to Doña Iris's in an hour."

"Thought you said you had work."

"That *is* work. Besides, my mom gets home soon. She'll kick your ass."

"Let her try." He laughed, letting out a cloud of smoke.

Maricarmen avoided his gaze, kept her eyes on the sugarcane.

"Doña Iris is work now?"

"Carmelo."

"I'm just asking. Isn't that—"

"Isn't that *none of your business*?" she said.

"Don't shit where you eat, nena," Carmelo said under his breath.

Maricarmen shot up out of her chair. "I think you need to go now."

"You serious? I just got here." He narrowed his eyes at her.

"Why do I have to explain myself to you? You're not my man."

"So, you saying you explain yourself to your man." He stifled some laughter.

"Don't be a fucking asshole."

"What? How am I the asshole?"

She kicked his chair leg. "Time to go."

"Mari. What the hell? This isn't you." He dropped the half joint on the grimy balcony floor. "Fuck."

Maricarmen stepped on it, stubbing it out. "How would you know? You don't even know what's going on with me!"

He looked her in the eye, holding his hands out in front of him, a peace offering. "I'm not trying to fight with you, Mari. You just blew up for no reason. What's going on?"

In the distance, she noticed the sun high in the sky over the cañaverales. It would be setting soon, she thought.

"Rey loves me, Carmelo," she finally said. "And his mom loves me. And his little brother." She didn't say she loved him back, even though she wanted to. But from the look on Carmelo's face, she knew she didn't have to.

"Mari," Carmelo said. He opened his mouth to speak again, then looked up and stopped. He put his hands on the railing, then hoisted himself over the balcony. He took off, running toward the caña.

She watched him run toward the edge of el Caserío.

"Pack your shit, and get out." It was her mother, standing in the doorway, her arms crossed. "Now."

MARICARMEN WAS YOUNG and in love and Rey was hers, and so it didn't faze her that Blanca beat her with a chancla like she hadn't done since Maricarmen was a ten-year-old. It didn't matter, Maricarmen told herself, that her own mother had asked her, like it was a real question, *Who the hell will have you when you're left alone and disgraced and roaming the streets like una perra preñá?* Or that her own mother said Maricarmen was "una cuero barata," and put her out on the street.

She was seventeen, still in high school, and now her mother insisted she had to go.

In her bedroom, Maricarmen picked up the dresses Blanca had pulled from their hangers in the closet, dropped on the floor.

"What am I supposed to do?" Maricarmen asked.

"Figure it out," her mother said. Blanca opened Maricarmen's dresser drawers and dumped out her clothes. Bras and panties and socks, shorts and T-shirts. Everything strewn on the floor and Maricarmen's bed. "Get your shit and get out of my house."

Maricarmen wiped tears from her face, but she said nothing. She wanted to defend herself, but she knew her mother. How could she convince her that Rey was good, that he loved her, when all Blanca saw was that he was Black? She didn't want to debate her—not about this. It was better to get out of her way right now, come back later.

She set her clothes on the bed, then pulled a duffel bag from her closet. Her mother watched as she threw dresses and shorts and underwear into the bag, half folded. The more Maricarmen packed, the angrier she got. It didn't matter, she thought. She wouldn't *let it* matter. Once she was out of her mother's house, Maricarmen's life would belong to *her*. She would go stay with Rey. She would take care of Doña Iris and Tito, and her mother would regret treating her like this. Maricarmen had always been a good student. She was respectful and polite. She never missed school, never missed an assignment. She had worked since she was thirteen years old, cleaning, but also taking care of kids in the neighborhood, washing clothes by hand and hanging them out to dry. She had worked and worked, and always helped her mother.

On the way out the door, she lugged her bag and looked around the living room. Where was Loli? She had no idea where her sister was, or who she was with, and she was sure that Blanca would let her have it whenever Loli came home. She wished her little sister was there, to wrap her arms around her, to tell Maricarmen she'd be okay, to yell at their mother for treating Maricarmen like shit, to stand up for Rey, who had always been kind and respectful. She threw the strap over her shoulder as she shut the door.

"Se Me Fue"

DOÑA IRIS'S APARTMENT was a short walk from her mother's, but after Maricarmen moved in with Rey and his family, she didn't see Blanca or Loli for weeks. Every time Maricarmen thought about what her mother had said to her, she fought back tears. She missed Loli, who hadn't shown up to work at El Paseo since Maricarmen left home. She even missed Blanca, although she didn't know why.

Living with Rey and his family was more work than she'd thought it would be—Maricarmen spent all day taking care of Doña Iris and Tito, cooking and cleaning, and now that she lived with them, Rey didn't help much. He went to his band practice and came home expecting dinner before taking off again. Or he came home only to change for his weekend gig at El Paseo and barely said a word to his mother or Tito. By the time Maricarmen had to get ready for her shift, she was always so tired, she considered quitting El Paseo. But she needed the money. Somehow, she had to make a life for herself. She loved Rey, but she couldn't make this her life.

As the first day of school approached, Maricarmen knew she wouldn't go back. It would be her last year of high school, but she was so consumed with everything that had to do with Rey—Rey's mother, Rey's little brother, Rey's house, Rey's breakfast, lunch, dinner—she barely had time for herself. And she still had to make it to work. She didn't know how she would have time for school. Besides, her school uniforms were old and faded, raggedy. She desperately needed new uniforms, and she didn't want to spend the little money she'd saved. She kept making excuses whenever Rey asked about school.

"Maybe I'll sing with you or something," she said once when Rey asked what she would do. He spent day after day practicing in Don Ojeda's makeshift studio, his second bedroom. Maybe after a while, she thought, they'd let her sing backup.

Rey laughed. He didn't take it seriously, Maricarmen thought, and she didn't bring it up again.

On the first day of school, Maricarmen got up early while everyone else slept. She stood at the bedroom window, watching as all the other schoolkids headed in groups toward el pueblo. It would be the high school students first, she knew, then the little kids headed to the elementary school, and then the junior high kids. Would she see Loli? Would Loli decide to go out of her way and walk past Doña Iris's building, on the off chance that she could run into her sister?

Loli. The thought of her little sister made Maricarmen's throat hurt. She swallowed, waited. She wouldn't walk this way. Maricarmen knew it. By now, she was probably past the main entrance, right by their building. If Maricarmen went now, she could catch Loli, join her on the walk to Ana Roqué.

She moved quickly, trying not to wake Rey, pulled her uniform shirt out of her bag, not caring if it was wrinkled. She threw it on and grabbed a pair of uniform trousers and stepped into them, pulled them up, tried to button them. But they were too tight. Damn it. She peeled them off, went for a pleated skirt she hated because it made her look like one of her mother's Pentecostal friends from Patagonia. She fought with the zipper on the side of the skirt, tried pulling it up, but it wouldn't budge.

"Puta madre," she said, then gasped.

No.

She walked to the mirror over Rey's old dresser, examined herself, her hips, her belly. No. No no no. Her breasts. She turned, watching herself. The hair on her arms stood straight up.

How could she let this happen? This was exactly what her mother had said would happen.

No.

She needed her sister. She tossed the skirt on the floor, put on a pair of sweatpants she only wore in the winter. She couldn't go to school like this, in her pajama bottoms. But she needed to talk to Loli, *now*. She would stop by the apartment, even if her mother was there, to see if she could catch Loli.

She shut the door behind her and flew down the stairs, taking them two at a time. Outside, she crossed the street without checking for cars. It was still early, only the high school kids headed out of el Caserío in packs, the folks who worked the early shift at La Central Patagonia getting into their cars. Maricarmen broke into a sprint, looking at the faces of all the high school girls she saw, but none of them was her sister. She turned the corner toward the basketball courts, ran past them, then stopped in front of their building. All the lights in their apartment were off. The balcony door and windows were shut.

Maricarmen put her hand in her pocket, but then realized she'd forgotten her keys. Shit. She'd have to knock, and her mother would probably come to the door and scream at her. She wondered if Loli had already left for school, but it was still early. She could still be doing her hair or washing her face or trying to get another five minutes of sleep, for all she knew.

Maricarmen knocked hard. She didn't care what her mother said. She waited, then knocked again. Blanca would be pissed, but Maricarmen needed to see her sister. She knocked and knocked, harder, louder.

"Open the fucking door!" Maricarmen kicked the door, then tried the knob. It was open.

At first, it seemed strange, the living room appearing both larger and smaller than she'd remembered it. But how was that possible? It was dark. She turned on the overhead lights, and there, in the middle of the empty room, was a skinny black cat. Filthy, its eyes blazing, one ear clipped. A stray.

What the hell was a stray cat doing in her mother's living room? And it came to her in small bursts, like a slap in her face, then another, and another. She walked past the empty living room toward the kitchen, the empty kitchen, the door to the back balcony cracked, and she realized that's how the cat had gotten in. She shut her eyes. She fought the urge to collapse right there in the small kitchen that had been theirs, her mother's and Loli's and hers. She couldn't take this. Not today.

She walked toward her bedroom, where the door had been left open. It was completely empty. Everything was gone.

"Loli!" She ran across the hall toward her sister's bedroom.

In the empty room, only the dust bunnies in the corner, Maricarmen finally did collapse, onto her knees. She breathed deeply, thought she might vomit, but didn't. On the linoleum floor in front of her, she noticed a dull round coin. Una peseta. She picked it up. That was it. Her mother and her sister were gone, and that quarter was all that was left of their old life in this apartment.

Maricarmen lay facedown on the dusty floor, her cheek pressed into the linoleum, and cried.

HOURS LATER, THE sun filling her sister's bedroom, her face wet and grimy, sweat running down her back and chest, her scalp damp, she peeled her body off the floor. Rey would wonder where she'd run off to so early in the morning, but she couldn't bring herself to care. She wanted her sister, her own mother. Maricarmen got up finally, wiped her face on her sleeve, and walked out, leaving the apartment door wide open behind her.

She walked slowly past the canchas, ignoring the guys when they called her name, past the granos vendor pushing his cart down the street, past the dilapidated post office that was somehow still running, past a teenage boy on a bike who clearly should've been in school but instead was posted up outside la plaza, she assumed, as a lookout for los tiradores. He would see los camarones coming, haul ass to warn them, and the guys would scatter, taking off before the cops got there. She should know this kid. Was he in school with her? Suddenly, all at once, she felt so old. They were probably the same age, but she felt like an old woman.

How long had her mother and sister been gone? How long had it been since she saw Loli? A couple of weeks? A month? How long had it taken her mother to pack up the apartment, sell off whatever she could? And why hadn't Loli come to warn her? To tell her where they were going? Once, she'd had a mother and a sister, a whole life, and now, overnight, Maricarmen was alone.

At least she had Rey, she told herself. At least there was that.

Rey wasn't home when she got back. Nobody was home. Maricarmen walked through the apartment, pushed open Doña Iris's bedroom door, but nothing. The bed was unmade, the room dark. She opened the curtains, letting the sunlight filter in. The room smelled like piss and sweat. She pulled the sheets off the bed, bundled them up, and carried them toward the balcony, where the old washer was.

"Mari!" Don Ojeda called for her from the living room.

"In here," she said. She dropped the sheets in the washer, left them there. She felt nothing. She was numb.

Don Ojeda's face was swollen, eyes bloodshot. He carried Tito, who was asleep.

When she came into the kitchen, Don Ojeda immediately handed Tito over to her.

"What's wrong?" she said, cradling Tito against her. But she didn't really want to know. Not today. She couldn't do this today.

THINGS IN EL CASERÍO weren't exactly like the early days, when babies were delivered at home by midwives, when new mothers had la cuarentena, healing and bonding with the baby, resting at home for forty days after giving birth. But when it came to elders, for Doña Iris, the community kept the tradition: She was washed and laid to rest in the apartment's small living room, dressed in her best outfit, the simple white wedding dress she wore when she married Rey's father. She had lost so much weight during her years-long battle with cancer that it was loose on her body. Maricarmen applied some of the woman's makeup—some loose powder, a simple mauve lipstick. She wasn't sure what to do, but she tried her best to be helpful. She cooked, laboring for hours alone in the kitchen, grating yuca, plátano, yautía, and guineo for masa de pasteles, until Doña Matos came over to help with the food, and Don Ojeda brought over a pernil he'd made at home. The pasteles were still boiling when people started arriving.

As neighbors filed into the house, hugging Rey or shaking his hand as they entered, Don Ojeda stood by him, shaking men's hands, embracing the women. Cano and Ismael arrived with the first group, and Don Ojeda nodded hello while Rey stood by the front door awkwardly. Maricarmen sat on the couch with Tito on her lap, watching Rey. He was nervous, she thought. He didn't know what to do, what to say, so he just didn't say anything at all. Tito fell asleep as she held him, so she didn't get up to serve the pasteles. She let Doña Matos do that, even though it wasn't her home. She was so tired. She looked around at most of the people crowding the small living room, and she realized that besides Tito, she was the youngest person there. It felt surreal to recognize this, that she was young, that she was a teenager still, that she should be in high school, but instead, she was now in charge of raising someone else's child. Soon, she'd be raising her own. She longed for her sister, for Loli's brave, no-bullshit advice, for the way she said things exactly as they were. Loli would know what to say to Maricarmen right now.

When Carmelo walked through the door, Maricarmen was surprised at how relieved she felt. Carmelo shook Rey's hand, pulled him in for a hug, then did the same with Don Ojeda. His mother, Evelyn, came in right after him, wrapping her arms around Rey for a long time. Carmelo shook hands with Ismael and Cano, then looked around the room. He met Maricarmen's gaze, then immediately came over to her, sat between her and Doña Matos on the couch.

Tito shifted, then sat up, wide awake. Doña Matos got up, took Tito in her arms. "I'll give you a break," she said to Maricarmen.

"Will you see if he eats something?" Maricarmen asked.

"Don't worry. He'll eat." Doña Matos set Tito down, took his hand, and together they made their way through the crowd toward the kitchen.

Carmelo took Maricarmen's hand in his, held it tight. She tried to hold back the tears, but they came anyway. She wiped her face and smiled at him, her friend since childhood. How far away those days felt now.

"I would ask how you're doing, but I know you're not okay," Carmelo said.

She squeezed his hand. She wanted to tell him everything, but she hadn't told anyone about the baby. Not even Rey.

"You don't have to say anything."

They sat for a while, quietly watching the neighbors come and go, until Carmelo let go of her hand. Maricarmen noticed him watching Rey.

By the door, Don Ojeda was talking to Cano and Ismael. But not Rey. Rey was staring at Carmelo, mouth like a fist.

Maricarmen turned to Carmelo, then Rey, and back again. She couldn't believe it. They were glaring at each other. In the middle of Doña Iris's velorio.

"What the hell, Carmelo?" Maricarmen shook her head. Before she could get up, Rey was standing in front of her, taking her hand, leading her outside.

As she stepped out of the apartment, she caught a glimpse of Carmelo. He sat hunched forward on the couch, face in his hands.

"What's going on with you two?" Rey said as soon as they got outside.

"I should be asking *you* that question. You know Carmelo's my closest friend."

"That didn't look like *just friends*."

Maricarmen exhaled. She was too tired for this. She didn't have it in her to fight. "You think I would do that to you? At your mother's velorio?" She looked into his eyes. She wanted to see what she'd find there, if Rey really did believe she was capable of that, or if grief was making him crazy. What she saw in his eyes was just pain, sadness, desperation. And she realized he was watching her the same way she was watching him.

"You might not see it, but I do," Rey said. "Carmelo's in love with you."

She shook her head, exhaled, then turned back toward the apartment, leaving Rey outside.

Maricarmen shut the door behind her, walked past Don Ojeda without saying anything, then went back to the couch, where

Carmelo was waiting for her. All around her, women prayed the rosary.

"Everything okay?" Carmelo whispered.

"Everything's fine." She sat back, watched the women, the men standing around, eating and drinking.

She expected Rey to walk in any moment. But each time the door opened, every time another neighbor came in and greeted Don Ojeda, Maricarmen was relieved that it wasn't Rey. She stayed up with the women, praying the rosary as neighbors left, as Doña Matos put Tito to sleep on Rey's bed, as Cano and Ismael and even Don Ojeda filed out of the apartment.

Rey didn't come back home that night.

AFTER THEY BURIED Doña Iris, it was Don Ojeda who came to check on Maricarmen, brought over gallons of milk, sacks of rice, canned beans, a dozen eggs. Rey came home late in the afternoon and barely talked to her before he was gone again. It became a pattern: He'd be gone for days at a time, until finally, he'd come home and crash. He'd sleep for an entire day, and then he'd wake up in the morning, act like everything was fine. He'd be happy—joyous, even—take Tito to the basketball courts, take her to the beach. Maricarmen would think they were going to be fine, that they'd be happy. And then he'd take off again, come home the next day or not at all.

Almost every afternoon, after Don Ojeda closed up el colmado, he came over for café. Sometimes he took care of Tito when she had to go to El Paseo. It was Don Ojeda she told first, late one afternoon, even before she told Rey.

"I'm having a baby, Don Ojeda."

He nodded, like maybe he already knew, or like he was trying not to say what he was really thinking.

Don Ojeda was still sitting at the kitchen table, the news heavy between them, when Carmelo came knocking and Maricarmen let him in.

Carmelo shook Don Ojeda's hand and gave her a hug. "How you doing, Mari?"

Maricarmen shrugged. "Hey." She served Carmelo a cup of café, pushed the porcelain sugar bowl across the table.

Carmelo sat down. "My mom says you can bring her the baby if you need to run errands and stuff. Or when you go to work. She can watch him."

"Tell her thank you," Maricarmen said.

Don Ojeda got up, left his empty cup on the table. "Gracias, Mari."

"See you tomorrow?" she asked.

Don Ojeda nodded. "You'll call if you need anything?"

She smiled.

Soon as Don Ojeda left, Carmelo relaxed. "Why didn't you tell me about your mom moving out?"

Maricarmen sat with him, blowing into her own cup. "What's there to say?"

"This mean you're leaving too?"

"I'm pregnant," she blurted out. "I'm pregnant, and my mother took my sister God knows where, and I haven't even told Rey." She spilled everything she'd been keeping inside. How her mother had moved out without even saying goodbye, without telling her where she was going, that she found out on the day she realized she was pregnant, and what was worse, that was all the same day Doña Iris died, so she didn't tell Rey.

"Damn, Mari. I'm sorry." He took her hand. "But she's in Miami. She called my mom. My mom got her address and everything."

Maricarmen wiped the tears from her eyes.

"We thought you knew," Carmelo said. "I thought you knew and just didn't say."

"I didn't know what to do."

"You know you gotta tell him."

She nodded.

"And you need to see a doctor or something, don't you?"

"I gotta tell him first."

Carmelo took her hand. "Mari, you know I can take you, right? To the doctor, or wherever you need to go. Say the word."

She squeezed his hand. She could count on Carmelo, this she knew for sure.

HE CAME HOME high that night. Stumbled into the living room and threw himself on the couch, ready to sleep. But Maricarmen shook him awake.

"I need to talk to you."

He sat up, opened his eyes wide. "Sorry, mama. I'm just tired, you know."

"Tired? You're high."

"Come on, don't be like that," he said, whining.

She didn't have the patience for this. She launched into her story, told him everything, how her mother left, how she'd felt so alone since her mother took Loli away, how she was pregnant, and she was having the baby, and how she planned on going back to her mother's apartment, where she would raise her child. She couldn't raise her baby in a place that didn't feel like her home.

"You can come, and you can bring Tito. But if you do, I'm not taking care of Tito alone, you hear me? He's your brother. *Your* brother."

Rey stared off into the distance, as if he were trying to understand what she'd just said. "A baby."

"If you want to do this with me, I need you here, Rey. You can't be leaving for days at a time. If you don't want to do this, tell me now. I'll do it alone."

"We just got a bunch more gigs. Ismael booked us a couple of jobs in New York and Miami. I can't just promise to be here when opportunities are opening up."

"Okay, and what about Tito?" she asked. "What about *his* opportunities?"

"What about him? He can't come with me." Rey was slurring now, and it was getting on Maricarmen's nerves.

"What the fuck, Rey. You can't abandon him."

Rey shook his head slowly. "It's just a couple weeks. I'll be back in a couple weeks. We'll have money. For the baby!"

She reminded him, again, that Tito was *his* little brother. "He just lost his mom, and you barely see him. He lost both his parents. Do you know what that means?" She wanted to say the word *orphan*, but she couldn't bring herself to do it.

"Of course I do," Rey said, sounding suddenly sober. "I lost them too."

"He needs you here. He needs his family."

"We're a family," Rey said. "You and me and Tito and the baby. We'll be okay."

She wasn't sure she'd gotten through to him, or if he would be around more. But she liked the idea of all of them being a family. There was nothing she wanted more.

Over the next few months, that was the way Rey calmed her when she was anxious: *We're a family. We'll be okay.* When she was upset with him: *Don't worry. We're a family.* When he said he'd be gone four days but came home two weeks later: *We're a family. I would never abandon you.*

In those months, Maricarmen turned eighteen, with only Evelyn and Carmelo around to cut her a small bizcocho de guayaba that they washed down with guarapo de caña. Evelyn brought over food all the time or sent something over with Carmelo. Eventually, when her apartment application came back approved, Carmelo, Cano, and Ismael helped her move. They carried the furniture from Rey's second-floor apartment to hers, and only Carmelo understood why she needed to move.

"It's bigger," she said whenever someone asked. "We need three bedrooms now."

Once she'd moved back, she made it hers. Even though it was filled with the old furniture that Rey's parents had collected over the years, she cleaned and organized and arranged the furniture however she liked. This was her home now, and she could do whatever she wanted. Nobody would tell her what to do again.

Sometimes Doña Matos stopped by, brought her caldo de pollo, took her blood pressure with her manual cuff and stethoscope, then talked to her about what would happen on the day the baby finally came.

Rey was around more than he'd ever been. He even took her down to the courthouse in el pueblo to get married. It was a quick ceremony, the two of them, Cano and Ismael as witnesses. There was no ring and no proposal, just a judge, the witnesses, Rey looking down at her. She was happy then. But even with him at home, as her belly got bigger, her loneliness grew.

The morning Nena came into the world, in May of '78, she arrived in silence. Rey was no help in the room—he just stood around, watching, getting in the way. Doña Matos kept reassuring them both, but Maricarmen was scared. And because Maricarmen was just a girl, because she didn't have her mother by her side during those months of pregnancy, or Loli to hold her hand during those last few minutes, that final push, Maricarmen froze. What if she couldn't push anymore? What if the baby never came? What if it came, but

Maricarmen bled and bled until she couldn't bleed anymore and it killed her? She'd heard of this. There were plenty of stories. Women died in childbirth all the time.

In the hospital room, there had been none of the joy other women described when they told stories of bringing children into the world. Maricarmen was scared when they didn't let her hold the baby, when Doña Matos took her without explanation, nurses running around the delivery room while Maricarmen held out her arms for her daughter. For the first time, Doña Matos stopped reassuring her, and worked silently. But the baby didn't cry, and Maricarmen knew something was wrong.

"What's happening?" she asked.

Rey stood by her side, watching, and Maricarmen snatched his T-shirt and shook him.

"Tell me what's happening."

And then the baby coughed, like she'd been drowning, like she was finally coming up for air.

Doña Matos put her in Maricarmen's arms, the infant's eyes searching for her mother, looking up at her face like she expected Maricarmen to keep her safe, and Maricarmen thought she would collapse with fear, from the weight of the entire world in her hands. Everyone would be looking to Maricarmen now—not Blanca, not even Rey—expecting her to be responsible, to know what to do. She was just a teenager, eighteen years old, and already she had to take care of Tito. While Rey was off playing the bars and nightclubs with Ismael, spending weeks in New York, in Miami, she would be at home, with kids. No school. Nothing she could call her own. Except the baby. She'd never felt so alone.

When Doña Matos asked what they would call the baby, Maricarmen didn't let Rey speak.

"Nenuska," she said. "Her name is Nenuska."

"Juanito Alimaña"

THE SUMMER OF '78, el Caserío was quiet. After years of harassment and surveillance and locking people up, los camarones slowly stopped coming around. Most of the hustlers had been locked up after one big bust. El Caserío Padre Rivera became known as the place you went if you were looking to get busted. Cano suspected that there had been chotas working with the cops. He didn't want los camarones around, but he didn't want all the drugs in the neighborhood either. Cano's friends, all in their twenties, were settled now. Ismael and his wife, Johanna, had twin boys, and though they still had their place in el Caserío, Johanna wanted them to move to a house in Patagonia, where her mother could move in with them, help with the kids. Cano and Jeannette, who he'd met and married in a matter of weeks, were expecting their first child. They lived with Doña Matos, and were planning on turning David's old bedroom into the baby's room. David lived out in el pueblo, at the Catholic parish.

These days, it was quiet—except for the children. Everywhere Cano went in el Caserío, there were children. Women pushing strollers, kids running around the front lawns, riding bikes and Big Wheels. Sometimes, pulling into el Caserío in his van after a long day of classes and a full shift at the library, he imagined that the neighborhood could be like the old days. Kids playing outside, throwing a ball around, without worrying about police raids or violence. Block parties to celebrate babies being born, birthdays, el Día de Reyes. In those days, his mom had walked down the street and left the apartment door unlocked, and never worried about a break-in. Kids could run around the block, climb the trees out back, and the whole neighborhood was watching, making sure they were all right. Everybody was poor, but they were poor together, so when one person struggled, everybody pitched in. They took care of each other.

After his daughter was born, Rey still took off for days at a time. But he kept missing practice with Ismael and the band. Nobody knew where he spent those days, but he'd come home looking like someone had scraped him off the road and dropped him off out front. Maricarmen took care of the baby and Tito all by herself. The band had started getting gigs all over Puerto Rico, opening up for big bands in Miami and New York, but sometimes, the night before they were supposed to travel, Rey went MIA. Cano thought these should've been the happiest days of his life—he had a baby girl, a hardworking, loyal wife at home, a dream job. Rey made money, real money, from singing and playing music. Rey and Mari should've been able to afford a house in Patagonia. Rey had everything he'd ever wanted and more. But even happiness couldn't keep him straight.

About a year after his daughter was born, Rey stopped showing up to practice altogether, stopped answering Ismael's phone calls. It happened without warning. One day, he just stopped playing, stopped showing up for their shows. Stopped making music.

Ismael was mad as hell.

"Let's go find him," Cano said. "Maybe he needs help. Something's going on with him."

But Cano already knew what was going on. Truth is, everybody knew.

The first time it occurred to Cano, he'd been playing dominoes in la plaza on a Saturday afternoon. The guys were drinking beer and talking shit, sitting around a plastic folding table outside Ismael's building, when Cano spotted him: Rey was watching them, smoking under the shade of a ceiba, his back against the trunk. Where had he come from? Had he been there the whole time? It was like he'd been hiding in plain sight. An apparition. He wore a Pittsburgh Pirates ball cap, a faded black T-shirt two sizes too big. He had one arm tucked inside his shirt, hiding something.

Rey looked around, all around him, checking out the perimeter. He was waiting, Cano realized. But who he was waiting on, Cano wasn't sure. Maybe he already knew what was coming. As Cano watched him, Rey checking out the balconies, the front and side entrances leading to the courtyard, he could see the shape of what was under Rey's shirt, its double barrel tucked inside his waistband. It was a sawed-off shotgun—Rey had let Cano see it once. It had been his dead father's, Rey told him, and he'd been trying to sell it, but who in their right mind would buy a sawed-off shotgun?

"I'll let you have it for two hundred," Rey had told Cano.

"Nah, man. Even if I had the money, I'm not trynna catch a case. Besides, I don't need that." Cano had looked into Rey's face. "And, brother, *you* don't need that."

What was he doing under that tree? Was he trying to sell the shotgun again, or just tempting fate?

Juanito, one of the other guys playing dominoes, saw Rey and chugged the rest of his beer. "I'll see you all later." He jogged over to the ceiba.

Rey and Juanito left together, heading toward el Caserío's front entrance.

Later, the rumors started. Los camarones were looking for Rey, and Maricarmen was looking for Rey, calling everybody she knew, asking around the neighborhood, the basketball courts. Cano always lied, said he hadn't seen him. How to tell her that every time Cano saw Rey, he was holding on to that shotgun, sometimes trying to hide it under a hoodie or jacket, sometimes just carrying it in plain sight like he was some vaquero on a mission? Rey knew los camarones were looking for him, people said, and he wasn't about to go down without a fight.

Doña Matos started leaving food for him again, café con leche and pan de agua out on the back balcony. Rey was out there, she told Cano. And she knew he was hungry.

When los camarones came knocking, asking Cano and Doña Matos about Rey's whereabouts, they just shrugged.

"Nobody knows where he is," Doña Matos said. "I haven't seen him." She turned to Cano. "Have you seen him?"

"Nah. He doesn't come around anymore."

It didn't matter that Doña Matos was feeding him or that half of el Caserío saw him come around with that shotgun every other day or that sometimes he showed up lugging cases of baby formula, diapers, gallons of milk, eggs, or bottles of rum to distribute around the block before going home to Maricarmen. Nobody was going to give up Rey. Nobody was going to say shit about how he showed up with a dozen packs of chicken drumsticks from Pueblo Supermarket and knocked on his neighbors' doors, one pack per family, handed them out until he was down to one pack, then took that home. These were his people. Everybody else—the cops, the government, the rich fucks who got richer while their factories sent black ash snowing over the homes of the poor? They were who Rey was out there waiting for. They were all fair game.

Rey, they said, became a master thief. He and Juanito drove out to el área metropolitana, breaking into fancy cars, even robbed a jewelry store, a nice joint run by an American couple, Spanish-speaking gringos who'd lived in San Juan for like a decade. Juanito had bragged all about it. The couple got on WAPA Televisión, talking about their horrific experience.

"¡Qué susto pasamos!" the wife said to the camera in accented Spanish. "¡A mi esposo por poco le da un ataque del corazón!"

"We're lucky to be alive," the husband said as he avoided looking directly at the camera. It seemed "el susto" had made him forget his Spanish.

This didn't sound like the Rey Cano knew. When had he changed like this? Cano worried that Rey and Juanito would get busted one day, or that they'd get shot by los camarones. But Juanito didn't seem all that fazed. Once, Juanito boasted to Cano, the guys stopped at a roadside restaurant, a place called the Harbor, one of those expensive American seafood joints that had just opened up in Fajardo. It didn't make sense—the place was packed, and they were at the bar having a couple of beers when Rey pulled out his shotgun.

"Put the money on the bar. Con calma. *Easy.*"

The bartender almost shit his pants. He opened the register, hands shaking, pulled out all the bills and dropped them on the counter without a word.

"Damn, Rey," Juanito had said, shaking his head. "I haven't even finished my beer."

Rey took the money and walked out. Juanito took his Medalla for the road.

Sometimes they stole cars, sold them up in Bayamón. Sometimes they drove a car home, used it for a few days' work, then left it behind at a junkyard in Juncos. Cano usually found out about their escapades from Juanito a few days later, when Juanito came home to sober up and eat his mom's home cooking.

"Where's Rey?" Cano asked once when he and Ismael ran into Juanito. Cano had just parked his van. Ismael was coming around the back.

Juanito shrugged. "I ain't his father."

"You two are always together now," Ismael said.

"What are you, los guardias?" Juanito said.

"He hasn't been home in God knows how long," Cano said. Cano had just become a father, and he could imagine what Maricarmen was going through, all alone with those two kids. "His wife has been looking for him, asking around about him."

"Maybe she hasn't been asking the right people." Juanito smiled.

Cano studied him, narrowing his eyes. He wanted to ask what he meant exactly—that Rey had another girl somewhere? That Rey had something more to hide?

"Look," Juanito said finally. "He's been hitting the H *hard* all weekend. He's probably getting himself cleaned up, you know?"

Cano nodded, but he knew that was bullshit. You didn't just quit music and stop going home to your wife, your little brother and baby girl, and then get "cleaned up" like it was that easy.

THAT FRIDAY NIGHT, Don Ojeda closed up el colmado and set up his table in the back for the weekend poker game. He had seven guys coming and exactly eight folding chairs. His brother Junior, God rest his soul, had been a gambler and a drinker. He'd started drinking at one of these games when he was just seventeen, and after that, Ojeda couldn't remember a single day in his life when Junior didn't have a drink in his hand. When Iris went into labor with Rey, Junior, drinking at some bar in Juncos, had missed the birth. The local places in Humacao had stopped serving him. But even though he'd watched his own brother lose everything time and time again, and somehow Ojeda always ended up paying his debts, he loved these card games—at the poker table on Friday nights, he remembered what it was like to be young, live a simple life filled with simple pleasures. A cold beer, some good company, some laughter after a week of working all day.

That Friday, the men started arriving as the sun set. Some guys from La Central, one of Ojeda's friends from the neighborhood, and a couple of guys from Patagonia who came around once in a while. The last man to arrive was Altieri, taking Don Ojeda by surprise. In the past, Altieri had come to a couple of games, but after what he'd done to his nephew, cracking his skull open so Rey almost lost an eye, Don Ojeda thought he'd never see the son of a bitch again. He'd have to get himself something to sit on.

Altieri didn't shake anybody's hand, not even Don Ojeda's—just sat down. He never greeted anyone before he sat down at Ojeda's table. He wasn't the type to come around el Caserío looking for friends.

Don Ojeda didn't want trouble. This was supposed to be a friendly game. Sometimes you won, sometimes you lost, but not too much. He wasn't trying to make enemies—nobody was trying to make enemies. They all just wanted to have a few drinks and play some cards, come back next week, do it all again.

"What are you drinking?" Don Ojeda asked Altieri.

Altieri looked around at everybody else's drinks. Beer, mostly Medalla. A couple guys had shots of Palo Viejo. Altieri scratched at his thick mustache. "I'll take a Heineken," he said.

Ojeda laughed. Everybody laughed but Altieri.

"Brother, we have Medalla, Budweiser, or Palo Viejo," Don Ojeda said. "Unless you want some pitorro."

"I'll have a Budweiser."

Don Ojeda went for his beer, and Altieri shifted in his chair. Altieri looked around the table at the other men. No one met his eyes.

Don Ojeda came back with a milk crate to sit on, Altieri's beer, and a cigar for himself. He set the beer down on the table, then slapped his hands together. "First round's on me."

Altieri raised his beer, nodded. "I got the next round."

The men played and drank for a couple of hours. Don Ojeda played a couple of hands and then bowed out, smoking his cigar, dealing, and serving drinks. Altieri didn't drink much, but he bought rounds of drinks for the other men whenever he won a hand. The more they played, the more they drank. The drunker they were, the more they lost. The more they lost, the harder they drank. Altieri was having one hell of a winning streak, so he kept buying. And the other men kept drinking, so he kept winning.

Don Ojeda had just put another round of drinks on the table when Rey appeared in the front of el colmado.

"I thought I locked the door," Don Ojeda said.

Rey jiggled his keys and pocketed them, smiling. He turned to the table, slow and steady, and raised his sawed-off shotgun, pointed it at Altieri's face.

"Put all the money on the table."

Everybody froze.

"Come on, Rey," one of the men said. "It's just a game. Not a lot of money."

Altieri was expressionless.

"Rey," Don Ojeda said, his voice shaking, "put it down. Please."

Altieri's eyes narrowed. "You know who I am." It wasn't a question.

"Rey, please," Ojeda said.

Altieri huffed. "You're making a big mistake, my friend."

And Rey, who took the word *friend* seriously, swung the shotgun and hit Altieri, cracked him once in the head and knocked him out cold.

"¡Dios mío, Rey!" Don Ojeda said. "¡Ese hombre es sargento de la policía!"

"Take your money and get out," Rey said calmly to the other men. But all the other men were frozen.

"Rey..."

One of the men, Don Ojeda's friend from the neighborhood, started pulling coins from his pockets, emptied his wallet on the table.

"I said, take your money. Take it."

None of the men moved.

Rey raised his shotgun again. "Before I start blasting motherfuckers."

Suddenly, all the men scrambled to take the money on the table, nobody counting anything, just taking handfuls of bills and coins. A couple of them left the cash and headed for the door. Don Ojeda's friend, still frozen, looked Rey in the eye.

Rey gathered the rest of the bills on the table, then bent over Altieri and searched his pockets. He folded up all the cash and turned to his uncle's friend, put the folded bills into his hand. "You didn't see nothing, you hear me?"

"My God, Rey," Don Ojeda said.

"I didn't see a thing." Hands shaking, beads of sweat collecting at his temples, Don Ojeda's friend headed straight for the door.

And that was how Rey el Cantante became Rey the Fugitive.

THE STORY SPREAD. Rey el Cantante had robbed Altieri but managed not to keep a single dollar for himself. Had served up justice the biblical way, an eye for an eye. And after that, Rey became known around el Caserío as the man you went to when you fell on hard times, when you couldn't feed your baby or pay your rent or get your kid that pair of skates for Día de Reyes. Your daughter needed uniforms for the new school year? You wanted to propose to your girl but you couldn't afford an engagement ring? Rey was your man.

A couple of times, he stole a pallet of diapers and a few cases of canned baby formula from the Econo Supermarket, tossed them into his car, then distributed them among families in the neighborhood. People said he just walked right up to the delivery truck and started unloading it, like he worked there. As a teenager, Rey had ridden around on a Sting-Ray he stole from Dios sabe dónde. As a kid, they say, Rey stole everything he could get his hands on: stop signs, the hubcaps off the school principal's rusty Chevy Nova, bell-bottom jeans hanging from clotheslines. His most infamous plunder had been a Chapulín Colorado birthday cake he swiped from some kid's party in la plaza de Humacao. All the Caserío kids were playing basketball when Rey showed up and started handing out cake. But now he knew better. He'd never steal from his people.

As the story spread, Cano couldn't believe how it got more and more twisted. He almost didn't recognize this Rey in the stories he heard, this Caserío myth: Rey had been evading los camarones for months, laughing behind their backs, humiliating them. They'd get an anonymous phone call—Rey having coffee at Panadería Ramalu, or Rey playing dominoes in la plaza, or Rey walking down la Calle Tres toward el pueblo—but by the time they showed up, he was gone. And Altieri was livid. How was it possible that they had not been able to catch this petty thief this small-time dealer this wannabe Caserío Robin Hood?

He'd been doing his vanishing thing for months. He'd show up in el Caserío in the middle of the afternoon, see the kids for a few minutes, and then, just like that, he was gone.

But one day, Rey came home like he meant to stay.

"WHAT ARE YOU doing here?" Maricarmen asked when Rey walked through the door with a small color TV and a tricycle for Tito.

"What do you mean, 'What are you doing here?' Don't I get a 'thank you'?"

"*Thank* you? Your daughter has a fever and hasn't slept in days! And Tito keeps asking about you."

When they fought, Maricarmen resisted the urge to remind him that Blanca had told her all along that Rey would leave her, that he'd turn out to be un tecato and she'd end up alone. Now she was so angry that she wanted to do exactly that. Instead, she reminded him that when Doña Iris died, Rey had promised he would be around to take care of Tito, how he'd used the word *family* again and again.

Rey didn't flinch. He set the TV down next to the sofa and picked up a toddling Nena in his arms. She was laughing immediately, reaching for her father's unshaved face, his long curls. He smiled at Nena, took her hand in his and kissed it, then pretended to bite it. Nena threw her head back, cackling with joy, and pulled her hand away. Maricarmen wanted to scream but bit her tongue. She could easily see the kind of father Rey was capable of becoming, a father like the one she'd never had. She didn't know how to get through to him. She loved him, but sometimes he made life impossible. These days, when she saw him, it was because he was making some grand gesture for the people in the neighborhood and had come home to accept praise. He wasn't happy when what he got instead was a lonely and exhausted Maricarmen who'd stayed up all night with a sick baby, who was often desperate for help with the laundry, or the cooking, or with bathing the kids.

And as much as it hurt to admit it to herself, she hadn't been surprised to learn that los camarones were looking for Rey again, although she was surprised when Don Ojeda told her about the poker game. That's all anybody could talk about anymore, that damn poker game.

"Where's Tito?" Rey asked.

"What are you doing here?" she asked again. "You know Altieri's looking for you."

"Don't you want me around?" Rey bounced Nena lightly, then reached over and caressed Maricarmen's bare shoulder over her tank top.

She pretended to feel nothing. "Since when do you care what I want?"

"Mari, come on."

Maricarmen reached for Nena, took her from his arms. "Tito's in his room. You wanna get him? It's lunchtime."

Maricarmen carried Nena into the kitchen and sat her in a high chair, set a small bowl of smashed pumpkin in front of her.

Rey came back with Tito sitting on his shoulders, smiling wide. "All right, lunchtime, brother." He lifted Tito high, then brought him back down slowly. "When did you get so heavy? You're like a baby elephant!"

Tito laughed.

Maricarmen pointed to a bowl already on the table. Rice and beans and a few pieces of chicken cut into small cubes. "He eats by himself, but make sure he eats it all, okay?" She went back to feeding Nena.

Rey served himself a plate, sat across from Tito, and ate.

Maricarmen fed Nena small spoonfuls, then watched Rey and Tito. They talked happily, not missing a beat, as if everything had always been normal. How easily Tito just forgave him, even though night after night, at bedtime, he asked about Rey, asked Maricarmen to call Rey and get him to come home. But how do you explain to a child that his brother couldn't come home, because he was on the run? She wanted him home, but she also didn't want the kids to witness Rey being dragged away by los camarones, or what could happen if Altieri had more than an arrest in mind. She didn't want to think about what Altieri would do when he finally caught Rey, and, yes, she was sure that Altieri would catch him. It was just a matter of time.

EVEN THOUGH REY was on the run, Cano saw him every other day. He saw him so much he thought maybe Rey wanted to get picked up. He sometimes caught a glimpse of him at la plaza, waiting for someone. Juanito, Cano imagined. Sometimes Rey came around Cano's house, and Doña Matos fed him. He was usually there a short time. Left a few dollars behind for Doña Matos and gifts for the family: a pair of 14K gold studs for Cano's baby girl, a Tonka truck for his son, now a toddler, a gold pendant for his wife, Jeannette. He gave Cano a quick one-armed hug, and then he was gone. Cano wanted to ask Rey if he'd seen his own baby girl and his little brother, but he never did. He wasn't sure how his friend would take it.

One afternoon, Cano came home from work to find Jeannette pacing in the living room. She held the baby in her arms, trying to soothe her.

Cano took the baby, rocking her gently.

"We're out of formula," Jeannette said.

Cano had no money until he got his paycheck from the library in a couple of days. Doña Matos was working her shift at the hospital, but Cano didn't have enough gas in the car to make it to the hospital and back. Why had Jeannette waited until they'd run out of formula to tell him? Jeannette hadn't been able to produce much milk, and he didn't want her to feel worse than she already did, so he didn't ask.

"I'll take care of it," he said.

He left the apartment, not sure where he was going. He could ask a neighbor for milk, maybe. He could walk a couple blocks to Ismael's garage and ask to borrow some money. But what if Ismael wasn't even there? He would have to swallow his pride, walk to the basketball courts or la plaza, see if anyone would lend him the money.

In la plaza, it was the usual guys smoking and playing dominoes. Cano tried to avoid his friends, anybody he'd gone to school with. He just couldn't look them in the eye and admit that he had a family at home he couldn't take care of, even though he had a full-time job and he'd dropped out of college to work more hours.

He went up to a crew of guys who slung dope, who were covered in gold. Rope chains, gold watches, pinky rings. They weren't exactly friends. Just guys he saw around all the time.

"Any of you think I could borrow ten dollars until Friday? I'm trying to buy baby formula, pa' la nena."

Most of those guys had kids of their own, and they'd known Cano for years. They knew his mother, his brother. They knew he had a newborn at home, that he worked, that his mother worked. Yet every single one of them took one look at him and kept slapping down cards like he didn't see Cano standing there, a knot in his throat.

So Cano moved on to the next group, some tiradores throwing dice under a flamboyán. When he approached them, they shook their heads.

"Nah, man," one of them said. "It's hard out here." The others didn't even bother looking up at him.

Cano was about to turn and go when Rey came up, shotgun under his jacket. He pulled it out but didn't point it. "Empty your fucking pockets," he said to them.

"Come on now, Rey," one of the tiradores said, shaking his head. "Don't do me like that."

And then all of them joined in, negotiating:

"Come on, pana, you know us."

"Don't do this. We're from the same barrio."

"I got kids," one of them said.

But Rey? He did not give a fuck.

"Put your fucking money down." Rey held up the shotgun, and they emptied their pockets immediately, dropping everything on the ground.

"I don't have anything," Cano said, turning his jeans pockets inside out.

Rey picked up their money. "Nothing happened here, you understand? I was never here."

Cano nodded, but then realized Rey wasn't talking to him.

Rey wasn't pointing the shotgun anymore, but the guys were still frozen in place.

"Get the fuck outa here," Rey said.

All the guys split in different directions, Cano heading back home. Rey took off running down the block, turned the corner out of la plaza, and disappeared.

As Cano made his way toward his building, before he turned the corner out of la plaza, somebody snatched him by his collar and pulled him behind a dumpster.

"Don't say a word."

It was Rey. He counted out about a hundred dollars, put the bills in Cano's hand, and took off running past Cano's building toward the cañaverales.

Cano didn't look back as he got in his van, as he drove it to Pueblo Supermarket and bought enough formula to last a couple of weeks, got some groceries, some diapers, and filled up his gas tank. He didn't mention anything when he got home to Jeannette, not a word about how he came up with the money or about how Rey had robbed all the tiradores in la plaza just to make sure their baby girl was fed. How his friend, his brother, was lost. Cano could see exactly where Rey was headed, and he wanted so much to protect him. But what could he do?

CANO DIDN'T SEE Rey for a few weeks after that afternoon in la plaza. Altieri and los camarones came around el Caserío every few days, pulled up to the basketball courts, and crashed the pickup games. They lined all the guys up against the chain-link fence, frisked them, and peppered them with questions.

"Where is Rey Ojeda?" and "Have you seen him carrying a

weapon?" and "What kind of weapon is he carrying?" and "Where does he sleep?"

But the guys on the courts always had the same story: Nobody had seen Rey in months. Weapon? What weapon? He took off one day and hasn't been back.

Altieri didn't believe a word they said, Cano could tell. He looked them up and down, scowling. Then the cops got back in their cruisers and drove away.

Another day, Altieri came back when Cano, Ismael, and Juanito were playing, pulled them all off the courts, along with some tiradores who were camped out on the benches.

"Up against the fence," Altieri said.

Cano, Ismael, and Juanito lined up right away, but Cano watched los tiradores. They took their time, staring at Cano, then back at Altieri, like they were trying to make up their minds about who the enemy was; they were the same guys Rey had robbed a few weeks back. When they finally lined up, leaving some space between themselves and Cano, los tiradores didn't say a word. Juanito stood there smirking under the sun. Ismael fidgeted impatiently. Cano prayed that Juanito wasn't holding.

"One of you knows where Rey Ojeda has been sleeping," Altieri said.

Juanito wiped the sweat on his upper lip with the back of his hand.

Cano watched the cops, then the guys lined up against the fence. All of them were Black Caserío guys. All the cops were white or mixed, but none of them was Black. It made Cano's face burn with anger. Over the years, he'd gotten used to it, but he felt it just the same.

One of the tiradores spoke up. "Listen here, papi," he said. "You find Rey, maybe you tell *me* where he's been sleeping, 'cause he owes me money."

Altieri grabbed the guy's collar, pushed him back against the fence. Then he let him go, spitting on the ground before heading back to his cruiser.

CANO AND ISMAEL sat outside Ismael's garage, a few blocks from el Caserío, listening to the radio and drinking beer. The shop smelled of motor oil and chemicals, the guava paint peeling off the outside. Ismael didn't do much work there anymore, so he hadn't bothered to repaint. Outside, the grass needed mowing, and the dumpster was overflowing with trash that hadn't been picked up. It was an old blocky building, and Cano thought it probably needed demolishing because it was rotting.

Ismael had just finished changing the oil in Cano's van.

"How much do I owe you?" Cano asked.

Ismael shook his head. "Keep your money, man. I don't even have to do oil changes anymore."

Ismael hadn't been working in the garage all that much since he'd started making money from music. He'd reformed the band with a different singer, another drummer, guys who were committed. But Ismael missed Rey, Cano could tell.

Ismael didn't make enough to stop working altogether, Cano knew, but at least he could spring for Heineken, which Cano appreciated. "Gracias, brother."

Ismael raised his beer. He was still holding it up when a blue Civic sped around the corner, screeching to a halt on the asphalt. The driver honked his horn three times, and Ismael and Cano both jumped.

"What the hell?" Cano said.

Juanito sprang out of the car, slammed his door. "They got Rey, man," he said. "Those motherfuckers got Rey."

"Who?" Ismael said.

"Help me get him out."

Rey lay sideways in the back seat, his body leaning against the passenger-side door. Juanito pulled the door slowly, holding Rey up so he wouldn't fall out.

"Is he shot?" Ismael asked.

"Who did this?" Cano said, although Rey had a lot of enemies—it could be anybody.

They held Rey, looking over his bloodied face, both eyes swollen shut, nose broken, a splatter of blood across his nose and mouth and shirt.

"I don't know," Juanito said.

"You don't know?" Ismael said.

"I picked him up outside el Caserío just now. They just left him there on the side of the road. In a fucking ditch, man."

Cano and Ismael hoisted Rey, threw his arms over their shoulders, and carried him inside the garage.

Juanito threw open the door to the dank office. Across from Ismael's desk, there was a small twin bed, haphazardly made.

"Shit," Juanito said. "You got a bed in your office? Your wife know?"

"Where do you think I was sleeping when we met?"

They lay Rey down on the bed. Cano couldn't tell if he was conscious or not, but Rey was moaning softly. Ismael lifted his shirt. No blood. Just dirt.

"Where does it hurt?" Ismael said.

"I think they just jumped him," Juanito said. "All the blood is coming from his face."

"And his head. We need a doctor," Ismael said. "Why didn't you take him to the hospital?"

The hospital? What did Ismael think would happen if Altieri found Rey in the hospital?

"I'll be right back," Cano said. "Stay here."

"Where you going?" Juanito asked.

"To get Mami," Cano said.

Juanito turned to Ismael. "His mom? What the hell for?"

Ismael shook his head. "She's a nurse, man. At Ryder?"

Cano took a moment, then gave them both a look. "What if he's not okay? What if…"

Juanito brought both hands to the top of his head. "Shit."

"He's gonna be fine," Ismael said. "He just took a nasty beatdown, probably has some broken ribs." Ismael looked Cano in the eyes. "Get Mari."

Cano got in his van and drove toward el Caserío.

"Las Caras Lindas"

CANO HAD GONE to Maricarmen with the news and brought back Doña Matos to patch him up. After that, Rey spent a few weeks living in Ismael's garage. As he started to heal, he told them how the guys from la plaza had jumped him. Those same guys he'd robbed caught him, beat him, and left him in a ditch.

Every day, Cano stopped by Ismael's garage to check on Rey, bringing Mari along. She brought food, toiletries, and clothes but never stayed too long. Ismael hung around those first couple of nights when their friend was so out of it he could barely move, giving him painkillers every four hours or so. As soon as Rey could sit up by himself, Ismael let him stay alone at night. The cops were still searching for him, the hustlers from el Caserío were looking to take him out, and Altieri was *hunting* him, so he couldn't leave the garage. Ismael hadn't even told Johanna, his own wife, that he was hiding Rey in his shop.

Cano brought Rey's car to the garage, and Ismael parked it in the back. A few weeks later, when he could finally get up and walk around, Rey left Ismael's.

Maricarmen came home from her shift at El Paseo one night and found him standing in the kitchen with a glass of water. "What do you think you're doing?"

"What?" he asked, taking a large gulp of water.

"What are you doing here? You know half the guys in la plaza want to kill you, and the cops are still looking for you."

"So don't tell 'em I'm here." He shrugged, sipped some more water.

"You were pissing blood a couple weeks ago. What the fuck are you doing?"

"I'm better now," he said. "I just wanted to see you. Where are the kids?"

"The kids are with Evelyn." She looked him up and down, threw her purse on the table. "It's one thing that you barely see them, and that I have to find people to babysit so I can go to work, while you're out there doing God knows what. But then I hear all about what you and Juanito get up to. And now there's people looking for you? I don't want you bringing that here."

"All right, so I won't," Rey said. "I won't get into any more of that shit. I'll stay here, and after a while, los camarones will stop looking for me, like always."

"And what about Altieri? You think he's gonna stop, after what you did to him?"

"What I did to *him*? What about—"

"Don't. He doesn't have a daughter and little brother to worry about. You do. Don't you want a better life than this? Don't you want a better life for Nena? And for Tito?"

He wrapped his arms around her, and she let him. She was so tired—she just wanted him to listen, to hear her.

"We'll have a better life. I'll figure it out. I promise." He pulled away so she could see his face. "But you know we can't stay here."

"I don't care about that," she said. And she meant it. "If you're serious, we should go now."

She watched him thinking, as if he was considering what she'd just said.

"My mother," she said. "She's in Miami. We could go there." She knew what she was saying, how her mother would never let them stay there. But Maricarmen was desperate. She needed to get her family away from el Caserío. If they could just find a way, she'd figure out the rest later, once they were in Miami.

Rey nodded. "We can leave in the morning."

THAT NIGHT SHE barely slept. She had so much to do. In just a couple of hours, she'd run over to Evelyn's apartment, borrowed one of Carmelo's duffel bags and a suitcase from Evelyn. She'd packed their clothes, left the bags by the front door, then stuffed a large diaper bag with Nena's things, a backpack for Tito. After packing, she'd gone to Cano's. If they were leaving, they'd need a ride to the airport—Mari, Rey, the kids, and all their luggage. She was sure Altieri would know Rey's car. But Cano had his van.

When Cano opened the door, he didn't seem happy to see her. "What's wrong?" he asked.

Maricarmen looked over her shoulder, keeping her voice low. "Do you think you could drive us to the airport in the morning? Me and the kids. And Rey. Like around eight?"

"The airport?" Cano narrowed his eyes.

Maricarmen could tell he was trying to work it out for himself, considering whether he should ask questions.

"Eight? No problem," he said.

"Thank you." She smiled.

"Mari," Cano said, taking a deep breath. "If he changes his mind, don't stay. Just go without him if you have to."

Stung, Maricarmen studied him, not sure what made him say this. "He won't change his mind."

Cano nodded. "But if he does…"

Inside Cano's apartment, she could hear the baby crying. Cano was a father now, she thought. She barely saw him anymore. Not like she used to when she cleaned his apartment, when David still lived with him and Doña Matos, when it still felt like it was Doña Matos's place. All of that seemed like a million years ago. When had all of this happened? When did they grow up? Suddenly, standing in front of Cano's door, she felt like she'd gone from being a girl to being a woman overnight.

"He won't," she said again.

IN THE MORNING, Maricarmen fed the kids and then headed toward Evelyn's building. She wanted to say goodbye to Evelyn and Carmelo, then stop by Don Ojeda's so he could see the kids one last time. She'd left Rey at home, told him that they'd be back in time to meet Cano out front.

As they walked, Maricarmen told Tito that after seeing Doña Evelyn and his tío Ojeda, they'd all be going on a trip.

"What about Rey?" Tito asked.

"We'll meet him at home, and then we'll go." Maricarmen walked up the sidewalk, Tito at her side, balancing Nena on one hip. The sky was gray, the sun starting to rise. It was still early, everyone getting ready for the day, headed to work or the basketball courts or la plaza or wherever else they were planning to spend the day. The granos man and his cart down by the entrance, a line of people already waiting as he handed over grease-stained paper bags full of fritters.

She couldn't believe this day had come, that they would all go. Together. She imagined Rey, how he'd spent all those fugitive nights on friends' couches, in Ismael's shop, wherever the night caught up to him. All those nights she'd stayed up, waiting to hear from him. She imagined him in that ditch, where Juanito had found him.

She was crossing the street when she saw them: a caravan of police cruisers, their flashing blue and red lights illuminating the dark street, the whole neighborhood. She turned back as soon as they passed her, took Tito's hand and jogged toward home, Nena bouncing with every step. And there was Rey, across the street from their building, getting in his car. What was he doing? Maricarmen thought. Was he leaving?

But she didn't have time to stop and think, because soon they were on him, police cruisers with their lights on blocking his car. And finally, an unmarked car screeched to a halt right in front of their building, and Maricarmen saw that Altieri, el sargento, had his gun drawn before his car had even come to a complete stop.

For years, everyone would tell this story, how the morning the cops caught Rey, all of el Caserío Padre Rivera watched: the young neighbors who didn't really know him, who were just coming home after a late night knocking back Medallas in a local bar; Evelyn, who'd seen him grow up, who'd known his mother when she was alive, who took care of Tito and Nena; Doña Matos, who'd fed him when he was just a kid dribbling a basketball around el Caserío, who'd patched him up so many times; his tío Ojeda, who'd bought him his first güiro, who'd put a pair of drumsticks in his hands, taught him to bang out songs on congas, to hold a tambor primo steady between his knees and *feel* the dancer; his boys Cano and Ismael; his little brother, Tito; and Maricarmen with baby Nena in her arms.

Maricarmen squeezed Tito's hand, held Nena tight. She watched as los camarones pulled Rey out of the car, grabbed him by the shoulders, slammed him facedown on the cruiser, pulled his arms behind his back. She flinched, the baby wailing in her arms. Tito tried to pull free, but Maricarmen grabbed him, held his body against hers.

The crowd gathered outside as Don Ojeda rushed over, tried to talk to Altieri, but another cop hit him with a truncheon to the ribs and Ojeda fell sideways on the lawn.

Altieri stepped over Don Ojeda and marched toward Rey, smiling wide. There he was, Rey el Cantante, cheek pressed against the cruiser's hood, handcuffs tight enough to cut his circulation. All his possessions tossed and spread out on the sidewalk or somewhere in the tall grass—his car keys and his cigarettes and his wallet and a few 8-tracks and a couple T-shirts and a pair of Adidas sneakers and a hair pick and a pair of drumsticks. And then, when they pulled it out of the trunk, Maricarmen saw the duffel bag where she had packed all his clothes. That's when she realized it, that Rey had planned on leaving them. But also, that she always knew he would leave.

Altieri opened the zipper on the duffel bag, rifled through the clothes, then left it for the other cops to deal with. He had something else in mind. Standing over Rey, as two uniformed cops held his body against the hood of the car, Altieri punched Rey once on the side of his torso. Rey flinched, and Altieri hit him again. Then he stepped back, patted one of the other cops on the back. He finally got his man. But that wasn't enough. One by one, all the other cops took turns punching him and then, as Rey slid off the hood onto the ground, kicking him while he was down.

The crowd grew larger, women on their balconies calling for los camarones to stop.

"Dios mío," they said, "think of his family, his baby girl."

And "What the hell is the matter with you?"

And "Stop! You're gonna kill him!"

And then they did stop, stood him up to face the crowd. Rey, el Cantante, husband, father, brother, fugitive, face turned up to the morning sun, the crowd watching, waiting, their voices loud, Maricarmen holding her breath. Jesus. Altieri had reopened the wound above his eye socket, and it was angry and bloody. She couldn't stop it, and she didn't want the kids to see. She thought about leaving, kids in tow, running past the side of the building, past the hole in the fence, not slowing down until she got into the cañaverales.

Forgive me, Rey, she thought, and closed her eyes, holding the children close.

Or she could just go home, get her luggage, get into Cano's van. Take Cano's advice. Take the kids and go.

And then she knew, right there on that sidewalk. She had stopped thinking of herself as that girl in his bedroom, had stopped thinking of the two of them, those two kids who'd met right here, at a block party in the street. Rey had left them all a long time ago—she just hadn't wanted to see it—but she had left him too. She had let him go.

Everyone watched as Altieri and two uniformed cops threw Rey, battered, bruised, bloody, and handcuffed, into the back of Altieri's car.

After they drove away, Maricarmen, with Nena in her arms, let go of Tito and tried to help Don Ojeda to his feet. Evelyn and Carmelo helped her, and together they got him inside.

"We have to bail him out," Maricarmen said.

Don Ojeda shook his head, holding his side. "Won't be any bail. What we need to do is get him a lawyer."

"Mari, I know you don't wanna hear this," Carmelo said, "but what *you* need to do is go."

She stopped suddenly as they all watched her, Carmelo, Don Ojeda, Evelyn. Cano had told her to go. He'd known Rey would change his mind. Carmelo was pushing her to go, even though he loved her. She knew it was the right thing, for Nena and Tito.

"After we get him a lawyer," she said.

DON OJEDA PAID a lawyer in el pueblo, one of el padre David's friends. He promised not to charge much, on account of his friendship with the priest, but Don Ojeda wasn't sure how long the trial would be or how long he'd be able to keep paying him.

Rey had been locked up for less than a week when Mari read

about it in her morning copy of *El Mundo*. Before the knock on her door, before the phone call from Cano, and before the news hit the street, the newspapers were already reporting it.

Rey had escaped from la Cárcel de Humacao, the story said. He'd spent almost a week in a bed at the infirmary, recovering from a serious beatdown. He had a nurse taking care of him day in, day out, but on that last day, he asked for help. He hadn't had a shit in two days, and needed something *now*. He was in so much pain, he told the nurse. She'd be back in a few minutes, she told him, before stepping out to the pharmacy for some medication. But Rey knew she'd probably take her sweet time. He was in a locked infirmary, on the second floor of the medical wing, and the pharmacy was on another floor, as far as he could tell. Rey managed to get the window open and, along with two other guys, jumped from the second story into a hedge. When the nurse came back, he was gone. Rey el Cantante, a twenty-four-year-old salsa singer turned thief from el Caserío Padre Rivera, had somehow managed to escape la Cárcel de Humacao. *El Mundo* referred to him as "el Houdini de Humacao."

That day, los camarones parked their cruisers by every entrance to el Caserío, circling the block every hour. There was no chance Rey would evade capture if he tried to come back home.

Maricarmen feared the worst. Every time the phone rang, every knock on her door, she could feel it coming: the news of Rey's death.

"He better not turn up here!" Maricarmen told Don Ojeda, Evelyn, and Carmelo when they came over that afternoon.

Everybody else in el Caserío had read the news, Carmelo told her, and most people found it funny as hell.

"El Houdini de Humacao," Evelyn said, chuckling.

But Don Ojeda and Maricarmen didn't think there was anything funny. They just wanted to know how to find Rey, *where* to find him.

Carmelo picked up the copy of *El Mundo* on the kitchen table.

"La Cárcel de Humacao. What kind of pendejos are running that place?" he said, flicking the front page with his finger. "I mean, Rey's not exactly a genius, you know?" He put the paper back down.

Don Ojeda just shook his head.

"Don't worry," Carmelo said, "I'll talk to the guys around the neighborhood. And I'll find Ismael and Cano. They gotta know something."

Soon after Carmelo left, there was a knock on the door. Maricarmen rushed to open it.

Altieri stood in front of her, both thumbs on his gun belt, like he was some kind of cowboy expecting a duel. Maricarmen felt goose bumps at the sight of him. He had a long jagged scar on his forehead. It was raw and red, and she realized it was where Rey had cracked open the man's head with the butt of his shotgun. Up close, she saw how bad it was, much worse than it had looked when she saw him in the street a few days before.

"Where is he?" Altieri asked. "I know you know where he is."

She shook her head, but she couldn't get any words out.

"We don't know where he is," Don Ojeda said over her shoulder, and she was grateful.

"I find out you're hiding him, you'll regret it," Altieri said, looking directly at Maricarmen.

Next to her, Evelyn took Maricarmen's hand. "Mira, mijo, if he shows up, you're the first person we'll call. Don't you worry."

Altieri took one step forward, leaned in closer. "One day soon, I'll be the one to transfer him to his new home. The fortress known as el Oso Blanco. Maybe you've heard of it?"

Maricarmen nodded, feeling tears sting her eyes.

"The Alcatraz of the Caribbean," Altieri said, laughing. "If you need a ride to go visit him, I'll drive you there myself. You just let me know."

Evelyn stepped into the doorway, in front of Maricarmen. "Thank you for your kind offer. It's always nice to see you, Sergeant Altieri." She smiled at him. "Have a good day."

Maricarmen watched Evelyn as she stepped back, as she ushered her and Don Ojeda gently inside the apartment and shut the door. She was still watching her when Evelyn closed her eyes, leaning against the door. "Don't look at me like that, Mari."

"Like what?" Maricarmen asked.

"Like you're judging me."

"I'm not judging you. I'm just trying to understand why you talk to that man like he's a friend."

"Why I talk to him like that? I have a Black son. You need to smarten up, Mari. You are raising Black children. You might be white, but when Nena and Tito go out into the world, they are Black children from el Caserío. You need to understand what that means."

MARICARMEN AND DON Ojeda stayed put long after Evelyn went home. They waited for the phone to ring, for the cops to come knocking, for Carmelo to come back with some news. But nothing.

After everyone went home that night, after all the lights went out in el Caserío, Juanito showed up.

"You alone?" he asked when she opened the door.

She looked him up and down. She didn't trust him and wasn't sure which answer was better. "Are *you*?" she said.

Juanito shook his head, then placed a folded envelope into her hand.

She looked at it, then tore it open.

Juanito looked over his shoulder, then turned back around and watched her.

It was a note. From Rey. He did want a better life for them, he said, and for his daughter, his little brother, and for her. *Let's run away together. You, me, and the kids, where no one will find us.*

"Who else knows about this?" Maricarmen asked Juanito.

"About what?" He turned and walked away.

She understood that to mean it was a secret Juanito would keep. Juanito knew where Rey was, and all she had to do was wait. Rey would come for her.

REY HAD BEEN stashed away at the garage for a few days. To Cano, it seemed like he was in no hurry to go back to el Caserío for Maricarmen and his family. Yet Mari was a nervous wreck, taking care of those two kids all by herself while cleaning houses and working shifts at El Paseo.

Cano parked his van on the gravel outside the shop and headed toward the door, carrying a bag of groceries and a new pack of drugstore underwear for Rey. Before he had a chance to knock, Ismael had opened the door, grabbed Cano by his shirt collar, and pulled him inside. They were all there, Ismael, Rey, and Juanito.

"Anybody follow you?" Ismael asked.

"Damn!" Cano pushed Ismael back, straightened his shirt. "Cálmate, brother. What's wrong with you?"

"Sorry, man."

"Cops are all over the place," Cano said. "Parked at every gate. But they're not moving. They just stay put, day and night." He handed Rey the paper bag, tossed the underwear onto the bed.

Rey ignored the underwear and searched the bag. "Gracias, brother." He broke off a piece of pan de agua and stuffed his mouth.

"You gotta get outa here, man." Cano walked over to the window, looked outside.

"It's true," Ismael said. "How long do you think you can stay here before Altieri finds you?"

Rey kept eating. "Let him come. I got something for him." He reached inside his waistband for his Cobra .38 Special, then flashed it at the guys. "Cleaned and loaded."

"Aw shit!" Juanito said. "Let me see that."

"Come on, now—don't encourage him," Ismael said.

"You trying to get killed?" Cano said. "You gotta think of Mari and your baby girl."

Rey nodded, reaching into the grocery bag for a banana.

Cano and Ismael exchanged looks. To Cano, Ismael appeared tired, exhausted with Rey, but Cano couldn't help feeling responsible somehow. Rey was like a little brother, too young to be living this kind of life.

"Rey, you gotta slow down, *think*," Cano said. "What do you think will happen if they find that on you? You gotta be smart."

"Look at me, Rey," Ismael said, sitting on the twin bed. He took his time, like he was preparing to say something important. Cano was hopeful—for so long, it had seemed to him that Ismael had given up on Rey. But maybe it wasn't like that at all. Cano and Juanito were quiet as they waited for Ismael to continue. "My whole life, I never met anyone with so much talent. You had a chance to do something *real*. You still do. We could be making music together! But you're throwing it all away. And for what?" Ismael turned from Rey to Juanito then.

Juanito narrowed his eyes. He checked his watch, squirming in a way that, Cano realized, made it seem like he was uncomfortable. "I gotta head out. I'm running late."

"Where you going?" Rey asked.

"Don't worry, man. I'll be back." Juanito swung the door so that it slammed on his way out.

"The hell's the matter with him?" Cano asked.

Ismael got up, watched from the window as Juanito walked to

his car. "That man ain't your friend," Ismael said to Rey. "You know that, right?"

"Come on, man," Rey said, exhaling.

"Rey, I'm being straight with you, as your friend," Ismael said. "You need to be on a plane to Miami *now*. Cano and I will make sure Mari and the kids get there after, but you need to go. At least until the heat dies down." Ismael looked at Cano. "Tell him!"

Cano watched the two of them, his closest friends. Ismael didn't say another word, and the silence in the room felt heavy. Cano wanted to say something, to remind Rey, again, about his family, all that he had going for him. He wanted to tell him about all the people who cared about him, who wanted him to succeed. Standing by the window in silence, Ismael widened his eyes. He gave Cano a nod, urging him to say something, to back him up. *Tell him*, his eyes seemed to say, *tell him that Juanito is bad fucking news.*

Maybe he would regret it for the rest of his life, but as much as his gut told him that Juanito *was* bad fucking news, in the moment, Cano said nothing.

Rey got up, reached for the underwear on the bed. "I don't need no babysitters. I know you're looking out for me, but I know what I'm doing." He tore open the plastic and pulled out a pair of white briefs. "Tighty-whities? Seriously?" He laughed and held them against his groin, shaking his head.

"Why don't you even consider it?" Ismael said.

"Look," Rey said. "I am considering it, but I don't know anybody in Miami. What would I even do there?" He held his hand up, like the question was rhetorical. "I know, I know. I'm not trying to get picked up here—I ain't doing no more time. But if I go, I need to get some money together, that's all. I just need a day."

"A day?" Cano asked.

"One day," Ismael said. "One."

"One day," Rey said. "Day after tomorrow, you drive me to the airport yourself, and I'm outa here."

"We'll be back tomorrow," Ismael said. "Tomorrow night."

Rey shook his head and laughed. "All right, all right. Tomorrow."

"Remember what I said," Ismael said.

"We'll see you tomorrow," Cano said. He fished his car keys out of his pocket, headed outside.

Ismael got in his Toyota and started slowly down the gravel toward the road. Cano followed in his van.

They were both headed toward el Caserío when they stopped at the intersection a block away. Ismael's left-hand signal light was blinking, but he wasn't turning. He was just idling.

Cano considered honking the horn but then checked out the traffic. He saw their lights first. And then, one after the other, the police cruisers crossed the intersection, passing Cano's van: Altieri's unmarked car, one police cruiser, then another, and another, all of them speeding in the opposite direction, toward Ismael's garage.

"Fuck!" Cano honked his horn, not sure what to do.

Ismael made a U-turn, doubled back.

"Fuck!" Cano couldn't believe it. Damn it, Rey. He slammed his fist on the steering wheel, then started turning. Across the intersection, parked in the corner, Cano spotted Juanito, sitting in his Oldsmobile. He shook his head, made a U-turn, and followed Ismael back toward the shop.

THE NEWSPAPERS, TELEVISION crews, and police press conferences that followed would get only part of the story right. They would not take into account the witnesses, Ismael and Cano, who watched as Altieri and his crew kicked down the garage door, the door to the office. How the cops dragged Rey, wearing only his fresh white briefs, threw him down on the gravel, and started kicking. How Cano and

Ismael ran over, but were tackled by the uniformed cops, spread facedown on the road, both of them handcuffed. How hearing Cano and Ismael shouting for them to stop, the neighbors from el Caserío and from Patagonia, the passersby heading home from el colmado, stood on the road and watched as Altieri pulled out his weapon. How Cano, his face pressed sideways against the hot tarmac, a uniformed cop's knee against his back, tried to breathe as Altieri stood over Rey, as he aimed his pistol. How Cano exhaled and Altieri pulled the trigger, and all the birds in the distance, the doves perched on the power lines above, a red-tailed guaraguao, a plague of grackles, exploded across the sky. Altieri aimed his pistol again. Pulled the trigger. A second shot to the groin.

Nothing in the police reports about how Altieri had been looking for Rey, or about how later, after getting a promotion and a raise, Altieri was heard bragging all over the city—at the barbershop, la barra, down at Pueblo Supermarket—about how *he* was the one who shot Rey el Cantante, the one who finally took him down.

Nothing about how everyone in el Caserío had a story about where they were on the day Rey el Cantante was killed: the granitos man pushing his cart down the street like every other day; Maricarmen in her apartment trying to rock Nenuska to sleep when she heard the two shots; Carmelo, Maricarmen's best friend, walking back from el colmado with some orange juice and a gallon of milk for Nena when he heard the two shots.

Nothing about how los camarones, parked around the corner, parked by the front gate and the back entrance, had been watching Maricarmen, waiting for him to show up. Or how when Altieri pulled the trigger, all the other cops had their guns drawn and pointed at Rey, and how after the two shots, Ismael screaming, eyes wide, Cano struggling to breathe, coughing, his hands behind his back, the cops tossed Rey into the back of a police cruiser, and there, Rey eventually bled out.

The newspapers would mention, briefly, that the Humacao prosecutor opened an investigation. They'd say that after Rey was driven to the Ryder Memorial Hospital emergency room, the police cruiser had been stolen from the hospital parking lot, and when it was found three days later, it had been doused in gasoline, set on fire. No evidence was recovered. They'd say Rey would be remembered as a loyal friend, that he was an addict, that he left behind a daughter, a wife, a little brother. The Humacao Houdini. El Caserío's Robin Hood. He was twenty-four years old.

THE CATHOLIC CHURCH refused to take care of Rey's funeral. Cano's brother, David, had moved to the Catholic church in Cidra, city of eternal spring, and the Catholic Diocese of Fajardo–Humacao denied Maricarmen's and Don Ojeda's requests for a funeral Mass. The two of them had gone down to the parish to talk to the new priest. Sitting together in his office, they just listened in silence as he explained that the church could not—*would* not—be involved with criminals. It had come down from the diocese, and his hands were tied.

In the end, the community showed up. Maricarmen and Don Ojeda held a vigil for Rey at home. Carmelo's father, who owned a funeral home, paid for the flowers. The community's donations paid for the pine casket. The viewing lasted twenty-four hours, the neighbors praying the rosary all night.

David the priest drove in from Cidra and led a small service in Maricarmen's apartment the next morning. Mari sat on the sofa, Tito sitting close, Nena on her lap. Their apartment filled up with people from the neighborhood, people who'd known Rey's parents and grandparents, who'd watched him grow up, who knew Ojeda and still called him a friend.

The pallbearers carried the casket out of the apartment and into the street. There was no hearse. There were no funeral cars. It was not a funeral procession. It was a parade, all of el Caserío walking together. Cano and his wife, Jeannette, his kids, Anthony and Jaqui, walking with Doña Matos. Evelyn and Carmelo walking side by side. Don Ojeda holding Tito's hand. Maricarmen pushing Nena in her stroller. People coming out of their apartments last minute, joining the march down the street. Neighbors, friends, strangers. Men who'd played dominoes in la plaza. The ladies who'd first started calling him Rey el Cantante. The guys from the basketball courts. The whole block lifting the casket over their heads, Evelyn taking over while Ismael went to Cano's van for his instrument. And as they marched up the street toward the front gates, Ismael strapped a conga to his body and started playing, the rhythm following them, the sound winding its way to the front. Ismael and his conga, a horn player, a trombonist, un cuatro, un güiro, and the whole barrio, the band singing Ismael Rivera's "Las Caras Lindas," Rey's favorite song.

"*Las caras lindas de mi gente negra...*" All the way to el pueblo, past the Patagonia suburbs, past la Catedral Dulce Nombre de Jesús.

They say the people of el Caserío Padre Rivera hummed along with the song as they marched, until the humming turned to singing, Maricarmen wiping tears from her eyes, holding Nena close. Maricarmen would lose more of Rey as the years passed, little by little—the way he smelled, the sound of his voice. But some things she would keep forever: how he was tall and lanky and brown skinned, his afro always picked out; how he'd lifted her up when he sang; how he was always going somewhere, always thumping out the beat to whatever song was on the radio, whatever song had been playing in his head all day.

The story goes that on the afternoon of Rey el Cantante's funeral, the people walked all the way from el Caserío, moving slowly, lifted the casket over their heads, the sun beating down on them, until they could see the entrance to the cemetery, the arch at the center of the wrought iron gates. Rey's friends and family carried the casket, carried the song, danced in the street.

THEY SAY HE was a thief, a hustler, that he ran from the cops, that it was Juanito who betrayed him, that he had it coming, even though everybody loved him. They say they found the police car, burning, out in the cañaverales. That there was no evidence left after everything burned. They say Juanito, the friend, was never heard from again.

Nenuska Ojeda Doval would not remember her father, but there were things she would always know to be true. How her mother loved him her whole life, even years after his death. How everybody called him Rey el Cantante. How he could summon ghosts, palms beating on a tambor primo, bomba y plena coursing through his veins. How he was all hustle and music, all loyalty and reckless abandon, all those things at once. How in the end, he was running. How in the end, he was lost. And how his name, Rey, means "king."

PART TWO

"Calle Luna, Calle Sol"

1993

"Periódico de Ayer"

NENUSKA OJEDA DOVAL was not the kind of girl people in el Caserío expected her to be. She didn't care about anything other girls her age cared about. When her friends at Ana Roqué de Duprey High School talked about crushing on Eduardo Palomo in *Corazón Salvaje* or the guys from *Beverly Hills, 90210,* which they bragged about watching in English, Nena could not relate. Nena didn't wear dresses. She wasn't crazy about lip gloss or eyeliner or getting her nails done. And she didn't care about the kind of boys who memorized all the lyrics to Vico C's "Saboréalo" just to get her attention.

She spent most of her time with Génesis, her best friend, or (when she wasn't at school) with her face buried in a book. So when her mom started planning a traditional quinceañera ceremony, which included a court of damas and chambelanes, Nena refused. Putting on a puffy pink dress, long gloves, a tiara, and high heels just so she could dance with some mouth-breathing boy and announce to the world that she was now a woman? *That* sounded like a damn nightmare, if you asked her. You couldn't pay her to do it. She would not be paraded like some child bride for the neighborhood men, she told her mother. Her mother insisted on throwing Nena a party, but it didn't have to be a traditional one. They settled on a regular Caserío block party, with a DJ, some dancing, some friends, and a lot of food.

The day of the party, as the sun set, everyone drank and danced in the street. In the buffet line, people moved slowly, getting in each other's way, laughing as they bumped one another. Nena and Génesis piled arroz con gandules and pernil onto their paper plates and ate sitting together at one of the long folding tables on the lawn. Nena leaned into Génesis, and when the streetlights came on, the two of them swaying to the music and licking grease off their fingers, Nena could smell a hint of perfume on her. The smell of Génesis mixed with the pork and herbs as Nena sopped up the juices and onions with a piece of bread.

In the buffet line, Génesis's older brother Jamil finished plating his rice and reached for a serving fork. Next to him, Tito reached for the same fork, but before he could grab it, Jamil held it up and away from him. For a second, the two teenage boys stood over the pernil, staring at each other aggressively.

"What's up with *them*?" Nena asked Génesis.

Génesis kept eating, her eyes on Jamil and Tito. She made a face, scrunching her nose. "Ugh. Ignore my brother. He's always catching beef."

Nena put her plate down, ready to get up. But after a tense moment, Jamil set down the fork and kept the line moving.

Tito watched him go.

Nena leaned back in her chair. She looked around, taking in the crowd: her mother dancing salsa with Carmelo; Génesis's brothers sitting at the table across from them, stuffing their faces with pork; Evelyn, who'd already finished her plate, wiping at the corner of her mouth with a paper napkin. Checking out the party, Nena didn't think there was anything special about her fifteenth birthday. It was like every other Caserío block party. The DJ would play all the same songs he always did, and her mother and Carmelo would dance all night, sweat running down their backs. All the kids would eat, toss their paper plates or leave them behind for someone else to clear. Tito would spend ten minutes with her and then sneak out when nobody was watching. She would spend all night with Génesis, and they'd have more time than they usually got together, since their parents would keep drinking and dancing, and nobody would have a bedtime. The two girls would wander home at two, three in the morning after her mother and Génesis's parents had fallen asleep.

The DJ played another salsa song, and Mami tapped Carmelo on the shoulder, then walked back toward the long folding table where Tito sat. She took Tito's hand, pulling him onto the makeshift dance space in the street. Tito smiled, towering over Mami with his long, lanky limbs, turning her mother to the rhythm of the music. He was a good dancer. Mami had taught him, so of course he was. But also, Tito moved like a dancer. Graceful and confident, strong, and a little effeminate. At the table in front of Nena and Génesis, Jamil watched Tito, and Génesis watched her brother, nervous, shifting in her seat every time Jamil moved.

This was like every other party. And that's exactly how Nena wanted it. None of that fancy shit. No ugly dresses, no girls wearing too much of their mother's makeup, no pimple-faced sweaty boys in rented tuxedoes. Her mother never had a quinceañera celebration herself, and Nena didn't like the thought of Mami working two jobs just to make sure Nena had all the things *she'd* never had as a girl. Nena didn't want the things her mother never had.

Her mother had told her about the block parties in el Caserío when she was Nena's age. She'd told her about the music, her job at the restaurant, the nights when she and Titi Loli would take off with the guys and end up at el malecón under the moonlight. How they'd all dance weekends away at las fiestas patronales where her father and his band played. How they fell in love. That was real. Nena didn't want fake shit.

Nena turned to Génesis then, watched her until the song ended. When the next song started, her mother and Tito suddenly stopped dancing. Carmelo, watching the dance floor from another table, stood. Some of the other dancers stopped, too, looking around, as if trying to figure out what they should do. Nena heard the trumpets and trombones, the congas. She thought she should go to her mother but wasn't sure how Mami would feel and didn't want to make a scene. Nena was frozen in her seat. As she watched Carmelo leaving his drink on the table and heading toward the DJ, Nena exhaled.

"What's going on?" Génesis asked.

"It's the song," Nena said.

Nena watched her mother and Tito as Carmelo talked to the DJ. The DJ, a young guy from some other barrio, probably had no idea. Slowly, the song faded, another one played in its place. Everyone started dancing again, but Tito took Mami's hand and walked with her back to the tables.

"What was wrong with the song?" Génesis asked.

Nena had never talked to her about this, had never told Génesis everything about her family. Everyone in el Caserío knew, or at least that's what she always assumed. People who'd known her father before he died all knew about the song. But Génesis's family had moved there after her father's death.

"Have you ever heard it?" Nena asked. "'El Entierro del Salsero'?"

Génesis nodded slowly, her eyes widening like she was just putting it together. "It's about your father."

Nena had always known this. Or, she couldn't remember when she learned it. She must've been small. But she had never said it aloud, not to Tito, not even to Mami. It had always been a thing they never talked about, just changed the station if it came on the radio. Her mother could not listen to the song, but Nena had listened when her mother wasn't around. She had listened again and again, memorized the lyrics, turned over every sentence in her head, every word. It was a tribute. It was a song about friendship and love and forgiveness, written by her father's closest friend after he was killed by the police. Nena hadn't known her father, or this friend, but there was something about the song that made her feel grateful. For how her father lived on in a way, even if her mother couldn't bear it.

"It is," Nena said.

Génesis took Nena's hand, interlacing their fingers, and held it.

The streetlights were brighter now, and people would see them holding hands, but Nena didn't care. She leaned in closer to Génesis, put her head on Génesis's shoulder, breathing in the scent of her perfume.

Across the intersection, Nena noticed a police cruiser coming from the direction of the far entrance to el Caserío. It turned away from the crowd, away from the people dancing in the street, toward Padre Rivera Elementary. The cruiser stopped in the middle of the street before it reached the school, made a U-turn, and double-parked, facing them so the cops would have a full view of the block party. There were no lights, no sirens, but there were two uniformed cops sitting in the car. Los camarones were watching, and, Nena knew, they would stay there all night, until every last one of the residents of el Caserío Padre Rivera had gone home.

AT SCHOOL A couple days later, Tito dodged Jamil in the hallways. He dreaded the walk from one class to the next, when guys would stare as he passed, his face down, his eyes on the floor in front of him. He'd look up before he reached Jamil's locker or his classroom, then keep walking when he'd made sure Jamil wasn't around. He was way too familiar with these types—the ones who acted all bad in front of their friends, who got rougher with a little encouragement, so he tried to stay out of their way. But sometimes there was no avoiding them. Guys would catcall as he walked into the locker room with his backpack, blow kisses as he entered one of the toilet stalls to change. Boys pulled open the doors in the bathroom stalls sometimes, if there was a broken lock. The locks were always broken. Sometimes they stood around and watched him pee. Sometimes they joked, *Look at him! I thought locas pissed sitting down!*

He never used the urinals. Even with a broken lock, at least the door between them and his body was *something*.

Tito was headed to the stall to change for PE when they blocked him. Four guys from his class, already changed and ready to run circles around the basketball courts.

"Where you going, loca?" one of them said as he stood in front of him. The other three crept up from behind.

Tito didn't speak. He waited for what came next—what always came next with these assholes. They were so predictable, always with the same stupid jokes, trying to impress their friends.

Behind him, one of them shoved his shoulder.

"Don't touch me," Tito said. He regretted it as soon as the words left his mouth.

"Or what?" the one in front of him said, standing up straight and looking Tito in the eyes.

"Can you just get out of my way?" Tito said, knowing it would do him no good.

From behind, he felt their hands on his shirt, his shoulders. They pulled him from the stall, snatched his backpack off, threw him sideways onto the floor. It was fast, so fast he didn't have time to think about what had just happened, only that he was on the floor, and one of the guys was straddling him, a hand on his chest, holding him down. Tito felt the blow to his face first, then the side of his head hitting the tile. He brought his hands up, then slapped at the boy on top of him. Tito's open palm connected with something in a satisfying *thwack*, and he did it again, one hand, then another, a slap, another slap. He was hitting him back, Tito realized. Tito, *fighting* back.

He rolled onto his stomach, trying to get the boy off him, slapping, jerking, aiming for anything he could hit. Somehow, the guy fell off, and Tito kicked him in the stomach.

And then, just like that, Tito was down again, his face touching the cold tiles. He braced himself for the shower of blows, bringing his arms up around his head, curling up into the fetal position. He took every punch and kick they gave him, and even though he tried to will his body to get up, keep fighting, his limbs felt so heavy. He was lightheaded. He was somewhere else.

The blows stopped, and he lay there breathing. Breathing.

"Fucking maricón," one of them said, and Tito recognized his voice.

Tito's vision was hazy, but he could make out Jamil's thick, messy curls, the baggy cargo shorts he always wore, his broad chest. Tito didn't move. He wanted to face the guys, face Jamil, but he couldn't fucking move. It was then that he felt it. A stream of hot piss raining down on his head and neck. He shut his eyes tight and jerked sideways, rolled over, trying to get away.

Somewhere a door slammed and Tito heard their footsteps scattering toward the exit, the big metal double doors opening, then closing again.

Mr. Peña, the basketball coach, stood over him. He helped him up, one hand under Tito's armpit as he struggled over to the bench by the lockers.

"Jesus. Who did this to you?" Mr. Peña shook the piss from his hand, then quickly went over to one of the sinks, rinsed it. He pressed and pressed the pump for the hand soap dispenser, but it was empty.

"Didn't see him." Tito pulled his shirt off and threw it on the floor. He coughed. He wiped piss from his face, unbuckled his jeans, unzipped.

"You can tell me," Mr. Peña said. "I won't let anything happen to you."

Tito peeled off his jeans and stood there in his underwear. He looked into Mr. Peña's eyes. What was he saying? Something had *already* happened to him.

Mr. Peña had a pained look on his face. Maybe it was sympathy. Maybe he felt sorry for Tito.

"If you want to get cleaned up," Mr. Peña said, looking down at Tito's soiled T-shirt on the floor, "I'll get you something else to wear." He turned to go, but then turned back to Tito. "Then we can talk."

TITO SHOWERED IN silence, letting the tears run down his face. He listened for the double doors that led out to the basketball courts, and the heavy metal door that led into the school hallway. He was afraid the guys would come back, but he wanted the hot water to wash over him as long as possible, wash off everything that had just happened.

In a few weeks, he told himself, school would be over. In a few weeks, he would get his diploma, and he'd finally be free. He stood under the shower head, letting the water fall over him.

When he turned around, wiping the wet hair from his face, Mr. Peña was standing there, a gray hoodie and sweatpants in his hands. Watching.

AFTER THAT, MR. PEÑA started looking out for him. Every day, Tito noticed, Mr. Peña watched Tito's every move on the courts, and then afterward, explained where he'd gone wrong. Mr. Peña taught him how to focus, how to glide across the court with style, when to use a head fake with a crossover. Mr. Peña, who now spent so many hours after school with Tito, teaching him layups, hook shots. Mr. Peña took care of Tito when he'd needed him that first day in the locker room, and every day after that. Mr. Peña stayed behind with him all that week every afternoon until all the other guys were gone, and sometimes drove Tito home.

Tito knew that Mr. Peña lived in el Caserío with his family, his wife, Maritza, and their baby. But when he drove Tito home, he always seemed interested in what Tito had to say, always asked questions, never mentioned his wife.

"Do you have a girlfriend, or maybe *a boyfriend*?" he'd asked that first day.

Tito had flinched at that, not sure why Mr. Peña asked.

"No boyfriend," Tito had said, and then, taking a chance, he added, "Not yet." He smiled, and Mr. Peña laughed.

Tito had been relieved that there was no judgment, no unsolicited advice, just silence as Mr. Peña drove. But even with the awkward silence, afterward, something between them became clear. They had an understanding: In Mr. Peña's presence, Tito could be himself. During their rides home, they could talk about anything.

During one of those rides home, Mr. Peña and Tito were singing along to Chayanne on the radio when they came to a red light. Mr. Peña glanced over at him. Tito was smiling, his curls still wet from the showers at the locker room a few minutes before. When Tito noticed his face, Mr. Peña seemed so full of sadness, close to tears.

"Something wrong?" Tito asked.

"If only you were older..."

Tito had wanted him to continue, say whatever it was he'd been thinking, but he was too shy to ask.

Even though it had just been a few days, it seemed that so much had happened since the incident in the locker rooms. Tito and Mr. Peña stopped dancing around their feelings. There had been moments in the car—when Tito slid into the passenger seat and Mr. Peña smiled at him, touched his knee. When Mr. Peña reached for Tito's hand, put it on the gearshift before shifting gears, his large fingers over Tito's. It felt nice to have Mr. Peña's hands on his—he felt safe. And it felt good to know that Mr. Peña wanted him. Mr. Peña wasn't really that good-looking, and he was a little corny, with his broom of a mustache and his too-tight jeans. He dressed like a dad, moved like a dad. He was definitely not like one of the guys from *Por Siempre Amigos*—Sergio with his long hair and his biceps, or Ricky, with those big brown eyes. But Tito liked the way Mr. Peña tried for him, the way he promised that once Tito got older, he would teach him things. Tito knew what he meant; there had been others. But he wasn't about to tell Peña that.

One day after basketball practice, Peña waited for him outside the locker room. After all the other boys left, once the school had emptied, they walked to Peña's car together.

"I have a surprise for you," Peña said.

Tito smiled. He didn't want to seem too excited and didn't want to say the wrong thing, so he didn't ask what it was. Maybe Peña had bought him some jewelry. Maybe he was taking him somewhere special. But in the car, Tito noticed that they were taking the same route they always took back to el Caserío. He tried not to get his hopes up.

Tito watched out the window as the car slowed down outside el Caserío but didn't turn. They drove past the entrance, past el colmado, toward La Central, past the rows and rows of lush green caña bursting next to Peña's small car. Occasionally, Peña got too close to the ditch on the narrow road, and the long leaves slapped the side of the car.

"Where we going?" Tito finally asked.

When they got to the first intersection, Peña turned left onto the dirt road that ran behind the cañaverales. "Don't worry. We're almost there."

They drove deep into the green, until you couldn't see la Calle Tres anymore, and when the dirt road sloped slightly downhill, Peña slowed down. He parked at a slant, the same way he drove in, close to the sugarcane.

Tito took it all in—the miles and miles of caña, the dirt road, not a single other person around. They were alone. Completely alone.

"So what's the surprise?"

Tito knew what he wanted, even though Peña had been nothing but nice. He'd taken care of Tito, watched over him when the other guys were around. He'd listened when Tito talked about all the shit they'd put him through day after day. He'd asked Tito questions about his family, about his plans after high school. Tito had started to really like him, considered him a friend, even.

Peña reached back and grabbed a plastic bag in the back seat, handed it over. Inside was a box wrapped in glossy gold paper.

"My birthday was last month," Tito said. He felt bad for thinking that Peña had brought him out here for something else, that he just wanted to fuck him.

"Open it!" Peña said, smiling. "I know it's a month late, but eighteen's a big deal."

Tito peeled back the tape gently, not wanting to rip it. He couldn't believe that Peña had bought him a gift, that he'd taken the time to wrap it and everything.

"I hope you like it."

Tito pulled off the paper and let it drop on his lap. It was a Polaroid camera. He opened the box quickly, pulled out the camera. It was not like the old one Maricarmen had. This one was brand-new.

"It's already loaded, look." Peña reached for it, took it in his hands, and pointed it at Tito. Tito covered his face with his hands, and Peña stopped. "Come on, now. Film is expensive. You don't want to waste it."

Tito rolled his eyes, then composed himself, smiling shyly for Peña.

Peña held the camera up, pressed the shutter, and the photo came sliding out. Tito snatched it quickly, then watched it change before his eyes. The colors looked washed out at first, but slowly they began to change: a washed-out Tito starting to brown, turning sultry and inviting.

"Mari has one of these," Tito said as he waited for the image to fully transform. "An old one."

"Look at me."

Peña was waiting on him, but Tito didn't know if he should smile, if he should pose or something. He looked out the window at the caña, holding up his chin with one hand, soft and pensive. Peña pressed the shutter. They both laughed.

"You're beautiful," Peña said. "You know that, right?"

Tito laughed. "Yeah, right. You mean like a girl."

"No. Not like a girl." Peña put the camera down between them and moved closer. He placed the tips of his fingers on Tito's collarbone. "Beautiful like a man is beautiful." He moved in closer and Tito leaned back.

Peña stopped. "I'm sorry. I was going to kiss you. I thought that's what you wanted."

"Oh," Tito said. He felt himself starting to get hard.

Peña pulled back. "I don't want to cross a line or anything, do something that you don't want. But if you want me to—"

"I do."

"I want you to be sure."

Tito leaned forward and kissed him first, not sure what to do with his hands, but Peña took care of that. He took both of Tito's hands, kissed them one by one, then kissed his throat softly, his jaw, his lips. They kissed for a few minutes until Tito forgot that they were in a car, out in the cañaverales behind el Caserío, and that this was his coach, his *teacher*.

But he was eighteen, he thought. He was an adult.

Suddenly, Tito pulled back. "What if someone comes?"

"Nobody comes here."

"How do you know?"

"I know." Peña picked up the camera again, held it up.

Tito smiled nervously.

"I want to remember that look," Peña said.

"What look? What do I look like?"

Peña held the camera with one hand, reached down into Tito's shorts with the other, and Tito felt himself get harder.

"I want to see you when you're not around, when we can't be together," Peña said. "I want to carry you with me."

Tito closed his eyes.

"I want you to take pictures of yourself. For me." Peña pressed the shutter. "Will you do that for me?"

Tito nodded.

"Happy birthday."

THEY SAW EACH other every day after that.

On practice days, Peña drove them into the cañaverales before dropping him off a block away from el Caserío. On the weekends, they snuck out separately and met in the caña in the middle of the night. On Tuesdays and Thursdays, when there was no practice, sometimes Tito found Peña in his office inside the gym. They'd lock themselves inside during the lunch hour, and Peña would make a show of taking off Tito's T-shirt, pulling down his jeans, and taking him into his mouth.

Afterward, they ate lunch together, talked about what they'd watched on TV the night before.

Once, while they sat together in Peña's office, the two of them still sweaty and smelling of sex, Peña put down his ham sandwich.

"Am I the only one?" Peña asked.

"What?" Tito said. He put a Dorito in his mouth.

"Tell me you're not fucking anyone else."

"Of course not."

Peña leaned over and took Tito's hand. He brought it slowly to his lips, kissed it. "I love you." Peña's face lit up with anticipation.

Tito didn't know what to say. He thought about it. He wanted to be honest. He wasn't sure what had changed between that first day in the locker room, when Peña had just been his coach, a car seat–carrying nerd with a weird mustache, and that afternoon in the office. For a while, Tito thought it was just fun, this older man who made him come every time they saw each other, who bought him gifts and gave him rides and made Tito feel like everything about him was perfect. For a while, Tito had thought it was one of those things you did in high school, before you go off to college or move away or whatever. Sowing wild oats. One of those things you do just so you can tell your friends, *Yeah, I fucked the basketball coach.* But Tito didn't have any friends. And the idea of telling Nena made him feel ashamed—not because he was gay, or because Peña was his teacher, but because Peña was married to their neighbor Maritza, and they had a baby, and hurting them made him feel like the worst person in the world.

Months ago, when he decided that he'd leave after high school, Tito had promised himself that he'd never again feel ashamed, that he would not let hypocrites and bigots tell him who he was, that he would hold the truth about himself with pride.

"What about your wife?" Tito said now. He wasn't sure he wanted an answer, or if it had even been a question. Peña talked about his marriage like it had always been a lie. He often said he was trapped and unhappy. But now the fact of Peña's wife and baby felt like an indictment of Tito.

"That doesn't have anything to do with us," Peña said.

"Oh." Tito felt stupid for letting himself believe, even for a second, that Peña had actually meant it when he said he loved him, or that he'd thought of him as something more than a piece of ass. Tito wasn't sure if he loved Peña or if he was just hurt because he felt used. He spent most of their time apart trying to figure that out.

"You don't understand," Peña said. "It's not that easy. We have a baby. And I could lose my job."

"That's not love," Tito said. "I don't think you even know what love is."

"That's not fair."

Tito tossed his half-full bag of Doritos into the metal trash can next to Peña's desk, wiped his hands on his jeans. He didn't want to hear anything about what was *fair*. He pulled his backpack off the floor, strapped it on.

"Where you going?" Peña asked.

"You're a good teacher," Tito said as he reached for the doorknob. "You taught me a lesson after all."

IN EL CASERÍO Padre Rivera, where the myth of his dead brother followed him—the tragic salsero, the thief with a heart of gold who died too young—Tito was just a minor character. If Tito died, he knew, nobody would be writing songs about him. Who wrote songs about gay boys who dreamed about leaving the only place they'd ever known? Who wrote songs about *gay boys*? In el Caserío, gay boys turned into men like Peña. They married women who loved them, had children who looked like them, and spent their lives pretending. Or maybe that was just Peña, who liked younger boys and insisted on being called *Mr.* Peña, even when he drove Tito out to the lechoneras in Carraízo or when they were out in the cañaverales under the cover of darkness.

Tito was tired of pretending. He was tired of being the boy on the side, watching from his balcony as Peña came home from a day out with Maritza and baby Kevin. Peña opening the car door for her, Maritza holding the baby in her arms, Peña carrying the car seat. A happy family. He was tired of all the people he knew, who insisted that there was only one way to be a man—*their* way. And he was tired of waiting for a man who would never love him. He wanted to be *adored*. He would not settle, he decided. He would speak the truth about himself and expect to be taken seriously.

THEY WERE MOSTLY silent during the ride, except when Peña talked about where they were going. Eros, where they could play a couple games of pool, dance, maybe have a drink. Tito had reluctantly agreed to go out—he wasn't sure it would be a good idea, but he'd never been to a gay bar before. So he let Peña take him.

Tito wore a shitload of cologne, his gold crucifix on a delicate gold chain, and a pair of tight jeans that maybe made him look like he was trying too hard. But he didn't care. He wanted to be seen.

"We're friends," Tito told Peña as they drove out to Eros. "Just friends." He wanted to make sure the night would unfold without drama.

"I don't know if I like the sound of that," Peña said.

Tito laughed. "Oh yeah? That's too fucking bad. You decided that. You're married, remember?"

"That doesn't mean—"

"Don't fucking play with me," Tito said, cutting him off. "That's *exactly* what it means. If you can't handle that, then we won't be anything at all."

Tito tried to keep from smiling. He was surprised at himself, his confidence.

Before they walked through the door, Peña told Tito not to worry. "You'll have a good time. Just be yourself, and all the guys will love you."

But Tito wasn't worried. He was ready for the night.

Inside Eros, Tito stood at the bar, watching the dance floor, sipping cranberry juice from a plastic cup, and swaying his hips to the rhythm of Eddie Santiago's salsa.

When Peña leaned up against him at the bar, brushed Tito's forearm softly with his fingertips, Tito pulled his arm away, said, "Don't."

"You wanna dance?" Peña asked.

Tito shook his head. "Maybe later."

Peña downed two shots and hit the dance floor.

Tito hung out by the bar. A tall, muscular trigueño not much older than Tito came up to the bar and sized him up, and Tito couldn't help but smile. This confident beautiful stranger stood out in the crowd with his red silk shirt, diamond earrings glittering under the dim lights, and the way he just looked people in the eyes like he was searching for something secret. The bartender put a bottle of Heineken in front of the stranger, and Tito realized that he must be a regular.

Red Shirt took a sip of his beer and smiled at Tito. Until then, Tito hadn't realized that he'd been watching the guy, so obvious. The opposite of smooth. Tito went back to watching the dudes on the dance floor.

The jukebox played a mix of salsa, merengue, and boleros, and

Tito sat on his stool, his back to the bartender, feeling out of place while Peña let the boys grind on him. Peña was older than all those boys, and much older than Tito. He was close to thirty.

Next to Tito, el trigueño in his red shirt looked like he was on fire. Un hombre de fuego, Tito thought as he watched him across the bar.

Eyes back on the dance floor, Tito recognized a few guys from school—nobody he knew, just people he knew *of*. They moved like they owned the place, like they were regulars, too, and Tito guessed that the novelty of a place where you could be yourself had already worn off for them. For Tito, maybe it would always feel like this— fleeting, precious. There had been so many of these guys, the ones who'd teased him and called him pato on the basketball courts or in front of the other guys, the ones who'd beat him in the locker room, the ones he'd forget, the ones who somehow came back to him, the ones who graduated and he'd never see again. The ones who didn't take off to New York or Miami would always end up in San Juan. It had never even crossed his mind that he'd run into them right here in el pueblo. Tito had never even considered staying. Soon, he knew, he'd be gone. He didn't know where, but he wouldn't be *here*.

The guys picked out an empty pool table by the far wall, crowded around it. One of them made a beeline for the bar. The rest of the group laughed and smoked and talked, some of them watching as one of them racked 'em up. Tito wasn't sure if they were all gay or if they were just a group of friends hanging out, but he smiled when they looked his way.

El Hombre de Fuego checked out the dance floor, glanced over at Tito like he was expecting him to say something. It was dark, nothing but the lamps over the pool tables lighting the place. Tito set his drink on the bar, moved with the rhythm of the song, watched the guys he knew. Back at school, their uniforms had made them all seem so young, but out here, even though it was just a small place, wood-paneled and smoke-filled, where you got your drinks in plastic cups, it was different. Inside Eros, it seemed like anything was possible. Tito snuck a peek at el Hombre de Fuego, smiling mischievously.

When he saw Tito's face, el Hombre de Fuego shot back the kind of smile that made Tito feel caught. Tito swallowed the rest of his cranberry juice, and when the bartender looked his way, Tito pointed down at his cup.

El Hombre de Fuego pulled up the stool next to Tito's, took a long swig of his beer and set it back down. "What's that? A soda?" He chuckled.

"I don't drink," Tito said. He gave him a don't-fuck-with-me look.

El Hombre de Fuego smiled, and Tito liked his dimples, the small gap between his two front teeth, the whitest teeth he'd ever seen.

The bartender snapped up Tito's empty plastic cup and set a fresh one on the bar in front of him. On the dance floor, Peña was shaking his head from side to side, singing along to Whitney Houston's "I'm Every Woman" with a pretend microphone.

The man offered Tito his hand. "I'm Ángel."

"Tito." Tito didn't quite shake it, just sort of held it there. It was the most awkward thing, shaking someone's hand at a bar, especially since it wasn't like men around there wanted to be known.

"How long have you been coming here?" Ángel asked.

"First time." Tito looked down into his cup.

Ángel laughed, angling his body toward Tito. "Same."

That was a lie, Tito knew it. But he decided to play along.

Ángel smelled faintly of cologne, sandalwood, and soap. Tito made a show of checking out the dance floor in the mirror behind the bar, took a sip of his drink. Peña was still grinding on the boys, except now he was wearing someone else's ball cap and smoking his cigar.

"That your boyfriend?" Ángel asked.

Tito laughed. "Why? You trying to take his place?"

Ángel put a hand on Tito's arm. "Mi amor, you don't have to pretend. Not for me."

Was he being condescending? Tito couldn't tell. Ángel's smile was warm.

"He's my neighbor," Tito said, "and I'm not pretending." He fiddled with his crucifix, shifting uncomfortably, then leaned against the bar.

Ángel touched the crucifix, then ran his fingers along the length of Tito's hand and up his forearm. "You religious or just spiritual?" he asked, looking Tito in the eyes.

Ángel's skin against Tito's felt surprisingly familiar—this was the same way Peña had tried to caress him. But the way Ángel looked into his eyes and held his gaze, it made Tito feel young and powerful, like he was asking something else.

"Hombre de fuego," Tito said.

Ángel threw his head back, laughing loudly. "Hombre de fuego? I like that. It's like you *see* me, like you already know exactly who I am."

"Why? Do you like playing with fire?" Tito asked.

"Maybe you'll find out."

Tito's eyes widened. "I bet you love being in charge."

"I like living, being present. I want to experience every single feeling. And, yeah, I am always in control."

Tito slapped Ángel's shoulder. "That's fucking beautiful. Why wouldn't you want to feel every single thing?"

"Some people are afraid to feel. Life is beautiful, but you know. Some people weren't meant for this life."

"That's corny as fuck," Tito said, laughing.

"You want a real drink?"

They sat talking, checking out the dance floor, laughing at each other's jokes. Ángel was sweet, and then a song would come on the jukebox and he'd change the subject, say, "I love this song," and ask Tito to dance.

Tito had already stopped watching Peña dance when the jukebox played Eddie Santiago's "Tú Me Quemas." He jumped off his barstool and Ángel did the same. The song was kind of ridiculous, Tito thought, definitely corny, but it felt right. Eros felt like the place to be real, to let yourself feel every feeling, just like Ángel said.

Ángel took his hand, their soles sticking to the greasy old vinyl, and they were in the roar of their own world for a moment. Soon those kids from Ana Roqué High were out there, and some guys who'd been watching the basketball game, and then they were all bopping and shuffling and shimmying and looking silly, even the bartenders and the big guy who checked IDs at the door. They danced until they were sweaty, until Tito could see that Ángel was so much more than just a boy. Ángel, in that red shirt, how freely he could take his hand, dance with him, touch him however he wanted, remind Tito that he was free, that they were both free to do what they liked. How long had Tito waited for Peña to make him feel like this?

After the song ended, after the guys from Ana Roqué High went back to their pool table, and the men from the bar went back to their Long Island iced teas and their beers, and the bartenders to their bartending and the waiters to their waiting and the big guy to his door, Ángel would take Tito's hand again and lead him out the door and around the side of the building, where he would look into Tito's face and smile and kiss him. And Tito would kiss him back.

AT THE END of the night, after Tito and el Hombre de Fuego had exchanged numbers and talked, as Tito and Ángel kissed outside the bar, the late-night tecatos hanging in the parking lot across the street, the other men leaving the bar headed to their cars, Peña found them. Ángel was twirling one of Tito's curls between his fingers, kissing along his jawline, Tito pulling Ángel against him.

"What do you think you're doing?" Peña yelled. He was half drunk and smiling. Jealous, wounded.

Ángel turned to find Peña standing there, arms folded across his chest. "Is he for real?" he asked Tito.

Tito laughed, glancing over at Peña. It was obviously a joke. Had to be.

"I didn't bring you all the way out here so you could run off with the first sucio to come along," Peña said.

Ángel flinched at the insult, the muscles on his neck and shoulders tensing, then sprang toward Peña, stopping when his face was just inches away. "You don't know me, man," Ángel said.

Tito nervously got between them. He put his hand gently on Ángel's chest, but focused directly on Peña. "I'm gonna need you to back off. I appreciate our friendship, I do, but I'm not your property." Tito looked into Peña's eyes, impressed with himself, how calm he was, how direct. "This is not cool."

"We came here together," Peña said, his voice shaky. "You and me." He breathed hard, and Tito wondered if he would cry.

"We talked about this," Tito said. "You made the call. And I was clear, we can't be more than friends."

Peña opened his mouth to speak, but Tito spoke louder, with purpose.

"No. You need to stop."

Ángel was still, letting Tito speak for himself. Tito appreciated that the guy had backed off when he needed him to.

"If you want a ride home," Peña said, "I'm leaving now."

Tito exhaled, disappointed. But he didn't argue. He would not argue. He smiled at Ángel. "Call me, okay?"

Ángel glanced from Tito to Peña to Tito again. "I don't wanna tell you what to do, but I can take you home if you want."

Tito considered it. "I'll be okay."

"Get home safe," Ángel said, a little too loudly.

In the car, Tito and Peña barely spoke. Tito was relieved that Ángel had smiled as he left. Tito was sure he'd call. He replayed the whole night in his head—the conversation, the dancing, all the kissing.

"So you just go around with whatever Fulano shows interest?"

Tito shrugged. He could see clearly now—Peña had never planned on leaving Maritza. He was perfectly happy in his marriage, pretending to be someone he wasn't, running around on her. He had always been happy in his marriage, and he had always protected Tito only because it meant Tito would be grateful.

"I'm not married," Tito said. "I can do what I want."

Peña slammed the steering wheel with both hands but said nothing. He pulled into el Caserío, driving slowly past the buildings, watching to see if anybody was out on the street. Tito watched through the open passenger window, letting the wind blow over his face and hair, feeling inside his jeans pocket for his keys. Peña parked a block away from their building.

"Mr. Peña," Tito said, "I appreciate everything you've done for me."

Peña smiled. "You're not mad at me, then."

"I don't think we should see each other outside of school anymore."

"What do you mean?"

"We're not friends. You're my teacher. And my coach."

"We *are* friends!" Peña's eyes were pleading, begging. "You're eighteen. You're an adult."

"This has nothing to do with *that*."

"There's nothing wrong with—"

"You're not listening!" Tito said, raising his voice. "I'm saying I don't want to see you anymore. I'm done."

"You're not done."

"You have a wife and a baby. You made it clear: That will never change. And that's okay. I'm good with that. But I don't want to see you anymore."

"You can't—"

"Go home. I'll see you at school." Tito opened the car door, but Peña reached for him, grabbed his wrist.

"You can't do this to me. I love you." Peña had tears in his eyes.

Tito pulled his wrist loose. "Please leave me alone."

Peña grabbed his T-shirt, pulled Tito back in the car. Tito fell into the seat. He sat very still, silent, waiting. He held his hand up calmly and just breathed. His heart was racing. Peña's hand was still gripping the side of his shirt.

"I'm sorry," Peña said. "I'm so sorry."

Peña let go of his shirt, and Tito jumped out of the car and threw the door closed. It slammed shut. Tito leaned down so Peña could see his face through the open window.

"I never want to see you again. Get that through your fucking head." Tito walked home, picking up the pace as he crossed the street.

"Tú Me Quemas"

THAT MAY MORNING, before dawn broke, Nena heard a chorus of coquíes across the cane fields behind el Caserío, calling for each other in the dark. Soon they disappeared with all other signs of life, the sound of night fading with the sunrise, the fires spreading over the caña. It was the burning season in Humacao, when cane fields were set on fire ahead of harvest and the air turned black with smoke, ash falling from the sky like black snow, over the playground and the basketball courts, over their chairs on the balcony, over the bedsheets that Nena and her mom had hung out to dry.

Since the American sugar mill in Humacao bordered el Caserío Padre Rivera, the black ash would rain down on el Caserío, and they just had to live with it every spring. Just as they had lived with it a few years before, when there was an explosion two towns over, in one of the pharmaceuticals factories in Ceiba. There was talk of toxic gas leaks. Those fires had burned for hours, smoke billowing over from across the main highway. There had been no cleanup, no explanation, and then, her mother said, only when people in Las Parcelas started dying, then the factory just closed, boarded up its windows and doors, padlocked the chain-link fence. Nena could still make out a strange sweet musky smell in the air when they drove by Las

Parcelas. *Some kind of chemical or gas leak*, people said. *That's the smell of the dead*, her mother said.

The sugarcane fires were the last controlled burns of the season. Every year, weeks before school let out, the fire ran down the fields of cane, unfurling across the green and gold, lighting up the night sky. Sometimes she and Génesis would sit on the balcony, watching. It would be hours before all the leaves withered and fell away, only the charred stalks left for the cane cutters and their machetes. Hours before the men arrived, in their boots and protective headgear, pushing aside the burnt stalks, a single machete strike taking down several of them at once. Hours before the sweet campfire scent of burnt sugar turned into something else. Hours before the men followed the stench down the fields, the ground still smoldering, the heat still rising under their boots.

NENA WALKED INTO the kitchen and Mami was already in front of the stove, pouring herself a mug of café from la greca.

"Good morning, mi amor," her mother said, and Nena nodded, still groggy.

Mami was dressed in her gray coveralls with the blue OSBORNE PHARMA logo over the right breast, her ID card clipped to the pocket. Her brown hair was pinned up in a tight French twist, her bangs swept sideways, her lips painted red, brown eyes lined in black pencil, cheeks dusted with blush. Nena didn't look much like Mami. She was brown, just like her father, her mother always said. But Nena didn't remember him. According to Mami, Papi had the same brown skin; the same coily curls, which he sometimes picked out and fluffed into an afro; and small almond-shaped eyes like hers. He was a free spirit, a salsero, tall and slim.

You have your father's eyes, people sometimes told Nena, *your father's smile, your father's temper, your father's long, slim neck. Do you sing like your father? Do you play? Your father was so handsome.*

Nena had always suspected that when people said she looked like her father, what they meant was that she was Black, that she would never look like her white mother. All her life, she'd wanted people to notice all the ways she *was* like her mother: How she was smart and hardworking. How she loved science, loved her family. One day, she would show them all. She would be a pharmacist, do what her mother hadn't been able to do. Mami would be proud of her, and everyone would know her as the successful hardworking daughter, not as a carbon copy of her dead father.

"Tito stayed out all night, so you'll be by yourself for a little while until he gets home." Mami blew into her coffee mug.

Tito didn't usually stay out all night. He didn't spend nights at boyfriends' houses, didn't go out to clubs, and didn't get into cars with men he'd just met. Nena knew he went on dates, but he'd always meet them somewhere out in town. He'd ask Mami for a ride to la panadería or the beach or wherever else he felt like going that day. He'd walk to the basketball courts if he was gonna ball, or to one of the galleras out in town, where he'd bet on cockfights and sometimes make a little money, meet men. But the men there were usually rough, Tito told Nena. They weren't interested in being out in public, and they weren't trying to fall in love. So he was careful. He always came home.

Mami never asked questions, because (1) she couldn't be bothered, (2) Tito was her brother-in-law, not her son, as he never wasted a chance to remind her, and (3) like most of the other women in el Caserío, Mami believed that men could do what they wanted and she was just letting Tito learn something about manhood. Secretly, Nena wondered if the reason Mami never asked anything was because she was afraid of the truth.

"Will you be okay by yourself for a little while?" Mami sipped her café and walked around the kitchen, gathering things to put in her bag: a *TVyNovelas* magazine on the table, all the food she'd prepared to take with her to her two jobs.

"I'll be fine." Nena opened the refrigerator and pulled out the gallon of milk.

Mami stood there a moment, watching her. She was so overprotective. If she only knew all the stuff Tito shared about men, what they wanted, about all the ways you could hide when people didn't really want to know the real you. Nena figured she knew much more about the world than Mami had at her age, but somehow, Mami could only ever see her as a little girl.

"Go!" Nena said. "I'll be fine!"

"You know how to reach me." Mami packed up her thermos, a sandwich she'd wrapped in foil, a banana, an old butter tub she'd been reusing since the beginning of time, filled with arroz, habichuelas, and leftover bits of chuleta. She took one last look at Nena.

"I'm *fifteen*!" Nena smiled, trying to reassure her. She didn't want Mami to be late for work or to call in sick because she was afraid of leaving Nena in the apartment alone. Nena could take care of herself.

Mami gulped down the rest of her café. "Okay, but I don't want you hanging in the street or running around with those bandoleros from the block."

"I have plenty of housework to keep me busy," Nena joked. Mami liked everything in its place. When she was off from work, she woke up early on weekend mornings to clean the entire apartment, a record on the turntable, salsa blaring from the speakers in the living room.

"If you feel like doing chores, start by cleaning your room." Mami laughed. "Te quiero, mamita. See you tonight." She left her lipstick-stained cup on the counter and grabbed her purse on the way out the door.

"I love you too," Nena called after her. She picked up the leftover café, swallowed the last sip, and then poured some milk into the same cup. She closed the front door behind her mother. She sipped the milk, watched out the living room window as Mami hustled to the car, her lunch bag and purse slung over one shoulder, her white pharmacy smock draped over her other arm.

Nena scanned the street, the sidewalks, what she could see of the neighborhood, for any sign of Tito. She imagined him coming up the block, waiting for Mami's car to pass the front gate and out of el Caserío so he could finally walk home. Maybe he was trying to avoid the questions, in case Mami asked where he'd spent the night. But Nena knew that would never happen—her mother wouldn't really want to know what Tito had been up to, who he'd been with. Maybe he'd gone to someone's house and he was still asleep. That didn't really sound like him, though. He would've come home, showered, then slept until the smell of huevos fritos, jamonilla, and amarillos pulled him out of bed. But it was Saturday morning, and Tito was eighteen. He could do what he wanted.

Nena ate a bowl of corn flakes while standing at the kitchen sink, not really awake enough to think, but hungry. She was going back to bed.

Her chancletas slapped the linoleum floor, echoing through the apartment. She stopped in the hallway in front of Tito's bedroom. On his door, an old life-sized poster of Michael Jackson in his red *Thriller* jacket, sleeves scrunched up to his elbows. The door was cracked. Mami must've left it like that—she hated closed doors. She liked to leave all the doors open and the windows cracked to let the air in. But what was the point, Tito said, if it was always hotter than un tubo y siete llaves in this place. Tito liked his bedroom door shut, and they were supposed to knock and wait for him to come to the door and let them in. If he wasn't home, his bedroom was off-limits, period.

Nena pulled his door shut, stared at Michael. Even all these years later, Nena and Tito still loved everything about *Thriller*. For Tito, it was Michael. His dancing, his swagger. For Nena, it was the zombies, the monster story, the possibility that there could be something terrifying lurking in the shadows. They'd watched the video like a thousand times when it first came out. And even now, teenagers, they still whooped and howled when it came on, ran toward the TV to turn up the volume, then danced like the undead in the middle of the living room.

Nena reached for the doorknob again. Tito would be mad, but she didn't care. He was the one who had explaining to do. His windows were cracked, the ceiling fan turning slowly, blowing air over his dark room. She kicked off her chancletas, climbed onto his bed. Outside, the birds were chirping. The coquíes had already stopped singing. The smell of charred leaves and cane slithered through the cracked windows. She pulled her tangled mass of curls over one shoulder, lay down sideways on top of Tito's blanket. She made herself into a ball, tucked her knees into her big T-shirt. Somewhere far off in the distance, a rooster screamed.

MARICARMEN WALKED TO her car, balancing her bags and purse slung over one shoulder, carrying her pharmacy smock on a clothes hanger, a thermos filled with café con leche in the other hand. Like every Saturday, Maricarmen had an early shift at the factory, then her night shift at the pharmacy, where she counted pills and bottled cough syrup until eight. The sun was on her face, but as she got closer to her car, she noticed a woman across the street, watching her. Maricarmen stopped in her tracks, almost stepped on a pile of dog shit. The woman had long black hair. She was pale and skinny, bags under her eyes, her mouth a bruise. And a jagged scar on her cheek.

Maricarmen crossed herself, and the woman just turned and walked off, headed up the street toward the front gate. Maricarmen had seen her before. Like so many others, she dropped by el Caserío to buy dope every couple of days. El Caserío was hot—it was where all the tecatos came to score their perico.

It took Maricarmen a minute, but she finally stepped toward the car. She slipped the key in the lock, got the door open, and flung her things into it. When she got in, she exhaled, and only then did she realize that she'd been holding her breath. She sat for a second, just a second, checked her reflection in the rearview, her hands shaking. She made sure her hair was okay and her gray coveralls' collar was neat, and then she crossed herself again and drove off.

At Osborne Pharma, once she'd showed her ID at the entrance, she clocked in and rushed past the double doors to the break room. She dropped her things in her locker, zipped up her coveralls, and headed to her line. On the factory floor, the rumble of machinery and fans all around her, she calmed down. The other women, all in blue or gray or green coveralls depending on their position, worked without looking up.

She found her place between conveyor belts and got started, inserting blister packs of birth control pills into their corresponding plastic dial packs, then clicking them shut and placing the disks inside small boxes. Ten dial packs to a box. Ten boxes to a plastic repack, which would get sealed, loaded onto trucks, and driven to pharmacies across Puerto Rico. The repacks would be emptied, sent back to the factory, and Maricarmen would fill them all again. She put the repack on the conveyor belt to be inspected.

She worked fast, picking up another blister pack, sliding it into the dial pack, clicking it shut, and shoving it into the box. She slid another pack on top, then another, like a filing system. One box and another and another and another, every damn day. At her second job at the pharmacy, she'd count pills by five or label the prepackaged birth control pills for their patients, leave them on the counter for the pharmacist to inspect and bag. She wiped the sweat from her forehead, set another repack on the conveyor belt, and sent it up.

As she worked, she lost track of time, let her thoughts drift to Rey, and Cano, and Ismael. She thought of her sister, Loli, how they'd been inseparable. Those days before Nena was born. With those friends she'd had her first cigarette, her first taste of marijuana, her first everything. How Mari and Loli were teenagers when Rey let them try scutter for the first time. How after that, they all went off together when they got off their shift at El Paseo. She remembered how Cano had parked his van on a hill in Carraízo once, overlooking the lake. They all got out, la Sonora Ponceña's "Omelé" blaring from the van's radio. They snorted perico out of a baggie using Cano's car key, shared a bottle of pitorro, and danced under the moonlit sky, el lago Carraízo dark and endless below. They were young and in love and invincible, all of them so damn happy. They would live forever, Loli y Mari, Rey and Cano and Ismael. How Don Ojeda had been like a father to her, how he'd supported her when Rey ran away, and once he was gone.

Maricarmen loaded up another repack, set it down on the conveyor, wiped her forehead with the back of her hand. Evelyn was standing at the end of the line, a clipboard in her hand. Maricarmen waved and kept working.

When she'd gotten the news last year, a Sunday morning before church, what she felt more than anything was regret. She'd planned on going to see Don Ojeda with the kids after church, but then it was too late: She got the call from the hospital as they were heading out the door. As she hung up the phone, she didn't cry. She pretended it was someone else, a wrong number, a neighbor calling. She would think about this later. In the car, as they drove into town, as Nena and Tito chatted about school, Maricarmen kept her eyes on the road, barely blinking.

She'd walked into la Catedral de Humacao with Tito and Nena just ten minutes after the phone call. And as they made their way toward the holy water font, Carmelo had pulled her aside, gave her a kiss on the cheek. She whispered it into his ear, and he crossed himself.

She tried not to cry in front of Tito and Nena. She needed to keep it together until they were home again. They were the only family Don Ojeda had, so it would be up to Maricarmen to arrange the service; Carmelo had taken over his father's funeral home, so she'd have to talk to him about it. But she couldn't do this, not yet. She needed a moment, a day, some time.

That morning, Maricarmen, Nena, and Tito had sat in the pews, the three of them listening as el padre Francisco held up the chalice with both hands, *the blood of Christ*. Tears slid down her face. She wiped them with the back of her hand, careful not to let Nena and Tito see her cry.

She took Tito's hand, put her arm around Nena's shoulder.

Blood of my blood. Sangre de mi sangre.

For so long, the only family she knew had been Rey and Don Ojeda. After Don Ojeda, it was just the three of them, Nena and Tito and Mari.

ON THE FACTORY floor now, Maricarmen pressed the red button to stop her conveyor. It wasn't break time yet, but she needed some air, some coffee, some silence, *something*. She waved at Evelyn to let her know she was headed to the toilets, and Evelyn held up her wrist, pointing at her watch.

"What do you want me to do, hold it?" Maricarmen called out to Evelyn across the crowded floor, but she knew Evelyn wouldn't hear her. You couldn't hear a thing over the conveyors unless you were close enough.

Maricarmen took off her goggles and pushed the double doors.

THAT MORNING AFTER church, the news of Don Ojeda's death still fresh on her mind, she'd driven home with the kids, her mind racing, her stomach in knots. As they walked through the door, she told them to grab their swimsuits, their chancletas and towels.

"Are we going to the beach?" Nena had asked.

"You have five minutes."

Tito threw on his swim trunks and grabbed his things before she could change her mind. But Nena was more difficult, always asking questions. Did she need suntan lotion? Sunblock? Would they get lunch while they were out or would she have to wait until they got home?

Mari had slipped on a pair of shades and packed a small bag. She pulled on her suit silently, ignoring Nena's questions until Nena knew to stop asking them. They were out the door in less than five minutes.

At la playa de Humacao, Mari had dropped her things on the sand and headed toward the water. Don Ojeda was dead and she wondered what she looked like to the kids. Don Ojeda was dead and there she was, Maricarmen floating in the ocean, face turned up to the sun. Don Ojeda was dead, and Nena and Tito walked barefoot on the water's edge, their toes sinking into the wet sand.

Nena walked along the shore, kicking up clouds of sand and sea, her wet swimsuit dripping salt water down her legs. She was fourteen years old, and Tito seventeen, but they still played like children.

Rey el Cantante, everyone had called him, once upon a time. Don Ojeda was the first to call him that, and then all the women made it his nickname. Treading water in the sea, Maricarmen thought about how she had called him that, too, only for a little while. *Before.*

Nena floated next to her.

Maricarmen didn't say a word, closed her eyes and pinched her nose as a wave fell over them.

That day on the shore, after Maricarmen got out of the water, Nena called after a sato that had come out of nowhere, abandoned on the beach, its soft brown fur dirty with grit and motor oil.

"It's probably been sleeping under cars or something," Tito had said. They'd reached out their hands, pretended to be offering food, snapped their fingers, blew kisses. The sato hopped around, wagging his whole butt.

"We should name him," Nena said, "train him to come when we call."

"We're not taking him home," Maricarmen snapped.

Tito got on his knees, clapped his hands. He was the kind of skinny that you noticed no matter what—long limbs, small shoulders, all cheekbones. His curls windblown. His nails were neatly cut, his hands soft. Later that year, he would take up basketball, and then overnight he'd start biting his nails, develop calluses on the palms of his hands, grow muscles. He would eat more than Nena and Maricarmen put together. He'd start going out every afternoon, to the basketball courts mostly, and every time she saw him walk through the door all sweaty, Maricarmen would say, *¡Mano, estás al garete!*

The sato had run from the rush of salt water, then back toward Tito, who was holding his arms out. The dog jumped into them.

"Mami! Please?" Nena said. She'd wanted to take the dog home, take care of it. She wanted so much to save him.

A few yards up the beach, where the sand dunes met rock, a pack of satos played.

NENA WOKE UP in Tito's bed a few hours later, the back of her neck sweaty, her armpits sticky. She got out of bed, pulling Tito's door shut behind her. In the kitchen, she listened to the birds singing outside, the neighbor's yard birds, roosters crowing, all of el Caserío's sounds right there in their apartment. The sunshine filtered in through the blinds. No Tito. Mami was gonna be pissed. But if *he* could do what he wanted, so could she.

She put on her jeans and a purple off-the-shoulder top Mami said looked good on her. She sprayed herself with Mami's perfume, a small round bottle with an embossed swan. She slipped on her pink jellies and walked back to the mirror, but she needed *something*, she wasn't sure what. She rummaged through her mother's makeup and found a shade of pink lipstick she liked. It would look good against her brown skin. She'd spent days trying on her mother's makeup, pretending to be a woman, like Mami, but she'd never worn it outside the house. She applied it slowly, making sure to trace the natural outline of her lips perfectly. Then, as she'd seen Mami do a hundred times, she blew herself a kiss and smiled.

She walked out of the apartment like it was any old day, pulled the door shut, and strutted up the street toward Génesis's building, expecting to run into Tito on his way home. She didn't know what she'd say to Génesis—she'd walk by her building, just in case Génesis happened to be outside. There were almost no cars on the block, since most everyone with cars in el Caserío worked the first shift at the pharmaceuticals factory, like Mami. It was Saturday, and most of the kids were outside on their skateboards or roller skates or bikes.

Maritza pushed her baby stroller up the street toward Nena. She wore a skintight tube top and shorts, her hair pinned up in a perfect dubi.

She grinned. "Nice lipstick, Nena!"

"¡Gracias!" Nena shot her back a smile.

When she reached Génesis's building, she couldn't tell if anybody was home. Génesis's dad's car was not out front, and there were no toys out in the front yard, no skateboard forgotten on the front steps, no bikes anywhere.

Nena pretended she was going somewhere else until she reached the end of the block, then looked both ways, the sun on her back, the heat creeping all the way up from her jellies to her scalp. Suddenly, up the hill, she saw them, all of them on their bikes: Génesis and her four brothers rolling down toward her. She checked her shoes, her jeans, her shirt, and felt ridiculous, like a kid stomping around in her mother's high heels.

"What's up, Nena?" Génesis called out. Génesis wore her favorite denim shorts and a red tank top, her long braids in a high pony. Her skin was a deep brown, her legs long and lean. Génesis was taller than Nena, taller than most of the boys their age, and everybody had something to say about her long legs, her broad shoulders, too boyish and muscular for a girl. Nobody ever kept their opinions to themselves when it came to Black girls. They loved pointing out how *these* girls, Nena and Génesis, were the opposite of what girls were expected to be. Always running around, climbing trees, too loud, too fast, too strong. It was only recently that Nena had decided to dress more like a girl, to make more of an effort with her hair, to try her mother's lipsticks.

Génesis's brothers whooshed past Nena on their bikes, one after the other, turned at the end of the block, and circled back. Génesis slowed down, then rolled her bike to a stop right in front of Nena.

"Whatcha doing?" Génesis asked, a little out of breath.

Nena's body clenched, the way it only did around Génesis. I came to see *you*, she wanted to say, but didn't, because how could she say that without sounding weird?

"Just going for a walk. Looking for Tito. He didn't come home last night. You seen him around?"

Génesis twisted up her face like she was thinking. "I don't think so."

Up the street, Jamil, the oldest brother, broke off from the group and rode toward the girls. He slowed down, then circled them. He looked Nena up and down, like he was trying to figure her out, then stopped.

"Who's your friend?" Jamil asked his sister.

"You know Nena," Génesis said. "No seas pendejo."

Nena could feel little drops of sweat trickling down her back.

Jamil's eyes widened. "Nena? Shit, you're all grown up! When did *that* happen?"

Génesis scowled. "Last month."

Jamil laughed. "You look good, girl."

"Don't be nasty," Génesis said. "Nena's looking for her uncle Tito. He's missing."

Nena flinched at the word *missing*. It didn't sound real, like it was an exaggeration.

"He went out last night and hasn't come home yet," Nena said.

"You seen him?" Génesis asked her brother.

Jamil didn't say a word, just eyed Nena. Slowly, his smile faded. He adjusted his grip on his bike's handlebars.

"You know Tito, don't you?" Nena asked, even though she knew he did. They all went to the same school together. She remembered that tense moment at her party as they stood in line at the buffet, how they stared at each other.

"Was he at la gallera last night?" Génesis asked.

"How the hell should I know?" Jamil said, a little too loud, like he was inviting the whole block into their conversation. "I don't hang out with faggots." He was talking to Génesis, but he wasn't looking at her.

"Jamil!" Génesis yelled. "What the fuck!"

Nena stepped back, and the side of her sandal scraped the edge of the sidewalk where it met the grass. She stumbled, almost fell, but caught her balance.

Jamil watched Nena, waiting for her to say something.

"Are you okay?" Génesis asked.

Nena was dripping sweat now, her armpits like puddles, large drops running down her temples and chest, hair sticking to her neck. She wiped her face with her forearm, but it did no good. She was so hot she thought she'd faint. She looked up at Jamil again, embarrassed. He was smiling.

Génesis also watched her, but there was something else on her face. She was embarrassed for Nena. Embarrassed about Jamil? Or worried about Tito, maybe?

"You look like you need some shade," Génesis said. "I'll take you home."

Nena turned, heading back toward her street.

Génesis hopped off her bike and walked it alongside Nena, then stopped, turned back toward Jamil. "¡Cabrón!"

Jamil gave her the finger.

She caught up with Nena and they walked silently for a while. But then Génesis, who hated when anyone was mad at her and always had to make things right, stopped again.

"I'm sorry about my brother," she said, squeezing her bike's handlebars tight.

"I know." Nena kept walking, the sun scorching her forehead. But *did* she know? Something was different now. No one had ever called Tito a faggot in front of her before. No one had ever said it out loud like that, not to her. It felt like Jamil was saying something about *her*, like he was calling Nena a faggot too.

GÉNESIS SET HER bike down on the lawn and followed Nena inside. They grabbed a couple of Pepsis from the fridge, went out to the back balcony. The patio chairs were hot to the touch, but they sat on them anyway, burning the backs of their legs on the plastic. They didn't talk about what Jamil said, even though it sat like a boulder between them, taking up so much space. Nena thought now of all the things she should've said to him, all the things she'd been too scared to admit. *Yes, my uncle is gay,* she imagined herself shouting, *but* you're *a fucking asshole!* Tito was a lot of other things: He was good at basketball, and he was the one person who really knew her. Nena took long swigs from her Pepsi, checking out the passion fruit vines along the chain-link fence that separated el Caserío from los cañaverales. Far off near the edge of the fields, at least half the cane had been burned, but at that distance, Nena couldn't tell if the caña was still smoldering from the night before.

Génesis held her Pepsi to her cheek, her neck. Nena watched the beads of sweat roll down Génesis's face. She imagined herself loosening Génesis's ponytail, the braids falling down her back. She wanted to press her lips against Génesis's the way she never had with a boy, the way she only ever had with Génesis. She had thought about it so many times, played the whole thing out in her head again and again. In Nena's fantasies, the next time Nena kissed her, Génesis always kissed her back.

They sat, pressing their bodies into the hot plastic, watching the back of el Caserío. All the clotheslines out back were bowed with the day's laundry, the overgrown passion fruit vines covering the fence, then the field of charred naked stalks of cane. The blackened shoots like spears, and beyond that field, the next one, and the next one, the rows of caña went on forever, a sea of black and brown and gold that stretched toward La Central Patagonia, where exhaust rose from the many stacks. La Central had a few buildings: Azúcar Patagonia, the sugar mill and packaging plant, and the Destilería Patagonia, where they made rum and spirits.

Even at fifteen, Nena already felt a certain way about La Central. She'd heard so many stories about how they didn't hire anybody from el Caserío except to break their backs cutting cane. Mami had tried to get a job there, as a receptionist, as a secretary, on the factory floor, anything, so she could be closer to home, make more money, finally quit her second job and get some rest, but nothing. And almost everyone they knew from the neighborhood always had the same story: The second they find out you're from el Caserío, those gringos want nothing to do with you.

They'd spent so many afternoons out there, Génesis and Nena, looking at the cane, at the stacks, sitting together on a picnic blanket, flipping through one of Mami's *Vanidades* magazines, Génesis laughing at all the silly things Nena's white mother was into. Nena thought *Vanidades* was ridiculous, too, and she wasn't sure what other girls her age were into—she wasn't into anything her classmates were into. And her only friend, other than Tito, was Génesis.

Now it was almost summer, the beginning of the never-ending heat, of rainy afternoons running through puddles, the moriviví overgrown and bushy. When they were kids, nine, ten, eleven, Nena and Génesis had spent whole summers together, all sweat and sugar, asking their parents for change, running down to Doña Evelyn's house to buy limbels de coco, the ice melting in the afternoon heat, juice running down their forearms. They would be twins in matching blue swimsuits, running and diving chest-first onto the yellow Banana Split Slip 'n' Slide, laughing laughing laughing as they slid. They would chase each other on their bikes, run through the sprinklers in the early morning, splash each other in the street when somebody's tío busted open a fire hydrant. They'd always been this close. All summer, Nena y Génesis, Génesis y Nena.

But something was different that afternoon. Maybe they had a sense that something was coming. Maybe they already knew. In the distance, in between the stalks, a man emerged slowly. Dark trousers, a blue polo shirt, huge goggles, not the kind of outfit you put on to go out into the cane, definitely not the visors, helmets, and coveralls the workers wore. He was odd, dressed like that. He would stain his nice clothes for sure. He stopped, dusting himself off, bending over to pick up something off the ground, and then stood up, turned in the girls' direction. He wasn't one of the cane cutters, and he wasn't one of the other workers, Nena could tell. The workers were usually out there by early morning.

He was a cop, Nena realized. He had a gold badge attached to his belt, and on the other side, his holstered pistol. He checked out each of the buildings, shielding his eyes from the sun with his forearm.

"What's he looking at?" Génesis said. She turned toward the building next door, extending her neck.

They'd learned to be afraid of los camarones. Everybody knew the stories about their raids, knew to run home and lock their doors when they saw them pull up and step out of their unmarked cars. When los camarones came into the neighborhood, they left chaos in their wake: A summer block party turned into an invasion, cops storming in and out of a building with four teenagers in handcuffs, a toddler and his mother shot dead on the street. Later, they'd find out that they had the wrong guys, that one of the teenagers had been thrown into the back seat of the cop car so hard they broke his neck, that the baby's mother had been mistaken for a kidnapper from some other barrio. And then there was her own father.

Two more men came out of the cañaverales, and then a woman, all of them with weapons holstered, badges attached to their belts. They stopped at the edge of the sugarcane, at the vine-covered fence, took off their goggles and talked for a while. And then they all turned to look up at Nena's building.

"I think they're all looking at *us*," Nena said, not sure if they should just go inside, lock the back door.

Far off in the caña, Nena saw more movement, some smoke. She could make out more people, blue ball caps.

Génesis shaded her face with her hand and stared. "What's going on?"

Nena followed Génesis's gaze, narrowed her eyes, trying to see. She stood, brushing the curls from her face. Deep in the cañaverales, past a downward slope, she could see them clearly now: more men, cops all around, and they were all heading toward the fence.

"What the fuck," Nena said.

At the fence, the cops gathered, inspecting the metal, touching the top of the chain link with their gloved hands. The woman, flanked by two male cops, was watching Nena and Génesis. Beside her, the other cops pulled on the chain link, and one of them held up a pair of small wire cutters.

"Go home," Nena said.

"What?" Génesis stood up, trying to see what Nena saw.

They were cutting the fence, Nena realized, the cops pulling it toward them as one of them cut all the way up, then across the top. Once the space was wide enough, the woman slid through the hole and walked on.

"You need to go home right now," Nena insisted. But Génesis didn't move.

The other two cops followed the woman through the opening in the fence. They headed toward Nena and Génesis.

Nena grabbed her by the arm, but Génesis was frozen in place.

"Something happened," Génesis said. "Something's wrong."

Nena pulled her. "We need to move."

"There's something in the cane," Génesis said.

As the cops came closer, the woman pulled her badge from her belt, held it up. "Nenuska Ojeda?" she called out.

Nena froze.

They approached the balcony, the two men a couple of steps behind the woman. "We've spoken to your mom," she said. "She's on her way home."

"What?" Nena couldn't understand how this woman knew her name, why they'd spoken to her mom, and why her mom was on her way home. "Why?"

The woman put her badge away. "I'm Detective Colón. Your mom is being escorted home by one of my colleagues."

Génesis grabbed Nena's hand, pulled her closer. "Oh my God, Nena."

"Tell me what's going on," Nena said. Beside her, she could feel Génesis's body shaking. Was she crying? Nena couldn't understand.

"Can we go inside and talk?" Detective Colón asked.

"What? No!"

"Let's go inside," Detective Colón said. "Please."

"Oh my God, Nena. It's Tito." Génesis squeezed her hand, hard, and for a moment, Nena didn't want to hear this. She didn't want to know.

"We're not going anywhere with you," Nena said.

One of the other cops stepped forward. "When was the last time you saw your uncle?"

"Why?" Nena asked. *What happened to Tito?* she wanted to ask, but she couldn't form the words. She didn't have it in her.

Years later, she wouldn't be sure what made her do it. Had she lost her mind when she jumped over the balcony's railing? When she took one step forward, two, three?

"Where are you going?" Génesis said.

"You can't go over there!" Detective Colón yelled after her.

Or when Nena searched the cane, trying to figure out what Génesis had seen? Was it Tito? Or when she broke into a run, the cops following her as she tried to climb the chain-link fence like she'd done a hundred times before, as she fell and got back up, considered the opening the cops had cut but climbed it again, tearing a small hole into the side of her shorts as she jumped to the other side, slipping on the passion fruit vines. The shuffle of cops behind her, the sting of cane on her skin, Génesis's voice calling her back. Or when they caught her, grabbed her shoulders, their fingers gripping her hard. Or when she tried to shrug them off, pulled and pulled her arms, tearing her shirt. How she shouted at them, "Let me go, let me fucking go!" How she would feel their hands on her skin, their fingertips digging into her wrists, her shoulders, feel the cuts on her bloody feet before she saw them, and only then realize she'd lost her sandals somewhere in the burnt cane. And the acrid chemical smell, rotten eggs and decaying fried meat, piss and shit, stinging her eyes and nose, everything still smoldering around them, the muffled sound of her own voice caught in her throat, "Let me go," as she dropped slowly to her knees and started vomiting.

The cops held her shoulders, her arms. Somehow, she was on her feet again, and they were dragging her back toward el Caserío. Nena pulled and jerked sideways, out of their grip, and then she took off running again.

The cops scrambled, calling out to each other. "Grab her! Don't let her go!" And then she had more cops on her, three or four, she couldn't tell.

She stumbled as they snatched her by the waist, her body tightening, uniforms and plainclothes, all of them yelling at once, holding on to her wrists, shoulders, arms, and no matter how much she struggled, this time she couldn't get free.

"Let me go." On the ground, surrounded by charred, downed sugarcane stalks, small yellow flags staked into the dirt, marking a boundary. "What is that?" she yelled, then raised her voice, repeating the question again and again. "What is that, what is that—*What is that!*"

"Jesus Christ," one of them said. "She's just a kid."

"Let me go!" She kicked at one of them. She stared across the perimeter, past the border marked by the stakes in the dirt. There, in the center, the source of the smell. She couldn't explain what she was looking at. A long strip of garbage strewn on the ground? A clump of burnt blankets?

And then she was facedown on the blackened earth, the heat rising, and she thought of flames, an inferno, hell itself. All those sermons she'd had to sit through at church with her mom, with Tito. All those things she'd heard about heaven and hell.

She turned her face toward it. She screamed, "What. Is. *That?!*"

A few yards away, Génesis stood on the other side of the chain-link fence, hand over her mouth, the cop next to her—Detective Colón—patting her shoulder.

It was when Nena saw Génesis that she knew: Génesis watching as they pulled Nena's arms behind her back, as they lifted her body off the ground; Génesis lowering her eyes, her tall frame slumped forward. Nena stopped fighting then, stopped pulling her arms, and let them take her.

"Nadie Es Eterno"

THEY GAVE MARICARMEN an estimate. Not the exact time, but they knew it happened in the night. She had been asleep in her bed, dreaming, or not dreaming—she couldn't remember.

The policewoman sat in the living room with them while the others were out in the caña, taking pictures, scribbling notes in their pads, measuring the distance between footsteps, waiting on the medical examiner. One of them walked up and down the caña with a dog on a long leash. Tito was still out there.

Some of the others walked in and out of the apartment. There were two in Tito's room. The medical examiner would take another hour, they said. And, God, Maricarmen would spend that hour fighting the urge to run out there, to scream, to rip the hair from her head. How could this have happened? And Nena, Jesus Christ, Nena. She took her daughter's hand, pulled her close.

They were both sitting on the couch in front of the policewoman, who was asking question after question, taking notes.

Detective Colón, she'd said.

Maricarmen had only ever heard of one or two female police officers, and definitely not a detective. She wasn't sure how she felt about that, but she didn't trust this Detective Colón either.

Maricarmen asked her to tell her everything, every detail about how Tito died, and Detective Colón looked her in the eyes.

"Señora—"

"I need to know," Maricarmen said. She let go of Nena's hand, stood up suddenly, ready to take the detective outside so she could get the whole story.

Colón stood up too. "We'll know more when the medical examiner—"

"We've been waiting hours," Nena said, wiping tears from her face.

Maricarmen ran her hands through her hair.

"Is there someone we can call for you?" Detective Colón asked.

Maricarmen stopped, glanced at Nena, at the detective. How to say that, no, there was no one else. How to say that it was just her and her daughter now. That years ago, she'd had a mother and a sister, a young husband and a daughter, and Tito. That she'd get the occasional letter from her sister, a picture here and there, but that her family had abandoned her. How did one say a thing like that?

One of the other detectives came into the room, and she stopped breathing.

"Medical examiner just pulled up," he said to Colón.

Maricarmen recognized him immediately. He was older now, but she hadn't forgotten his face.

"What are you doing in my house?" she said to him. She raised her voice, said it again. "What *the hell* are you doing in my house?"

Detective Colón placed her hand lightly on Maricarmen's shoulder. "This is—"

"I know who you are," Maricarmen said to Altieri. She would never forget his face. Or his name. Or the sound of his police cruiser screeching to a stop on their street, her pulse quickening as he reached for his weapon and pointed it at Rey. How he drove away from el Caserío with his men, with her husband in the back seat of his car. How the first night she and Rey talked, she had held him, pressed her hand to his bloody face after Altieri broke it open with his gun.

Maricarmen turned to her daughter, reached for her. She sat on the couch again, held Nena in her arms.

Nena just slumped on the couch, her mother's arms around her, her eyes so far away.

Altieri and Colón watched them a moment, then Altieri slipped outside without a word.

Detective Colón sat down again. "María, we can call someone to be with you. Family? A friend?"

She could have them call Evelyn and Carmelo, but that felt like too much. Maricarmen shook her head. Nobody called her María anymore, not since she was a child in school. And in this woman's voice, with that man just outside her door—it all felt like a threat.

The policewoman nodded. "I'll be here with you."

Maricarmen didn't want this motherfucker in her house, near her daughter. She wanted them all gone. She looked Colón in the eye. She wanted to thank her for being there, but she couldn't trust her. Maricarmen couldn't think, and there was a bomb in her chest, ready to explode. They had come into her home with their questions. They had stood in her living room, turned over Tito's mattress, opened drawers, put their hands all over his things, all over her things and Nena's things, and now the same man who beat her husband in front of the whole neighborhood, the same man who killed him, would be the one investigating Tito's murder.

Next to her, Nena was shaking. She could call Evelyn. She could call Carmelo. She could give this woman their phone numbers.

"Get out of my house," Maricarmen said. "All of you. Get out."

"Incomprendido"

A FEW NIGHTS after they found him, bees made a hive of Nena's body. In her mouth, her ears, inside her chest cavity. She felt them expanding as she lay in bed, thousands of wings brushing softly against her organs. The swell of a dark cloud pulsing until her body opened up, tearing from the inside, a seam, and a single honey-covered bee flew out. It circled her head, inspected her neck, her cheek, and then dug its stinger into her right eye. She woke up breathless, gasping.

After they found him, after she saw Tito in the caña, all those restless nights. Some nights, it was bees, but sometimes the dreams were all water. Nena out there looking for Tito, a stream appearing in between the rows of cane, cutting right through the middle, then the wide turn of water expanding into a river, carrying him off to some other place. Sometimes she'd dive in after him, but she was always too slow, too heavy, the bees buzzing inside her, all around her, gathering in her hair. Some nights none of it had happened yet, Nena and Tito were still young and alive and together, two kids on the shore, two teenagers sitting in front of the TV. Some nights he was there, standing over her bed, and Mami would come into the room, would embrace him, but slowly, in her mother's arms, he turned to ashes. Some nights, all those years later, everything came to her in those dreams: his broken body, her mother, Génesis, the burning season.

When they found him, he wasn't just battered. He was covered in piss and shit, parts of his flesh had been burned. This she read in the pages of *El Vocero*, every single detail out there for all to see.

AFTER, MAMI AND Nena could barely speak to each other, could barely say his name. They stood in the living room watching his closed bedroom door, the Michael Jackson poster.

After, her mother drove to the hospital morgue to identify Tito's body. She did not take Nena with her, and when she came home, she refused to talk about it, just sat with Nena on the couch, holding her without saying a word.

After, the news vans parked out in front of their building for days, WAPA-TV and *El Vocero* and the Channel 4 News crews, all of them waiting for Mami and Nena to leave the apartment, look out the window, step out on the balcony.

After, the phone rang and they just looked at each other, both of them too afraid to say the words out loud, to string the sentences together. It rang again and again, and when it finally stopped, Mami picked up the receiver, left the phone off the hook.

After, Nena stayed home from school, Mami stayed home from work for four days, all that her two jobs would allow. Mami shuffled around the house like a ghost, and in the kitchen, she piled cold leftovers into bowls, set them on the small dining table, poured them each a glass of milk.

You have to eat, she told Nena. You have to sleep. You have to get out of bed, shower, brush your teeth.

She filled glasses with milk, juice, water, set them down in front of Nena. She filled la greca with café. She cleared the table, washed the dishes, wiped and wiped and wiped counters.

For three days straight, Tito's picture was in the papers. Every day, the speculation, the rumors. What the neighbors said, what other people in some other barrio said, what strangers said. What had he been doing out there? Maybe he was dealing drugs, selling sex. No one knew for sure. Copies of *El Vocero* and *El País* and *El Nuevo Día* piled up. Mami and Nena looked for any mention of Tito, circled it, then left the papers on the kitchen table, the couch, the bathroom vanity.

Mami spent hours, days, nights on the sofa, in front of the TV. On the third day, she watched Walter Mercado deliver the horoscope on TV while she waited for the news, waited for signs, something that would tell her why, Dios mío, *how* could this happen. She watched him weekly, Walter on his golden throne wearing a green velvet cape, a ring on every finger, golden hair swept back, fates sealed with a wink, a delicate flick of the wrist. "Cáncer," Walter said, "there is no time for crying! It is time for love!" He shot the audience a smoldering look and started explaining the week's ritual for prosperity. "Dress in the colors of your zodiac sign. This is the year of magic in threes, so light three candles, or three pieces of camphor. But be careful—we are in a year of *fire*!"

When the news came on, they held their breath as pictures of Tito flashed across the screen. A school photo from ninth grade, taken more than four years before, his messy curls falling over his eyes, half smile revealing big crooked teeth that made him look like a little boy.

"Where did they get that picture?" Mami asked, turning to Nena.

Nena studied his face on the screen, but she had no idea. She'd never seen that picture before. That boy looked like Tito a million years ago, so innocent, so skinny. When she thought of Tito years later, she would always remember him as vulnerable as the boy in that picture, a kid who loved dogs and basketball and the ocean. She remembered that day at the beach, the two of them running around with a flea-bitten sato. How Mami had come out of the water and yelled at them to put it down. *"How do you know that dog doesn't have rabies? How do you know he hasn't given you some disease?"*

The screen changed, and then it was a slide show of Tito and a couple of girls in their school uniforms, standing outside in front of Ana Roqué, their arms crossed. Then Tito in a white T-shirt and a black leather jacket, looking at the camera under dark shades, his hair gelled and combed until his curls had been almost stretched into waves. He looked like a Black James Dean. Then what looked like faded Polaroid photos: Tito in his basketball jersey and shorts, a shot of his profile, in the middle of a game.

Mami was sobbing now. "Did you give them these pictures?"

"What?!"

"Don't lie to me."

"I've never even seen them before!" Nena got up, started pacing. She wanted to leave but didn't want to miss whatever they said.

Mami sat back, closed her eyes, wrapped her arms around herself.

On TV, the reporter Juan Santiago stood outside el Caserío by the chain-link fence, surrounded by cañaverales, yards away from the spot where they'd found Tito's body. He walked slowly, the camera following as he recounted all the details about how Tito was found: the Azúcar Patagonia factory workers had come to work in the morning just like they always did, the Central Patagonia crew was just getting off their night shift after supervising a controlled burn. Around lunchtime, some workers found his lifeless body between the burned rows.

They cut to interviews—random people talking about how they felt that someone had been murdered right outside their neighborhood. An older couple letting their dogs out, a shirtless man washing a car in front of his building. And then a woman pushing a baby stroller down their street. Nena recognized her immediately: It was their neighbor Maritza, Mr. Peña's wife, who had complimented Nena's lipstick a couple days before when she passed her on the street.

Maritza squinted in the sun, talked about how scary it was for her as a mother.

"What are these people doing here?" she said. "We have *children*."

"What?!" Nena said.

Maritza continued. "First, we had to worry about them coming here and spreading disease. Now they're killing each other. We don't want this around our children."

Mami stared at Maritza on the screen. "Hija de puta," she said under her breath.

"Spreading disease?" Nena slumped back down on the sofa, her heart pounding. Maritza and her husband, Mr. Peña, were their neighbors! Her husband was Tito's basketball coach, and Tito helped Maritza carry her groceries from the corner store. He helped her all the time! She hadn't been worried about any disease when she needed Tito to lug her fucking gallons of milk and boxes of diapers up the stairs to their second-floor apartment.

The camera cut back to Juan Santiago in the cañaverales, who explained that some people believed Tito was "a homosexual."

She tried not to look at Mami, but Nena could hear her sobbing softly.

Finally, they cut from Juan Santiago to a police spokesperson, Captain Altieri.

"We have been interviewing the victim's family, and everyone who knew him. Yes, we've received confirmation that he was a homosexual, but we don't know if this is connected to the crime. We're looking into what he was doing in the cane fields. We suspect that he was there meeting with other homosexual men."

Mami's hands shook, chest rising, falling. The last time Nena and Mami had sat like this, the two of them silent, was a few months before, when Mami had refused to sign a permission slip for a field trip to las Cavernas de Camuy. Her entire sophomore class was going, including Génesis, but Nena was grounded because she'd gotten a C on a math test. There would be no field trips, no sleepovers with Génesis, and no TV until she brought her grade back up. How Nena had cried and cried, like the whole world was ending, like her entire life was over. How she had told her mother she hated her, that she would never forgive her.

That was only months ago. How long ago that field trip seemed now, how ridiculous, all of it. Nena felt it in her body—that other life, that childhood, which was over now. It was someone else's. She had no idea who she was, but she was not that girl. Not anymore.

They went to a commercial break.

"Was Tito sick?" Nena asked. She walked over to the TV, turned it off. "Why do they talk about him like *he* did something wrong? Like *he's* the criminal? Why don't they talk about La Central, and how they start those fires? Who's making sure people don't get hurt out there? What if the fires spread?" Nena's mind was racing. She had so many questions.

Mami got up, reached for Nena, put her hands on her shoulders.

Nena looked into her face. Her mother had aged a decade in three days.

"Listen to me," Mami said. "These people, they don't know Tito, and they don't know our family. They don't care about us, and they don't care about him. Don't you listen to a goddamn word they say."

NENA LEFT HER empty glass in the sink, left the dirty dishes on the counter, and went down the hallway toward her room. She stopped when she reached Tito's bedroom, his door, Michael in his red jacket. She couldn't stand the sight of him, couldn't stand his bright smile or the way he stood there, like he knew everything. She peeled back the tape on one corner, then ripped the whole thing off. She tore it in half, then tore those pieces in half, tore it to shreds.

Mami called from the living room. "Nena?"

She ignored her, letting the bits of poster fall to the floor.

She'd spent days waiting for Génesis to show up, listening for the sound of knocking on the front door, footsteps in the hallway outside her room. She'd considered calling, but she didn't want to hear Jamil's voice, his breathing in her ear until Génesis picked up the phone in her room. So she didn't call—she waited.

She went for walks around el Caserío, stopping in front of Génesis's building just to see if anyone was home. She'd stand out front for a few seconds, then head toward the elementary school, find a spot out by the twisted trees at the edge of the swamp forest, and sit. Shaded by a red canopy of flamboyán, Nena thought that there was no one left who knew her hiding places, no one who would know to find her there. Sometimes she'd sit, her back against the trunk, knees against her chest, and she'd feel just how alone she was in the world. She had a grandmother somewhere and her titi Loli, her mother's family, but she had never met them, and Mami didn't really talk about them. She had a couple of pictures Titi Loli sent from Miami, but that was it. She didn't understand why, if they had people out there in the world that they belonged to, she and her mother were so completely alone. Why there had never been any birthday cards or Christmas cards or phone calls, why her mother worked and worked and never asked for help. Why no one had called after Tito died.

It had been out by the twisted trees, Nena listening to the birds, that she spotted Jamil one afternoon, a baseball cap shading his eyes from the sun. He rode his bike on the dirt road leading to the forest but stopped a few yards away when he caught a glimpse of Nena. Nena froze. He watched her, menacing, she thought, although she could barely make out his expression, because the ball cap was shading his face. For a moment, he balanced himself on the bike, then slowly turned and went back the same way he'd come. As his figure disappeared in the distance, Nena got up. She slapped the dirt off her shorts and started walking back home. She didn't go back out to the edge of the forest alone after that.

A few days later, while her mother was reheating leftovers in the kitchen, Nena shut herself in her bedroom, sat on her bed, and was absentmindedly turning the pages in Tito's copy of Manuel Puig's *Kiss of the Spider Woman* when she heard a soft knock on the door.

Génesis opened the door, then stood in the doorway as Nena wiped tears from her eyes. She shut the door behind her.

"Your mom says food's ready if you're hungry."

"Why didn't you call?" Nena closed the book and set it on the side table, then moved over, letting Génesis climb into bed next to her.

"I didn't want to bother you," Génesis said. "I didn't think you wanted me to."

Nena reached for the book again. "That's bullshit."

Génesis looked down at her hands.

"Was it Jamil?" Nena asked.

"My parents said I shouldn't give people reason to talk."

"What does that even mean?"

"They're just worried. I think they're afraid for me."

Nena wanted to ask so many questions—like what exactly Génesis's parents were afraid of—but she wasn't sure she was ready to hear the answers. Recently, she'd started to understand why her mother never asked Tito where he was going, who he spent time with, never asked about a girlfriend, like the other women in el Caserío who always joked about how Tito would grow up to be a heartbreaker, asked how many girlfriends he already had.

Génesis reached over and took the book. "Kiss of the spider woman," she said out loud.

Tito had always loved reading. He loved novels but also had books about bugs and cars. About the US military, about motorcycles, all the things Nena assumed boys liked. Nena preferred to read about women athletes, Angelita Lind and Jackie Joyner-Kersee and Flo-Jo. She didn't have to explain anything to Génesis about what she was looking for in that book. Génesis, she knew, understood that she was looking for Tito.

"What are people saying?" Nena asked.

Génesis tried to hand her the book. "Tell me about *Kiss of the Spider Woman*."

Nena leaned back against her headboard. "I hate them all." She closed her eyes. "I wish I could leave this fucking place."

Génesis wrapped her arms around Nena, pulled her close, and they sat there for a while, Nena wiping tears off her face with the back of her hand.

"Would you come with me?" Nena asked.

Génesis pulled away to get a look at her. "What do you mean?"

"If I left. We could go together." Nena knew how young she sounded. She knew this sounded like a fantasy, like a dream. But it was what she needed.

"You mean run away."

"I'm serious," Nena said. She couldn't remember the last time she'd asked Génesis for anything, not a single thing.

"You can't just run. Shit doesn't work like that. You need a place to live. You need food, money. How are you gonna take care of yourself?" Génesis was trying to make her voice comforting, but she just sounded frustrated.

"We could take care of each other."

"You haven't even finished high school."

Nena sat up. "Fuck high school. We can do whatever we want." She watched Génesis, waiting for a reaction.

"My parents worry, Nena."

Nena realized they were having two different conversations. She had imagined the two of them running away together, risking everything, but Génesis had never even considered that. She couldn't remember the last time Génesis had held her like she had today. Suddenly she felt the weight of that long-ago field trip she never got to go on, how she'd told her mother she hated her, the dampness of the wet soil against her shorts, against her body, as she sat under the flamboyán, and it was like she was there, too, in all those other places, like she'd always be sitting under the tangle of branches, always a girl, always alone.

Nena lay down, trying not to look at Génesis. Génesis lay on her side and put her arm across Nena. Any other day, Nena might have been nervous or anxious—Génesis's body so close, Génesis's face right up against her cheek. But now she was just so tired, her body heavier than usual, her eyes watery. She was too tired to feel anything, too tired to care.

"You can sleep if you want to," Génesis said. "I'll be here when you wake up."

Nena closed her eyes. She wasn't sure if she believed her. Not anymore.

TWO WEEKS AFTER he was found, Maricarmen and Nena finally got the call that Tito's body was ready to be released to the funeral home. They got in the car early that afternoon, and Mami drove them into el pueblo. Nena knew to keep her mouth shut, even though she wanted to ask so many questions. They were going to make arrangements for Tito's funeral, Mami had told her.

A funeral seemed so final.

In the car, they said nothing.

Mami had dressed like she was going to a job interview, a pantsuit and heels. She wore no jewelry except for a small crucifix on a delicate gold chain, the one piece of jewelry she wore all the time. Tito had given it to her as a Christmas gift last December. Mami had asked where he got the money—he didn't have a job, and he wasn't the kind of boy who mowed lawns around the neighborhood. He told her not to worry about it, and that was enough for her. She never asked about it again.

Mami parked the car a block away from the Catholic church, across the street from la plaza de cuatro fuentes, where she'd taken Nena when she was little. They'd spent so many Sunday afternoons there, Nena and Tito tossing pennies into the fountains, running into the flocks of pigeons that gathered outside the church waiting to be fed. Nena remembered how once, Mami bought a small bag of birdseed from a vendor on the corner and handed it to Nena. Nena and Tito had run toward them, Nena holding the small paper bag open in her cupped hand, waiting for the pigeons to fly at her. And when they did, she threw the thing, ran screaming toward Mami as the pigeons fought for the scattered seed. Tito had laughed so hard, bent over holding his stomach.

But there were no pigeons that afternoon. Just a guaraguao floating above, its red tail feathers lighting up the sky.

The city center was bustling with pedestrian traffic, the narrow streets busy with cars and bikes, like every other day in el pueblo. A pack of satos walked right in front of a car, and when the driver slammed on the brakes, they all bolted. At the crosswalk, Nena thought to take Mami's hand like she had when she was a little girl but then changed her mind. They crossed the street.

As they walked through the glass door at the parish office, Mami turned to Nena.

"Wait here," she said, pointing at the three chairs by the door.

Nena sat under a giant crucifix, a little nervous that it would come crashing down and crack her skull open. She fought the urge to move or look back at it.

"Buenas tardes," Mami said to the receptionist. "I'd like to arrange Catholic funeral services for my brother."

The receptionist, a middle-aged short-haired woman with large glasses, looked at Mami, then over at Nena. "I'm so sorry for your loss," the woman said, then turned to Nena again. She took a step back, turning from one to the other, and exhaled softly. Nena could tell she was just figuring it out.

"El padre Francisco, he was the one who…" Mami paused, searching for the words. "He gave him his First Communion."

Mami worked so much they didn't really go to church all that often anymore. Nena couldn't remember the last time they'd been here, or the last time she'd seen el padre Francisco. Maybe a few months before.

The receptionist frowned. "El padre Francisco is here, but he only leads Catholic funerals."

Mami narrowed her eyes. "My brother was Catholic. This is our church."

The woman took off her glasses. "I'm so sorry, Miss—"

"He was baptized here. He was confirmed here."

"I'm really sorry. There's really nothing we can do."

"El padre Francisco *knows* us. I told you, he gave him his First Communion! Is he here?"

The woman glanced back at Nena, then lowered her voice. "I know how you feel. I do. But your brother was a—"

"Mire, doña," Mami said, cutting her off. She raised her voice. "Is he here or not?"

Nena sat up straight. Her mother was not one to raise her voice or disrespect her elders. How many times had she told Nena that she would smack the teeth out of her mouth if she ever heard her disrespecting her elders?

The woman raised her voice too. "The Catholic church won't be performing funeral services for homosexuals. Do you know what a scandal that would be? Un escándalo." She really emphasized the word *es-cán-da-lo*, dragging it out and pronouncing every single syllable.

"What the hell is *wrong* with you?" Mami yelled across the desk.

Suddenly, el padre Francisco appeared behind the desk. Nena hadn't noticed him walking across the lobby, but he must've come out of his office after hearing all the shouting. He wasn't wearing his usual priest garb, his full collar shirt and cassock. Instead, he wore a short-sleeved white shirt and gray trousers.

"María del Carmen, please," he said to Mami. "Please." Hearing her mother's name, so formal, made Nena flinch. No one ever called her María, let alone María del Carmen. It was like the priest was reprimanding her. Mami fell silent, exhausted. She let him speak.

"We aren't just trying to avoid a scandal," he said. "We want to avoid leading others toward sin, weakening the faithful. You understand."

And then Mami lowered her head, brought her hands up to her face.

Nena stood up, not sure what to do.

"I know how you feel," the receptionist said again, which made Mami look up.

"You know how I *feel*," Mami said, but it wasn't a question. She turned before the woman could respond and headed for the door.

Nena followed her out and tried to keep up as her mother hurried to the car.

As Nena waited at the intersection, watching the guaraguao perched high on top of the church's crucifix, she thought about the cruelty of those words, *weakening the faithful*. She swallowed back tears—every breath like sandpaper in her throat. She wondered what el padre Francisco saw when he looked at her. If when he searched Nena's face, he saw only sin. If he thought she was weak. And why was it that even when you had lost everything, people still expected you to be strong? As the pigeons finally appeared, gathered all around, her mother crossing the street before her, Nena remembered that afternoon, Nena and Tito chasing each other around one of the fuentes, Tito tossing a coin toward the gentle arch of water, a wish for luck or love. As they walked past the fountains, which Nena and Tito had passed every day on their way home from school, she thought of all the coins in the four fountains. How many of them were Tito's? How many wishes would stay underwater forever, never to be granted?

I know how you feel, the woman had said. Nena wondered if she was telling the truth, if her brother or uncle or son had been murdered, if she'd been taken into a hospital morgue to look at his lifeless, unrecognizable body, and asked to identify him. To say, *Yes, this is my brother, this is my uncle, this is my son.*

MARICARMEN DROVE THEM home without a word, taking all the turns way too fast. She couldn't help herself, speeding past curves on the road back to el Caserío. Nena had questions, she could tell, but kept them to herself. She worried about Nena. She was too smart for her own damn good, just like Tito. Just like Rey. She wasn't sure how to fix what had been broken, how to look after her girl. How much more could they take, when they'd already lost everything?

When she pulled up to the front gate, Maricarmen crossed herself. She drove past the flamboyanes, then stopped in front of their building.

She spotted them before she knew who they were. They were leaning against a fancy car—a black BMW with tinted windows parked outside her building. She hadn't seen that kind of car around el

Caserío, ever. It was not the kind of car the reporters drove around. But it was definitely waiting for her, she thought.

Her heart pounded when she realized who it was. Ismael and Cano. In the flesh.

They had been so close once. But that was such a long time ago. After Rey's funeral, they scattered like fucking roaches.

Cano, Doña Matos, Jeannette, and the three kids had left el Caserío. He was running a liquor store in Fajardo, making good money. Had himself a business, a wife and kids, even a mistress, she'd heard.

And Ismael, who'd once been Rey's best friend? After Rey died, he'd written that song.

When Rey stopped playing, after he started coming and going with the tides, disappearing again and again, Ismael's band kept changing. Singers came and went, other percussionists tried to replace him. Ismael had always been the bandleader, even though he couldn't sing. He was a percussionist, producer, and writer. After Rey, he went out and got himself another band, and together they toured the island, even spent a couple summers playing in New York and Miami.

After Rey died, Ismael wrote the song that made him famous. Called it "El Entierro del Salsero." It opened with a funeral march.

The first time she heard it on the radio, the description of the burial, the chorus about a betrayal, a murder, she'd been driving to work. She had to pull over on the side of the road. Car in Park, she screamed and screamed, spit flying out of her mouth, tears in her eyes, screamed until she lost her voice. Motherfucker wrote a song. A tribute, he called it.

Now Ismael drove a BMW. She'd known him when he was just a mechanic, barely making ends meet, living from job to job, who couldn't even afford to pay for his instruments. He'd had to buy congas on layaway, and who gave him the money? Rey did. It was always Rey. Now every one of his songs climbed the *Billboard* charts, and he hadn't shown his face around el Caserío in more than a decade. And now, there he was, parked on her street.

"Get inside," she told Nena.

She slammed the car door and slung her purse over her shoulder. Nena hurried across the lawn, climbed the two front steps, and went inside their apartment.

"Mari," Cano said as she approached, "I'm so sorry about Tito." His eyes were bloodshot, and she could tell he'd been crying. "He was just a kid." He leaned down to hug her, wrapped his arms around her.

His shoulders shook. It felt so different after all these years. How strange it was to see him now, to touch him and feel like she was touching a grown man, not like he was when they were friends. They'd been kids, barely older than Tito.

"How you doing?" Ismael asked.

She stepped back from Cano.

"Where were *you*?" She looked from one to the other. "Where the fuck have you been? Huh?"

Cano's face dropped. He wiped his eyes.

Ismael didn't cry, didn't apologize, and for that she was grateful. He pulled a pack of Winstons from his shirt pocket. He lit up a smoke and offered her one. She took it without thinking, then looked around for Nena before letting him light it for her.

"Cops know who did it?" Ismael asked.

"Why do you care? You gonna write a song about it?"

Ismael shook his head slowly, then took a long drag off his cigarette. She couldn't tell if he was embarrassed, or something else.

"You know I loved Rey," he said.

Maricarmen tried to hold it together. She didn't want to cry in front of them. All she wanted was to bury Tito and keep Nena safe, but everything about Ismael just made her angry, so angry. Here he was now, in el Caserío, when he hadn't shown his face in so long?

"You *loved* Rey?" She turned to Cano, then back to Ismael. "What the fuck do you know about love? The two of you loved Rey so much you couldn't even come see his brother? His daughter? Did you love me too? 'Cause I'm alive, and I've been here this whole time, taking care of Rey's family."

"Mari," Cano said. "We're here for you now, and we're here for Nena."

"I'm surprised you remember her name."

Ismael pulled a folded envelope out of his pocket and put it in her hand. She felt the weight of it, and she didn't have to open it. She knew it would cover Tito's funeral. And maybe, after that, she'd have enough to put Nena on a plane to Miami.

"You mind if we come inside?" Ismael said.

Maricarmen took one last drag off her cigarette, tossed it at their feet, then looked Ismael in the eye. "The only thing you ever gave my daughter was a song about her father's murder. Get the fuck outa here. You don't live here anymore."

CARMELO CAME OVER that afternoon, straight from his funeraria. Sitting in her living room, he handed her a slim photo catalog of wooden caskets and prayer cards with el Sagrado Corazón de Jesús and la Virgen María in different styles. He was tall, lean muscled, almost skinny. All these years and he still had that boyish body, a mess of dark brown curls that fell over his forehead. They'd been friends their whole lives, Carmelo and Maricarmen. Best friends, just like Tito and Nena.

Carmelo talked about a payment plan, how much Maricarmen would have to pay each month, while Nena opened cabinets in the kitchen, poured what Maricarmen assumed was flat Pepsi into a mug, snacked on whatever she found. People had stopped dropping off food ever since Maritza went on the news and told the world that Tito had brought a disease into their neighborhood.

"I'm not charging you, Mari," Carmelo said. "You'll only pay what I have to pay the suppliers. And I'm asking for discounted rates, as a personal favor to me."

"Don't worry about the money," Maricarmen said. "I have some savings."

In the kitchen, Nena slammed a cabinet door, opened the refrigerator. Maricarmen wasn't even sure if they had any food left. They hadn't gotten groceries in two weeks.

"No open casket," Maricarmen said. "I know you know this. I just want to make sure."

"Of course."

"No viewing, none of that. And we want this to be private. Family only."

"I understand."

"We'll bury him in the morning. Just a burial."

"What about flowers? Do you want to think about that for a while?"

"Lirios, something simple. It's just the two of us, you, and your mom, no one else."

"What about—"

"None of that," Maricarmen said again.

They talked for a while, Carmelo asking question after question, and Maricarmen trying her best. And then the conversation turned.

"Mari, I need to ask you something else. Don't take this the wrong way, but we just have to know. We have to take precautions."

"Have to know what?"

"We have to take precautions," he said again. "I don't know if it's true, that Tito…"

"Carmelo." Maricarmen's voice was measured, a warning.

"We just need to know. To take precautions. Because of the body. You know."

"Spit it out already!"

Carmelo took a deep breath. "Was Tito sick?"

She narrowed her eyes, incredulous. "He was *murdered*."

"I know this is hard."

"He was just a boy."

Carmelo was stuttering now. "I'm sorry, Mari. I am. It's just that *El Vocero*, and people around el barrio...We'll find out when we get the paperwork later today, but I just wanted you to hear it from me. We need to know if Tito was sick. And I didn't want to go behind your back."

"Tito wasn't sick, Carmelo. He was just a kid. And he wasn't like *that*."

Maricarmen's hands shook. She leaned forward, listening for Nena in the kitchen, trying to catch her breath. She hoped that Nena hadn't heard her. She regretted it now, the way she'd emphasized, *Tito wasn't like that*. Whatever *that* was, she'd made it sound like it was the worst thing you could be.

"I know it's hard," Carmelo said. "Nobody deserves this. But sometimes kids get into shit, you know. You remember how we were?"

She lowered her voice, thinking of Nena in the kitchen. "Carmelo, you don't *know* anything."

Carmelo put his hand on hers. She closed her eyes.

"La Cura"

MAMI WAS BACK at work, but with only three weeks left of school, she let Nena stay home.

At home alone, Nena started seeing police cars everywhere. They drove around el Caserío a few times a day, parking up the street for a couple of hours. Every evening, when Mami came home, as she pulled up to their building, los camarones turned their lights on, circled the block before leaving for the night. Nena watched them from the balcony, learning their routines. She knew when to look for them, when they left, when they'd be back. She knew it would always be Colón, the woman detective, driving. She knew the older one from the news would be riding shotgun. Altieri, the one Mami knew from before. Her mother wouldn't talk about him, but Nena knew he'd been the one who arrested her father and, later, shot and killed him. Nena had caught glimpses of the story on the news, even though Mami always turned off the TV when they started talking about Altieri's history with her father. She'd read all about it in the pages of *El Vocero*. All these years later, Altieri still referred to her father as a lowlife, and insisted that every person in el Caserío who'd protected this "hardened criminal" was a lowlife too. Mami would be surprised by how much Nena knew. How everyone underestimated her intelligence, not even seeing her when she was in the room. Except for Génesis, there was no one left who really knew her.

Every day, los camarones watched, waited, and Nena started to wonder what they were waiting *for*, if it had something to do with her not going to school, and why they left as soon as Mami got home from work. If they were protecting Nena, what exactly were they protecting her *from*? But Nena knew better. Los camarones weren't known for protecting anybody—her mother had taught her that much.

Standing at the window one afternoon, Nena watched the parked car for a while. It wasn't a police cruiser, and it wasn't one of the news vans she'd learned to just ignore, but nobody in el Caserío drove those big fancy cars. Everybody they knew had small rusted-out hoopties, if they even had cars. She wondered what they actually knew about who killed Tito, if they knew anything, if they even cared, the way they talked about Tito on the news and in *El Vocero*, like he was some kind of criminal, like what happened to him was his own fault.

Nena stepped away from the window. She wanted to understand how people could be this cruel, how even the community who'd known her and Tito their entire lives, the same folks in el Caserío who'd loved her father, would just forget about Tito overnight. And her mother—she talked to her like she was a kid who understood nothing about the world. Whenever anyone called, Mami talked in a hushed voice even though Nena had been right there with her at the parish when el padre Francisco said that Tito couldn't have a Catholic funeral, even though it had been Nena who saw Tito's body.

She headed toward her room but then stopped in the hallway, in front of Mami's door. It was closed, which wasn't like her mother at all. Nena turned the knob, stepped inside. The smell made her gag: dirty laundry, rotten milk, a bowl of three-day-old rice and beans abandoned in some dark corner. Her mother's bed was a mess, her curtains drawn to keep the room dark. She flipped on the lights. There were used coffee cups and bowls and glasses all along her dresser, on the side table, on the floor next to the bed. Her dresser was overstuffed, the drawers jammed almost shut, the clothes spilling out of it like her mother hadn't bothered to fold them. And there was that smell. In all the years she'd been alive, Nena had never seen her mother's room like this. Her mother kept an immaculate house.

Nena's room didn't look like this, didn't smell like this. Her clothes were folded neatly in the drawers, her dresser and mirror wiped clean, her bedsheets newly washed. Her room was neat because her mother had cleaned it, had folded her clothes, had swept and mopped and dusted. Mami had made sure Nena's room was spotless. Nena's face burned with guilt.

She got to work. She picked up all the dishes and cups, old receipts, gathered the dirty laundry that lay in a pile. In the kitchen, she washed and dried all the cups, put them back in their places in the kitchen cabinet. She went to Mami's room with a spray bottle and a rag and started wiping the dresser, mirror, side tables. She pulled open the drawers and started folding, pairing socks, organizing. In the bottom drawer, there were a couple of towels, and underneath them, a stash of pill bottles, an overstuffed envelope, her mother's address book. Nena picked up the envelope first and realized it was stuffed with twenty-dollar bills. She was tempted to count it, but she put it back and picked up a pill bottle instead. It was a prescription in Mami's name. She counted six different medications, all dispensed in the last month.

There was a knock on the front door, and suddenly she realized that Mami would be really upset if she thought Nena had been doing more than just cleaning. She rushed to put everything back in the drawer, dropped the rag and spray bottle on the kitchen counter on her way to the door.

Through the peephole, she saw the older cop, the one from the news. She took a step back.

"Hola," the detective said from outside the door. "Captain Altieri here."

Nena remembered what her mother had told her at least a hundred times: *You never talk to los camarones, you hear me?*

She wasn't sure if she should open the door. Mami had been very clear. But there was so much Nena wanted to know.

Captain Altieri knocked again, softly.

Nena was desperate to make sense of it, to know if they had found the guy. But she doubted this cop would tell her. Nobody told her anything. All that she knew she'd learned on the news or in *El Vocero*. She remembered how on the news, Altieri had acted like maybe Tito had deserved what happened to him, like he should've known better. If she opened that door, Mami would be so upset. She thought about the pill bottles, all the secrets Mami had been keeping. What if her mother was sick? Why wouldn't anybody tell her anything?

"Can you ask your mother to call me?" Altieri slipped a business card under the door.

Nena took another step back, then turned for her bedroom, leaving the card exactly where it was. She was nervous and exhausted, but somehow, she was able to stop in the middle of the hallway. She forced herself to turn around, make it back to the door, and even though her mother had been clear, she reached for the doorknob.

She pulled the door open in one hard swing.

But he was gone. Altieri was already walking up the street toward his car.

A FEW HOURS later, Maricarmen dropped her bags on the kitchen table and poured herself a glass of water from the tap. She was still wearing her white pharmacy technician smock, the hideous, comfortable nurse's shoes she always wore to work. After she set the water down, Nena placed a business card into her hand.

Maricarmen was livid. "Who the fuck do they think they are?" On her way back to the front door, she knocked her purse and lunch bag off the table.

She could hear Nena's chancletas slapping the sidewalk behind her as she headed down toward the police cruiser. Maricarmen usually tried not to let Nena see her anger, her fear, but she couldn't help it this time. Her white smock blew back against the wind as she approached the car. Nena called after her. How many times had she told Nena, *You don't just step to los camarones without some kind of consequence*? She'd taught her that. And yet there she was.

Maricarmen turned back to Nena, pointed at their apartment building. "Get back in the house!" As she crossed the street, she noticed the three vans: WAPA-TV, WVSN News, and an unmarked one she knew was probably the photo crew from *El Vocero*. They'd printed all those bloody crime scene photos on their front page. They could all go straight to hell.

"Who do you think you are, coming for my daughter?"

On the driver's side, Detective Colón opened her door, but Captain Altieri stayed in the car, got on the radio. Maricarmen kept her eye on him.

Suddenly, the reporters all got out of their vans. She ignored them as they filmed her, ignored the camera flashes, even as they got closer to her and the cops.

"She's fifteen years old," Maricarmen said. "Why don't you go bother los tiradores in la plaza?"

"Mami!" Nena yelled from across the street. "Please!"

One of the photographers walked toward Nena, his camera turned in her direction.

Maricarmen pointed her finger at Nena's face, her nostrils flaring. "I told you to get in the house! *Now!*"

She regretted it as soon as the words had left her mouth. She'd never talked to her daughter like that, especially in front of other people. She'd spent every day of her life trying to be the exact opposite of her own mother. She had promised herself she would never hit her, would never scream at her, would never humiliate her or belittle her the way her mother had done with her and Loli. And now here she was, sounding exactly like her own mother. And the reporters probably had her on tape. Her stomach tightened into a knot.

Nena wiped tears from her face, turned toward their building. She crossed the street.

Maricarmen turned back to the cops. Now both of them were out of the car.

Carmelo was standing out front, smoking a cigarette. "You all right?" he called out to her from across the street.

Maricarmen nodded but then realized that, no, she was definitely not fucking all right. She just wanted to bury Tito, keep her daughter safe, away from the cops.

Carmelo dropped the cigarette, stepped on it, and crossed the street. "Have some respect," he said to one of the guys filming Maricarmen. "Come on, let's get inside." He barely looked at Altieri, and took Maricarmen's arm.

She wouldn't budge. She didn't know how else to say *Stay the fuck away from my daughter*. She looked into Altieri's eyes, hoped that he could see in her face how much she hated him, that murdering piece of shit.

"Don't come knocking on my door again unless you have a warrant. And leave my daughter alone. You do *not* have my permission to talk to her. Ever."

Carmelo put his hand on her shoulder, like he was holding her up, giving her strength.

Altieri's face was stone. He had always hated her and she knew it.

And now she'd probably pissed him off. She tried to compose herself, feeling the pressure of Carmelo's hand on her. She didn't want Altieri to go after Nena just to get back at her.

"What I mean is," she said, "I would appreciate if you left my daughter alone. She's been through enough."

Detective Colón nodded. "I'm so sorry, María. We were actually just hoping to speak with *you*, ask some follow-up questions?"

"What, so you can get on the news and spread lies about my family? I got nothing else to say to you."

Altieri got back in the passenger seat, shut his door.

"I know it's been hard," Colón said, "and I know you're not ready right now. But we're trying to find out who did this." She gave Maricarmen a look that was meant to be comforting, then got in the car. "Please reach out when you feel ready. The sooner the better."

Maricarmen wondered how long she'd been a cop, if she was like the rest of them, how long it would take before she was also accepting bribes, falsifying evidence, brutalizing innocent people.

As the car slowly drove off, reporters hurled questions at her.

"Mrs. Ojeda, do you know who wanted to hurt your brother-in-law?"

"Señora Ojeda, how's your family dealing with your brother-in-law's death?"

"María, is it true that Tito was dating several different men?" said one of the younger reporters, a man who looked no older than Tito.

The last question made her flinch. Who did this fucking guy think he was? She'd started to turn around when Carmelo took her arm.

"Leave us the fuck alone!" Maricarmen yelled across the yard, the sidewalk, the street.

The police car made a right turn at the gate and disappeared.

AT THE ECONO supermarket just outside el Caserío, people stepped aside as Nena and Mami walked by, watched as Mami picked up a shopping basket and hung it over her forearm. Nena did the same with her own basket and followed Mami up and down the aisles.

Mami wasn't really looking for anything specific—she hadn't made a shopping list or cooked one of her elaborate meals since Tito died. She just picked things off the shelf: canned gandules, salsa de tomates, Spanish olives. In the cereal aisle, Nena dropped two boxes of Frosted Flakes into her basket.

"Do we have rice at home?" Mami asked.

"We don't have anything but mayonnaise. Maybe ketchup." Nena grabbed a box of farina, then headed toward the milk.

They went around Econo like that for a while, Mami shopping for a meal she was never going to make, and Nena trying to figure out what she could easily put together. Lately, all Mami cooked were things that went in a bowl. There had been a lot of cereal, boiled eggs. Nena knew that this was Mami's way of trying to be her mom, the mother she'd been before Tito died.

At the checkout line, as they stepped up to the counter and Mami started unloading her groceries onto the conveyor, the cashier put an orange CLOSED sign in front of her register.

"Sorry!" she said, and walked off.

Mami watched her go, then looked around, checked if someone else was coming. She tossed her groceries back in her basket. "Come on," she said to Nena.

They got in the 10 Items or Less lane. When the woman ahead of them saw Nena and then Mami, she stepped aside, then quickly walked past them to get out of line, bumping Nena's elbow hard with her full basket.

"Ow!" Nena said under her breath.

"Excuse me!" Mami called after her, but the woman got in another line, pretending not to hear her.

"I'm fine," Nena said. She stood up straight. "I'm okay."

Mami set her basket on the floor and took Nena's. "You sure?"

"Yeah. No big deal." Nena forced a smile.

All around them, people had started moving, getting out of line, walking over to the other end of the supermarket. A woman lifted her baby out of the shopping cart's child seat and left her cartful of groceries blocking the aisle. When they got to the front of the line, again, a different cashier placed a sign on the conveyor: CLOSED. They watched her go, no apology this time, no explanation.

Years later, Nena would remember this moment as part of the beginning, when everything had already started shifting. How they stood there, Nena and her mother, watching all the people around them, the disgust in each of their faces, the fear. How much Nena would change that year, how she'd learn to hide her pain, her own fear. As the crowd gathered around them, Mami's face changed. Nena didn't know what she'd do, but what she felt was beyond anger or sadness. Her mother's eyes filled with tears, her hands shook a little. Her mother, who'd raised her on her own, who'd worked two jobs to put a roof over their heads and food on the table, who had always made Nena feel loved. Mami exhaled, looked into Nena's eyes, took her hand. And what Nena saw in her face, even at fifteen she understood, was an apology.

Nena took her basket then picked up Mami's too. "Come on," she said.

Slowly, they walked toward the next register, where an older Black woman with short gray curls smiled at them. Nena placed both baskets on the conveyor.

"Buenas tardes," the woman said.

Mami watched her but didn't say anything.

"Buenas," Nena said, unloading the baskets quickly, as fast as she could. She placed cereal, bananas, milk on the belt before the woman figured out who they were. She tried not to look directly at her.

The cashier bagged their groceries in big paper bags as Nena went through Mami's small purse and found her wallet.

The cashier counted out Mami's change, put it in her hand.

Nena picked up both bags, balancing them on her hips. "Thank you." She looked into the cashier's face, and when their eyes met, Nena saw that the woman was much older than she'd thought. And also, it was clear, she knew exactly who they were. She knew.

"Take care of your mom," she said. "Madre hay una sola. And before you know it, she's gone."

DRIVING HOME, MARICARMEN tried to think of something to say, something to comfort Nena. She remembered when Nena was a baby, how right after Rey was killed, sometimes she found herself listening for his singing, how sometimes she thought she could hear his voice coming from the bedroom as she prepared dinner. Sometimes she'd look for him, close her eyes and reach into the darkness for his face, his hands. She wanted to know exactly how it happened. How after they shot him, los camarones put him in that car, drove him away. She wanted to know where, exactly, he'd drawn his last breath, if he'd thought of her, if he'd called out her name. She'd heard Ismael's version and Cano's version and the version los camarones had testified to in court. When she thought back on that day, all she could see was a blur, her body going from one place to the next: Maricarmen and Evelyn at the police station asking about Rey. The uniformed cop at the front desk looking at them like he had no idea what they were talking about. Not a single cop at the station able to tell them anything about any arrest. How after they were sent home, she went back to Nena and Tito and Don Ojeda, waited all night for a phone call.

Maricarmen slowed the car as they drove past the back gate. She felt her body weighed down as they passed the elementary school, the basketball courts, the kids roller-skating on the sidewalk. Every night after working her second job, Maricarmen sat in her car in front of her building, waiting for God knows what. She couldn't go inside, face Nena. All those questions she didn't have answers to, how Nena needed her so much, how Maricarmen didn't know what else to say, what else to give.

Over the years, as Nena got older, Maricarmen had looked for traces of Rey in her face, her hair, her voice, and he was always there, in her almond-shaped eyes, in her dimpled cheeks, in her thick eyebrows. Sometimes when she'd held Nena in her arms, she would sing her to sleep, the same songs Rey had sung to her in her crib. But as Nena got older, she looked less and less like her father. Sometimes Maricarmen looked at Tito and she could see Rey clearly, so clearly. But now, with Tito gone, she couldn't remember Rey's face anymore without scouring the photo albums. Would Tito's face fade from her memory too? It was just the two of them now. And Maricarmen didn't know who would take care of Nena once she was gone. There was her mother and Loli in Miami. She hadn't spoken to them in years, hadn't even told them about Tito. She'd only sent letters. She wanted better for her daughter. She hated to imagine Nena's life without her, with only Blanca and Loli around to take care of her.

"Mami?" Nena said, pulling her back from wherever she'd been. She'd stopped the car in the middle of the road, in front of their building. She hadn't pulled into the parking spot, just stopped there, frozen.

Slowly, she slid the car into the spot. Nena unloaded the groceries silently.

Maricarmen wasn't sure she could do it, not tonight, not again. She could not go back into that living room, that kitchen, that bedroom. She needed someone else to be with, someone who wouldn't look at her with disgust, like she was carrying around some contagion. She needed to just *be*.

As Nena came back for the last bag, Mari got out of the car.

"I'll be home later. Make yourself something to eat."

"Where you going?"

"I need to talk to Carmelo."

At Carmelo's apartment, she stood in front of his door a minute, maybe two. There she was, so unlike herself. She closed her eyes, took a breath. She wanted all this to disappear. She wanted to wake up from this nightmare—a girl again, with Tito a small boy, Rey by her side, music filling their apartment.

Finally, she knocked.

CARMELO'S APARTMENT WAS smaller than hers. Just one bedroom, a compact living room, a hallway, a tiny kitchen; all the places in el Caserío looked the same, boxlike and dark, unless you opened all the curtains on a sunny day. But Carmelo's was especially bleak. At least she had painted hers a few months before. She'd done it over a weekend with Tito and Nena, each with their own roller. Touch of Sunshine was what Tito had picked for his room, a cheerful shade of yellow. Now that seemed like so long ago, a lifetime ago, a life.

In Carmelo's bedroom, she sat on the bed, kicked off her shoes. He handed her a can of Medalla. It tasted watered down, but at least it was cold. She didn't even like beer—she preferred rum. She drank it anyway.

"I didn't think I'd see you tonight," Carmelo said.

She shrugged. "Here I am."

He took off his shirt, dropped it on the floor, his faded jeans falling below the hips. He had a handful of dark hair on his chest, a five-o'clock shadow coming in. His curls were damp, as if he'd just showered. The bedroom was barely furnished—just a bed, a chair with some clothes draped over it, piles of magazines on the floor, a small table that held an ashtray and half a dozen empty beer cans. Everything about him was messy—the way he walked around barefoot, the way he never, ever combed his hair, the way he left his half-empty cans here and there, the mountain of dirty dishes in the sink.

He had always been this way, back in the day, running around with her and Loli. Maricarmen knew that he had loved her then. But all she'd cared about was Rey. She never even considered Carmelo—not once.

He swiped her beer and downed most of it. After leaving the can on the table, he took her hand and kissed it, then leaned in to kiss her on the lips. He smelled of cigarettes, Irish Spring soap, shampoo. Somewhere else, maybe all over the apartment, she could make out the fading scent of something like Elmer's glue—that shit he liked to smoke.

"I thought about you all day," he said.

She blinked. There he was, staring at her, studying her.

"You all right?" he asked.

"I didn't come here to talk." She tried to blink away their faces, the women at the supermarket. Tried not to see them. She took his hand and pulled him close, and he kissed her again, then slowly got on top of her. They kissed for a while, until Maricarmen pulled away, and they traded places. Carmelo lay there with his jeans on, Maricarmen straddling him, kissing him, numb. She wasn't sure what she wanted or what she was trying to feel. She took off her shirt and he sat up. When he unsnapped her bra, she closed her eyes. She imagined she was somewhere else, someone else.

Carmelo had stopped kissing her. He was watching her now.

"What?" she said.

"Tell me the truth. You okay?"

"Everybody keeps asking if I'm okay." She slid off, lay down next to him, then rolled onto her side.

He waited a moment before covering her with a blanket. She

closed her eyes, listened to the ceiling fan above her awhile, then drifted off.

Her dreams were all sound. A man's voice singing. A bird flapping its wings, blowing the hair from her face. Only there was no man, no bird. Only the echoes of them, reverberations, something she felt in her body.

SHE DIDN'T REMEMBER falling asleep, but she woke an hour later. The ceiling fan was still going, but the bedroom was darker. Beside her, Carmelo was sitting up in bed, wrapping a pantyhose tourniquet around his upper arm. She watched him, her eyes half open, as he tied the pantyhose into a slipknot, the same way Rey had done all those years ago. During that last year, Rey had spent day after day shooting H. He was barely there during that last year, and yet there were signs of him everywhere. At first, she'd found his fresh syringes where he'd stashed them, in shoeboxes at the bottom of the closet. But after a while, he wasn't so careful anymore. She found them under the bathroom vanity, left on their bedroom nightstands. The needles, the pieces of cotton, the bottlecap cookers and burnt spoons, the makeshift tourniquets. She would not raise their daughter like this, she'd told him again and again.

And now Carmelo.

This was her pattern.

The needle was already in his arm.

He mainlined it, his head falling sideways, slowly.

THE MORNING AFTER the supermarket, Mami was not about to leave Nena home alone, in case los camarones came knocking again. Mami seemed quieter, nervous. She'd locked every door, every window, checked them two, three times before bed. She was trying not to show it, but Nena knew: Mami was afraid.

That morning, Mami called up Doña Evelyn, who was her floor supervisor at the factory, and told her she was bringing Nena with her. It was temporary, Mami told her, until she could find someone to stay with her.

"Just one or two days," Mami said into the phone.

"I can stay by myself," Nena said loudly.

Mami put her hand over the receiver, opened her eyes wide. Nena had gone to work with her before, but it had always caused a problem. No kids allowed in the factory, the manager had said. It was a safety hazard. Never mind that Nena never went near any factory equipment—she'd never even been outside the break room—or that she wasn't exactly a child. But they'd told her, if Mami broke the rules again, she was done.

"I'm not a kid," Nena said. "I'll be okay."

Mami waved her away. "One day," she said into the phone. "Obrero won't even know she's there. You know he doesn't leave his office."

Mami sounded desperate. Nena wished she could show Mami that she could be trusted, that she could take care of herself.

"Gracias, Evelyn," Mami said into the phone. "You won't regret it. I promise."

Doña Evelyn had known Mami since before Nena was born. She was like a second mother, is what Mami said, but Nena knew Doña Evelyn was a big pata, that she was in love with Mami. It was so obvious, and Nena was sure everybody could tell. There was so much bochinche around el Caserío, Nena couldn't believe Mami didn't know. Or maybe she did.

Mami finished getting herself ready, and Nena packed their lunches—two ham and cheese sandwiches, two bananas. She made the coffee and poured it into Mami's thermos, like it was something she'd been doing her whole life.

They walked to the car, Nena balancing the lunch bag and Mami's purse slung over her shoulder, and she couldn't help feeling like she was grown, like she was a person with responsibilities. Making their lunches, carrying things to the car—she wanted to show her mother that she'd always take care of her.

"We're running late," Mami said.

"I could've stayed home."

"You can hang out in the break room, watch TV."

At Osborne Pharma, they rushed through the double doors and up the stairs to the second-floor break room. Mami stuffed her bags in her locker and zipped up her coveralls. She gave Nena a handful of quarters for the vending machines. "If you need the bathroom, go across the hall."

"I know the drill." Nena did know—her job was to do what Mami said, period.

Mami took Nena's chin, hard, looked her in the eye. Nena froze. Her mother's fingers dug into her face. "You stay up here and keep your head down." She let go of Nena's face, finished zipping up her coveralls. "Obrero doesn't leave his office, but don't give him an excuse."

Nena's eyes filled with tears. Her mother had never touched her like that, so aggressively, so violently, like her body was not hers anymore. She was humiliated. She fought the urge to cry.

"You hear me?"

"I heard you," Nena said, her voice hoarse. She could still feel the heat of her mother's fingers on her cheeks after Mami had left the break room, after the door had clicked shut behind her.

From the floor-to-ceiling windows, Nena had a view of the factory floor below. She left the lights off and kept her distance from the glass so she wouldn't be easy to spot from below. She felt the rumble of machinery, giant fans buzzing all around her, her body vibrating, her face still hot. The other factory workers, mostly women in blue or gray coveralls, didn't even look up as Mami passed them on her way to her line among the conveyor belts.

Mami started filling small boxes with pill packets. She had tried to tell Nena all about the pill a few months before, and Nena had reminded her that she already knew all about birth control.

"Are you learning about human growth and development at school?" Mami had asked.

Nena had looked at her mother in disbelief. "Is this your way of asking if I need a sex talk?"

Mami had ignored the question and just spat out every damn thing she knew about the pill, how the first-ever birth control pills had been tested on women right here in Humacao, how before that, the government had forced women to get sterilized with surgery.

"Maaaami." Nena had exhaled dramatically.

On the factory floor, her mother picked up the packets from one conveyor belt, slid the flat oval dispenser into a small box, then another, and another, one on top of the other, then tossed that into a plastic container. She worked fast. The sight of her made Nena want to weep. Mami had grabbed her face without even a second thought, had walked away without even apologizing. Once her mother had filled a plastic container, she set it on the conveyor belt and off it went. No sweat. She filled another one, set it down and watched it go, filled another. She moved fast, set one down expertly, picked one up. But no matter how fast she moved, the work kept coming. Someone was always building the small boxes. The conveyor belts were always moving. There were always more pills.

Nena caught a glimpse of Evelyn moving from one belt to another with her clipboard. She looked so masculine in her dark blue coveralls, her hair cut short, shaved on the sides, short on top, her protective goggles dangling under her chin. Nena didn't know why she even wore those stupid goggles. And, God, Evelyn was such a marimacha. She even moved like a man. Evelyn stopped by her mother's line, and they chatted for a minute, until Evelyn wrote something on her clipboard, then left. Mami went back to her pill packets.

The hum of the machinery all around her, all the conveyors moving, watching her mother, she fought back tears again. She felt like the floor beneath her was pulling her down, like she might fall to her knees, let herself lie on the carpet. She took a breath and it was like a punch to the throat, the pain expanding all the way down to her chest. She exhaled and her entire body deflated. Even though she knew this place, even though she and Tito had spent hours hanging in the break room doing exactly this, something had changed. It was Nena—*she* had changed. Now that there was no Tito, now that her mother was so tense, now that she'd reached for Nena in anger, now Nena saw things clearly. Her mother trying to keep it together, her mother's rage bubbling underneath the surface, her anger at all the people who'd always known her but had abandoned them after Tito's death, her anger at Nena. Nena, who was always around to remind her that her husband was gone. Nena, who had to be fed and clothed and taken care of, which is why she had to keep coming here to collect her paycheck. This job, this factory. This is what her mother did. This was her mother's life. Every morning when she left el Caserío, this is where she came. And she did it again, and again, and again. Every damn day. This was exactly what she'd been doing when los camarones found Tito.

They had not told Nena anything, even though she'd seen him there in the sugarcane. They'd refused to answer her questions, or even confirm that it was him. But she knew what Mami knew—it had happened at night. And later, when they found him, Nena out back with Génesis, Mami was here working her shift at the conveyor belt. They had waited for her mother to make it home, Colón and Altieri sat there while Nena paced the living room and asked questions they wouldn't answer. Why wouldn't they say it was Tito? Why couldn't Génesis stay there with her? Tito had still been out there when Mami came home.

Mami filled another plastic container, set it down on the belt. Nena had waited for him all day, and the whole time, he'd been out there in the caña.

Mami stopped, wiped her face on her sleeve, then got started on another one.

When Mami asked the detectives how Tito had died, she had demanded that they tell her everything. They were keeping things from her, she'd said.

In the break room, Nena put her hands up against the glass, feeling it vibrate under her fingertips. It occurred to her then—watching Mami, Evelyn, the conveyor belts, all the other women on the line, most of them Mami had known her whole life, girls she had gone to school with who had turned into the women she worked with, all of them filling boxes all day every day—that she did not want her entire life measured out in pill cartridges on a factory floor. Dear God, she did not want this life. Her mother's life. She did not want to be anything like her mother.

Nena's fingers slid down the glass, and even though she knew, she *knew* she should've stepped back, away from the windows, where no one could see her, she stayed put. She stood right there for all to see, even as Evelyn made her way quickly down the floor to Mami's line, as Mami looked up at her, pulled her safety goggles off. And as Obrero staggered toward the two women, then stopped. Looked up at the glass. As their eyes met. Obrero looking up at Nena. Nena looking back at him, her cheeks burning where her mother's fingers had squeezed.

AN HOUR LATER, Nena sat quietly in the front seat while her mother drove them to her second job at the pharmacy. Mami hadn't said a word about what Obrero said on the factory floor. She'd come into the break room, started gathering her things, and said, "Let's go."

They rode in silence, her mother watching the road, stone-faced, Nena waiting for her to say something, anything.

When they pulled into the Walgreens parking lot, Nena put her hand on the door handle.

"Did he fire you?" Nena asked.

"You can sit in the waiting room in front of the pharmacy, read magazines. No one will bother you." Mami turned off the ignition.

Nena nodded. She watched her mother gather her things mechanically, still no expression. She wanted to ask if she was all right, if things would be okay between them, if she would talk to her again, if she needed Nena to go back to school. She wanted to ask her mother if she could, or would, forgive her.

NENA CALLED GÉNESIS as soon as they got home that night, desperate to hear her voice, to be reminded of all that was still possible. It was the night before el entierro, and Nena wanted to make sure Génesis would be there, that she'd come meet her in the morning so they could go to the cemetery together for the private burial.

The phone rang and rang.

She was so tired. She decided to wait for Génesis to call her instead. She sat in front of the TV, Mami on the couch. Together, they watched the news.

Nena should've seen it coming, should've known it would only get harder. But somehow, that night, the two of them exhausted and barely able to look at each other, it took them by surprise.

The press conference outside the police station, the crowd full of people they knew, their neighbors, their community. Somehow, every last one of them had known that this press conference would happen. Everyone, except Nena and Mami. Somehow, they had all known to be there together, the exact time and place.

Nena felt herself reach for the remote. She wanted to change the channel, turn it off, fling the fucking thing at the TV, shatter the damn screen into a million pieces, but it was out of reach. And she was so tired. She sank back into the sofa cushions, let herself watch. Captain Altieri spoke into a mic.

Tito was gay, he said.

Tito was having "relations" with several men, he said.

They had reason to believe that one of those men held grudges against Tito, he said.

Even though a few reporters had raised the question, at this time, he could not confirm if Tito was HIV positive, he said.

The hair on Nena's arms stood up, her throat closed up. Next to her on the couch, she could hear Mami's breathing, but she could not bring herself to look at her.

One of the reporters on TV called out to Captain Altieri. "Captain," she said, "are you saying you have a suspect?"

Captain Altieri took a moment, scanned the crowd, and frowned. "That's all the information we can share right now."

In the crowd, the reporters talked over each other, asking question after question:

"Do you have a suspect?"

"Is this case connected to the killings of two gay men in Fajardo last month?"

"What is taking so long?"

Captain Altieri watched the crowd, waited. When the reporters quieted down, he spoke into the mic again. "I will take one question. One." He pointed: "Mr. Santiago from WAPA Televisión."

Juan Santiago stood up. "Captain, what is your response to the critics who say that your police department does not care about this young man's murder, because he was a homosexual?"

"Mira, Juan," Altieri said, raising his voice. "You and me, we've known each other a long time." The crowd went quiet. "These people, they go around dressing like they do. It's not like they're innocent. These guys, having sex with other men, showing it off. What did they think would happen?"

Juan Santiago pressed him, raising his voice too. "Captain, are you saying that Tito was asking for it?"

Altieri shook his head. "Look, that's not what I said. But do you want that around *your* children?"

"What about the other critics?" Juan Santiago asked. "Those who claim that your history with Tito's older brother, Rey Ojeda, makes you unfit to investigate Tito's murder?"

The crowd exploded, people shouting at each other, yelling at Juan Santiago, at the police. People shoved each other out of the way. The camera pulled back to capture the whole crowd: uniformed police officers herding people, pushing them back. The camera cut to Altieri again.

Altieri shook his head as Detective Colón walked past him and stepped up to the microphone. She started speaking over all the noise. "On behalf of the Humacao Police Department, we want to extend our condolences to Tito's family." The crowd quieted down. "Tito was only eighteen years old. He was still in high school. He was set to graduate at the end of this school year. He was beloved by his teachers, his friends, and of course, his family."

Nena's hands shook.

"Are you investigating anyone at La Central Patagonia? Was it an accident connected to the sugarcane burning season?" Juan Santiago asked.

Detective Colón glanced sideways at Altieri, who nodded his approval.

"We have determined that the incident was not connected to La Central Patagonia's controlled burns," Colón said. "The killer used a different accelerant."

"What—"

"The killer used gasoline," Colón interrupted Juan Santiago. She ignored all the raised hands and continued speaking: "We will do everything we can to bring this killer to justice, for Tito and his family. Thank you."

Nena couldn't catch her breath. She felt like she'd been for a run around the block. She closed her eyes and tried not to hear the noise from the TV.

When she opened her eyes again, Mami was standing over her, her mouth a straight line.

"Come on, mamita." Mami pulled her up by both hands and suddenly Nena was on her feet. "Let's get you to bed."

"What?" Nena said. When she looked around, the TV was off. "I'm not tired."

"We both need some rest."

"I'm not..." she started to say, then stopped.

YES. HE HAD fired her. After a decade, after she had showed up day after day, even if she was sick, even if she was depressed, even when the world was threatening to collapse on top of her. She had come in, zipped up her coveralls, and stood on that line. And the one time she'd needed just a little help, he had let her go, just like that. Those ten years a blur—fuck her and her family, fuck the food on the table and the roof over their heads. She was not his problem. He had a factory to run. Never mind that it was Evelyn doing all the running, that it was women on the line, because he only hired women. It was women, mothers, who carried that place. And yet, how easily he'd told her to clear out her locker, take her kid and her shit and go.

That night, after Nena was asleep in her bed, Maricarmen made her way to Carmelo's for a drink, for some conversation. That's what she told herself.

At the door, Carmelo's skinny shirtless frame moved aside and let her in. She took the cigarette pinched between his lips, brought it to her own, smoked it like it was the last day of her life.

"You want a drink?" he asked, but he was already on his way to the kitchen.

She walked over to the large boom box on the corner of his small living room, bent down to take a closer look. There was a tape in the tape deck.

"You remember when we were friends?" she asked, her voice echoing through the hallway into the kitchen. She pressed Play and the music blared, filled the room. "Plástico." Willie Colón y Rubén Blades. She took a long drag, blew the smoke, and started moving with the music.

"We're still friends, Mari." He handed her a glass, rum and Coke, not enough ice.

She only tasted rum, some lime. "I meant all of us. When we were kids."

"I try not to think too much about the past." He turned for the bedroom and she followed.

She suspected that was a lie, that it was easier to pretend he didn't think about the days when they were teenagers running around like the whole world belonged to them, Carmelo and Mari and Loli, and how everything changed when she met Rey, when Carmelo became *just a friend*.

After she met Rey at that neighborhood block party, all their friends dancing out on the street, how easily she'd fallen for him. That first year, after Maricarmen and Rey got together, she spent a lot of time trying to explain her friendship with Carmelo: They'd been friends since they were kids, she kept telling Rey. He was *just* a friend. He didn't like her *like that*, but Rey was convinced that Carmelo was in love with her.

In Carmelo's bedroom, Maricarmen gulped down the rest of her drink, set the glass on the dresser. She watched herself in his mirror as she stripped off her sweaty clothes, pulled the clip out of her French twist, let her hair fall down to her shoulders. She wanted to feel like someone else. Like the sixteen-year-old girl she'd been back in those days, Carmelo's friend, Loli's big sister. She knew nothing, that girl.

Carmelo watched her as she undressed, swallowed the rest of his drink, reached for her hand and pulled her against him. He put his face against her neck and breathed, then kissed her shoulder, her collarbone. She pulled back so she could get a look at him—she wanted to *see* him wanting her.

Rey had been right the whole time. She could see that now. Carmelo had always loved her. This beautiful mess of a man, who'd never stopped looking at her like she was everything.

The first time she'd come over like this, just days after Tito was gone, she'd just wanted to feel something. Now, she realized, she liked the way he wanted her, the way he fucked her, how he put his face between her legs like he had always known her body.

All those years ago, it was Rey who had cooked it for her, fixed the shot, pulled the slipknot loose. She'd just wanted to know what it felt like. It had been just the one time. Now she wanted to disappear.

After, when Carmelo pulled out his kit, she sat up in bed next to him, the two of them naked and sweaty.

She held out her arm. "Do me first."

THE NEXT MORNING, Nena called Génesis about ten times as she and Mami got dressed for the service. No one picked up, even though Nena knew someone was always home. Génesis's brothers, her parents, her abuela. They all came and went, and no one carried keys, because there was always someone around. Maybe, Nena thought, they'd seen all that shit they said about Tito on the news.

The cops were sitting out front when Mami and Nena got in the car. Nena sat in the front seat, playing with the hem of her blue dress, watching them in the side mirror. She prayed for Génesis to pull up alongside the car on her bike, or get dropped off by her dad before Mami drove away.

Mami wore the only black outfit she owned, a cocktail dress that fell just below the knees, her heavy locks pulled up in a messy twist, heavy makeup, the crucifix Tito gifted her. As they drove down the street, Nena checked the rearview mirror, the side mirrors, then stuck her head out the window. No Génesis. She felt the tears starting to sting, then sank back down in the passenger seat. Her mother was drenched in sweat, Nena noticed. Two dark pit stains were growing under her arms, and her foundation was running down her neck. Nena reached for the fast-food napkins Mami kept in the glove box, pulled out a handful, and handed them over. Her mother took them, rubbed at her face and neck, and balled them up.

The detectives were parked by the cemetery gates.

"Look at that," Mami said. "It's our own private security." She pulled the parking brake, stepped out of the car, slammed the door. She stared at them hard as they got out of their unmarked car.

They wore plain clothes—their usual dark trousers and button-down shirts, their detective badges on their belts, holstered pistols. Colón opened the back door and pulled out her blazer, put it on before walking in their direction.

Mami watched Colón and Altieri approaching. "I don't remember sending out invitations."

"We're so sorry for your—" Colón started to say.

"Yeah," Mami interrupted. "So you keep saying." She adjusted her purse and came around to Nena's side of the car.

Nena got out of the car, and Mami slammed her door, too, then took Nena's hand. Los camarones followed them toward the entrance but stopped there.

THE CEMETERY WAS made up mostly of small monuments and aboveground tombs, with one large mausoleum. Don Carmelo was already waiting by the tombs close to the dirt road, an aboveground cement burial vault, an older man standing at his side. His brother, Nena realized, since they looked almost exactly alike. They both wore gardening gloves, faded gray trousers, and white polo shirts. They were sweaty in the morning sun. Carmelo looked sick, his face gaunt, almost gray. He was wet with sweat.

Mami approached Don Carmelo first and shook his hand awkwardly. He pulled her in for a hug, and she leaned into him, collapsing in his arms. He wrapped his arms around her and looked up at the sky, like he was praying silently. Mami looked small in his arms.

When she pulled away, Carmelo crossed himself.

"Bendición," Nena said softly to Don Carmelo, not really sure what she was supposed to do, since he wasn't a priest or a relative. Nena had never been to a funeral without a priest—she'd never been to a funeral that wasn't Catholic.

"Que Dios te bendiga," Don Carmelo said, wiping tears from his eyes.

Mami took Nena's hand, squeezed it.

Nena kept her eyes on the front gates, checking for Génesis. But instead of Génesis at the entrance to the cemetery, there was Evelyn heading toward them in an ill-fitting dress.

Nena held up her hand to say hello. Evelyn's loose dress blew sideways in the wind. It was the strangest thing, seeing Evelyn in women's clothing, wearing makeup, lipstick. All of it like some kind of costume. She'd look better in a man's suit, Nena thought. She already had a man's haircut.

Evelyn hugged Nena first, pulling her close, and Nena smelled her flowery perfume, something else that didn't fit.

"How you doing? You okay?" Evelyn said.

Nena shrugged.

Evelyn hugged her mother next, and they held each other for a long time. It was a strange sight, her mother and this gay woman hugging for all to see. Nena wondered if Carmelo and his brother knew that their mom was gay. Did Mami know? Maybe it was just like Tito—her mother oblivious, when it was so clear. Nena wondered, for the first time in her life, if this is what she and Génesis would look like one day, if everyone would be able to tell.

Génesis. She scanned the cemetery for her again, and this time, she saw Ismael and Cano waiting by the entrance, near the hearse. She didn't know that much about them—they'd been her father's friends, and she knew about the song. She knew that Mami didn't care for either of them, and she definitely hadn't invited them.

Evelyn noticed them too. As Mami pulled away, Evelyn adjusting her dress, tucking a curl behind one ear, she asked, "Is that Ismael?"

"From Ismael y Su Banda de Pillos," Nena said. "The one who wrote that song."

Evelyn turned to her, face full of questions.

"I've heard the song," Nena said.

Mami wiped tears from her face, and even though her makeup had looked flawless when they left the house, she had dark circles under her eyes now.

Evelyn took Mami's hand. "Want me to ask them to leave?"

"Let's just get on with this," Mami said to Carmelo.

Carmelo and his brother got to work, sliding the cement slab off the top of the tomb, setting it aside carefully. Then they walked over to the hearse, talked to Ismael and Cano for a minute. They pulled the wooden box from the back, and together, the four men carried it. The box had a simple varnish, not like the elaborate glossy coffins Nena had always seen on TV, with polished metal handles. The handles were black and simple. It was just a plain wooden box. The four men held on to it, carried it toward the grave, where Mami, Nena, and Evelyn waited.

Nena struggled under the hot sun, sweaty and exhausted. Her clothes felt loose. She'd lost some weight over the last couple of weeks. But still, she felt so heavy—heavier than she'd ever felt. Watching the men approach with Tito's coffin, she felt even heavier. She knew the reason no one came to the funeral, the reason there were only four pallbearers. How an entire community, the people who had seen Mami grow up, the people who had known Tito when he was a baby—none of them were there in the end. Not even Génesis.

It was then that Nena started to cry, her entire body heaving, her breath caught in her throat. She crossed her arms across her stomach, hugging herself. Mami put her arm over her shoulder, pulled her close, started praying el padrenuestro. Under the hot sun, Don Carmelo adjusted his grip, and then the men lowered the box into the open panteón.

Nena checked the gate one last time. Génesis wouldn't come— Nena knew that now. She'd wanted to believe that things would go back to the way they were, at least with Génesis. She'd wanted to believe that she could depend on the people she loved. But as she watched Don Carmelo and the other men lowering Tito's casket into the small space that would keep him forever, she knew that things would never be all right, that people would always let her down the way they'd let her mother down. How stupid she had been to believe anything else. Her mother had tried to tell her—all those stories about her father. Her mother had loved him so much, but he'd been taken away from her, from all of them. And what followed, everything that came after Rey el Cantante's murder, had been a curse.

When the men were done, the box finally inside el panteón, Don Carmelo and his brother heaved the slab on top. Don Carmelo stepped aside, and his brother bent to pick up a metal pail filled with cement. He pulled a trowel out of the pail, slathering cement around the slab, working quickly, unceremoniously spreading it onto the seams, sealing it. As he finished, Mami and Evelyn crossed themselves.

He took the pail and trowel back to the hearse and returned carrying a large wreath. Lirios, some carnations. He placed it on top of the slab, crossed himself.

Carmelo, Ismael, Cano, all just stood there watching the tomb. Cano's eyes were bloodshot. Ismael hid behind a pair of dark glasses, an expensive suit, a gold pinky ring, a gold watch. Carmelo was a scrub of his former self, a ghost. Nena could not imagine any of them in the before times, when Tito and even her father were still alive, a bunch of Caserío kids running around trying to impress girls like her mother. She could not imagine her father and this Ismael making music together. This man who'd written a song about his murder, then got famous, who'd barely even said two words to Nena her entire life. Did he know that he'd escaped a curse? She wished she were brave enough to tell him.

Tito deserved so much more than a quick burial, a box sealed into a panteón like a brick into a wall. She stepped up to the tomb, ran her fingers over the flowers, then placed her hand on the stone slab.

Beside Evelyn, her mother wiped at her face with a fistful of fast-food napkins. Nena couldn't tell if Mami was wiping away tears or just sweat. Her mother seemed more tired than usual, sleepwalking through the morning. She had barely even hugged Nena since Tito died. Had Mami even called her grandmother and aunt in Miami? They should've been there. Did they even know?

She remembered that day on the beach, Tito and Nena, the two of them on the shore, the clear blue water catching them both in its wake, then receding. Tito held that sato tight against his skinny chest, so close. It was then that it happened, Nena remembered, a recognition, a new kind of awareness passing between them: Nena knew, and Tito knew that Nena knew. Tito was soft, and she loved him for it. But it was the kind of soft the world would not accept, because the world was hard. She'd known that, too, even if she didn't have the language for it back then.

They'd both known the dog would not go home with them that day, that Mami would never allow it. But Tito held the sato anyway, for as long as he could, let himself pretend the dog would be theirs.

Next to the hearse, Ismael joined Carmelo, his brother, and her mother in a conversation. He shook Carmelo's hand and his brother's, but he didn't hold out his hand for Mami.

"She'll be okay," Evelyn said, touching Nena gently on the shoulder. "You just gotta be strong for her."

Nena tried not to be rude, just nodded. Evelyn hugged her tight, and when she finally let Nena go, Cano was standing in front of them.

"I don't know if you know me," Cano said to Nena. "I was your father's friend."

Nena shook her head, even though she knew *of* him, knew that most of her father's friends stopped coming around after he died. She wanted to hear what he had to say. "I didn't know my father."

"You were just a baby," he said.

Nena nodded. Evelyn put her hand on her shoulder again.

"Your father and I," he said, "we always talked about our kids, you know. I have a daughter your age."

His eyes met hers, and Nena thought she saw his lip quivering. Maybe he was nervous. Maybe it was the cemetery. She looked away, started walking back to the car, Cano and Evelyn following in step.

Cano caught up to her. "He always said he would be my daughter's godfather. And I would be yours."

Nena stopped. "What?"

Cano's hands were shaking now. He talked fast, like he was unsure if Nena would hear him out. "I know I haven't seen you all these years, but your father was my brother, and I know I can't speak for Ismael"—he pointed at Ismael, who was still talking to Carmelo and her mother—"but he was his brother too." Cano looked into her eyes, searching her face.

Maybe what he wanted was forgiveness, Nena thought. Maybe he'd come back just for that. She fought the urge to remind him that her father had a real brother, and they had just buried him.

"I'm so sorry about Tito," he said, as if he'd read her mind.

In the sky, a red-tailed guaraguao, wings extended.

Tito was gone. The one person who knew her, who really saw her. In that moment, standing in the cemetery, walking away from all that was left of her uncle, she'd never felt more alone. She wished more than anything that she could touch him, that she could see him again. All those promises the church had made about eternal life, about heaven. How many times had she heard heaven described as a kingdom where Jesus sat on a throne? And how many times had she heard them describe the sins that would keep Tito—and Nena—from the kingdom of heaven? But hell wasn't real, and heaven was no kingdom. *This*, she wanted to tell them all, *this is the only kingdom*. Everything else was a lie.

"Calle Luna, Calle Sol"

IN HER BEDROOM, Nena hadn't been able to stop thinking about Génesis, why she hadn't made it to Tito's funeral, even though she had promised she'd be there. Maybe Génesis was in the hospital, unconscious. Maybe she was dead. Nena didn't know what she'd do if she lost her—Génesis was the beginning, was the world, was everything.

They had spent most of their days alone, riding their bikes around the city, into the plaza, past the tangle of trees by the winding country roads. They did what they wanted in those days—everyone else had stopped paying attention.

It was Génesis who'd been there when her tío Ojeda died a year before. Mami had kept the news from Nena and Tito as long as possible. Had kept it to herself as she and Tito and Nena spent the morning at church, as they spent a whole day at the beach, as they stopped in la plaza de cuatro fuentes on their way back home in the late afternoon.

That day, Mami had parked outside the church, left the windows down, and started walking toward one of the fountains. "Come on!" she called back to Nena and Tito.

Mami sat on the ledge, watching the pigeons.

Tito dipped his hand into the water, reaching for a quarter.

"Don't do that!" Nena said, peering back at her mother.

But Mami just sat, staring off into the distance. "Your tío died early this morning," she finally said, just like that.

Tito sat next to Mami, quietly took her hand. "We knew it was coming," he said, trying to reassure both of them.

But Nena had so many questions. When did Mami get the news? And why was she just telling them now? And how come they went to church first, then the beach, and not straight to the hospital?

Her mother wouldn't say why she'd kept it from them. Instead, she talked about how Tío Ojeda had always been like a father to her. How in the early days, Don Ojeda's family dog, an old mutt they called Peposo, once bit her on the butt as she walked across their front yard.

Nena had told the dog story to Génesis as they worked in the parish office a couple of days later, printing copies of the program for Tío Ojeda's Catholic funeral. *Celebration of Life,* the sheets said. Nena and Génesis were to print and fold them in half, leave them on the table. They were fourteen, and it was the only way they were allowed to help, even though Nena had told her mother that she wanted to help—she *needed* to.

Nena and Génesis had worked in the office alone while everyone else made preparations. They stacked the papers on the table, folded them one by one, then made neat piles, working mostly in silence—they'd reached a phase in their friendship when neither one ever said the right things, when there was no way to say what was on their minds. Nena was sure she could feel Génesis's eyes on her as she refilled the copier's tray with a fresh ream of white paper, as she picked up the warm sheets and smelled the ink on them. Génesis watched her, brown eyes rimmed with too much eyeliner, her lips turned upward into a confident smile, sideswept braids falling over one shoulder.

How many copies were they meant to print? Had they been

counting? Nena had studied the writing on the sheets. *Celebration of Life.* She hadn't felt all alone in the world then, because Génesis was always with her.

But now, Nena was lost.

Mami was sitting alone in the living room when Nena came out of her bedroom, dressed and ready to go. Her mother was drinking café, listening to Lucecita Benítez's "Amor Mío" on the radio. She barely looked up when Nena came in, didn't ask where she was going, just drank her coffee, her eyes glazed over like she was in some other place.

Nena slipped out the door. She didn't really know what she'd do, what she'd say to Génesis, or to her brothers if they came to the door, but in her head, she rehearsed a hundred different scenarios.

In front of Génesis's building, Nena watched her balcony, her door, trying to work up the courage to knock. She imagined herself climbing the two front steps, then tapping softly on the door, but she didn't want to end up face-to-face with Jamil, or any of Génesis's brothers.

Before Nena could knock, Génesis stepped outside. "Hey," she said, closing her front door behind her.

"You didn't come." Nena could see the brothers at the window, all of them watching.

"What are you doing here?" Génesis hurried down the front steps, then across the front yard.

"Where were you?" Nena followed her.

"I'm not allowed out."

"How come?"

Génesis circled the lawn, then moved to the sidewalk. Nena realized she wasn't letting her get too close.

"I saw your uncle on the news."

Nena didn't understand. Génesis had heard everything they said on the news, had heard the hurtful things people in the neighborhood had been whispering about Tito, and then the day of his funeral, she didn't show, didn't even call?

Génesis met her eyes. "Is it true?"

"Why are you acting like you don't even know him? *Those people* don't know him. But you?"

"But they had all those pictures," Génesis said.

Nena wasn't sure what to say to that. "So what!"

She'd raised her voice, Nena realized. She glanced back over her shoulder. At the window, Génesis's brothers pushed each other out of the way. It was how they'd always been, ever since they were little—always fighting, loud, taking up space. Tito had been so different from them.

"I'm sorry he died," Génesis said, tears in her eyes, and Nena knew she meant it.

Génesis reached for her, wrapped her arms around her, and Nena just let her.

The front door flew open and all of Génesis's brothers burst through it. Génesis pulled away quick, then stepped aside.

"Keep your fucking hands to yourself!" Jamil said.

Nena wasn't sure she'd heard right.

Three of her brothers took Génesis by the shoulders, ushering her back toward their apartment, like they were trying to protect her. From Nena.

Jamil looked Nena dead in the eye. "Keep your faggot hands off my sister."

"Jamil!" Génesis yelled. She pushed her brothers off her, stepped up to Jamil and pushed his chest. He grabbed her hands, glaring at her until she stopped.

"Please," Génesis said.

He nodded, like they had some kind of understanding, then turned back to Nena, calmer this time.

"Look," he said to Nena, "what happened to your uncle was fucked up. Nobody deserves that."

Génesis was crying now.

Jamil pushed Génesis's shoulder. "Tell her!"

"My dad said I'm not allowed to hang with you anymore," Génesis blurted out. "He said I'm not allowed over your house, and you're not allowed over here."

"Don't come around here no more," Jamil said. "Just leave my sister alone."

Nena turned back toward her building. She was halfway up the street when she heard Génesis call her name.

Nena didn't turn, but she could hear Génesis running after her. When she caught up to Nena, Génesis wrapped her arms around her again. Nena was tempted to push her away, keep walking, but instead, they held on to each other, Génesis's breath in Nena's hair.

Nena knew then that this would be the last time they'd see each other. She tried to memorize her scent, lemon and coconut hair oil, soft braids brushing Nena's face. But Nena also remembered how she'd spent the morning of Tito's burial waiting for Génesis, waited for her all day, was still waiting. Now, as they started to pull away from each other, the blocky buildings looming over Génesis's shoulder, Nena spotted Jamil and the other brothers headed toward them. Jamil walked behind them, a baseball bat in his hand. Nena's breath caught in her throat, limbs heavy, Jamil tightening his grip on the bat, and although it hadn't happened yet, Nena knew that they could never go back to the way it was before.

When Jamil reached them, Génesis grabbed his arm, started pulling him back while the other brothers gathered around Nena, soldiers waiting for orders. Nena took a few steps back, and she knew, saw it in Jamil's eyes: There was a lesson he wanted to teach her, and if she didn't run, he and all his brothers would make sure she learned it good. She turned for her building, broke into a sprint, and the boys all chased her, all of them calling after her, "Come here, you fucking pata!" and "That's right, run, bitch!" She ran past the side of her building, past the backyard, the red-orange sunset bleeding across the sky, and jumped the fence.

In the parish office all those months ago, Nena hadn't told Génesis how she felt. But she was sure Génesis knew when Nena had touched her face unexpectedly, when Nena kissed her on the lips, sent her pile of sheets flying, scattering all over the carpet like feathers, dozens of the *Celebration of Life* programs, Génesis smiling down at her, looking at her with those big brown eyes.

Now Nena ran, the brush of cane against her as she passed, cutting her, tiny slices across her bare legs and arms, her shoulders, her cheeks. She pumped her legs as hard as she could, stopped feeling her body, the caña just a blur as she sped past, trying to cover her face. She could get lost in here, she knew. Like Tito.

He came to her then, not as she'd known him, but how she'd seen him that last time, his body in the cane, so small. She slowed down, came to a stop. What was she doing in there? She tensed, her jaw locked, her limbs tightened. Was she shaking? She felt her chest tightening, too, like something was squeezing her, and she tried to catch her breath, but her body was not the only body out there. She couldn't see them but she sensed them all around her, ghosts chasing her, pushing her, flinging rocks at her.

She turned, but there was no ghost, just wheezing, and then a gurgling wet breath that she realized was coming from her. She coughed into her hand and saw that it was bloody, but she had no idea where the blood had come from. Had she been hit?

Tito had looked so small out there that day, so strange. She'd closed her eyes when she realized it was him.

Nena turned again, her whole body clenched, and touched her own face. She couldn't tell what she felt. She was numb. She was throbbing. She felt nothing and everything. Her nose. She held her face, held herself steady, let herself look.

There was nobody chasing her. There was her own body, standing in the cañaverales among the ghosts. And there was Génesis, facing her, holding the baseball bat, her brothers watching, waiting.

"Do it," Jamil said.

In the parish office, Nena had pressed her body gently against Génesis, and Génesis had pulled at her shoulder blades, pulled her entire body toward hers. They had kissed and breathed softly into each other, and the only words either one of them could say were *Oh God* until their kiss became a prayer.

Génesis stepped closer. Dropped the bat.

Nena exhaled. Her head throbbing, pain radiating down her spine, her body swaying until she thought she might fall over. All around her, Nena heard the soft rolling moans of the cane toads. She realized she'd stopped at the edge of the field where the land opened up, the edge of the world, half of it burned black in the fires, the other half golden.

"Do it."

Génesis swung at her, landing a punch on her right cheek, and Nena fell.

Bowled over, on her hands and knees, trying to breathe, she wet herself. Somewhere in the cane, she heard laughter.

Génesis kicked her on her side and she flinched, feeling the pain not on her side but her head.

The sun was setting. The land beneath her felt warm. Nena let herself drop all the way down, stomach to the ground. She lay down sideways at the edge of the caña.

Her father, her tío Ojeda, and now Tito. Somewhere in the cane, all her ghosts were calling.

PART THREE

"He Chocado con la Vida"

1993–1996

"Dicen Que Soy"

MARICARMEN AND NENA arrived in Miami Beach that summer, stepped out of a taxi just before sunset, their two large suitcases dropped on the sidewalk at Meridian Avenue and Twelfth Street. The bags held mostly Nena's things—Maricarmen had done all the packing, but she barely brought anything for herself, just some toiletries and a few changes of clothes in a backpack.

Maricarmen checked out the block, strapped her backpack on tight, and picked up one of the suitcases.

"It's that one there," she said to Nena, pointing at a colorful two-story building with cat palms fanning the front entrance. This would be the first time Maricarmen saw Blanca and Loli since they left Humacao, the first time Nena met them. Nena only knew them from pictures.

"It's nice," Nena said softly. Maricarmen observed how Nena looked at everything with curiosity—the wide canopy of trees blocking out the sun, people walking their dogs in the park across the street. For the first time in weeks, Nena didn't seem fidgety or anxious. Like some of the fear and sadness had lifted as soon as they got off the plane.

Maricarmen was sweating from her scalp all the way down her back, her hands shaking slightly. She was worried about Nena, about how Blanca would treat her, considering she'd never made a single attempt to know her. Maricarmen had prepared her mother and sister, had told them everything on the phone, all that Nena had been through in the past three months, starting with Tito's death. She'd warned her mother that if she didn't take care to watch her mouth around Nena, to treat her with the respect and love a granddaughter deserved, she would never see either of them again. She'd warned Loli too. But Loli was another story—she had contempt for Maricarmen, but not Nena.

"She needs her family," Maricarmen had said to Loli on the phone. "She's been through so much."

And Loli had snapped back, "She's always had her family. And she will always have *me*. I'm not the one who abandoned her."

That stung, considering how abandoned Maricarmen had felt when her mother and Loli left el Caserío, but she bit her tongue, not wanting to rehash it all again over the phone. She was too damn tired. All she wanted was to get her daughter out of el Caserío, away from the reporters always camped out in front of their building, and los camarones, and all the questions. She had no faith in the police—she was sure the investigation would go nowhere, that there would be no justice for Tito, just as there had been no justice for Rey—and she wanted to keep them away from her daughter. Nena had been through hell already.

At the airport in Miami, before handing their tickets to the airline clerk, Maricarmen had said her daughter's full name out loud, "Nenuska Ojeda Doval." She'd taken out her large manila envelope with all of Nena's documents—birth certificate, passport, social security card—not sure what she'd need. Maricarmen had never taken Nena out of Puerto Rico. The airline clerk had smiled, told her not to worry, she could put those all away. Then Maricarmen repeated it in her head, like a mantra, *Nenuska Ojeda Doval.* Like she was trying to remind herself that Nena was real, that her fifteen-year-old daughter was alive. She still had bruises on her body, the fading black eyes from the broken nose still visible, three broken ribs. She'd spent the last couple of weeks crying in her room, but she was *alive*, gracias a Jesucristo. There were still the nights when it got worse: Nena's nightmares, the moaning in her sleep when the pain lingered.

The flight had been quiet. It was their first time flying, their first time traveling anywhere, and Maricarmen had been glad for the quiet, for the plane full of strangers. When they took off, Maricarmen had closed her eyes, thinking, *Dios Dios Dios*, but not much else. She'd stopped believing in prayer. She hadn't asked Nena to translate when the flight attendants rolled the food cart over. Maricarmen tried to remember the little bit of English she'd learned in school, but it was no use. She took what the flight attendant handed her. Nena had drunk three Coca-Colas, closed her eyes, moaned softly in her sleep.

On the sidewalk outside Blanca's building, Maricarmen and Nena dragged the old heavy suitcases toward the side entrance. Suddenly, a tall, skinny figure appeared in front of them. She was barefoot, wore cutoff denim shorts that were two sizes too big and an orange bikini top, her black hair in a tight low bun.

"Oh my God! You're all grown up!" Loli said in a husky voice, then ran up and caught Nena in her arms.

Nena, who'd dropped her suitcase, winced, then held her ribs. She looked at her mother as Loli shook her happily and did a little dance, right in the garden outside the building.

Loli finally let go of her, stepped back. "Let me look at you!"

Nena clutched her side, taking short breaths.

"You okay, mamita?" Maricarmen asked her daughter.

Nena nodded quietly.

Loli touched Nena's hair, and Nena flinched. "Look at you, you're gorgeous! The pictures didn't do you justice, girl." Then she turned to Maricarmen like she was a stranger. "Isn't my niece beautiful?"

"Hi, Loli," Maricarmen said.

"Make sure you get that bag?" Loli said, pointing at Nena's suitcase, then snatched Nena's hand and pulled her up the two steps and into the first-floor apartment.

Maricarmen grabbed ahold of Nena's suitcase, shaking her head.

"Here she is!" Loli yelled into the apartment. "Ma! She's here!"

Maricarmen lugged the heavy bags up the two steps and inside. She was annoyed at her sister, but at least she was being nice to Nena.

Her mother's apartment in Miami Beach smelled exactly like her apartment had during her childhood in Humacao, the faint smell of rice and beans on the stove, her mother's Bal à Versailles floral perfume, sweat and salt, and dirty laundry. It was like she was standing in their old living room, before it had become the home she'd shared with Tito and Nena. It was like Maricarmen was thirteen again, coming home to her mother's wrath. It was all too much. She recognized the 1970s sectional, just like the one they'd had back home, but was it the same one? She couldn't tell, but the rest of the furniture looked new. A set of modern glass-topped marble coffee and side tables, a new dining table and chairs, leather-upholstered stools at the kitchen counter. It all looked expensive. Somewhere inside the apartment, a dog barked.

She walked around the living room, looking at old family photos. Framed school pictures of Maricarmen and Loli in Padre Rivera Elementary, their uniforms ironed and clean, their hair brushed and neat. How close they were back then. All over the living room, all the photos were of Maricarmen and Loli as children: chubby cheeks, missing front teeth. In one photo, eleven-year-old Loli was as tall as thirteen-year-old Mari. But there wasn't a single photo of Nena, and not a single photo of Maricarmen as an adult. All those pictures she'd sent over the years, Maricarmen and her daughter, how she'd dressed her in frilly dresses that'd cost a fortune, shoes shined, her curls tidy and perfect, her daughter always smiling brightly for the camera. Maricarmen felt her stomach turn. What if this was a mistake?

She headed for her mother's bedroom. "Nena?"

Inside the room, Nena and Loli sat at the edge of the high four-poster bed, Nena petting a small brown mutt. Blanca, her mother, was sitting up in her bed, listening as Nena told the story of how she got her two black eyes, her broken nose: how Jamil had come after her with a baseball bat, how Génesis and her brothers jumped her, how it had been Génesis, not the brothers, who'd done most of the hitting. The broken nose, the kick to the ribs, all of it.

"They could've killed her," Maricarmen interrupted.

Blanca, who looked much older than Maricarmen had imagined, scowled. Her bone-straight brown hair was cut in a short bob with blunt bangs, a style she'd been wearing for decades. Her mother had spent her life working as a hairstylist, and Maricarmen thought she probably still cut her own hair. She had never trusted anyone else to do it.

"Killed her?" Blanca asked. "She got beat up by a girl and her little brothers."

"One of them was her *older* brother," Maricarmen said. "Eighteen years old, six feet tall. A goddamn baseball player."

"Fucking asshole," Loli said.

"They hit her with a baseball bat!" Maricarmen said, looking directly at her mother. "She's lucky to be alive!"

"They hit you with the bat?!" Loli said. She turned to Nena, searched her face for the truth. But Nena was quiet. Loli turned to Maricarmen. "Why isn't that fucker in jail if he's already eighteen?"

"I don't think they used the bat," Nena mumbled. She wiped tears from her eyes.

Maricarmen reached for her, then realized she still had her backpack strapped on tight. While she loosened it and set it down, Loli wrapped her arms around Nena.

Nena cried in her arms, and Maricarmen watched. When she glanced at her mother, she realized that Blanca had been watching *her*, not Loli and Nena.

"Why don't you take Nena into your room?" Maricarmen asked her sister. "Help her unpack?"

Loli looked up at Maricarmen, patted Nena's back. "Come on, Nenu. I've got cable in my room. You can unpack tomorrow." She led Nena away. "Oso, come!" The dog jumped off the bed and followed them.

Blanca didn't waste any time. As soon as Loli and Nena were out of the room, she said, "How long do you plan on being here? I hope you told her this is not a hotel. She has chores to do, and as soon as she's old enough, she needs to get a job. I hope you got her papers in order."

Blanca's words stung, silenced her. This is your granddaughter, she wanted to say, your blood. She just lost her uncle, and I almost lost *her*. It surprised her, how much her own mother felt like a stranger. She wanted to tell her about that afternoon, how she'd found Nena, bloodied and beaten, out by La Central, surrounded by the kids she'd grown up with, all of them taking turns hitting her while she just lay there. She wanted to tell her how Nena had seen Tito, what was left of him. How they were just kids, all of them, and she didn't know how to explain any of it. She wanted to tell her mother everything.

"I got all her documents for school registration," Maricarmen said. "Everything she needs." She waited a moment for her mother's reaction, then said, "I'll be gone soon."

NENA AND TITI LOLI made the small twin bed together, covered it with brand-new sheets, a new thick blanket that Nena wasn't sure she needed. Miami Beach was as hot as Humacao, and it was the height of summer. The small bed was new, Titi Loli told her. She'd had her boyfriend drop off the mattress, box spring, and frame after they picked them out at the Flea Market USA.

"He drives a truck," Loli said. "We're so glad you're here, Nenu. I've been looking forward to finally getting to know my niece."

"Sorry we're, like, taking over your bedroom." Nena forced a smile. She could tell her aunt was glad she was there, but she wasn't so sure about her grandmother. Nena pulled a pillowcase over a brand-new fluffy pillow. Oso sniffed around the twin bed.

"It's okay. Your mom will be out in the living room. It'll just be you and me in here. Like a long sleepover." Loli folded down the blanket neatly, then picked up the remote on the side table next to her own full-sized bed, turned on the TV. "We could watch movies or music videos. You like MTV?"

Nena nodded, pretending she knew what MTV was. They'd never had cable back home—even though her mom worked two jobs, they never had money for anything extra, no fancy sneakers or expensive jeans like her school friends, or like Génesis. Génesis's parents both worked, and their kids always had brand-new bikes, Nintendo games, whatever they wanted, even if her parents were always crying poor.

Nena found herself deflated, thinking again about Génesis and her family. Every time she thought of Génesis, of her brothers, she felt as if she'd done something wrong, even though Mami kept telling her that she hadn't done anything, that she didn't deserve what they did to her.

Loli turned off the TV, took Nena by the hand, and sat her on her bed. "You're okay now. You're safe." She adjusted her bikini top, then reached into her side table and pulled out a pack of Newports and a lighter. She brought one to her lips, then offered the pack to her niece as if Nena were grown.

Nena thought of her mother and grandmother in the other room, then shook her head. She appreciated the gesture, how Titi Loli went out of her way to make her feel like she cared about her, and now, this felt like a secret between them. She wished her mother were somewhere else. She needed Titi Loli to know that she wasn't rejecting her.

"My mom would kill me."

"She was smoking by the time she was your age." She lit the cigarette, dropped the pack and lighter on the side table, then blew out the smoke. "There was *a lot* she was doing by the time she was your age."

"How come you guys barely speak?" Nena asked.

Loli took a long drag off her cigarette, exhaled. "I probably shouldn't tell you this, because she's your mom, but...Let's just say your mom was the kind of person who betrayed people, abandoned them."

Her titi's words were like a punch to the gut. The hair on her arms stood straight up. No one had ever talked about her mom this way. No one. "What do you mean?"

"It's amazing that one of the worst people I've ever known had such an awesome kid. You're nothing like your mother."

It seemed that she was surrounded by terrible people, Nena thought, or the kind of people who were capable of doing terrible things. She wondered what her mother had done to make Loli talk about her like this. *What made her so bad?* Nena wanted to ask, but she couldn't bring herself to. She didn't want to hear the answer. But she knew from her own experience that the people you loved and trusted could hurt you most of all.

"What happened, Nenu?" Titi Loli patted Nena's back softly. Oso jumped onto the bed and snuggled in between them. "Is it true? What your mother said about the baseball bat?"

Nena couldn't remember everything, and every time she tried, the memories came with sensations. Any mention of the baseball bat—something her mother kept bringing up to anyone who would listen—and her stomach clenched, her bladder felt like it would burst. Right then, sitting on Titi Loli's bed, Nena thought she could feel the urge to pee.

Her mother had found her just outside La Central, outside the Azúcar Patagonia lot, where sometimes you could see the employees on break lining up for the roach coach, the small food truck that sold granos, sandwiches, and café in the mornings. Nena wasn't sure how she'd ended up there—she remembered running into the cañaverales, not turning into La Central. And she didn't know how her mother had heard the commotion all the way in their apartment. Her mother had come outside because she'd heard the scuffle, she'd told Nena. She'd heard what sounded like a dying animal, and then realized it was Nena screaming, calling for her. Mami swore that when she finally got to her, Génesis and her brothers took off running but left the bat behind.

Nena couldn't remember if she'd been hit with the bat—she remembered Jamil holding it, Génesis dropping it, a flock of birds exploding across the sky. Her mother holding her against her warm body, how cold Nena had felt then. She remembered waking up in a hospital bed, her mother and Doña Evelyn always hovering somewhere above her head, and how every time she asked for water, one of them came quickly. She remembered dreaming about her mother in a hospital bed, a tiny body in a huge bed, and Nena woke up choking, like she was swallowing her own tongue. How her mother had come to her, had held her hand, said, "You're fine, mamita, I'm here," and then Nena, only half awake, had asked her, "Mami, are you sick?" Her mother hadn't answered, hadn't said a word, just touched her face softly, and whispered, "Shhh, shhhh."

There was a knock on the bedroom door.

"Dinner's on the table," her mother called from the other side.

NENA SAT NEXT to her mother, keeping her eyes on her plate. She tried not to look at her grandmother too much—she didn't want to answer any more of her questions, but also, she was afraid of her. Blanca had straight dark hair and big pillowy lips that seemed unnatural on a white woman, especially one her age. But nothing about her grandmother betrayed her age. She still worked at a salon, according to her mother. They were all forbidden to ask how old she was. And Nena was not allowed to call her Abuela.

"What are you waiting for?" Blanca asked from across the table. "Don't you like arroz y habichuelas?"

"Sorry." Nena started eating.

"My God, Maricarmen, haven't you taught her how to sit como una señorita?" She leaned toward Nena. "Close your legs, girl, and keep them closed. Tú no eres un macho." When she spoke, Blanca's big white teeth were *so* big and *so* white they didn't seem real. Nena wondered if she wore dentures. One bite from those horse teeth and you could lose a finger.

Nena picked at her chicken, then licked her fingers, keeping her head down.

"Ave María. Licking your fingers at the dinner table? Maybe your mother didn't teach you any manners, but in this house—"

"Leave her alone, Ma," Loli said. "She's a kid. Let her eat." Loli ate quickly, eyeing her pack of Newports on the table. Nena was grateful for her aunt, who did what she wanted, smoked when she wanted, dressed however she liked, even wore bikini tops like they were shirts. Mami just sat there quietly, letting her grandmother talk to her like that.

Blanca ignored Nena after that. As they ate, her grandmother asked Mami about the people in the old neighborhood, about Don Ojeda and Doña Evelyn. How was Ojeda? Was he still handsome?

"He died last year," Mami said.

"Why didn't you say anything?" Blanca crossed herself. "My God, I would have made the trip for his funeral!"

"I wrote you a letter and never heard back. Just like all the letters I send." Mami took a bite of her chicken.

"Letters? Who has time for letters? I work for a living."

"I have two jobs and somehow still find time to write," Mami said.

"Why don't you call?" Titi Loli said. She set her fork down and snatched her cigarettes, pulling one out and placing it between her lips. She lit it, smoking feverishly. "You know, maybe *I* would like a letter once in a while. Since you never call. You have a phone, no?"

Mami glanced at Loli quickly but didn't acknowledge her. She turned back to Blanca. "You didn't bother with Tito's funeral, and you definitely didn't bother with Rey's, even though I begged you to. You never came to see your granddaughter, so why would you come down for Don Ojeda's?"

"You know I didn't plan on leaving. It was *you*—disgraceful. You drove us away."

Nena watched her mother. She hadn't known this—that Mami had begged Blanca to come to her dad's funeral, but she still didn't show. Blanca met her mother's eyes. They sat there, watching each other.

Nena put her fork down, and for the first time, when she looked at Blanca, she caught a glimpse of her mother's face. She tried not to see it. She knew enough about how she'd treated her mother, how she'd abandoned her. Maybe that had made her young mother more rebellious, intensified everything Mami had seen in her father all those years ago, the myth of him. How Mami had always described him to her: He had been beautiful, his dark skin, those lovely long eyelashes, the high cheekbones.

Mami had always said Nena looked just like her father, the man whose death had broken her mother's heart. She had heard so many stories about those years after her father died, when Mami had needed Blanca most, and this whole time, her mother had been keeping from her how, alone with a baby and with Tito, she had needed her own mother, but in the end, she'd had to do it all alone.

Nena looked into her grandmother's eyes, and she felt sick. She didn't want to be there, in her grandmother's house, sitting at her table, eating her food. And then, when she looked at Mami, it was like looking into a mirror but not seeing herself, seeing something else: what she'd never be. Nena didn't belong here.

Loli ashed her cigarette into her plate. "Everything with you was always about Rey. You stopped living your own life and became his shadow."

"What?" Mami said.

"And then you spent all those years taking care of Rey's little brother. You had a sister of your own, did you forget? Did you ever think that maybe I needed you?"

"I had a baby. I lost my husband. Tito lost his whole family. What did you expect me to do?"

Nena's stomach felt sour and her mouth watered, like she might vomit. If only Loli would put out that cigarette. Nena reached for her glass. She gulped down all her water.

"You were never there for me," Loli said, raising her voice. "You only ever cared about Rey. And you took care of his brother because you have a fucking martyr complex."

Mami slammed both hands on the table, and everything shook, making Nena jump. "I'm not your mother! You have a mother right here!" She pointed at Blanca, and Loli exhaled a cloud of smoke. "You wanna talk about being abandoned? At least you had a mother. At least you didn't get kicked out to live in the streets…"

Loli's eyes widened. She looked from Blanca to Mami, to Nena, to Mami again. "She didn't kick you out," Loli said, lowering her voice. "You left."

"Is that what she told you?" She turned to her mother. "Is that what you said?"

Nena suddenly felt like she needed to pee. Her bladder was full. She looked around for the bathroom.

"You brought that on yourself," Blanca said. "I told you what would happen."

Nena held it. Closed her eyes. In some other universe, she imagined, there was another version of her, another version of her grandmother, not this one. In that other life, her mother and aunt didn't fight and Tito was alive and her grandmother loved her and Génesis was the same Génesis she'd been before. Blanca spoke again, but Nena didn't hear it. She was no longer in her grandmother's dining room. The sun had set and she could make out the sound of cane beetles in the distance, a chorus of coquíes. In the sky, vultures soared.

"I told you what would happen."

Nena was on the ground, the moonlight filtering through a canopy of bright green cane leaves. Was she really out there, or in her grandmother's kitchen? What if she was still out in the cañaverales? What if no one found her? Her head—she raised one hand to the back of her head and felt a spike searing down her spine. She would die out there. Would anyone find her? She would die alone among the cane toads.

She pissed herself.

MARICARMEN HELPED NENA into the shower, peeling off her soiled shorts and underwear. She tossed Nena's clothes into the sink and let the water run—she would wash them, hang them outside to dry somewhere out of Nena's sight. Nena was silent, like those early days after she got home from the hospital, when she refused to answer any questions about Génesis and her brothers. As the water streamed down on Nena, Maricarmen wondered if she'd made the right choice. She'd needed to get her daughter out of el Caserío, but was this the right place for her? This was not how she'd expected their first night to go. She pulled the shower curtain closed when Loli came in.

"Don't worry," Loli said. "I took care of it." She handed Maricarmen a clean towel for Nena. Oso came in after her, wagging his tail, looking for Nena.

"Thank you." There was so much she wanted to tell Loli, about how fragile Nena was, how she needed time, how she still had nightmares, how sometimes she froze and her body turned into a child's body and there was nothing to do but hold her, make her feel safe. She wanted her sister to understand that it wasn't just the fight, or her best friend's betrayal, or the hospital—as bad as all of it had been. It was also Tito. How Nena had found him, had seen him like that, and even though she'd tried to be strong, it was all coming out now. She had put it all in a letter for her, all of it. She hoped Loli would forgive her. Nena, she knew, never would.

When Loli stepped out of the bathroom, waiting for her in the hallway, Maricarmen followed. The dog came out and sat next to Loli.

"I'll talk to Mom," Loli said. "Don't worry, I'll get her under control."

Eyebrows raised, Maricarmen crossed her arms. "How exactly?"

"This is my house too. I pay half the rent."

Maricarmen nodded. A few minutes ago, she'd been so angry at her sister, at her unwillingness to see her side, at her selfishness.

"I'm sorry," Maricarmen said. "I know it was hard, being alone with her all these years. I know she wasn't easy on you."

Loli wiped her face with her forearm. "I didn't know she put you out on the street."

"She did. And I need you to make sure she doesn't do the same to Nena." Maricarmen went back inside the bathroom to finish washing Nena's clothes, help her get dressed.

NENA SLEPT A lot those first few days, getting up only to use the bathroom or drink water before heading back to bed. She ate the sandwiches her mother brought her, the bowls of cereal Titi Loli made her sit up to eat. Blanca went to work at the salon, Mami went down to the local high school to get her enrolled, and Titi Loli went out with her boyfriend, but Nena didn't even notice. She was still in bed when her mother walked through the door, when her grandmother came home from work and immediately started complaining that all the windows were open, letting out all the cool air, and that the meal Mami had cooked for all of them smelled like fried fish, and when Mami confirmed that, yes, it was fried fish, and that's why she'd opened all the windows.

Nena didn't want fried fish. She didn't want to hear Blanca—who had probably sold her soul to Lucifer in exchange for immortality and big-ass teeth—complain about how Nena sat with her legs spread and how Nena walked like a boy and how if she didn't start sitting and walking like una señorita, everybody would think she was a goddamn pata. Or how Nena needed to tame that hair, and if she didn't put a brush through that hair or do something with it, she would take her down to the salon and make her presentable, because no granddaughter of hers was going to walk around looking like una fokin cuero barata. Or how Nena needed to get out of bed and get down to the Publix supermarket on Alton Road, where they needed cashiers, and she'd seen young girls her age working as cashiers already so why couldn't Nena.

Every hour of every day, Blanca complained. She complained about the weather and the price of cable and the phone bill and the pain in her hip and the upstairs neighbors stomping across the floor when they walked from one room to another. She complained about a man walking his dog on her street, as if her street were a public toilet for every Fulano and his mutt. She called down the angels from heaven when anybody left a light on because she was going to go broke with this light bill, and nobody thought about how hard she worked so they could all have lights and food and a roof over their ungrateful heads. The minute she walked through the door, she started narrating her awful day at work, all her demanding clients who only ever wanted *her* to take care of them because all the other stylists were inexperienced and slow and did terrible work, except this new Dominican girl who was always talking talking talking and kept interrupting her to tell stories. How inconsiderate! She would get more clients if she could just shut her damn mouth.

Nena quickly learned to tune her grandmother out as she tramped around the apartment. She wasn't sure how Titi Loli had managed to live with her all these years, or how she and her mother were going to make this work, but she hoped it wouldn't be for much longer.

LATE ONE MORNING, after Blanca had left for work, Nena woke up to the smell of fried amarillos, jamonilla, and eggs. When she looked around, the strange twin bed, the messy room, blinds closed, she couldn't remember where she was. When she saw the TV, it came to her. Loli. Blanca. Miami Beach. She and her mother were in Miami Beach now. She pulled off the covers.

In the kitchen, Loli put a mug of café con leche in her hand. "Careful. It's hot."

Nena blew into her coffee and Loli handed her a plate. At the table, as Nena dipped amarillos in her egg yolks, nothing but silence between them, Loli put an envelope down. On the front, in her mother's sloppy cursive handwriting: *Nenuska*.

"Your mom…She left this for you."

Nena looked at her name on the envelope, then at her aunt. "*Left this?*"

Titi Loli nodded.

Nena wanted to ask one question, just one, but she knew the answer would be inside. She picked up the envelope, tore it open. Money. A few twenties, a couple of fifties, and two one-hundred-dollar bills. More money than Nena had ever held in her hands. And tucked behind the bills, her mother's delicate gold chain with the crucifix. A parting gift. There was also a letter.

Nenuska, hija, mi corazón…

Under the table, she felt Oso's wet nose on her bare foot, sniffing her toes.

"This was always her plan, wasn't it?" Nena asked. "She leaves people behind. That's who she is." She couldn't bring herself to read the letter in front of Loli.

Loli took Nena's hand across the table, squeezed it. "You got me, kid. I got you. Your mom's just dealing with everything back home, and then she'll be back. She wanted you to be safe while she's taking care of things. And to get some rest." Her aunt went on about how they were family and they were going to be okay, and how her mother loved her, and a bunch of other shit that Nena didn't hear, because she was so tired of people lying to her. She was just *tired*.

So that was it. It was early morning and her grandmother was at work and her mother was gone. She was alone. Abandoned. Nena left the envelope on the table and finished her breakfast.

Later, alone in her small bed, while her aunt took Oso for a walk, she would read her mother's letter once, twice, three times.

Nenuska, hija, mi corazón, perdóname.

But she would not find anything in those pages that she didn't already know.

Afterward, she'd take Loli's portable phone, hold it against her chest, fall asleep waiting for her mother's call.

Her mother would be back for her, she would tell herself again and again. But she knew it wasn't true, because that summer, Génesis had taught her the most important lesson Nena would ever learn: One day, you wake up and realize that people move through your life like the seasons, that everything you thought you knew about them, and yourself, was a lie.

ALL SUMMER, TITI LOLI worked days at the Salt Life Surf & Skate shop, selling Rollerblades and surfboard wax, pushing expensive skateboards and surfboards, and hustling T-shirts, three for twenty dollars. She only went to work every other day, and the rest of the week, she and Nena hung around South Beach. Nena loved how large everything seemed, the wide streets and sidewalks, the row of ancient oaks that lined Meridian Avenue, the sand that went on forever until it met the sea. But she especially loved how foreign everything looked, the colorful old buildings in aqua, pastel pink, bright orange, the circular windows and glass blocks. Some buildings looked like spaceships, others like the side of a cruise ship she'd seen once at the Port of San Juan. She also loved that nobody knew her, that she could hide in plain sight, that she could forget her old life in el Caserío. Nobody in Miami would know about her family curse, about her dead father, about Tito, about her mother's abandonment. She could be whoever she wanted.

Titi Loli taught her to Rollerblade, taught her some English, introduced her to people when they walked on Española Way. That was one of Nena's favorite streets, with its palm trees, balconies overlooking the cobblestoned street, and tile roofs that made it look like they were in some European city she'd only read about in geography textbooks. Sometimes South Beach seemed huge, with its different neighborhoods, but other times, it was like a small town where every day you ran into someone you knew. Loli seemed to know everybody on South Beach, and they were always going to the beach or to a friend's house, never to work. Loli, who lived in her bikinis and shorts, was always tan, always trying to get darker. Nena, who had her father's complexion, was always brown. Out on the beach every other day, sitting in the sun or strolling the boardwalk, she got darker, her brown cheeks with a bronze glow, and the tips of her curly hair turning golden.

You're so gorgeous, Loli was always telling her. Nena wasn't sure if she should believe her. Nobody had ever told her she was gorgeous. Nobody had ever commented on her looks, except to tell her she looked like her father or to point out what a tomboy she was. And then there was Blanca, who pursed her lips whenever Loli paid Nena a compliment, was always nitpicking about the way Nena walked, the way she sat, her posture, her hair, the way she smelled. Nena tried to be done with dinner, showered, and in Loli's room by the time Blanca got home around eight thirty, so that they didn't have to interact. She didn't want to hear all her grandmother's complaints, how Miami Beach was overrun with maricones, how there was no safe place for families anymore, now that all the patos were spreading their gay disease. Nena kept her head down, tried not to give her any trouble, even though she wanted to scream every time Blanca opened her mouth. Her job was to stay in school, learn English, and eventually get a job. She hadn't told Loli, but secretly, Nena dreamed of her escape: What if she could get a job when she turned sixteen? What if she could get her own place? What if Nena's days didn't have to depend on Blanca's mood, how angry Blanca was when she got home? Nena didn't know where she could go, or *if* she could go, but she knew her mother would never come back for her, and she had a year to figure things out.

In Miami, she started learning English, spoke with an accent, and all the boys in their neighborhood stopped whatever they were doing when she walked by. "¡Mira mira!" they called out to her, and then they all busted up laughing like they were fucking comedians. "¡Mira mira!" Nena didn't give any of them the time of day—she had no interest in boys, and she would never be interested in men. The truth was, she couldn't see a future where she'd ever be interested in anybody. She tried to erase the memory of Génesis, the smell of her skin after a day riding her bike in the sun, the curve of her clavicle, her wild unibrow, all the things she didn't know she loved until it was too late.

Nena spent most of that summer on the beach with Loli, not saying much when Loli's friends joined them on the boardwalk, skinny women who spent small fortunes on Ocean Drive boutique bikinis only so they could go topless as soon as they hit the sand. Nena tried not to look directly at them once their tops came off. She didn't want them to think anything was weird about her. She preferred when she and Loli could just be alone—she could just be herself then, listening to Loli's stories about fighting with her boyfriend, having sex with her boyfriend, the boyfriend before this current boyfriend. Sometimes Loli even brought Oso along so he could get out of the apartment. Oso loved Nena. He didn't bark much, didn't chase the seagulls or go after any of the millions of stray cats that lived in the dunes. He was always by Nena's side. He was shy, she thought, like her.

And Nena loved the beach. In Puerto Rico, her mother hadn't taken her and Tito to the beach all that much, even though it was a ten-minute drive away. Now Nena tried to do everything Mami had never let her do. Mami might have abandoned her, but Nena had decided to abandon her right back. She'd no longer go by Nena—that had been her mother's nickname for her. Loli preferred Nenu, and so did she. She stopped wearing the clothes Mami had bought—all those cute pink and purple tops that she'd worn when she was fourteen, the colorful shorts, the ballet flats and strappy sandals. She was done with all of that. Instead, she wore Loli's hand-me-downs, cutoff denim shorts, bikini tops, sneakers. She'd buy school clothes with the money her mother left, but for now, while she still had three weeks left of summer, she ignored her mother's phone calls, her letters, and her wishes. She was alone now, grown, and she would wear whatever the fuck she wanted.

Still, sometimes she wore her mother's crucifix, sometimes she caught herself thinking of her mother. Sometimes she could remember the sound of Mami's voice when she said goodbye before leaving for work in the morning. Sometimes, as she walked Oso down to Flamingo Park, or toward the candy store on Española Way, she thought she could feel the soft grip of Mami's phantom hand holding hers.

ONE SATURDAY AFTERNOON, there were so many people on the beach Nena and Loli could barely find a spot on the sand. Nena lugged her backpack and Loli carried their beach towels, walking along the shore until Nena heard a man's voice call Loli's name.

Loli turned back, then smiled wide. "Hi!" She took Nena's hand. "Come on, Nenu."

"Who's that?" Nena asked. A black-haired blue-eyed man with so much chest hair you could make a shag carpet for Oso. He waved them over. Nena sighed but let Loli pull her along.

"You haven't introduced me to your niece yet," he said.

"This is Nenu. Isn't she gorgeous?"

Nena pulled her shorts up, trying to cover her belly button.

"The famous Nenu."

"Fabian lives upstairs with his sister," Loli said.

"Agnes," he said, pointing at his sister, who sat next to him on a colorful striped towel. She was Nena's age, sixteen at most, with the same striking blue eyes as her brother and smooth black hair that hung down her back in thick waves.

She scowled at Nena. "What kind of name is Nenu? Sounds like the alien on that show."

Nena pulled up her shorts again.

Loli threw her head back, laughing. "It's short for Nenuska. She was named after a powerful Russian witch."

Nena glanced sideways at Loli. That was bullshit—her mother had found her name in some beauty magazine. Nenuska was a Puerto Rican model her mother thought was beautiful.

"For real?" Agnes smiled.

"Careful," Fabian said, "she might put a spell on you."

Loli laughed and sat next to Fabian. Agnes moved over so Nena could put her towel down. Loli leaned in close to Fabian, smoking his cigarettes.

"Russians are *white*," Agnes said to Nena.

Nena immediately hated her and her hairy brother, whose back hair was matted with sand.

"Yeah," Nena said, "I guess."

"Where you from, anyway? We're Cuban. Fabian was born there, but I was born here."

"Puerto Rico."

Agnes nodded. "Yeah, I could tell from your accent."

"What accent?" Nena studied the girl's face.

Agnes laughed. "I didn't know they had Black people in Puerto Rico."

Nena raised her eyebrows, forced a smile. She remembered how Mami had said that people in Miami wouldn't be so ignorant, that the kids wouldn't be like the blanquitos out in Palmas del Mar. Nena had tried to believe her mother, even though she'd known better. Her mother was a white woman and didn't really get the shit she and Tito had to put up with every other day. And here was more proof: Whiteness was everywhere, and no matter where she was, it would always be like this.

"They have Black people in Cuba too," Nena said, "in case you didn't know."

Agnes chuckled. "Okay?"

"Do you live with your parents?" Nena asked, changing the subject.

Agnes shook her head and reluctantly started telling the story of how they came to be in Miami. Her parents had left Cuba with her brother. Four years later, Agnes was born. Her mother died three years ago, and a couple months later, her father. It was just the two of them now, Agnes and her brother, Fabian.

"Fabian goes to the University of Miami. He's gonna be a doctor."

Nena was tempted to ask how her parents had died, one after the other, but didn't want to be disrespectful. She knew something about death, about grief, about the things people say because they don't know you, or because they don't care.

"I'm sorry about your parents," Nena said.

"Oh," Agnes said. "Thank you."

"My dad died when I was little." Nena wasn't sure why she said this. She'd been trying to find something they had in common, but she felt stupid for saying it. She tried not to say much more.

"How did he die?" Agnes said.

Nena hesitated. "Um…" She glanced at Loli, but she and Fabian were deep in conversation, not even paying attention to Nena and Agnes. "He was killed."

Agnes's eyes widened. "Whoa. Do you mean, like, murdered?"

Nena took a deep breath. She regretted saying it when she realized that Agnes seemed intrigued.

"Wow," Agnes said. "It must be awful to have a family member *murdered*."

Nena shook her head. She shaded her eyes from the sun. "No, not *murdered*. Killed. There was an altercation. The police were going to arrest him."

"The police!" Agnes put a hand to her mouth.

Nena thought she was being dramatic but couldn't tell if she was being dramatic on purpose or if she was just really surprised. She wanted to change the subject. Why had she brought this up? "It all happened when I was a baby. I don't even remember."

"Okay," Agnes said. "It's probably better that you have no idea what it's like to really lose somebody."

Nena was quiet, pushing the hair away from her face. She watched a couple of surfers in the water riding a wave. She wanted to say something, but she could feel tears starting to sting her eyes, and she did not want to cry in front of this girl. They sat quietly, Agnes rubbing sunscreen into her pale arms, and Nena just watching the waves. She wanted to tell this girl about Tito, to let her know that she did, in fact, know all about losing the most important person in your life, but she didn't know this Agnes. And yet, the longer Nena sat there, pretending to be fine, pretending that this life of walking around South Beach and tanning on the shore and rollerblading on the boardwalk was the only life she knew, the more she felt like she was betraying Tito's memory.

"My uncle died too," Nena confessed. "Recently."

"Oh my God, you poor thing! I'm so sorry! What happened?"

Nena told Agnes about how she came to live in Miami Beach. All about Tito. Agnes listened, placing her hand over Nena's. She shook her head at the worst parts and occasionally interrupted Nena to say things like *I'm so sorry* and *You are so strong* and *That's just so awful*. Nena kept talking, told Agnes about the last time her mother had held her in her arms, how that morning, she'd woken up and found out her mother was gone, her mother's letter, how she claimed she was doing what was best for Nena, but Nena thought she was just giving up. Maybe Mami didn't want to be a mother anymore. Maybe she'd *never* wanted to be a mother. She told Agnes about Humacao, that city next to the ocean where the air smelled of salt and seaweed and the nearby cañaverales and La Central, sugarcane always burning, all the American factories that covered the air with black smoke, dumping their toxic waste outside the poorest neighborhoods, people dying of cancer, el Caserío, the projects, the small cinder block buildings, their balconies overlooking the rows of caña, the stray satos that roamed the streets in packs. The place that had held her all those years, how leaving it had felt like she had also left Tito.

Before Nena realized it, they were lying side by side on their towels, the sun on their backs, hair blowing softly, the wind wafting Titi Loli's cigarette smoke in their faces.

"You didn't leave him," Agnes said. "He's still with you."

Nena realized that this was probably the most honest conversation she'd had in a long time. Maybe the best day she'd had in the past year. With this girl she didn't even know but who also knew something about grief.

But then, when she sat up and wiped the tears from her eyes, Nena looked into Agnes's face and thought she saw a smirk? A smile? She didn't quite trust her, but there was something else there. Nena blocked the sun with her hand and watched her.

Agnes slowly got to her feet. "I'm going in the water." She walked off.

Wait. What had just happened? Agnes just got up and left her sitting there. Nena looked around, but Loli and Fabian were too distracted by each other to notice if anything was off.

As Agnes walked into the ocean, the waves breaking, Nena just watched. She felt a knot in her stomach. Why had she cried in front of some girl she just met? And how could Agnes just roll her eyes, then leave her sitting there wiping tears from her face? She didn't understand—something about Agnes felt strange. Nena closed her eyes, remembering Génesis, how she'd been her best friend one day, and overnight she'd turned against her. How could she have let herself say all of that in front of Agnes, the most private things? Nena had given Agnes the only thing she had left of her family. She thought back over their conversation and slowly realized that this girl had disarmed her, then robbed her. And Nena had given her everything.

"Hey, Nenu? You okay?" Loli said, the wind blowing her hair.

All around them, seagulls and sandpipers picked at the sand.

NENA STARTED SCHOOL at Miami Beach High that fall. It was an open campus—three main wings separated by courtyards, and then the music buildings. The music complex was huge, made up of the auditorium, the marching band and jazz band rooms, the rock ensemble room, and the choir room, plus other music rooms, maybe for private lessons? Musical theater? Music took up at least half the school. Back in her old school, they'd had a single music room, which was also used for storing all the sports equipment. The only instruments they'd had were tambourines and recorders. Walking through the double doors that led to the first wing, Nena was overwhelmed with the urge to call her mother, to tell her all about this music school. How excited she'd be, offering up stories about her father back in the old days, how he'd tried to teach Mami to sing, how he'd written songs for Nena when she was born.

She found the door to the administration office and walked inside.

NENA KEPT HER head down through most of her classes that fall. She didn't talk at all unless the teachers called on her, and then she stumbled through her answers in English. She knew she was smart, though, and she tried to learn at least five new words a day, studying more than what was required by her teachers. She did her homework, then read ahead in her textbooks, turning to the dictionary whenever she didn't understand a word. She took home novels from the library, things the school librarian suggested she read, like *The Great Gatsby* and *Pride and Prejudice*, but they just depressed her. She wanted to learn English, but she took so long to finish these books, and they just didn't feel real to her. She didn't know any people like these—rich folks whose big houses had *names*, who had pianos in their homes for entertainment, who were so caught up in proving that they were rich that they had to throw fancy parties. All their problems seemed superficial. Everybody she knew had real problems: like her mother, working two jobs to make rent, to put food on the table.

After school one day, she stopped by the library and searched the shelves herself, ignoring the librarian's recommendations. It was just a single shelf in the entire library, but there, she found names that spoke to her, names that sounded familiar, like people she might know from around the neighborhood. Esmeralda Santiago and Judith Ortiz Cofer and Julia Alvarez and Sandra María Estevez, women who sounded like they could be her mother's friends, or Titi Loli's, but were writing in English. She pulled one book off the shelf, then another, and another.

She was excellent at algebra—she always had been—because she didn't have to know English to understand it. She memorized the rules and always got A's. But it was in her Chemistry class that she wanted to shine. All her life, Nena had heard about her mother's jobs at the pharmacy and the pharmaceuticals factory. Everything about medicines and pills and mixing liquids seemed like a mystery to her, and she wanted it to make sense. In Ms. Rosado's Chemistry class, at the lab table she shared with Agnes, Nena felt like the smartest girl in the room. Chemistry was all around us, Ms. Rosado said. It was matter and its changes. Chemistry, Nena knew, would be a subject she could use in the real world.

In the Chemistry classroom, as they waited for class to start, Nena tried to be friendly to Agnes, asking questions about Agnes's favorite books, about what TV shows she liked. She'd wanted to practice her English, and she didn't feel like hearing Agnes talk about how much she hated Chemistry, World History, and Algebra. Agnes hated school and homework, anything that required her to read.

"Don't you like *any* books?" Nena asked one day.

Agnes nodded slowly. "I like the Bible."

Nena laughed. "Really? No you don't!"

Agnes just looked at her, deadpan.

"You're not serious!" Nena said, unsure.

Agnes turned back to the board, ignoring her, started copying the notes on the three states of matter: solid, liquid, and gas. *Gas has no definite shape, no definite volume, and particles move in random motion...* Class had started, and Nena hadn't even noticed.

"Sorry," Nena said. "I didn't know you were for real."

Agnes clicked her pen, clicked it again. "Maybe *you* should read the Bible. I don't know if Puerto Ricans believe in God, but you could learn something real."

"What?"

Again, Agnes clicked and clicked her pen.

"I'm Catholic," Nena said. She pulled her mother's crucifix from under her shirt and held it for Agnes to see.

"That doesn't make you Catholic." Agnes clicked her pen one more time, and Nena wanted to stab her in the hand with it. She couldn't understand what she'd done to make Agnes dislike her so much.

"What are the characteristics of plasma?" Ms. Rosado asked from the board.

"I was baptized by a priest," Nena said, a little too loudly. All around them, the other students were starting to listen in.

"That doesn't mean shit if you're a fucking tortillera."

"What?" Nena's hands shook. Nobody had ever called her that. She didn't know what it meant—she'd never even heard that word.

"A dyke," Agnes said to the whole room.

Every other student turned to face them. Nena couldn't stop her hands from shaking. The classroom buzzed around her with whooping and hollering, kids laughing. "Damn," somebody said. "Daaaamn."

Strangers, all of them. They didn't know her. She didn't know them. Except Agnes, who lived upstairs and knew all about her family. But *that*? Nena had never told her *that*.

"You gonna let her talk to you like that?" some kid yelled from the back of the room.

Nena could feel the urge rising, her body aching. She needed the bathroom.

Somewhere in the room, Ms. Rosado told everybody to quiet down, find their seats.

Somewhere, somebody was laughing, but she couldn't tell who.

Somewhere, Ms. Rosado was asking her if she was okay. "Nenuska?"

Nena needed the bathroom, now.

Nena touched her crucifix again, got up from her stool, and made for the door. She threw it open and ran down the hall and into the girls' bathroom and into a stall and pulled down her jeans and pissed. Relieved. Embarrassed. Then angry as hell.

On the wall of the bathroom stall, she read NENU OJEDA EATS PUSSY.

THROUGH THE REST of her school day, fourth and fifth and sixth periods, she imagined how she'd catch Agnes outside, by the flagpole in front of the school. Everyone would be chatting before running off to catch their buses or hitching a ride with friends. They'd all be watching, and none of them would even know her name, since they all just called her Spanish Girl, even though she'd told them she wasn't Spanish, she was Puerto Rican. But after she gave Agnes a Caserío beatdown, everybody would learn her name.

She didn't even get to the flagpole, though. At two thirty, after the bell rang, she found Agnes in the spill-out area where everybody hung out during lunch, and suddenly they were surrounded by girls in baby doll dresses, crushed velvet bodysuits, and Catholic school skirts, basketball jerseys and baggy jeans, a few boys in their football gear who should've been headed for practice, all of them ready to watch a fight.

Agnes had that same smirk on her face, looking her up and down, and it was then that Nena knew.

It was so clear as Agnes checked her out, as she moved closer, threatening, "What you gonna do?"

Nena understood exactly what she was seeing: why Agnes had been so loud, why everything about Nena pissed her off, how the words written on the bathroom wall were not just an accusation but a confession. Agnes knew, because Agnes *knew*.

"I feel sorry for you," Nena said, and she meant it.

"Fucking tortillera. That's why your uncle is dead, 'cause he was a fucking fag."

"Oh damn," another girl said. "Is your uncle dead for real?"

"It runs in the family!" somebody called out, and everybody *ooooohed*.

"That's not cool, Agnes," the first girl said, and then all around them, other girls started weighing in.

"So people should get killed for being gay? She's so wrong for even saying that!"

"Maybe he was hitting on another dude and homeboy didn't like that shit."

"Oh, that's definitely *crossing a line*."

As Nena stood there, numb, and all these people she didn't even know debated about what Tito's life was worth, she *hated* Agnes. Agnes was every single person who had ever done her wrong, every single asshole with an opinion about Tito on the news, every single thing that was wrong with the world.

Nena took the first swing, a powerful open-handed slap that echoed across the field and the parking lot and left Agnes holding her face, her eyes watering, and made all the girls burst into laughter and "Oh shit" and "Damn, girl, you gonna let her do you like that?"

In a split second, Agnes lunged for Nena, and Nena lunged for Agnes, and then they were rolling around in the dirt, throwing hands and pulling out fistfuls of each other's hair, until somebody pulled them apart.

"Dime Por Qué"

EL CASERÍO LOOKED exactly how Maricarmen had left it: The small dilapidated two-story buildings, a complex that hadn't seen fresh paint in decades. A couple of old hoopties parked here and there, an abandoned bike left out in somebody's yard. Women gathered across the street; a kid doing wheelies on his bike; her neighbor Margó on her second-floor balcony, braiding her teenage daughter's hair; the girl sitting on an upside-down milk crate. Maricarmen parked in front of her building and noticed the same pack of satos trouncing the same trash cans and chasing the same stray cat. In her apartment, she took in the too-small living room that opened up to the balcony, the cinder block walls, the old brown sofa, everything adorned in 1970s drab. None of the colorful glitz and glamour of her mother's Miami Beach. It was like she was seeing it all with fresh eyes, all this ugly shit she had inherited from Rey's mother when she died or hand-me-downs she'd collected over the years. But now, she realized, she wanted none of it.

In her bedroom, Maricarmen dropped her backpack, kicked off her shoes, and shut her door. She used to hate closed doors. She'd wanted to know what Nena and Tito were doing at all times, that they were happy, that they were safe. But in this new life—the neighbors talking, los camarones harassing them, the reporters always shoving their cameras in her face, Tito's pictures out there for everyone to scrutinize—the world was loud, hard, and she wanted to shut it all out.

She stood in front of her mirror, peeled off her sweaty clothes and dropped them on the floor too. She watched her own reflection for a while, like she was seeing some other woman standing there, her eyes red-rimmed, black mascara running. She'd looked like this when her mother kicked her out, when Rey died. Tired, *exhausted*. Only she was older now. How she'd tried to pretend she was fine, for Nena. All these years, she'd tried to make sure Nena and Tito had everything.

She hit the light switch, and the ceiling fan blew spirals in her bedroom. Her hair was greasy with sweat. She picked up the jar of Pond's Cold Cream she always kept on her dresser, turned the lid slowly. She didn't take her eyes off her own reflection. If she looked away, even for a moment, she might disappear.

Who would she be now, without her daughter? She dipped her fingers into the jar, slathered cream on her face, rubbed it in. She dipped her fingers again, slathering some more, then picked a tissue from the box on the dresser, wiped off her eyes, her lips, her cheeks, kept wiping until her face was clean. She was thirty-four years old, but she felt so much older.

Maricarmen picked up the telephone on her side table and dialed her sister in Miami.

"How's Nena?"

"She's in bed. Hasn't said much."

"Did she read my letter?"

"Give her a day or two."

"Will you ask her to come to the phone?"

Loli cleared her throat. "I'll get her."

Maricarmen had thought the letter was a good idea, a way to make sure she said every single thing Nena needed to hear in order to understand.

Loli got back on the phone. "She's asleep, Mari."

"She's asleep? In the middle of the afternoon?"

"Why don't you try back tomorrow?"

Maricarmen twisted the telephone cord with one hand. "Tell her I love her?"

"She knows. I will, but she knows."

Maricarmen hung up.

That night, she told herself, she would write another letter. No excuses, just the truth. She wanted to keep Nena safe while she took care of things at home. She hoped that Nena would one day forgive her. Maricarmen had never forgiven her own mother for putting her out on the street. Sometimes she wondered if she would've stayed with Rey if she'd had another place to go. Truth was, maybe they wouldn't have stayed together. Maybe they wouldn't have had Nena.

EACH DAY AFTER that, Maricarmen called and called, but Nena refused to talk to her. Each time she hung up the phone, she walked over to her dresser, where she kept her stash of pills, picked up a bottle, swallowed an Ativan. For days, she took pills. She'd started with one that would put her to sleep. Eventually, she woke up and took another one. After a while, she was on a two-hour schedule, taking one pill every two hours, until she fell asleep. She didn't need to be sober—Nena was in Miami.

She didn't get the door when Evelyn came knocking around lunchtime on a Saturday. They hadn't talked since she left for Miami. Maricarmen had wanted to call, but she didn't want to hear all about the factory floor, how Evelyn was getting too old to be dealing with so much work, so many hours, while they were understaffed and underpaid. She didn't want to hear how she should go to Obrero, ask for her job back.

"He'll let you come back, Mari," Evelyn had told her last time they talked on the phone, the night before the trip to Miami. "He said so himself."

No. Maricarmen was done with all of that. She'd been working herself to death since she was a girl, and now she was tired. All she wanted was rest. She hadn't even made it to her job at the pharmacy. She didn't bother getting up for her shift, just called them, told them she was sick, popped two pills, and went back to sleep.

That Saturday, she waited for Evelyn to leave, then opened the door to find a loaf tin on her front step. It was Evelyn's pastelón, leftovers from the night before. She picked it up and pulled her door shut behind her, then headed toward Carmelo's place.

At Carmelo's, she handed him the pastelón and made her way to the kitchen. He was in the middle of pulling on a T-shirt, but he took it anyway.

"Your mother brought it over," she said.

"When did you get back?" He set the loaf tin on the kitchen counter and pulled down his shirt.

Maricarmen opened his fridge. "Got anything to drink?"

He pulled two glasses from a cupboard, then the bottle of rum he always kept on top of the refrigerator. Maricarmen got an ice cube tray from the freezer and filled the glasses.

"How's Nena?" He topped off the glasses with soda.

Maricarmen opened the cupboard where he kept all his pills. "She won't talk to me." She pulled bottles off the shelf and read the labels. She wasn't sure what she was looking for—just something strong. When she found the Percocet, she opened it, popped one in her mouth.

Carmelo took a sip of his drink. She handed him a Percocet.

They ate cold pastelón in front of the TV, the sweet plantains and beef congealed together, licked their fingers while they laughed at Walter Mercado. They stared at the screen in a stupor when the reruns of last week's *Siempre en Domingo* started, watching Daniela Romo dancing across the stage, her long long hair swaying from side to side, watching Juan Gabriel singing his heart out, his dark eye shadow and eyeliner stunning, his cheeks glossy. Eventually, Carmelo went to the bedroom for his kit.

She woke up on Carmelo's couch a day later when she heard church bells. Or she thought she heard bells. Maybe she'd been dreaming. The TV was still on, but the room was bright with daylight. Her mouth tasted like dirt. She was alone in the living room, and she guessed Carmelo had left her there when he went to bed. Had she heard bells? Her ears were ringing, but she couldn't be sure. She couldn't even remember most of the night before.

She got up, turned off the TV, looked around for her empty glass. And then she heard them again, loud, like they were ringing right outside el Caserío. Church bells. She hadn't been dreaming. She waited for the bells to stop, left behind her glass, Evelyn's greasy loaf tin, and headed home.

SHE PULLED UP to the Osborne Pharma parking lot at around noon the next day, much later than the start of her regular morning shift. She wore a T-shirt and jeans, her safety shoes, her hair loose, no makeup. She had showered, she was clean, but not her usual put-together self. She wasn't ready to return to the factory—she wasn't sure she ever would be. But she would walk in there, swallow her pride, ask for her job back. She wasn't sure how long Colón's investigation would take, how long it would be before she could sell the car, get rid of the furniture, pack whatever she had left, and go. Get back to her daughter.

When she walked into Obrero's office, he was just getting off the phone, putting the receiver down. Evelyn had let her into the factory, swiped her ID and walked her past the factory floor and into the corridor, patted her shoulder, said, "You'll be fine, don't worry."

Obrero's mustache was overgrown and bushy, his eyebrows thick. He leaned back in his chair when he saw her, pleased with himself.

"Evelyn said you'd be coming in."

"You have a couple minutes?" Maricarmen sat in the old plastic chair in front of him. Suddenly, she felt naked without her full face of makeup, her perfume. Here she was, sitting in front of this boorish, unpleasant man, and she felt like a child. An ugly, sad child.

"You look...different."

Maricarmen bit the inside of her cheek. "Evelyn said you need all the help you can get. I'd like to come back, if you'll let me."

"You do something different with your hair?" He reached into his desk drawer, pulled out an ID card. "Oh yeah. You definitely look different." He held it up and looked from the small picture on the ID to her face, back to the ID.

He'd fired her several weeks ago. Why did he still have her ID in his desk? Had he always expected her to come crawling back? She bit the inside of her cheek.

"We need the help, and you need the work." He tossed the ID across the desk. "What we definitely don't need is your kid running around all over the factory floor."

She picked it up, checked out her small face. "No problem."

"I mean it, Maricarmen."

"My kid is in Miami. She lives with my sister now."

He smiled. "You can start today, then?"

She nodded.

"Good."

NENA HADN'T SLEPT well since she'd arrived in Miami Beach. It wasn't as hot as Humacao, but at night, she tossed on her twin mattress, sweating through the sheets. Mornings, she pulled the top sheet back to air it all out, so her grandmother wouldn't find yet another thing to complain about. Since everything about Nena offended Blanca, from her posture to the way her hair smelled, even though she now washed her hair every day—something she never did back home.

That morning, after Nena got out of the shower, Blanca found a curly hair. Pacing all over the apartment, Blanca demanded that Nena scrub the shower before leaving for school. Before Nena could get into the bathroom with a scrub brush, Blanca doused the shower with bleach.

"What kind of woman," Blanca said to the whole apartment while Nena scrubbed, "leaves her pubic hair for others to clean up? Disgusting!"

Nena kept her mouth shut, refusing to cry in front of Blanca. She would not give her the satisfaction. Later, as she walked to school, lightheaded from the bleach, headphones over her ears, La Lupe's "La Tirana" the soundtrack to her morning walk, a single tear ran down her face.

After the fight with Agnes, when Nena came home with the official notice of her three-day suspension for fighting, her grandmother had assumed it was all Nena's fault. She'd dissed Nena's attitude, her smart mouth, the way she walked into every room like she owned it, touching things that didn't belong to her. The way Nena tossed her limbs around when she spoke, waving her hands in people's faces. And always, *always*, the way Nena sat with her legs open, like un macho. How did she expect people to treat her, Blanca asked, when everything about her said that she was una callejera?

Nena didn't throw her hands around. She didn't have a smart mouth—if anything, she kept most of her thoughts to herself so she wouldn't set Blanca off. At school, Nena was polite. She spoke softly, too softly sometimes, so that when teachers called on her, they asked her to speak up, her classmates whispering and giggling behind her. Nena didn't have friends, but she didn't need them. She wasn't planning on sticking around for long.

And she still hadn't taken any of Mami's calls, wouldn't until Mami came back to get her. Her mother had left her alone in the world, to live with a woman who despised her, who made her feel like everything about her was repulsive. Titi Loli tried to make her feel welcome, but she'd never feel welcome in Blanca's place, and when Blanca was going off on Nena, where the fuck was Loli? Loli was in her room, watching TV, pretending she couldn't hear any of it. Nena would never forgive Mami.

Nena would lie in bed, imagining where she could run away to. During her walks home from school, on the avenues she passed on the way back to Blanca's, Collins, Washington, Española Way, Pennsylvania, Euclid, she imagined the inside of all those apartment buildings, those small boutique hotels and hostels. She could run away. She didn't know where she would go, or how she would live once she got there, but one day, she would find a way. She always walked by the youth hostel, the Clay Hotel, on the corner of Washington Avenue and Española Way. One afternoon, she saw a girl she recognized from school sitting at the front desk. She didn't know her name, but she knew she was also Black and Latina, a cute thick girl she'd always noticed in the halls. Nena stopped, stared. She wanted to ask how she ended up a front desk attendant. Did she need experience? A work permit? An ID? She probably needed one, Nena thought. She made a mental note to get herself some sort of ID that wasn't just her high school card for the bus.

Back at home, in the yellow pages her grandmother kept on the kitchen counter, she found the address for the closest driver's license office. From the top drawer of Loli's dresser, she snatched the manila envelope that Mami had left with her. Inside, she found all the documents her mother had used to enroll her in school. The next afternoon, she took the S bus to the DMV in North Miami Beach with her social security card, birth certificate, vaccination records, and report card in hand—more paperwork than anybody would ask for.

The day after that, she walked right into the Clay Hotel, found the girl from school at the front desk.

"Can I help you?" Her name tag said CLAUDIA. Her black hair was pulled into a tight bun, and her dimpled cheeks were covered in creamy foundation, her brown lipstick freshly applied. She looked more made up than she ever had at school. Up close, Nena noticed that she was younger than she looked from a distance.

Nena smiled her most professional smile. "Hi. I'm wondering if you're hiring?" Nena wasn't sure if she sounded professional, but she didn't sound like some kid. Maybe she sounded adult enough.

"I don't think so." Her hoop earrings looked like they were real gold. Her perfume smelled expensive. Probably her mother's. "Do you go to Beach High?"

"Yeah," Nena said.

"I'm not sure if we need anybody. I can ask the manager, but he's at our other property." Claudia looked her up and down. "How old are you?"

"Fifteen."

"Fifteen is good, but you can only work a few hours a week. Once you turn sixteen, you can work forty. And you need to be eighteen to work past ten p.m."

Nena nodded, not sure what to say.

"Why don't you fill this out and bring it back?" Claudia put a form on the counter. APPLICATION FOR EMPLOYMENT.

"Thank you." Nena took the application and slid it into a folder in her backpack, feeling the most adult she'd ever felt in her life. Outside the Clay Hotel, her chest expanded, her smile widened. This is what Nena needed to do. She needed to ask for things, walk right into a place, ask for a job. Or at least a job application. She needed to become the kind of person who got shit done. That was who her mother had been all her life—she got shit done. And even though Nena was mad as hell at Mami for leaving her, she realized that if her mother couldn't be that person for her anymore, Nena needed to be that person for herself.

After that day, every single afternoon after school, Nena stopped at all the businesses between Miami Beach High and home—restaurants, shoe stores, boutiques, thrift shops, hotels, sandwich shops, supermarkets, pharmacies, the dollar store, even the pet shop—and asked for job applications. Even if they said they weren't hiring, she'd ask for an application, take it home. She filled them all out and dropped them off. Then she waited by the phone for someone to call and offer her a job.

AT SCHOOL MOST days, Nena sat quietly in all her classes, taking notes, her shoulders slumped. At lunch, she sat alone outside the library, eating her sandwich on a bench, watching the other students walk by, sit together on the picnic tables, the sun beaming down on them. She loved sitting outside alone instead of eating in the cafeteria with the other losers, all the other kids with no friends. Most of the popular girls drove off campus, headed to Taco Bell or

Burger King, but Nena didn't have friends, let alone a friend with a car, and she definitely didn't have money for fast food. She just sat there silently, letting the lunch hour pass, ignoring the world and all its noise. She'd been at this school almost an entire school year, but still, every person here was a stranger. There was no one in this school who knew her. If she died tomorrow, who would even care? Who would even *know*?

One afternoon as she pulled a can of warm Coca-Cola from her backpack and took a long sip, she noticed Agnes, walking across the courtyard toward the picnic tables. Agnes rolled her eyes at her, then sat down with a group of girls. If Nena died tomorrow, Agnes would notice. Agnes definitely wouldn't care, but she would use the opportunity to talk shit about Nena. If Nena flung the half-empty can of Coca-Cola, would it make it all the way across the courtyard, hit Agnes in the back of the head? That would be hella satisfying.

When the bell rang for fifth period, Nena got up first, headed to the locker room to change for PE before Agnes. Nena tried to avoid her most days, but Agnes, who was always with her friends, enjoyed talking shit about Nena, giving her dirty looks across the field, laughing loudly when Nena missed a three-point shot on the basketball court, which was always. It seemed like Agnes spent more time watching Nena, talking about Nena, laughing at Nena, than she did doing anything else.

Nena's class was already running laps around the soccer field when Agnes and her friends started their jog. There were two classes in the mix around the crowded field, so Nena decided to put as much distance between them as she could. She picked up the pace, passing one student, then another, and another. There was no way Agnes would catch up. Nena had gotten used to walking everywhere, jogging, being on the move. She made her way around the field until she passed the edge of the volleyball courts where she'd begun, and started her second lap. She glanced back over her shoulder, looking for Agnes and her friends, but couldn't make them out. The field was too large and too crowded. Nena kept running.

Suddenly, she saw them in front of her, Agnes and three of her friends, jogging slowly. Nena slowed down so she wouldn't pass them, tried to stay behind, but they slowed and then just walked. Nena hesitated for a second, then felt some of the guys behind her catching up. They went around her, passing her. She followed the guys and kept their pace for a few yards, until she passed Agnes and her friends. Then she picked up the pace, running fast, faster, zooming past all of them, trying to put another lap between them, a whole field between them. She'd put a whole city between them if she could.

Nena walked off the field and headed toward the water fountain. She drank, let the cold water run over her face, the sun against her back. She straightened herself, stretching her arms out in front of her, then noticed Agnes and her friends walking off the field too. There was no way they'd finished the required four laps—Nena had passed them twice. But there they were, all of them talking loudly, a show for the whole group.

"How did she get so fast?" one of them asked.

Agnes laughed. "It's 'cause she's half man."

"Yeah, she does look like a dyke, doesn't she?"

"I thought that was just a rumor?" another one asked.

"Rumor?" Agnes said. "Look at her. She walks like un macho, talks like un macho, and runs like un macho."

Nena considered what would happen if she just went right up to them, right up to Agnes. What if she punched her in the face? Would she get suspended again? Would they just kick her out of school? Did she even *need* a high school diploma? Her mother didn't have one.

Nena stood up straight. She had nothing left to lose. She had no one. She hated this school, these people. She put one hand on her hip, stared at the girls, daring them to say one more thing. One more.

Agnes glared at her, but the other girls stopped talking. One of them looked down at the ground, at her own sneakers. Another watched Nena nervously, then pretended to look at something behind her. She couldn't meet Nena's eyes.

Nena pulled at her scrunchie and undid her messy ponytail, slowly, not taking her eyes off the girls. She neatly picked it up again, smoothing the sides, the hair on top of her head, the hair at her nape, until she had a neat low ponytail. She tied off the scrunchie, then twisted her curls into a bun and tucked the hair. Once it was tight, she cracked her knuckles, all show. If Nena was gonna get in trouble, she might as well do it right.

Another time, another place, another girl, she might have been nervous. She might have been afraid. But this was the right time, the right place, the right girl, and she had nothing left to be afraid of. She didn't feel anything anymore. She waited until Agnes realized what was coming, until her face registered that she knew Nena was coming for her. And then, satisfied, Nena sprang.

They rolled around on the grass, all of it unfolding as if in slow motion, four girls all over Nena, on top of her, underneath her, and Agnes's hair wrapped tightly in Nena's fist. Agnes trying to open Nena's fist to free her ponytail, then Agnes's friend trying to grab Nena's hands. The more they pulled at her fist, the more she pulled on the ponytail, the more Agnes yelled.

"Let me go, you fucking bitch!"

Nena would not let it go.

Someone kicked the back of her leg.

She pulled harder.

Agnes screamed.

Suddenly, the other girls got off of her, scattered.

They were surrounded by the coaches and school security. One of them grabbed Nena by the shoulders, another pulled her forearms up, up, trying to lift her entire body. She would not release Agnes's hair.

"Let go of her, *now!*" Nena didn't recognize the man's voice. He was a stranger. Everybody in this school, in this city, was a stranger, but they all thought they knew who she was.

Agnes pulled at Nena's T-shirt collar, slapped at Nena's chest, her neck, but got the security guard instead, slapped him once, twice, three times.

He flinched, then straightened himself, put his face in Nena's face. "You will let go of her right now, or I will slam you facedown right here, you hear me?"

And then, Nena let go.

The other girls were laughing now, taking in the show. Her entire PE class, all of fifth period was out on that field, watching as the security guard gripped her upper arm and led her toward the front of the school.

Nena could see everything clearly then, all that she was to these girls, all that she'd ever be in this school, in this city. She could see the way they were exactly like her grandmother, how they believed they knew the truth about who she was, what she was, even though she had never spoken the truth for herself. She could see what her life would become, if she let it. She would be nothing more than the story these girls had made up.

The security guard led her away, walked her past the basketball courts, pulling a walkie-talkie from his belt, past the entrance to the east wing. He was about to speak into the walkie when a group of kids ran into him.

"Get back to class!" he ordered.

He pulled Nena along, past the auditorium, past the orchestra room and the rock ensemble room, toward the principal's office. He opened the door, shoved her inside.

"Sit!" He pointed at the three seats in front of the check-in desk. She sat.

The security guard left without another look at her.

"Bye!" she said as the door closed behind him, surprising herself.

She meant it. She did not intend to see him again. She tried to adjust her PE uniform's top. Her gray shorts were covered in dirt and grass stains, her white T-shirt was filthy, the collar stretched out, a rip in one armpit.

She sat outside the principal's office for five minutes, ten minutes, fifteen. She waited and she waited. When the bell rang, the noise filling the hallway outside, she slipped through the door quietly, joined the chaos in the hallway, and slid between all those sweaty, loud boys, all the girls in their baby doll dresses and too much hair gel, back to the locker room.

In front of the mirror, Nena washed her face with hand soap. She slicked her hair back into its ponytail, tucking loose strands, smoothing them out. She peeled off her T-shirt and washed her armpits in the sink, then changed into her jeans and a tank top, tossed her PE clothes into the trash, strapped her backpack on one shoulder, and walked out of the locker room and out of the school. She kept walking, past the east wing, past the flagpole, past the parking lot, until she was crossing the street. She kept walking until she was at the bus stop four blocks away, and hopped on the S to South Beach.

SHE GOT OFF on Washington and Fifth, then made a right, headed toward Alton. She hadn't come this far south when applying for jobs, so she had a lot of ground to cover. She stopped at the ice cream place, at the surf shop, at the medical supply warehouse, the flower shop,

Burger King, Dunkin Donuts, Tap Tap Haitian Restaurant. She collected applications, slipped them into the folder in her backpack, and went on to the next place. When she got to the Eckerd Pharmacy on Fifth and Jefferson, she saw the sign on the sliding glass door, NOW HIRING, and headed inside.

This store was brand new, not like the pharmacy where Mami worked in Humacao. The floors were white and polished, *gleaming*. The shelves were almost empty, plastic merchandise tubs stacked in front of them, ready to be unloaded. She wasn't nervous. She had just walked out of school after a fight with four girls—the best decision she'd ever made. She was ready to take charge of her own life. She was excited, breathless.

She made her way to the back of the store, toward the pharmacy.

The pharmacy technician, a slim, effeminate Black boy wearing lip gloss and mascara, a pristine white pharmacy smock, stood there looking at her, expressionless.

She smiled. "Hello."

"Aren't you *a vision*?" he said sarcastically. He looked her up and down.

"The sign up front says you're hiring?"

"Rob!" he called over his shoulder, then turned back to Nena. "Talk to Rob. He's the pharmacy manager."

Rob was a very round white man, with perfectly arched eyebrows, thin from tweezing or waxing. "Hi there." He put his hands in his lab coat's front pockets.

"I'm Nenuska. Nice to meet you, Rob. I'd like to apply for the job? I can start right away."

Rob smiled. "Let me get you an application." He reached into a drawer beneath the register, pulled out a slim booklet. "Do you have time to fill it out now?"

Nena perked up. "Yeah."

He tore off a sheet and handed it to her. "Do you have pharmacy experience?"

"No," she said. She noticed Rob's mouth start to turn downward, and immediately filled the silence. "But I can learn."

"Are you in school?" he asked, checking out her backpack.

"I'm finishing high school. But I want to study pharmacy. I mean, I can start as a technician, but I'm going to be a pharmacist. My mom's a pharmacy tech at Walgreens in Puerto Rico." She realized she'd said way more than she intended to. Behind Rob, the technician was opening up boxes.

But Rob's face had lit up. "You're Puerto Rican?"

She nodded. "From Humacao."

"I'm from San Juan."

She smiled, studied his face. He looked like a gringo. She wanted to say he didn't look Puerto Rican, but that would've been a lie. She knew white Puerto Ricans with blond hair and blue eyes, she knew chinos boricuas, árabes puertorriqueños. And of course, Black Puerto Ricans—her own family was a mix.

"How old are you?" he asked.

"Fifteen."

He nodded. "Have you ever had a job before?"

Nena frowned. "No."

"When do you turn sixteen?" he asked.

"In May."

He smiled. "Okay. We can start you off as a cashier, but you have to be sixteen to be a technician."

"I can learn," Nena insisted. "I'm a fast learner. And I'm bilingual."

Rob smiled again.

Nena took her time, making sure her handwriting was neat as she filled out her name, her birth date, all the information about her school. She wrote in Loli's address but left the phone number blank. She didn't want them calling, just in case Blanca answered the phone. Once she was finished, she handed the application over.

Rob read everything over, then stopped, looked up. "No phone number?"

"Not yet," she said, which was the only thing she could think of.

He kept reading. "Can you come in tomorrow at three thirty? Bring your social, ID, birth certificate. We'll have you fill out some paperwork, and you can start training."

Her eyes widened. That was it? "I'll be here," she said.

"See you tomorrow, then."

Behind him, the pharmacy technician was stocking the shelves. She nodded. "Thank you!"

BLANCA WAS STILL at work. Loli was in the shower, getting ready for her shift at the Surf & Skate shop.

Nena hustled it to Blanca's bedroom, backpack still on, opened the door, peeked inside. She moved fast, flipping light switches, opening drawers, running her fingers through Blanca's clothes, her perfumes, searching. Then she found it: the envelope with the rent money. She counted out $400 in twenties, put the rest back in the envelope. She wasn't sure exactly how much Blanca needed to pay the rent but hoped she'd left her enough. She closed the drawer shut and then slid the cash into her back pocket. In the old Royal Dansk Danish Butter Cookies tin on the dresser, filled with Blanca's sewing kit, random buttons, sewing scissors, and ribbons, she found the paper bag where Blanca kept her quarters for the laundry.

"Get it, bitch," she said to herself, dancing a little. For all those times Blanca called her machúa, told her that she was a burden on her mother, for all these months of Blanca telling her to sit up straight, close her legs. All those years she'd never sent a birthday card, never called or wrote, pretended Nena didn't even exist. And for this morning. She couldn't believe her mother had abandoned her in this woman's house. Fuck them both.

Nena switched the light back off, closed the door behind her.

She could still hear the shower.

She ran into Loli's room, moving faster. Loli's wallet on the dresser. One credit card, a Visa. And about sixty dollars cash. But then she quickly changed her mind—she couldn't take Titi Loli's money, or her card. Instead, she pulled her own duffel bag from under the bed, threw all her clothes in there. On the dresser, she found her deodorant, her Right On Curl conditioner and gel, all her other hair accessories, and tossed them in the duffel bag too. She left behind whatever was in the bathroom with Loli, threw the strap over her shoulder, hustled down the front steps toward the back alley, not looking back. She picked up the pace. What if Blanca got off work early? She turned left.

She took alleys toward Española Way, five blocks, six, seven, turned right, kept walking. On the corner of Española and Pennsylvania, she stopped to catch her breath. And then she hoofed it all the way to the youth hostel. She wasn't sure what she was doing, but she was happy for the first time in months.

In the dark lobby of the Clay Hotel, Nena walked past the girls in bikini tops and shorts, past a bone-thin tecato who smelled like dirty laundry and malt liquor, and found Claudia smiling at the front desk.

Claudia gave her the rundown: The Clay Hotel was a sanctuary for young surfer boys who slept rough and spent all their money on weed and Taco Bell and then needed a place to crash before heading back to wherever they came from. For spring breakers who'd pooled their money together for a single room and a shared bathroom in the hallway, a few blocks from the beach. It was a no-tell motel, and a haven for teen runaways, and a weekly rental for single-parent families.

On the strip, there was a liquor store, a dollar store, a French café, a candy store, and a bunch of other hostels and weekly rentals. But the Clay Hotel on the corner was the one, overlooking both Española's cobblestoned street and Washington's high traffic, right across the street from the Cameo Theater. And, Claudia said, if you walked one block toward Collins, you were at the Warsaw Ballroom, where you'd find drag queens and gay club kids under disco lights seven nights a week.

Most of the people who worked there also lived there for discounted rent, except Claudia, who still lived at home. The Clay had it all: a bar, with a tiny kitchen that served up burgers and fries, and the bartender who gave Claudia unlimited free sodas; an old cigarette vending machine where Nena could buy a pack of Marlboro Lights like a grown woman; a jukebox that took quarters. And of course, Claudia, who offered up smiles willingly.

That first night, after Nena paid for the week and checked into her small room, she dropped her duffel bag on the carpet and collapsed on the bed. She closed her eyes. Tomorrow morning she'd start a new job, a new life. She opened her eyes, stared at the popcorn ceiling. She was on her own, in a huge city, in a strange room. She missed Tito. She was furious at Mami, but she missed her fiercely. And although she hated to admit it, she missed Génesis too.

Nena sat up in the bed, saw her own reflection in the mirror, her disheveled hair, her greasy face. No roots, untethered. She was running, but a strong wind could carry her away. It hit her then: She was fifteen years old and she was all alone in the world. She had never, in her entire life, been so alone.

In the privacy of her room at the Clay Hotel, a short walk from her grandmother's neighborhood but so far from home, from her mother, from anyone who really knew her, Nena cried.

"El Gran Varón"

EVERY AFTERNOON, NENA trained alongside Jay and two other cashiers. She had to learn how to work the register, how to count out the customers' change when they paid in cash. She had to remember to get them to sign the credit card slips when they paid with cards. Once she finished the cashier training, Rob started teaching her the computer systems, how to process insurance claims and prepare medications for the pharmacists' approval. Nena took her job seriously. She counted and bagged on the prescription counter, while Jay and the other techs worked at the pickup window. She printed labels for bottles of medication, organized and cleaned the refrigerator, kept the prescription bins in order, kept the shelves neatly stocked, processed orders using the inventory scanner, sanitized the sink for prep and cleaning. Eventually, Rob said, she would learn how to mix compounded medications.

Nena and Jay opened large bottles, spread pills on a counting tray, and used a wooden-handled spatula to count pills by five. Nena loved the ritual of counting out the medications that would heal their patients, even though everyone else called them "customers." She loved learning which drugs were controlled and kept in a locked cabinet, learning the names of the pharmacy regulars, who came on the first of the month, every month, like clockwork. She learned their nicknames, their partners' names. She read everything she could about prescription drugs—what they were for, which drugs were covered and not covered by which insurance, the brand names and their generic equivalents, which medications were usually dispensed together. Motrin (which they called Vitamin M) and ibuprofen, the more popular generic version. Tylenol with codeine. Antibiotics like penicillin and amoxicillin. Pepcid, Prilosec, and Zantac, for GERD. Zovirax and Valtrex for herpes. Xanax, Ativan, and Valium. Premarin hormone replacement therapy for menopause. Generic prenatal vitamins with folic acid for pregnant women. Whenever Nena reached for prenatal vitamins or contraceptive pills, she thought of Mami. Mami going off to work each morning, to the factory and then the pharmacy. Mami coming home in the evening, throwing some dinner together. How she'd admired Mami in those days.

Jay taught her everything she needed to know about South Beach. Since arriving from Atlanta two years before, he'd become himself there, had started dating men for the first time. South Beach, Nena came to learn, was full of gay men and lesbians, and most of them had moved there from somewhere else, had met their partners once they arrived. Almost everyone who worked inside the pharmacy, from Rob down to the cashiers, was gay.

They'd come looking for community, Jay told her. "South Beach is just a big ol' gay city."

He told her everything: about people in the photo lab, made predictions about which one of the women would get pregnant in the next year, which one of the stockboys would try to get with the fine-ass girl who worked in cosmetics. Together, Nena and Jay guessed which of the three full-time pharmacy cashiers was gay (all of them) and which of the photo techs up front was gay (none). And when he was in the restroom or the break room, they talked about Rob.

"He lives in my building," Jay told her as they restocked the shelves. "We met in the laundry room."

"So he got you this job?" Nena placed a box of Z-Paks next to a bottle of Zithromax.

"Told me to apply, and here I am." Jay reached up and put a large bottle on the top shelf, lined it up neatly next to the other bottles. "He drove me to Lindsey Hopkins to take my GED test so I could get my high school diploma. He's cool, and so is his partner, José. He's a chef. Makes a mean arroz con pollo."

"GED? You mean you can just take a test?"

"Girl, yes. You gotta study, though. It's every subject. Mathematics, reading, writing, science, all of it. It's like four years of high school in a single test."

"How long did you study?"

"By the time I met Rob, I'd been studying, like, five months. Then I took another couple weeks."

"Damn," Nena said, considering it. "You're fucking smart if you can do all of high school just like that."

"That shit was easy. I got a book with all the subjects. You just study the book." Jay winked at her. "As soon as the diploma comes, I'ma go down to Miami-Dade Community College and start taking classes."

Jay finished restocking and went back to the computer to enter insurance information for refills. He was always on task, always working, even when he was having a conversation. Nena admired his work ethic, but also the way he worked—he moved with a dancer's grace, and he was so clean. He always, always, washed his hands at the sink after handling cash. He sanitized his hands often. And he always left spaces cleaner than he'd found them. Nena imagined his apartment was probably spotless.

"Where do I get one of those books?" Nena called to Jay from her shelf.

"You can have mine. I don't need it anymore."

"Really? How much?"

"Girl, please. I'll bring it tomorrow."

Nena smiled, giving Jay a look that said she appreciated him.

At the counter, Rob was labeling a bottle when the phone rang. He snatched up the receiver, then spoke into the phone for a couple of minutes. After a while, he called out to Nena and Jay, "You all feel like arroz con pollo for lunch?"

Jay threw his head back with laughter. "Yes I do!"

"I haven't had arroz con pollo in *forever*!" Nena said.

"All right. I got you." Rob whispered into the phone, then waited on the line.

"Thank the Lord!" Jay said.

When the food arrived, Rob, Jay, and Nena sat on the pharmacy's carpeted floor, behind one of the shelves, eating arroz con pollo from Larios, where José was the chef. Nena scooped hers up with a spoon and shoveled it into her mouth, like it was her last meal. She'd been living on cereal since she left Blanca and Titi Loli's, microwaving Hot Pockets in the break room during her breaks. She chewed on a Spanish olive, licked her fingers.

"Told you it was good," Jay said.

"Thank you," she said to Rob.

Sitting on the floor with Rob and Jay, she thought of Mami. She couldn't remember the last time she'd had her mother's cooking, but she remembered the last time her mother made her arroz con pollo, how they'd turned on the radio while Nena washed dishes, how Mami danced around the kitchen as she cleared the mess. Now Nena couldn't remember how long her mother had been gone. It was months, but Nena had stopped counting. Almost May now, almost her birthday, and then it would be summer, and then fall, and then winter, and her mother would still be gone. There was a space there, between Jay and Rob and Nena, an emptiness, a moment of silence. She wanted to tell them how grateful she was for their kindness. How nobody had been kind to her in a really long time.

Sometimes she didn't know what the hell she was doing, what the future looked like, if she even had a future. Tito often came to her in those moments when she felt most alone, when she could not see how she'd make it. But then she remembered she had this place, a job, and that was something. She had Rob and Jay, and maybe someday they'd be friends for real.

She wasn't sure if she believed that—she'd been through too much to trust anyone completely. She could not rely on anybody to take care of her.

She chewed some chicken. Maybe she'd have a real kitchen someday, and she could make her own arroz con pollo.

"I'm gonna do it," she said to them after a while. "I'm gonna get that diploma and start taking classes at Miami-Dade. And then, I'm going to be a pharmacist."

THAT SPRING, NENA studied hard, took the practice tests in English, and studied some more. She studied in the break room, while the guys from the stockroom chatted about their cars. Jay quizzed her on slow nights at the pharmacy. After work, on the bus back to the Clay Hotel, she read her GED prep book. She thought she might be ready, but she wanted to be sure. The test only cost twenty dollars, but she didn't want to have to retake it. She couldn't waste a single dollar—her paychecks went to her weekly rent, food, toiletries, and bus fare. And she needed to save enough to move into a real apartment someday.

As the months went by, Nena never missed a day of work, even if she wasn't feeling well. Sometimes, after work, she and Jay went to a movie or got dinner at Puerto Sagua, a few blocks away. She went on with her life, trying to live as normally as she could, missing her mom, and always keeping an eye out for Blanca and Loli. At first, Nena had thought they would call the cops on her, that they would find her. Maybe they *had* called. Now she thought maybe Blanca was so happy to be rid of her, they hadn't even bothered. She wondered if her mother knew that she'd left Blanca's house.

One afternoon, when they got a big order of AZT, Rob told them they all needed to make sure their count was perfect.

"We need to keep a close eye on the inventory," Rob told Nena and Jay. "We're one of the only pharmacies in South Beach that has it in stock."

"But it's like a bestseller? How come?" Nena asked.

Rob didn't say anything.

"Because Rob ordered it," Jay said as he sprayed and wiped the counter, "and ordered extra."

"That's it?"

"Why do you think all the gay men in the city shop *here*, get their scripts *here*?" Jay sprayed and wiped his counting tray.

"Why?"

"Rob is one of us," Jay said. "We take care of each other." Jay was twenty years old, but sometimes, Nena thought, he sounded like he'd lived a whole life before they met.

Once everyone found out that their pharmacy always had AZT in stock, Jay explained, theirs became the first stop for patients with HIV/AIDS. When they went to other pharmacies that didn't have it, patients were sent to Fifth and Jefferson. At the end of the month, when it was nearing time for refills, they got calls nonstop—other pharmacies across the city, patients calling in their refill orders, nearby clinics. It was flying off the shelf—the more Rob ordered, the more they needed.

Together, they moved all the bestsellers, the HIV and AIDS medications, and any medications that their patients used regularly to a special section behind the drop-off window. Medicines to treat any HIV-related conditions, opportunistic infections, and anything that affected patients with HIV. Medications for oral thrush and pneumonia, antibiotics, and vials of testosterone for intramuscular injection. Every night at closing, someone took an extra fifteen minutes to do an inventory check.

On the first of each month, when Nena got to work, there were already a dozen customers standing near the counter with their prescriptions. It seemed as if HIV and AIDS were all over Miami now. But their little pharmacy on South Beach was where everyone went.

Day after day, as patients came to pick up their prescriptions, their consultations with Rob started to change. He asked not just about their symptoms, but about their families, their partners, their dogs, their weekend film festival plans.

"How was your trip to Key West?" Rob asked one of the customers at the drop-off window.

As they listened from the prescription counter, Jay looked up from his counting tray, elbowed Nena softly.

"He's always making friends," Jay said, laughing.

Nena took notes: When she finally became a pharmacist, she wanted to be just like Rob. She would take care of people, get to know them.

That year, Nena would stand at that register day after day, and at the end of the month, anticipate how many people would already be waiting when she came in at 8:00 a.m. on the first. She would be surprised each time. How much the faces of people she knew had changed, how many people would stop looking like themselves. How their regular patients stopped showing up, one after another, their names disappearing from the roster. Every day, they got news of a death. A lover came in, a mother, a neighbor, a friend. *My partner died. My son passed away two weeks ago.* Sometimes there was no news, but Nena would know, every Friday at the end of the day, when she cleared the bins of the abandoned prescriptions, AZT and Bactrim and a handful of others, never picked up. How much demand there had been a few months before, how much hope. Nena would open the bags, empty out the capsules and the tablets, place the bottles back on the pharmacy shelf. Process the return for the insurance.

Sometimes she couldn't stand the sadness. But Rob cared, Nena thought, because he believed he'd be able to make a real difference for their patients. That one day, they would all be saved with the right combination of medications.

Jay was that way too. He *knew* the people who came to the pharmacy. He also knew about their dogs and their nights at the club and what year they moved to Miami from Detroit. It was just Nena, she thought, who had been too afraid to get to know people, too guarded: What was the point of getting to know someone if you were going to lose them anyway? If they abandoned you. If they died.

As she watched Rob and Jay interact with their customers, she began to realize it had nothing to do with believing in a possible cure. Rob and Jay knew that most of their HIV/AIDS patients would die, but they did it anyway. They cared for them, invested their time and energy, got to know them, whether they had two weeks or ten years. Maybe, Nena thought, she hadn't been paying attention. Maybe she'd been seeing it all wrong. Maybe the people who came into your life, even if you only knew them for a little while—a lifetime or a few months or a week—were a gift.

ONE FRIDAY NIGHT, Nena got home after ten thirty, after all the gay club kids were already lining up outside Twist and Warsaw, and Washington Avenue was gridlocked with cruising lowriders and motorcycles. Jay walked her home from the bus stop, on his way to Twist, hugged her goodbye on the corner, and crossed the street. Nena took off her pharmacy smock as she walked into the lobby, wiped the corners of her eyes, where her mascara tended to run.

Claudia was sitting on a tall stool at the front desk, drinking from a mug. She was short, barely five-two, so the stool made her look taller. "Welcome back," she said as Nena walked in.

"Hey," Nena said, trying to sound cheerful. Every night, when Nena came home from work, Claudia was there to greet her. And every night, Nena looked forward to coming home to the hotel, to seeing Claudia at the front desk.

"You hungry?"

Nena shrugged. She wasn't really hungry, but she'd made a habit of eating with Claudia on weeknights. All she wanted was Claudia's company. Claudia was pretty and confident, but also the friendliest person she knew from her high school. No one at Miami Beach High had been friendly to Nena, but Claudia made her feel like she was fun and smart. Claudia, Nena could tell, liked her company too.

"You want me to send you up a cheeseburger?" Claudia asked.

Nena knew she wasn't really asking. Claudia made it sound like a question, but she usually got what she wanted. It made Nena laugh, her confidence. There was nothing uncertain about Claudia, like she wanted you to know she thought you were cool, and she wanted you to know she liked you.

"Onion rings?" Nena said.

Claudia looked at her watch. "I get off in half an hour."

In her room, Nena cleared the small table for them. She picked at her onion rings while Claudia took great big bites of her cheeseburger, gulping down half her Coke in one go. She watched Claudia, the way she held her food with her small hands, the way she let the grease run down the corners of her mouth. She ate like a cheeseburger was the best thing in the world. She wasn't a skinny girl—she was chubby and curvaceous—and she didn't let anybody else's ideas about women's bodies decide how she would live her life. She was beautiful and she knew it. She moved like she loved life, loved food, loved making friends. Being with Claudia, Nena usually forgot about all the awful shit in her life, although sometimes she thought of Génesis and just felt sadness.

"Something happened. What happened?" Claudia put her burger down, took a sip of her soda, watching her.

Nena picked at her onion rings, trying to avoid the question. She wasn't sure if she could talk about it without crying, and she definitely didn't want Claudia to see her cry. She took a small bite.

"Tell me," Claudia said.

Nena wasn't sure if she could say, or where to start. "Remember I told you about my mom?"

"How she lives in Puerto Rico? Yeah."

Claudia had this thing about her, a way she could make Nena feel like they'd known each other forever. She wasn't pretentious or snobby. She was just cool. But Nena hesitated, remembering how she'd offered up her whole life story to Agnes, and how that turned out.

Claudia took another sip of her soda. "Okay, I'll start, then," she said. She grabbed a handful of napkins and wiped her mouth and hands. "In case you didn't know, we *all* have fucked-up families." Claudia told Nena how she and her brother were always fighting. He was an asshole, she said. Her parents were always working and didn't bother getting involved in their fights. They were busy, and tired, and it was up to Claudia and her brother to grow up, get over it. So

Claudia put up with it. She couldn't wait to move out. Next year, she was going away to college. Finally.

"College where?" Nena asked.

Claudia shrugged. "Haven't decided." She sat back, ready to hear her story.

Nena figured she should just start at the beginning. She told her about her mother, and Tito. Claudia listened quietly, covered her mouth when Nena told her how they found him. She told her about Génesis and her brothers, and about how they left Puerto Rico, and how she ended up left behind at her grandmother's while her mother went back home to take care of business. How she never came back for her. How tense things finally got with Blanca. How she couldn't stand it anymore, so one day she left.

Claudia reached across the table and took Nena's hand with her greasy fingers.

Nena wanted to wipe the grease off, but she liked feeling Claudia's hand on hers. She told her about Agnes and the girls at school.

"Eventually, I kicked all their asses," Nena said, laughing. "Me against all four of them."

"All this 'cause you're gay?"

Nena froze. She hadn't said she was gay. Never even suggested it.

Claudia took another gulp of her soda. "Relax, girl. It's fine. Takes one to know one, right?"

Nena said nothing.

"Really? Oh my God, crazy girl. We live on South Beach. If you're gay, just be gay." She picked up her cheeseburger again. "Besides, Agnes probably had a crush on you or something. You ever think of *that*?"

Nena thought about it. "Nah."

Claudia nodded *hell* yes.

Nena laughed. "That bitch."

"I'm sorry about your uncle," Claudia said. She sounded serious now. "I'm sorry you had to go through all that, and that you're here under these circumstances. But I'm glad you're here."

After that night, Nena would start changing. She'd stop hiding. She'd be more open about her sexuality with work friends.

After a while, she felt free in their little gay gang. Some shifts, they were all so gay that when a straight person came to work in the pharmacy—a cashier from the photo lab filling in for the day, or a tech from another store helping out when they were short-staffed around the first of the month—it was so strange that they were all on their best behavior. Nena was the only girl, and even though everyone knew that most of the pharmacy staff had moved to South Beach to find other gay people, straight people always assumed Nena was straight. She didn't correct them—she figured they'd get it eventually. Most outsiders, the photo lab cashiers or boys from the stockroom, realized Nena was gay only after a masculine lesbian came to the drop-off window and a chorus of gay boys called out, "Nenu, come take care of your patient!" Or when Queen Latifah's doppelgänger came to pick up a prescription while Nena was in the break room, and Jay got on the loudspeaker and paged her: "Nenu, come to the pharmacy immediately for customer service."

Whenever she felt like hiding, Nena would think of Claudia. She'd never known someone who was so completely herself, so happy being exactly who she was. But also, Claudia made her happy.

IN ALL THE months she'd been working at the pharmacy, even though most of their HIV/AIDS patients were getting treatment, Nena had thought of AIDS as a death sentence. That was how everyone she knew had always talked about it, and it didn't help that every first of the month, the number of regulars coming to fill their prescriptions started diminishing. They were disappearing. Sometimes it made Nena angry as hell that so many people were dying, that even though they were all there, working day after day, it didn't make a difference. Sometimes all she could feel was sadness. But then, one day in December, patients started coming in asking about "the cocktail": Retrovir, Epivir, and Invirase—a new lifesaving drug combination. Nena and Jay had listened as Rob talked to the pharmaceutical sales reps. Even though the cocktail hadn't been approved yet, all their patients had been asking about it, doctors calling to talk to Rob. Everyone was getting ready. Nena started to feel a little bit of hope—maybe things would finally change.

One morning at the end of December, Nena came in late. She'd stayed up studying for her GED test, and overslept. Jay was already at the drop-off window, taking prescriptions. He barely looked up when she walked through the pharmacy door, but set a bunch of prescription printouts and labels on the counter for her to work on.

"Good morning," Nena said.

"Morning."

She could tell something was wrong. Jay had become one of her closest friends, with the same taste in music, and they could spend a whole shift just singing and talking shit. She'd been to his apartment; he'd been to her room at the Clay Hotel. They'd walked each other home, looked out for each other. Sometimes he cooked too much and brought her leftovers for lunch.

She looked over her shoulder for Rob. She could hear him moving around behind the shelves, probably eating his breakfast.

"Sorry I'm late," she said.

Jay laughed. "Oh, sweetie, it's fine. Been quiet all morning except for those refill requests."

Nena picked up the printouts and labels and gathered the giant bottles, placed them on the counter. She counted tablets, dropped them into the vials, sealed them, labeled them without a word, then placed the vial on top of its corresponding printout with all the drug information for Rob to check and bag. She'd gotten so good at this, working quickly, without making mistakes. She felt a sense of satisfaction every time she filled a prescription—how she could bring order to people's lives, how she could help take care of them. And there was also something calming about the ritual, how it took her mind off the world.

As the counter filled up, Jay still didn't say anything.

When Rob came from the back to check her work, he tapped her softly on the shoulder. "How you doing, Nenu?"

"I'm all right."

The cashiers were organizing the prescription bins quietly, pulling bagged prescriptions to see which had been left behind and never picked up. They didn't say a word. Rob was checking her work silently. Jay didn't look up from the computer.

Nena worked with a bunch of loud, energetic queens who joked and laughed all the time, even at eight in the morning, not some zombies. Usually, when she got to work, there was cafecito ready, a greeting with a kiss on the cheek, and definitely gossip about something that went down the night before, or the argument in the photo lab, or how somebody got caught shoplifting. She couldn't tell if Rob was disappointed that she'd been late or if something else was wrong.

"What happened?" she asked finally.

Jay walked over, handed her more printouts.

Rob checked and bagged the vials on the counter.

She put her hand on Jay's arm. "You okay?"

Jay met her eyes and spoke softly. "I'm okay. But I'm not."

"What?" She didn't understand.

The printer rolled out another label and its corresponding printout with all the prescription information. Nena leaned down and picked up the single sheet, added it to her stack. It was warm in her hands. She read the label: JAY RODRÍGUEZ. SAQUINAVIR.

"I'm positive," he said.

Nena looked across the pharmacy at the two cashiers, who kept working like they hadn't heard anything, then Rob, who kept verifying her scripts and bagging them. Had Jay already told them? Had they been talking about this before she arrived?

Nena met his eyes. She wanted to hug him. They stood there looking at each other, so much between them. She took his hand, held it.

They said nothing.

WHEN APPROVAL FOR the AIDS cocktail finally arrived in January 1996, everyone came to the pharmacy at the same time, a dozen people waiting when they opened at eight o'clock. Nena answered phones, taking calls from other pharmacies all over the city calling to check if they had the cocktail in stock; patients calling the pharmacy, the photo lab, cosmetics, the front register, to check on availability; doctors holding for the pharmacist so they could call in prescriptions for their patients. Nena on the phone, four people on hold, three patients at the register, two at the drop-off window, everyone asking about the cocktail.

Nena and Jay didn't really talk about his health. But by the time they got the cocktail, Nena had noticed that he was losing weight and he looked like he was aging. As Jay pulled out a bottle of lotion and rubbed it into his hands and forearms, Nena noticed that his arms seemed much thinner. She feared the worst but tried not to think about it.

All day she counted pills by five, filled the vials, labeled them. She poured cough syrup into smaller bottles, mixed amoxicillin powder with distilled water for oral suspension. She ran insurance authorizations, processed refills, printed labels. She counted. She counted. She sang under her breath. She had to keep working, stay focused, control the things she could control. She had to stay strong for him.

That night, as they were about to close, a guy walked up to the pickup window, stood by the register.

"I'm here for a prescription?" he called into the pharmacy.

"I got it," Nena said to Jay and Rob.

At the register, she immediately recognized him. His five-o'clock shadow, the dark hair poking out over his collar. Hairy-ass Fabian, Agnes's brother. Nena remembered how she used to see him sometimes while she was out walking Oso around the neighborhood, or when she went out for a jog in the park. How his thick chest hair poked out under his shirt collar, how he had a five-o'clock shadow even at 8:00 a.m. He always smiled at her.

Nena tried to keep her professional composure, but she hadn't expected to see him here. This wasn't his neighborhood pharmacy.

"What's the last name?" she asked, pretending she didn't know him.

"Hernández," he said.

Nena walked to the bins, stacked in alphabetical order, and found *H*, her back to him. Shit. She thought of Loli. He would tell her he'd seen her niece, and then eventually, Blanca would find out she worked there. Shit.

"Hernández," she repeated over her shoulder. "What's the first name?"

"Agnes," he said like he was talking to a stranger.

Maybe he didn't recognize her. She could be anybody. A girl, just turned seventeen, who happened to be a pharmacy technician working at this pharmacy on South Beach. Not the kid who went to school with his sister, the friend turned enemy, turned nothing. Maybe he didn't recognize her in her new clothes, a sundress and wedges, the makeup she now wore every day. She'd been a kid on the beach when they met, when he saw her every morning as she walked Oso on their block. So much had happened since then. Who even remembered that girl? She was nearly a woman now, taking care of herself.

She picked up the bag with Agnes's prescriptions, read the label slowly, her heart pounding. Retrovir. Epivir. Invirase. She walked back to the register, hands shaking.

"It's for three prescriptions?" Nena asked.

He nodded.

She pulled the three signature labels off the patient literature sheets, stuck them on the clipboard for him to sign.

He signed his name on each one, a quick scribble. *Fabian. Fabi. Fab.*

"Do you have any questions for the pharmacist?" Nena asked.

He shook his head.

She nodded, stood there holding the bag, studying his face. He looked so much like his sister. Same eyes. Same dark hair.

He took the bag. She watched him walk slowly down the aisle, all the way to the front of the store, and before he made a left out of the store, he turned back to look at her one last time.

THEY WORKED QUIETLY most of that busy week, Jay entering prescriptions into the system, Nena counting pills at the counter, labeling the vials, Rob checking and bagging them, the cashiers ringing up customers. They worked like an organized front, all of them moving slowly but steadily. She was tired, but grateful for the distraction.

"Can I help you?" Nena said as someone approached the window.

"Hi."

Nena almost wasn't surprised to see her. She wore black shades and a big floppy hat, a bikini top and shorts, and she was balancing on in-line skates. She took off her shades and Nena felt her heartbeat quicken. Loli, not surprised to see Nena at all.

"Are you dropping off a prescription?" Nena asked nervously, even though she knew Loli was here only because Fabian had told her.

"How are you?"

Nena nodded, took a second, and then realized she hadn't said anything. "Fine. I'm fine."

"Where are you staying?"

"I have a place. I'm fine."

Loli looked her up and down, trying to take her all in. "Does your mom know where you are?"

"Do you have a prescription?" Nena asked.

"Nah." Loli laughed. "You didn't ask, but I guess I'll tell you anyway. We're okay. Your grandmother and I. And Oso. Even though you stole the rent money, we're doing just fine."

"I'm gonna pay you back. I promise."

"We've been worried about you, Nenu. You just fucking left. I called the police! You know how hard it was to call the fucking cops? I hate them bastards! We thought you were dead."

"I get paid on Friday. And then I can pay you the whole thing."

Loli shook her head. "Did you even hear me? I don't give a damn about money. You're my niece! I need to know where you're staying. Who are you living with?"

Nena checked over her shoulder. Rob had disappeared to the back, probably to give her privacy.

"I'm sorry," Nena said. "I just couldn't do it anymore. She was fucking torturing me. She made my life hell."

"That's the way she is—"

"And you let her. Maybe you weren't flinging racist insults at me, forcing me to scrub the shower with bleach after finding a fucking hair, but you *let* her treat me that way. You could've stopped her. You heard her and saw her and you pretended not to."

Loli opened her mouth to speak, then didn't.

"I will pay you her money, I promise you that. But don't come here expecting me to forgive her or *you*, or to let you back into my life. You don't get to know where I live. And I don't care if you tell my mother or not. She doesn't get to know either."

Loli grabbed hold of the countertop, balancing on her skates. "You're right. I should've protected you. I'm sorry. But I am your family, and I love you. You can come home."

Nena was close to crying. She checked for Rob again, and when she turned back to Loli, she couldn't fight the tears. She wiped her eyes. "I'm old enough to take care of myself. And I'm fine. I'll drop off the money on Friday."

"Please come home."

"Hell. No." Nena wiped her face, let out a nervous laugh.

Loli exhaled. "Okay, then what do I tell your mom?"

"Whatever you want. I don't fucking care. She abandoned me."

"She left you with family."

Family. Nena was tired of having this conversation. She didn't want to talk about Loli's idea of family, or her mother's. She was done with them all.

"Please, don't come here again."

NENA AND CLAUDIA were friends, but maybe more. Nena wasn't sure how to bring it up, or even if she should. She just let it be this thing between them. Nena liked her, dreamed of kissing her, but what if Claudia didn't feel the same? Nena let herself doubt, and then Claudia started coming over even on her days off. Nena was sure she felt the same, but neither of them would say.

Nena had never taken Claudia on a date. Not to the movies or the mall or wherever it was people went on dates. They saw each other at the Clay Hotel and went up to Nena's room, or they sat at the bar drinking their Cokes and waiting on their burgers and fries while pretending to be just friends. But she finally got up the nerve, and on her day off, Nena asked Claudia to go out for a walk. They planned to walk on Ocean Drive, like tourists.

Nena was getting ready when she got the phone call: Jay's sister, who came down from Atlanta to be with him.

"Come now," she said. "He doesn't have very long."

"What?" Nena said. "I don't understand. He was fine yesterday." Nena remembered that Jay had seemed like his usual self, working steadily, washing his hands after handling cash. She didn't remember anything wrong with him.

"He was at the ER all night with a fever. They were finally able to get it under control. I picked him up this morning."

Nena was still on the phone when Claudia knocked on her door.

When she opened the door, Claudia's smile faded. "What's wrong?"

Nena explained that she had to go, that Jay was really sick.

"I'll come with you," Claudia said.

"Are you sure?" Nena asked. She explained again what it meant, that Jay was sick, that his sister would be taking care of him, and that her other friends, Rob and José, would be there too. Nena wasn't even sure how she would introduce Claudia.

"He's your friend, and you love him," Claudia said. "That means something to me. I want to meet him, and I want to be there with you."

Nena felt something expand in her chest. A space? Her heart? She wasn't sure. But she was sure that this friendship was more than a friendship. They'd been moving slow—so slow—not holding hands, not kissing, just being together. But this felt like they'd jumped ten steps. Jay was family, and she was bracing herself, getting ready to lose him. And Claudia wanted to be there for her. *With* her, she'd said.

So Nena took her to Jay's.

They all gathered in Jay's living room, Rob and José, Jay's sister Angie, Nena and Claudia. Angie served them all drinks, and José served them arroz con pollo he'd made in Jay's kitchen. Jay sat with his legs propped up on the couch, eating from a bowl, and the rest of them sat around on the floor, their plates on the coffee table. Jay was skinny. Now that she really let herself look at him, Nena realized how much she'd been in denial. She hadn't wanted to see.

Nobody asked how he was feeling. Angie had warned them against that, said Jay didn't want any of that. No sympathy or pity. He just wanted his friends. A normal day, like any other day.

"Just be with him," Angie said. "Like you've always been. He's still the same Jay he always was. Just be who you are, together."

And so Jay made his usual wisecracks and jokes. Nena talked about her GED test, how she'd studied for so long, and she'd finally made an appointment. As soon as she passed, she'd go down to Miami-Dade Community College and register for some classes.

Jay told her he was proud of her. "You worked *hard*," he said, smiling at her.

Rob and José talked about food, this new restaurant on Lincoln Road that made the best overpriced yuca con mojo, and how the neighborhood was changing.

Angie turned on the radio. "This okay?" she asked Jay.

Jay nodded. "I love this."

They talked while listening to salsa.

"So," Rob said to Nena. "Are you going to tell us about *this*?" He waved his hand in the air in a circular motion at Nena and Claudia.

"This?" Claudia asked, giggling.

Nena tried to sidestep the question, complimenting José's food. Claudia stuffed her mouth with arroz con pollo, nodding, and everyone laughed at them.

When the song ended and the next one started, the trumpets and congas and keyboards, Ismael Rivera's "Las Caras Lindas" playing softly, a salsa celebration of Black beauty, Nena smiled. The song felt like home, the warm breeze blowing through their apartment in el Caserío, where all the doors and windows were always open because they had no air-conditioning, where they always had music playing, her mother sliding a salsa album onto the turntable for Saturday morning cleaning. This song, "Las Caras Lindas," was one of her father's favorites, her mother told her once. Nena imagined that it had reminded him that he was beautiful, that to look out at the world and see Black people looking back at him was to understand what real beauty was. To be surrounded by Black people smiling, dancing, crying, loving, fighting, *living,* was to be truly blessed. As flawed as he'd been, her father had loved his Blackness, his people, and they had loved him back. She wondered now if her mother had really grasped what her father had been talking about when he said he loved this song. She'd understood back then that Mami was trying to pass something on to her and Tito that she couldn't quite understand herself, a white Puerto Rican woman raising Black children. But now it occurred to Nena that her mother didn't understand what it truly meant to love somebody, to stay. Did her mother even see how much like Blanca she was? That what she'd done to Nena was exactly what Blanca had done to her?

The song ended again, and then La India and Marc Anthony's "Vivir lo Nuestro" rang into the living room. Jay set his bowl down on the coffee table, smiled at Nena from across the room, swaying a little to the rhythm of the song. Everyone kept eating, drinking. Angie sat next to Jay on the sofa, and he draped his legs over hers. Angie took his hand. Rob and José were mouthing the words, singing to each other, giddy. Nena took Claudia's hand, and Claudia smiled.

Her father had been a singer, her uncle had been her best friend, and she hadn't really known her mother at all. But they were all gone now. This was her family now, and Nena felt grateful, lucky to have them, however long that might be. She didn't need to hide—she could be exactly who she was, and they would love her anyway. She looked at each of them, listened to the end of the song. This was it. Everything she'd ever wanted.

"Todo Tiene Su Final"

SUNDAY MORNING, LIKE every other Sunday, Maricarmen woke to church bells. It was her only day off, and she usually went right back to bed after a quick piss and a cigarette. But that morning, there was also a knock at her door.

"Fuck." She looked around. She couldn't remember if Carmelo had stayed the night, but he wasn't in bed. "Carmelo, get the door!"

Nothing. The knock came again, harder this time. "*Fuuuck.*" She was in a long T-shirt, no underwear, so she pulled on the same pair of jeans she'd left on the floor. "Coming!"

She found Detective Colón standing in front of her door, looking more tired and much older than she remembered, considering it had only been months since Maricarmen last saw her. Detective Colón just stared at her, lips pressed tight, like she was preparing herself to say it.

The question came to Maricarmen more as a feeling, not words. *Did you get him?* she wanted to ask. *Did you find the guy?* But the words didn't come. All Maricarmen could do was breathe, and when she looked over Colón's shoulder, there he was, that fucking diablo. Altieri. Waiting. She did not want him here, not for this. When she exhaled, it was as if someone had punched her in the stomach, all the oxygen leaving her body at once.

Detective Colón nodded like she knew the question without her having to ask it, and when Maricarmen nearly collapsed onto the floor, Colón reached for her, catching her in her arms. "We got him," Colón said. "We got him."

MAY 1993. Friday night, the air thick with mosquitoes and cucullos, Tito glanced over his shoulder before jumping the fence, the stars shining so bright in the sky he could almost forget where he was. Sometimes he did forget, when he snuck out after dark to meet the men among the cañaverales. He swatted at a mosquito around his face, tried not to think about what could be lurking out there. Toads. Snakes. Rats.

It was close to midnight, and the house party down the block was still going, the salsa and merengue spilling out into the streets, the kids passing around cans of Medalla, taking sips from bottles of Ron del Barrilito stolen from their parents' kitchen cabinets. Tito didn't go to a lot of parties. He usually didn't get invited—he didn't have what everyone called "friends."

That night, as he walked into the cañaverales, Tito heard rustling, someone moving in between the rows toward him, and he walked faster, away from el Caserío, where Maricarmen and Nena were asleep. He was supposed to stay home with Nena the next day, but she didn't need a babysitter. She usually woke before him, hustling up some café con leche and fried eggs, and he'd help with the dishes. After school they watched *Por Siempre Amigos*, that novela starring the boys from Menudo as students at a Catholic high school in Argentina. Menudo in Catholic school was ridiculous—who would believe a Puerto Rican boy band going to school in Argentina with their Puerto Rican accents?—but Tito loved to fantasize about which one of the boys would be his boyfriend in the real world, which one would keep his secrets, which one would carry his books in the hallway. That's how things would go if they were all in Catholic school together, the school where all the rich kids from Palmas del Mar went, Nuestra Señora del Perpetuo Socorro, where all the signs were bilingual. Tito and Nena walked by it on their way home from Ana Roqué High sometimes. He loved stopping in front of the old neo-Gothic buildings of the Catholic school, checking out the kids' fancy uniforms with the gold crests on the breast pockets, reading the golden Scripture on the wrought iron gates, in English, then Spanish. HE WILL COMMAND HIS ANGELS CONCERNING YOU, TO GUARD YOU IN ALL YOUR WAYS. A SUS ÁNGELES MANDARÁ ACERCA DE TI, QUE TE GUARDEN EN TODOS TUS CAMINOS.

They talked about that a lot, Tito and Nena. Catholic school, God, heaven, hell.

"I don't know if I'll make it to heaven, Nena," he told her once while they watched the boys from Menudo sitting in their classroom.

But Nena looked him dead in the eye. "You will. I'll be there too. We'll make it together."

Nena was probably the only person in the world who *really* knew him, and loved him anyway. He'd never come out to her. He just *was*, and it made sense. He'd asked her once how the world was so easy for her to make sense of when it had always been so hard for him, when he felt like he might spend his whole life hiding.

Nena never said so, but he knew that she'd been hiding too.

In the last few weeks, he'd finally stopped hiding. Finally broke things off with Peña.

Tito walked into the middle of the cañaverales, where the space was wide enough for him to squeeze in between the rows. He pushed aside some cane, careful not to slice his fingers on the sharp leaves, and turned left, made his way deeper into the dark, where the fields stopped at la Calle Tres, the main road into Humacao. He tried to forget what could happen if anyone found him, if Maricarmen found out, if she heard about who else went out there, the men who hid in the cane night after night, reaching for another man's body, reaching for *him*.

Sometimes he came back out of the shadows with a bruised neck or a swollen lip where one of the men had sucked, then bit down hard. Sometimes they'd ask, *How old are you?* Sometimes all they really wanted was to know when they'd see him again, how easy it would be to get him back out into the dark, his jeans around his ankles. *Old enough*, he often said.

At eighteen, Tito already knew more than any boy should know at that age: The smell and taste of a man who spent long days sitting at the wheel of a truck, chain-smoking Winstons and tossing the butts out the window. The coarse brush of la vecina's husband's beard against his face and neck. The desire on Mr. Peña's face as he watched him shooting hoops, watched Tito peeling off his sweaty T-shirt and wiping his forehead. Tito standing there, shirtless, staring right into his face, waiting for his reaction, even in front of all the other boys on the court. He could always feel him watching, even as he pretended not to.

Tito knew all about pretending, had spent years doing it. But fuck that—he didn't care anymore. He was counting down to the end of summer, and then he'd be off. He wouldn't have to see any of them again.

When Tito got to the edge of the caña, close enough that he was sure he'd be able to hear a car, he turned to find a path of downed rows, and then a large clearing. He always met them out here, close to the road, where they'd park their cars and make their way toward him. *Ángel*, this one had said when Tito asked his name.

He slapped at a mosquito around his face again but hit something soft instead, a cane beetle maybe. He felt a mosquito bite on his thumb and slapped at it. He sped up, feeling around his jeans pocket for the small flashlight on his key chain. When he heard more rustling, he shined his light across the darkness, signaling the way for his date. But they always found their way, always found him.

Tito wanted to be found.

He stepped slowly, shining his flashlight, breathing. He'd only met him a couple of times before this and didn't want to seem nervous. The cane shook, another flashlight beaming back at him.

"Ángel?" Tito called into the darkness, the light growing brighter as it got closer.

Tito felt it before he saw him. The blinding light in his face, the ringing in his ear, his whole body flung by the blow to the side of his head, then his face in the dirt, the pain in his eyes, his mouth, another blow to his ribs, and then another blow, and then another, so many, his head, his ribs, his stomach, until his vision went dark and he felt himself drifting and couldn't feel the ground anymore, tried to hold himself up, to move away from the blows, his body convulsing, his lips his cheeks his hair, something breaking, his entire body screaming. Maybe he called out for Maricarmen that night, or for Nena. Maybe in those last moments, he tried to remember his mother, Doña Iris, or his brother, Rey.

He tried to move his hand.

Please, he thought he heard himself say, but in his mouth the words were wet and heavy.

He wanted to say his name.

In those last moments, he could see the flashlight he'd dropped, his swollen body throbbing, his own pulse too much to bear, but then he stopped feeling anything. He didn't think about heaven or hell. He closed his eyes and saw the Catholic school, Nuestra Señora del Perpetuo Socorro, the gardens, the sand, the ocean. Tito and Nena and Maricarmen on the beach. The dog in his arms. The wrought iron fence. FOR HE WILL COMMAND HIS ANGELS. The ornate gilded letters. QUE TE GUARDEN EN TODOS TUS CAMINOS.

On the ground, wet and out of breath, before everything burned, Tito saw his face. He recognized him. They saw each other, Tito and Jamil, looked into each other's eyes, and they both knew exactly what this was.

I see you, Tito wanted to say. *I know you.*

And then Jamil poured the gasoline.

"He Chocado con la Vida"

MARICARMEN WOKE UP without her alarm on Monday morning, coughing violently, the ceiling fan blowing over her, sheets sticking to her bare arms and legs. She was drenched in sweat, but next to her, Carmelo seemed fine. He breathed heavily, his naked body wrapped in the soft pink sheets. Her side was wet. Her knotted hair stuck to her neck, her forehead. She was so tired, like she hadn't slept at all. She looked at the time, realized she'd turned off her alarm and she was running late.

In the shower, she tried to move quickly, running the bar of soap over her armpits, her arms, her breasts. She was going to be late if she made herself a lunch, and Carmelo couldn't be counted on to make coffee. She couldn't even remember the last time she saw him eat, or drink anything other than beer. She'd grab something from the roach coach at work. She wasn't very hungry anyway. She barely had any appetite these days.

She rushed out of the shower, wrapping a towel around herself, and went back into the bedroom to get dressed.

"I'm going to work. Lock the front door on your way out."

Carmelo sat up.

She pulled her coveralls over her shorts. She couldn't find a T-shirt to pull over her bra. "Damn it." She picked yesterday's shirt off the floor, sniffed it, then dropped it where she stood. "Fuck." She put her arms into her coveralls' sleeves and decided that it would be a no-shirt kind of day anyway. It was too damn hot for layers.

On the drive to the factory, she kept her eye on the gas gauge, reminded herself to stop for fuel on her way home. She coughed and coughed, turned the radio on, but it was too much, she couldn't concentrate with the music. She turned the volume all the way down, drove in silence, shaky hands gripping the steering wheel tightly. She hated the silence, the sound of her own breathing. It reminded her of how alone she was, how stuck she felt. She'd meant to come back to take care of things, pack up their apartment, sell the car, but she hadn't called Nena in months. After all her phone calls went unanswered, she'd given up. She told herself she would get her shit together, pack up the apartment, sell the car, and go. She'd get her daughter back, get a job in Miami, and they'd start over. Just the two of them. But she wasn't sure how long that would take.

She pulled into the factory parking lot, slid the car into a spot in the sun, and parked. She fished a small baggie from her purse, and with her car key, she scooped out a bump, brought it to her nose, and snorted it. She snorted another one, then resealed the baggie, dropped it back in her purse, then wiped her nose on the back of her hand.

Once she was on her line, she worked fast and steady, like she'd always done, fitting slim blister packs of birth control pills into small cartridges, loading the boxes onto the conveyor belt and letting them roll along. She sliced her cuticle on the cardboard as soon as she let the first box go. She wiped her forehead. She was fed up with this shit, couldn't remember what she'd hoped to accomplish by asking for her job back, except that she needed money. Maybe she could get a different job, waiting tables, bartending. She'd done it before. But, fuck, she didn't have the energy to smile at people, pretend to care if they liked their food. At least in the factory, she could do the job without thinking, without smiling, without pretending to care about all the new people Obrero had hired. Men, mostly. She had enjoyed working there once, even if the pay wasn't all that great. At least back then she had only worked with women. There was a feminine energy to the place, everyone worked hard, and during their breaks, they laughed a lot. They were friends, a bunch of women sweating and listening to loud music, and by the end of a day, they were exhausted, but it still felt good to be tired from a day's work. Back then, she'd even had the energy to work a second job at the pharmacy. Now she felt like there were eyes on her everywhere she went. If she took a bathroom break, there was always some man watching her ass as she walked by. If she was sitting with a few other women during their lunch break, some man would come into the break room and insert himself into their conversation. And everywhere she went, some idiot was telling her to smile.

Maricarmen was loading another box onto the conveyor belt when Evelyn stepped up to her line, clipboard in hand. Maricarmen exhaled dramatically.

"Lost my count, so don't even ask," Maricarmen said, coughing.

"Where's your goggles?" Evelyn said.

"You serious?"

Evelyn opened her eyes wide. "Take a look around. You're the only worker not wearing goggles."

"If I get stabbed in the eye with a packet of Loestrin, I'll say you told me so."

"Mari."

Maricarmen reached across the back conveyor for a slim box, then started building it. She quickly picked up the blister packs and slotted them in, then closed the box.

"Maricarmen."

"I don't have goggles. I don't think I ever did, to be honest."

"You did."

"I don't anymore, then."

Evelyn looked her up and down. "Come with me."

Maricarmen followed Evelyn down the line, past the other women loading their boxes onto the conveyor. They walked past a man Maricarmen didn't know.

"Can I come too?" he said.

Maricarmen gave him a dirty look. "Asshole," she said under her breath.

As she followed Evelyn toward the stairs that led up to the break room, another woman got out of her line, walking along with Maricarmen. She glanced at her, then noticed another two women getting out of line. Evelyn was already halfway up the stairs.

It wasn't break time, and it was too early for lunch, but half a dozen women were headed to the break room with Evelyn and Maricarmen. Evelyn opened the door and went inside quickly.

"Something's wrong," Maricarmen said as soon as she stepped inside. "What is it?"

Evelyn stood by the door, pointed toward one of the tables. As soon as the other women were inside the room, Evelyn locked the door.

"Something's definitely wrong," one of the women said as she sat down.

All the women sat at Maricarmen's table. She crossed her arms across her chest, waiting.

"The men have been talking," Evelyn said.

"They talk a lot," the other woman said.

Evelyn nodded. "They do."

"This isn't about my goggles," Maricarmen said.

The other woman fidgeted in her seat. "It's Obrero. All the men he hired? Every single one of them is getting paid more than me. Three dollars more at least. One of them, this idiot, the one who works on my line and won't shut up about how his wife left him? Well, the wife is Obrero's niece."

"So what?" Maricarmen said.

"I've been here seven years," the other woman said. "Seven years. He's been here a month. Obrero just brings in whoever he wants, his family and friends, to make more than any woman here."

"I've been here ten," another woman said. "How much does he make? How much do all of them make?"

Maricarmen started to tune out as the women talked. She didn't have the energy to deal with this. She couldn't make herself care. She hadn't told Evelyn that they'd found Tito's killer, that they had arrested him yesterday, and it would be a matter of hours before everyone found out, if they hadn't already, and the whole media circus started again.

"Last week, I was in the office," Evelyn said, "and tried to talk to Obrero about it."

"How much does he make?" asked another woman.

"Obrero's guy? Fifteen dollars an hour, he says."

"Fifteen?" the woman said. "I make seven!"

All the other women started talking at once, shouting about how they'd all been at the factory six, seven, eight years, and that new guy made more than every single one of them.

"Listen!" Evelyn said, raising her voice.

The women all quieted. Maricarmen measured the distance between her seat and the door, wondered if they'd be upset if she just got up and left. She just couldn't do this.

"Listen," Evelyn said, "I've been here fifteen years, and I'm a floor supervisor. I just started making fifteen dollars an hour. That guy who just started last month is making the same as me. Before he got here, I was the highest-paid employee, except for Obrero."

The women started arguing again, getting up out of their chairs.

"Listen!" Evelyn said again. "I need you all to listen. We don't have much time."

The women quieted down.

"Last week I tried to talk to Obrero about it. He said he would think about it, and then this morning, when I asked again, he said he'd thought about it, but that productivity wasn't high enough and we couldn't afford to raise wages."

"Obrero doesn't care about any of us," the other woman said. "He's a sexist piece of shit."

"You're right," Evelyn said. "Obrero doesn't care about us. He doesn't care about you or me. But you know what he cares about?"

"What?" someone said.

"Productivity. He cares about looking good for those Osborne Pharma assholes. The more productive we are, the better he looks."

"So let's go on strike," someone said. "Let's see how good he looks when most of his workers are gone."

"Exactly," Evelyn said.

Maricarmen looked up at Evelyn. She hadn't been serious, right? Or at least, she didn't think most of the women would agree. They all had families. How were they supposed to make ends meet if they all lost their jobs?

Evelyn kept talking. She had a plan. They had to be strategic. They had to be organized. They needed to listen to her, let her do all the talking.

Maricarmen got up, headed to the door.

"Where are you going?" Evelyn said.

"I need the toilet." Maricarmen saw the disappointment on

Evelyn's face. "Go ahead. Plan without me. I'll just follow your lead. You're doing all the talking, right?"

All the women were staring back at her now.

She turned and walked out.

WHEN SHE GOT back from the bathroom, all the women were ready. They headed back down, wearing their coveralls and their safety goggles, watching as the men moved slowly, packing the birth control pills, paying the women no mind, taking it easy as they always did. The women walked past the floor, every single woman in the factory heading toward Obrero's office. Sixty women.

Evelyn knocked on Obrero's door but didn't wait, just let herself in. The women went in after her, as many as could fit in his office.

Obrero looked up from his roach coach breakfast, a Styrofoam container with scrambled eggs and pan sobao and a café con leche.

"Yeah?" he said. He wiped at his lips with a napkin. "Something happen on the floor? Someone hurt?"

Evelyn talked slowly, professionally. "We're here, all of us female employees, to have a conversation."

Maricarmen coughed into her fist.

"Who's on the factory floor?" Obrero said.

"We've come here as a union of working women," Evelyn said. "We work hard and fast, and our production numbers clearly show that each one of us, individually, is doing twice the work as male employees who are paid more than all the women here."

Obrero rolled his eyes.

Evelyn continued. "We want to be paid fairly for the work we do."

"You're not working now!" Obrero said. "You're standing in my office."

"We would like to be paid equal salaries to those of the men."

"Listen," Obrero said. "Those men have families to support."

Maricarmen took a step closer to his desk. That had touched a nerve. "What, you think I don't have a family? I've been a single mother for the ten years you've known me. I can't even afford childcare on the wages you pay." Evelyn touched her arm softly and Maricarmen quieted.

"We all have families," Evelyn said. "Every single one of these women has a family to take care of. And every single one of these women deserves equal pay."

"We don't have the budget for raises right now," Obrero said. "At the end of the year, when you have your reviews, each of you will get a raise." He stood up, pushing his chair back. "And let me make this clear: We don't have unions here. There is no union, and there won't be any negotiations. You will be reviewed when the company decides that it's time for your review. Right now, it's time to get back to work, if you intend to keep working here."

Maricarmen was ready to lunge, but Evelyn took her arm.

"We came here as a union of working women," Evelyn said. "We've discussed this, and we have agreed. We are ready to go on strike until you are ready to negotiate, and until we are satisfied with your offer."

"What offer? There is no offer. Didn't you hear what I just said?"

"Please make your offer in writing. Until then, we are on strike."

Evelyn turned and the women opened up the ranks to let her pass, then followed her out of Obrero's office.

Maricarmen stayed as long as she could, to enjoy the dumbstruck look on Obrero's face. Once all the women were out the door, she left too.

The women strutted down the hallway, pushed open the double doors, and made a show of coming back onto the floor, so the men could see them leave. They walked past the men, filing down the floor, and climbed the stairs to the locker room. Some of them took their purses and lunch boxes, leaving behind their coveralls, their goggles, and made their way downstairs again. But others lingered, probably not ready to risk their paychecks. Evelyn probably hadn't expected that, Maricarmen thought. Evelyn's son Carmelo was grown. She only had to worry about herself.

Maricarmen coughed and coughed, her chest feeling tighter than this morning. She wasn't sure this strike would work. She expected Obrero to come out of his office with threats, fire half of them on the spot. She left her coveralls on, since she didn't have a shirt on underneath, but grabbed her purse out of her locker. She stopped in the bathroom on the way out.

She'd spent the last two nights on the couch with Carmelo, drinking and snorting perico, and that was all she wanted to be doing. She went into the first stall and locked the door. She listened to the silence, pulled the baggie out of her purse, and used her car key to scoop the perico. She snorted and snorted it, taking a short break, wiping her nose, then snorted some more. Fuck it. She didn't have to go back to work anyway. She snorted the whole bag.

In the parking lot, she made her way to the roach coach, got herself a café con leche, then found Evelyn. She didn't even want a coffee—she just needed something to hold in her hand.

Evelyn was holding a sign: EQUAL PAY FOR EQUAL WORK in big, bold black letters.

Maricarmen wondered when she'd had time to make a sign. Had Evelyn brought it from home? She broke into a coughing fit.

"You feeling okay?" Evelyn asked.

Maricarmen shrugged. "I've been better."

"Have you been smoking?"

"You know I don't smoke."

"Has Carmelo been smoking that shit?"

"No," Maricarmen said. "Carmelo is fine, and I'm fine. What's with all the questions?"

Evelyn studied her, searching her face. "Mamita, you don't look fine. You look like you're coming down with something."

"I'm gonna sit in my car and have my coffee," Maricarmen said.

She didn't like feeling like Evelyn's kid. Evelyn was her supervisor, not her mother-in-law. Sometimes she took it a little too far. Maricarmen was a grown woman. She adjusted her purse on her shoulder and walked off. The women lined up next to Evelyn, who held up her sign toward the entrance, so anyone leaving the factory or looking out the window on the second floor could see it. If Obrero looked out his office window, he would see them clearly.

EQUAL PAY FOR EQUAL WORK.

Maricarmen leaned against her car, took a sip of her café, and listened to the women. They chanted, but Maricarmen couldn't make out what they were saying, just the rhythm of their chants. The sun was beaming down on her face, her chest feeling so tight she couldn't breathe. The women kept chanting. The sun was getting hotter. Maricarmen reached into her purse for her car keys, dropped her coffee on the gravel.

"Fuck!" she said. Suddenly, she felt like she would vomit.

"Equal pay for all!" the women said.

Was that what they were saying? She thought so.

She searched and searched her purse and finally fished out her keys. She dropped the keys into the coffee.

"Equal pay for all!"

She reached for them, dropping her purse as she leaned down, holding on to the car door to keep herself steady. She was so exhausted.

"Equal pay for all!"

She snatched the keys, wet and sticky with coffee and dirt. She leaned her entire body against the car, took a breath, then another.

"Equal pay for all!"

The women were loud, steady, all of them facing the factory.

Maricarmen tried to catch her breath before she opened her car door.

In the sky, some kind of bird, a hawk or vulture. Floating, tilting sideways, its body swinging this way, that way. Un guaraguao. The women were singing now, the bird dancing in the sky, swaying to the rhythm of their song. The women facing the factory, Obrero watching from his office window.

Maricarmen saw him then, standing among the women, the sun beaming down on all of them. He was facing Maricarmen, *seeing* her—Tito. Those curls framing his sad face. He wore his crucifix, just like the one he'd given her. Maricarmen reached for her own crucifix, but then, when her hand touched her bare chest, she remembered she'd left it for Nena.

But he couldn't really be there, standing among the women.

"What are you doing here?" Maricarmen said, a wet gurgling stuck in her throat. She coughed, hacked up some phlegm, spat it onto the gravel.

The women singing. The guaraguao in the sky. Tito watching her, waiting.

Maricarmen losing her balance, falling, falling. Her body shaking violently.

AT THE PHARMACY, as Nena entered insurance information into the computer at the drop-off window, she looked across the aisle to the front of the store and saw Loli skating toward the pharmacy. She was swaying slowly across the linoleum floor. For a moment, Nena wondered why no one ever asked Loli to leave a store when she skated in, or take off the Rollerblades. Then she remembered, she hadn't paid Loli what she owed her. She'd told her she'd pay back the money she stole, but then never thought about it again, completely erased it from her mind. Fuck.

"I have your money," she said as soon as Loli reached the drop-off window. "I just have to go into my locker. Give me a couple minutes."

Loli was trying to catch her breath.

Nena searched Loli's face.

"It's your mom."

CARMELO PICKED THEM up at the airport in San Juan, Loli and Blanca carrying their old suitcases, and Nena carrying a duffel bag, her backpack strapped on tight. Nena didn't know how long they would stay, or where Blanca and Loli would sleep, or how she would even be able to speak to her mother. She'd met Loli and her grandmother at Miami International and hadn't been able to speak a word to her grandmother at the airport, or on the plane, or once they landed. She had handed over the money she stole, and that was that. As far as Nena was concerned, they had nothing left to talk about.

When she saw the black Honda Civic drive up, she half expected her mother in the driver's seat, then realized how stupid the thought was. Carmelo popped the trunk and got out, taking Blanca's suitcase first, then Loli's. Nena dropped her duffel into the trunk. Before Nena could stop him, Carmelo took her into his arms, hugged her hard.

"I'm glad you're here, Nenu," he said.

She hugged him back reluctantly. "How is she?"

He pulled away, glancing at Loli, Blanca, and back at Nena. "I'm not gonna lie to you—she's not good. But she's gonna be better now that you're here."

Nena sat in the back seat, backpack on her lap, and slid her dark shades on.

Blanca sat in the front. "What does that mean, 'not good'?"

"She almost died. But she didn't. She's home now. And she has other things she needs to tell you, but she's gotta be the one to tell you."

"Why all the secrets?" Loli said. "Jesus Christ, just tell us." Sitting next to Nena, Loli was the only one to put on her seat belt. "If we're gonna find out anyway, what's the big deal?"

"Shut up," Blanca said from the front. "Just shut your mouth."

In the back, leaning up against the window, Nena cried quietly.

AS THEY PULLED into el Caserío an hour later, in the middle of the afternoon, Loli and Blanca just stared out the window. They hadn't set foot there in over seventeen years, Nena realized. It had probably changed since they were last there, but not much, she imagined. Nena watched the street as they drove in. It looked exactly as she'd left it. It was still downwind from La Central Patagonia, and they were still breathing the toxic fumes, still living with black snow raining down on them during the burning season.

There was a police cruiser parked at the end of one street, and another parked in front of the basketball courts.

"See that?" Carmelo asked, pointing at the police cars. "Now we have young people dying of overdoses every other week, los camarones swooping in day after day to collar the heroin dealers and the perico slingers, day in, day out, all they do is put bodies in el Oso Blanco and Bayamón Correctional."

Blanca side-eyed him, and Nena just knew she'd be talking shit about him later.

Carmelo pulled up to their building, parked right in front.

Nena slid out of the car, shut the door behind her, and reached the apartment first. It was open, so she slipped inside quietly. Loli and Blanca followed, Carmelo carrying Blanca's suitcase.

Nena looked around, taking it all in. The living room smelled like cigarettes and feet. There was a thin layer of dust over the coffee table. She dropped her backpack on a chair and headed straight for her mother's bedroom.

Mami was sitting in her bed, Evelyn in a chair by her bedside. It was then, when she saw her mother, that Nena knew. Nobody had to tell her that Mami had almost died of a drug overdose—she looked rough, and nothing could have prepared Nena for it. Her mother was skinnier than Nena had ever seen, her beautiful face hollowed out, cheekbones protruding.

How long had her mother been like this? Back in this apartment, this place where Tito was murdered, where her husband was killed, where the people who claimed to have loved him, loved her, had all turned away? Nena stepped closer, and Evelyn smiled at her, stood up.

"You can sit here," Evelyn said, and got up. She stepped out of the room.

But Nena couldn't bring herself to sit. Her chest was hurting. She had a stabbing, searing pain that didn't let her take a breath. All these months, she had hated her mother, vowed never to see her again, tried so hard to forget her. All these months, she had so willingly thrown her away, doubting her love, her capacity to even *feel*. She had thought the cruelest possible reasons for her mother's absence. Except this—she hadn't thought of this. Her mother, suffering without her.

"You can sit if you want," Mami said softly.

Nena stepped closer, kicked off her sneakers, and climbed into her mother's bed, crawling over the bedspread and lying next to her, wrapping her arms around her mother's torso like she had when she was little, when her mother read magazines in bed and Nena wanted attention. She pressed her face into her mother's side, felt her mother's hand on her head, caressing her hair, and she wept like she hadn't done in years, like she hadn't done her whole life.

Nena opened her eyes. Evelyn stood in the doorway as Blanca and Loli let themselves into the bedroom. Loli started weeping as soon as she saw Mami. Blanca was quiet, her mouth a fist.

"Obrero called," Evelyn said to Mami. "He said Osborne Pharma is reviewing every employee and considering raises. But he can't promise equal pay. He says if we don't get back to work tomorrow, we're all fired."

Maricarmen laughed. "That son of a bitch. Tell him he owes me money."

Evelyn smiled. "Let me know if you need anything."

Blanca just stood, expressionless, as Evelyn left. Loli sat in the chair, took Mami's hand. Nena sat up.

"I'm gonna get my things from the car," Nena said, and got out of bed.

In the living room, she found Carmelo sitting on the sofa, elbows on his knees, palms drawn in prayer. Maybe he was praying. Maybe he was just thinking. She didn't want to interrupt him. She picked up the car keys on the table and went outside.

She opened the trunk and pulled out her heavy duffel bag, pulled the strap over her shoulder, wiped her face with the back of her hands.

She felt her before she saw her.

Across the street, on her bike, staring right at her, was Génesis. She looked older, her hair pulled back in a messy bun, her face sweaty and ruddy. Nena slammed the trunk shut.

So here she was, back home in el Caserío, the sun on her face, bright clouds spreading across the sky, the overgrown weeds and morivivi, the paint peeling off the corners of dilapidated buildings. She had loved this place so much. She had loved Génesis so much. And yet now, as they stared at each other, Nena wiping off tears, Génesis nodding at her, a gesture she wasn't sure she understood, Nena felt nothing. She didn't even feel the urge to pee. Was that head nod an apology? An acknowledgment that Génesis saw her? A hello? A *Sorry I sent you to the hospital, my bad*? Whatever it was, Nena didn't care. She turned, headed back inside.

In the kitchen, Blanca opened cabinets, searched, closed them. Nena looked around for Carmelo, but he wasn't on the couch anymore. She went into the kitchen.

"What do you need?"

"Coffee? La greca." Blanca put both hands on the counter, her body bending slightly, her brown bob shaking. She was crying, Nena realized. Blanca was crying.

Blanca let out a breathless shriek, an animal sound, then straightened her body again. She turned to Nena.

She thought Blanca might fall, that she might let her body slide down onto the kitchen floor, break down. Maybe she would ask forgiveness. Maybe she would finally tell her that she had been wrong all these years about her father, about her, and admit that she had abandoned her own daughter out of spite, finally admit that she regretted everything. Had Blanca asked for Mami's forgiveness? Maybe she'd told her that she loved her.

Blanca's eyes were narrow, studying Nena. "I bet you're enjoying this. I bet you think I'm finally getting what I deserve. I bet you're glad your mother almost died just so you can see me suffer."

It took Nena a minute to realize what she'd said, that she *had* heard her clearly, that she had not imagined it. Her grandmother had really said those words to her. It was the single most vile thing Blanca had ever said to her. Blanca would never, Nena realized, ask her forgiveness. She would never work for it, never earn it, never deserve it. But that was okay, because Nena would never offer it, and she was fine with that.

Nena opened a cabinet, pulled out la greca and a bag of Café Oro, and placed them on the counter.

"You did this," Blanca said.

"What?"

"You drove her to this!" Blanca yelled at her. "You drove her crazy when you ran away. We thought you were dead! All this time, we thought you were dead! All this time, you never thought about anybody but yourself."

Nena tried to keep calm. "What are you even doing here? You left her when she was a kid, and now you try to act like a mother?"

Blanca picked up la greca and flung it at Nena, but she ducked out of the way.

Nena reached for la greca, and as much as she wanted to throw it back, she just held it. "I don't hate you, and I don't wanna see you suffer." She slid the coffee maker back on the counter. "Hating would require that I *care*. Truth is, I don't even care enough to pity you."

Nena reached across the counter for the sugar, put that next to the coffee and la greca, and left the room.

In the bedroom, her mother was still sitting up, Loli next to her in bed. They were talking, but quieted when Nena came in.

Loli got up, leaving them to talk. Taking Loli's place, she squeezed close to her mother. Mami took her hand.

"I'm glad you're here," Mami said. Her body next to Nena's felt hot.

Nena wanted to ask so many questions, but she didn't want her to feel like she was being interrogated, or like she needed to apologize. She wanted her mother to know she was okay. She wanted their time together to matter. And more than anything, she wanted to take care of her. Even though Blanca had left her, Nena would not leave. She would be the one to stay.

"I'm taking you home with me," Nena said.

"Home where?"

"To my place in Miami. We can get you treatment, a doctor, if that's what you want."

"Of course that's what I want." Her mother paused, deep in thought.

"What?" Nena asked.

"I thought you were coming home."

"One day," Nena said, "we'll come home. We'll come back to Puerto Rico together, once you're better. We'll figure it out, find some other place, but right now, we just need to get you sober, Mami. So I'm taking you with me."

Her mother wiped tears from her face and nodded.

"You know," Nena said, "it was hard at first, but I'm all right now. I was never alone. And I have people who love me."

Mami squeezed her hand but didn't say anything, and Nena felt stupid for saying that. She wanted to tell her mother she loved her, that she'd missed her, that she'd been lost without her all these months. But she didn't say any of that. She thought of Angie and Jay, how Angie had said that what Jay wanted most was his friends, for them to be as they always were. To remember him as he lived.

Before Tito died, before Miami Beach, her mother had lived her whole life for Nena and Tito. She'd spent her whole life working, making sure they lived a good life. Nena thought about what her mother wanted, what her mother could want, more than anything. She'd spent so long telling herself that her mother had abandoned her, but now she thought back to the days before Miami, and what her mother had wanted most had always been for Nena to be happy, for her to be safe. As complicated as their relationship was, as hard as the last two years had been, she knew her mother loved her.

"I have friends in Miami, good friends. I have a job. I'll be starting college soon."

Her mother turned to her and smiled. "Really?"

Nena nodded. "I'm gonna study pharmacy," she said, laughing.

"Oh God, don't do that. Do something you love." Her mother's eyes were watery, trying to focus on her.

They both laughed.

"I want to tell you something," Nena said. "I've wanted to tell you for a long time." She looked into her mother's eyes, trying to gauge whether it was the right thing to do. She was still her mother, she told herself.

"You can tell me anything. You know that."

Nena knew it was true. "I met someone, and I think I love her. I think I'm gay."

Mami squeezed her hand again. "I know," she said. "I know."

"You do?"

"I always knew."

"You did?" Nena's hand started shaking. She tried to keep still.

"Of course I did." She took Nena's hand in both of hers. "Love who you love, mamita. That's everything. Don't get to the end of your life and realize all you have left is regret."

Nena was full of questions now. Was there something Mami regretted?

"There are things I did," her mother said. "Things I wish I hadn't."

"Mami, you don't have to—"

"I'm sorry I left you. I didn't want you in danger while I handled things here. I was always gonna go back for you. Then I got sick." Mami wiped her nose with the back of her hand. "I knew I was sick, but I didn't want to accept it. I tried to hide from it."

Nena didn't know what to say, but when her mother said it, she knew it was true.

"Listen to me, Nena. Don't you waste your life hiding."

"Okay," Nena said.

"I have more to tell you."

Nena listened quietly, afraid to interrupt.

"I want you to know who your parents were. Your mother and your father. We loved each other, but it wasn't some perfect love story. That's just the version I've been telling you, and myself, all these years."

"I thought he was the love of your life."

Mami frowned. "Truth is, maybe he didn't love me enough. *You* were the love of my life. You and Tito."

Nena let her continue, and her mother told her the whole story: How everybody started calling him Rey el Cantante. How the first night they talked, she'd held him in her arms as he bled. How when she heard him sing "El Ratón" for the first time, she knew she loved him, and at once, knew he would never be hers. How at sixteen, she had made a family of them, Rey and Tito, took care of their mother before she died, before Nena was born. How she'd tried to make a home for all of them in this place she had loved and hated, where she had lost everything, el Caserío Padre Rivera. The place that made them, where they had been their whole lives, this housing project built for the poor—people like *them*—and even after they were gone, Rey would live on. Rey el Cantante, the myth of him, how he could move an audience, how he could summon ghosts. How he was all music and loyalty and reckless abandon. How in the end, he could not be the star, the hero, the father, everyone wanted him to be. How Altieri killed him. And how his name, Rey, means "king."

LINER NOTES

1. "El Cantante," Héctor Lavoe, written by Rubén Blades
2. "El Ratón," Cheo Feliciano & Joe Cuba Sextet, written by Cheo Feliciano
3. "Se Me Fue," El Gran Combo de Puerto Rico
4. "Juanito Alimaña," Willie Colón & Héctor Lavoe, written by Tite Curet Alonso
5. "Las Caras Lindas (de Mi Gente Negra)," Ismael Rivera, written by Tite Curet Alonso
6. "Periódico de Ayer," Héctor Lavoe, written by Tite Curet Alonso
7. "Tú Me Quemas," Eddie Santiago, written by Luis Ángel Márquez
8. "Nadie Es Eterno," Tito Rojas, written by Darío Gómez
9. "Incomprendido," Ismael Rivera, written by Bobby Capó
10. "La Cura," Frankie Ruíz, written by Tite Curet Alonso
11. "Calle Luna, Calle Sol," Willie Colón & Héctor Lavoe, written by Willie Colón
12. "Dicen Que Soy," La India, written by Guadalupe García & Sergio George
13. "Dime Por Qué," Ismael Rivera, written by Pedro García Díaz
14. "El Gran Varón," Willie Colón, written by Omar Alfanno
15. "Todo Tiene Su Final," Willie Colón & Héctor Lavoe, written by Willie Colón
16. "He Chocado con la Vida," Tito Rojas, written by Ivette Ayala

THE LIFE AND DEATH of Reinaldo "Rey el Chino" Santana Reyes, from el Caserío Padre Rivera, is remembered in Pedro Conga's 1984 song "Rey el Chino," sung by Axel Martínez. In the real community of el Padre Rivera, Rey was beloved by family and friends. I grew up hearing stories of Rey el Chino, who gifted me my first pair of gold hoops, and who was killed by los camarones when I was two years old. My tío David performed his funeral Mass.

But this is not the story of Rey el Chino or his family. *This Is the Only Kingdom* is the story of a fictional family. All the characters in this novel are fictional, and the events are imagined. The fictional rendering of el Caserío Padre Rivera is not the real place, which is now called Residencial Padre Rivera. The setting of the novel is a place that exists only in my imagination. It is in some ways a tribute to the real people I know and love, who are complex and hardworking and loving and talented and flawed and beautiful. And they pass stories down.

ACKNOWLEDGMENTS

MY DEEPEST GRATITUDE to Aracelis Girmay, for your poetry and your light. I'm so grateful that I got to witness your brilliance and grace advocating for Black Puerto Ricans during the 2023 Letras Boricuas gathering in Fajardo. I carry your words with me. El ojo es negro. Thank you to Mayra Santos-Febres, Yolanda Arroyo Pizarro, Anjanette Delgado, Esmeralda Santiago, Vanessa Mártir, Carina del Valle Schorske, Xochitl Gonzalez, Justin Torres, and Xavier Valcárcel, for your words. Xavier, gracias por tomarme de la mano y presentarme a Yolanda. Gisselle Yepes, your words have kept me on this earth. I am so grateful for you.

For your generous support during the years it took to write this book, thank you to the Columbia University Hettleman Summer Grant Program in the School of the Arts, the Alonzo Davis Fellowship at the Virginia Center for the Creative Arts, the Mellon Foundation, la Fundación Flamboyán and the Letras Boricuas Fellowship, the Shearing Fellowship at the Black Mountain Institute at UNLV, the Atlantic Center for the Arts, Yaddo, Lynn Harris Ballen and the Jean Córdova Prize for Lesbian/Queer Nonfiction, Lambda Literary Foundation, and the Whiting Foundation.

My heartfelt gratitude to the team who rallied behind this book: To Kathy Pories, who saw the real story in the fractured mess of those early pages, this book would not exist without your guidance. Thank you to Nadxieli Nieto, Gregg Kulick, Pat Jalbert-Levine, Jovanna Brinck, Brunson Hoole, and the many, many folks at Algonquin,

Little, Brown, and Hachette. Gracias, Eliani Torres, for your meticulous copyedits, and for seeing me. To my agent, Michelle Brower at Trellis Literary Management, who found me at Sewanee all those years ago. I'm so lucky to have you in my corner. To Amelia Possanza at Lavender Public Relations, for your enthusiasm and humor as we plot to take over the world. To Sara Ortiz at the Lyceum Agency, for your advocacy and your friendship, but especially for those Las Vegas nights dancing to Bad Bunny until the break of dawn.

I am indebted to the musicians who hustled when salsa was political, anti-colonial, and focused on storytelling: Rubén Blades, Héctor Lavoe, Cheo Feliciano, Ismael Rivera, and so many more; los salseros de Humacao, Pedro Conga y Su Orquesta Internacional, and Tito Rojas, nuestro Gallo Salsero. And to the women whose voices bring me back to my most authentic self: La India, Myrta Silva, La Lupe, Blanca Rosa Gil, and Lucecita Benítez.

Thank you to the Randolph College family. I'll miss you all. To my colleagues in the Writing Program at Columbia University, especially Deborah Paredez and the Nonfiction coven, for your support during the darkest times. And to my students: You make it all worth it. I am so proud to have known you and taught you. To Lance Cleland and A.L. Major at Tin House, for karaoke and dancing and all that you do. To Laura Pegram and all the folks at Kweli. Thank you, Leah, Adam, Gwen, Travis, and all the folks at the Sewanee Writers' Conference (too many to name) for bringing me back year after year. To Briana and Plum: Here's to dancing to Madonna's "Like a Prayer" and casting spells under the full moon. I wish you joy, music, art, queer liberation, and so much love.

With so much gratitude for the friends who held me down and lifted me up when I needed it most. There was a time when I thought I had to do this work alone. I'm so glad I was wrong. Much love to Deesha Philyaw, Ansel Elkins, Natalie Lima, Sreshtha Sen, T Kira

Madden, Cleyvis Natera, Quiara Alegría Hudes, Stephanie Elizondo Griest, Lupita Aquino, Vanessa Micale, Alex Marzano-Lesnevich, Elena Passarello, Melissa Febos, Natasha Oladokun, Jamila Minnicks, Ofelia Montelongo, Cecilia Rodríguez Milanés, Philip B. Williams, Kavita Das, Mira Jacob, Keith Wilson, Kenyatta Rogers, Eric Sasson, Sarita González, Laurie Thomas, Sheree Renée Thomas, Maaza Mengiste and Marco Navarro, Margaree Little and Rebecca Seiferle. Lars, I was lucky to find you in Tbilisi, and then again in Nairobi. Thank you for the years and for your friendship. You held me during the darkest days. Thank you, Aisha Sabatini Sloan and Lydi Conklin, keepers of my secrets, for the badminton and so much queer joy. Remember that time we all joined a secret society? Much love to Familia from Scratch for this incredible community. Much love to El Gran Combo, who took the time to read these pages and who give so much: Lilliam Rivera, Boricua horror queen and fashion icon; Angie Cruz, wellspring of community building; and Caro De Robertis, King of Kink. I am so grateful for our friendship, for the ways you show up, and for your work. Thank you, Jacqui Rivera, for seeing me, and for believing in the work. We'll make that TV show someday. One time for Walton Muyumba, brilliant friend, confidant, critic, and Book Whisperer, who listens to me talk shit, always there with the jokes and sage advice. You give so much of yourself. The world is lucky to have you. I am lucky to have you. Much love to my fellow library kids, my sweet friends, Jennifer Hope Choi and Aurvi Sharma. Joe Osmundson, I love you, you sexy bitch. Gabriel Louis, who once overnighted a care package across the country just so I'd have fresh-baked cookies. Thank you. I still smile when I think of you singing "Bésame Mucho" in Tbilisi. I was tempted.

To my chosen family, who somehow still love me after all these years: Martha Socarras and Fabian Socarras, Angie Vega, Claudia López, Yasmine Monserrate, Yesenia Monserrate, and Max Rivera.

To Massiel Bellina, Venus Morejón, Evy Edelman, Amalie Vega, Cesar Vega, Alfredo Ortega, Luis Viera. Thank you to David Horn, Melissa and Eileen Webb, Liz Horton, and especially Sheridan Horn, for giving me a home in the UK, and for making me feel like family. Gracias a todas las titis de Humacao: Sandy, Pily, Johanna, Lournna, Waleska, Lizza, Jodaly, Sonia.

To Demian San Martin. Someday, when I'm finally ready, I'll write it all down.

Gracias a mi pueblo de Humacao. Gracias a mi gente del Caserío Padre Rivera. Millie Herrera, in another life, I made you laugh, and you promised to remember me forever. Thank you for believing in me. Thank you for finding me in this life. I'll find you in the next.

Y a la familia, Jeannette Doval Sánchez, Petra Matos Ramos, David Díaz Matos, y Rafael Díaz Matos, who told me all the stories.

ABOUT THE AUTHOR

JAQUIRA DÍAZ was born in Puerto Rico and raised between Humacao, Fajardo, and Miami Beach. She is the author of *Ordinary Girls: A Memoir*, winner of a Whiting Award and a Florida Book Awards Gold Medal, a Lambda Literary Awards finalist, an American Booksellers Association Indies Introduce Selection, a Barnes & Noble Discover Great New Writers Selection, an Indie Next Pick, a Library Reads selection, and finalist for the Discover Prize. The recipient of a Letras Boricuas Fellowship, the Jeanne Córdova Prize for Lesbian/Queer Nonfiction, the Alonzo Davis Fellowship from VCCA, two Pushcart Prizes, an Elizabeth George Foundation grant, and fellowships from MacDowell, Yaddo, the *Kenyon Review*, the Wisconsin Institute for Creative Writing, and the Black Mountain Institute at UNLV, Díaz has written for *The Atlantic*, *The Guardian*, *Time*, *T: The New York Times Style Magazine*, and *The Fader*, and her stories, poems, and essays have been anthologized in *Best American Essays*, *The Breakbeat Poets Vol. 4: LatiNext*, *Best American Experimental Writing*, and the Pushcart Prize anthology. She lives in New York and teaches at Columbia University.

RAISING READERS
Books Build Bright Futures

Thank you for reading this book and for being a reader of books in general. As an author, I am so grateful to share being part of a community of readers with you, and I hope you will join me in passing our love of books on to the next generation of readers.

Did you know that reading for enjoyment is the single biggest predictor of a child's future happiness and success?

More than family circumstances, parents' educational background, or income, reading impacts a child's future academic performance, emotional well-being, communication skills, economic security, ambition, and happiness.

Studies show that kids reading for enjoyment in the US is in rapid decline:

- In 2012, 53% of 9-year-olds read almost every day. Just 10 years later, in 2022, the number had fallen to 39%.
- In 2012, 27% of 13-year-olds read for fun daily. By 2023, that number was just 14%.

Together, we can commit to **Raising Readers** and change this trend. How?

- Read to children in your life daily.
- Model reading as a fun activity.
- Reduce screen time.
- Start a family, school, or community book club.
- Visit bookstores and libraries regularly.
- Listen to audiobooks.
- Read the book before you see the movie.
- Encourage your child to read aloud to a pet or stuffed animal.
- Give books as gifts.
- Donate books to families and communities in need.

Books build bright futures, and **Raising Readers** is our shared responsibility.

For more information, visit **JoinRaisingReaders.com**

Sources: National Endowment for the Arts, National Assessment of Educational Progress, WorldBookDay.org, Nielsen BookData's 2023 "Understanding the Children's Book Consumer"